# THOR'S REVENGE

## DONOVAN COOK

Boldwood

First published in Great Britain in 2024 by Boldwood Books Ltd.

Cover Design by Head Design

Cover Photography: Shutterstock

A CIP catalogue record for this book is available from the British Library.

Paperback ISBN 978-1-80483-829-7

Large Print ISBN 978-1-80483-830-3

Hardback ISBN 978-1-80483-831-0

Ebook ISBN 978-1-80483-828-0

Kindle ISBN 978-1-80483-827-3

Audio CD ISBN 978-1-80483-836-5

MP3 CD ISBN 978-1-80483-835-8

Digital audio download ISBN 978-1-80483-833-4

Boldwood Books Ltd
23 Bowerdean Street
London SW6 3TN
www.boldwoodbooks.com

*To Phil*

# CHARACTERS

## FRANKS

Charles – son of Torkel and grandson of Sven the Boar
Hildegard – mother of Charles and abbess of Fraumünster
Bishop Bernard – bishop of Paderborn
Duke Liudolf – duke of Saxony
Roul – spy for King Charles of West Francia
Father Leofdag – priest from Hedeby
Father Egbert – priest from Hedeby
Gerold – former slave and spy for Duke Liudolf
King Louis – king of East Francia

## DANES

Sven the Boar – former jarl of Ribe, grandfather of Charles
Thora – former shield maiden
Rollo – son of Arnbjorg
Alvar – hirdman of Sven's
Jorlaug – daughter of Thora's cousin

Sigmund – son of Rollo
Audhild – Thora's aunt
Ivor – son of Guttrom
Jarl Torgeir – jarl of Hedeby
Steinar – Torgeir's son
Jarl Hallr Red-Face – ally of Torgeir and Ivor

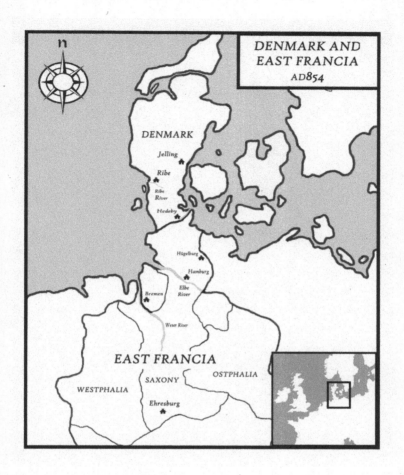

# 1

## THREE DAYS AFTER THE BATTLE AT JELLING

*Thora!*

Thora woke with a start and groaned as the pain tore through her midriff. Her hand went to her stomach, and she frowned when she felt the bandage, but then she remembered. She had been stabbed by Ivor Guttromson and Charles was gone, taken by bastards who had claimed to be friends and allies of Sven. Thora cursed the gods, but knew she could not blame them for what had happened. They only had themselves to blame.

Lying back down again, Thora stared at the wooden rafters above her head and sensed a presence in the bed next to her. She then remembered Alfhild, the young thrall badly injured by one of Ivor's men when she had tried to warn Charles of the danger he was in, and turned her head, expecting to see her short dark hair, but saw thick red hair instead. Under the hair was the freckled face of a girl about six winters old, her eyes closed as she slept peacefully.

'Jo... Jorlaug?' Thora grimaced as her niece's name struggled to come out of her dry mouth.

Jorlaug opened her eyes and blinked a few times before a

smile appeared on her face. 'Aunt Thora!' Moving faster than even
the most skilled warriors that Thora had faced before, Jorlaug
jumped up and wrapped her arms around Thora's neck. Thora
gasped at the pain in her stomach and Jorlaug jumped back, her
face paling. 'Sorry, sorry, sorry—'

Thora forced herself to smile through the pain. 'I'm fine,
Jorlaug. I'm happy to see you, too.' She stroked her niece's face
and was glad to see her infectious smile.

'I stayed here the whole time! Not even the giants could carry
me away. And I prayed to Frigg and to Eir every day.' Eir was one
of Odin's Valkyries, but she was also known for her healing abilities and would often be called upon when someone needed
healing.

'Aye, she did. Refused to leave your side,' Ingvild, Thora's aunt,
said as she sat on a chair near the bed. 'How are you feeling,
child?'

'I'm hungry,' Jorlaug said and then laughed when she realised
the question wasn't aimed at her.

Thora laughed before she could stop herself and winced at the
pain as she clutched her stomach again. 'I live.' She looked
around the room and remembered that she was in the sleeping
quarters at the back of the main hall. The room where the jarl of
Ribe would sleep, but Sven never could, so she and Charles had
used it instead. The room was big, with a large bed covered with
thick furs, and two chests, where Thora and Charles kept their
belongings. There were also a few chairs, like the one Ingvild was
sitting on, and a bucket by the door. In one corner was a small
table with a wooden cross, a shrine Sven had made for Charles,
who was a Christian. Thora glanced at Charles's chest at the foot
of the bed where his few possessions were kept and felt the lump
in the back of her throat.

'Get your aunt some water,' Ingvild said and, as Jorlaug

jumped off the bed, she turned back to Thora. 'You did all you could, Thora. But even you could not have stopped Ivor and his men.' Thora nodded as she remembered fighting the men Ivor had brought with him to Ribe while most of the warriors were away with Sven fighting the king of Denmark. The only warriors left in Ribe were those loyal to Oleg, an old warrior who used to be one of Sven's hirdmen when he had been jarl many winters ago. 'At least you killed that treacherous dog, Oleg, for betraying us and siding with Guttrom. We chopped his body into many pieces and scattered it along the river. That worm will never see Valhalla or Hel,' Ingvild said as if she was reading Thora's mind.

'I still failed to protect Charles.' Thora lowered her head as the tears ran down her cheeks. She closed her eyes and saw Charles thrown on the back of Ivor's horse and disappearing into the distance.

'No one could have done more than you did,' Ingvild said. 'Sven should never have trusted Guttrom, but his greed for vengeance blinded him.'

Thora looked up and sighed. 'We were all blind. And not just about Guttrom, but Oleg as well. Sven didn't trust him. That's why he left him behind. He was worried Oleg would stab a knife in his back during the battle.' Thora took the cup filled with water from Jorlaug and returned her smile. She emptied the cup without taking a breath and winced as her empty stomach churned. 'Alfhild?' Thora asked about the thrall.

Ingvild shook her head. 'We did what we could, but her injuries were too much. The bastard must have ruptured her stomach when he kicked her.'

'Sven gave her a funeral and buried her in the graveyard,' Jorlaug said, her eyes wide. Thora understood why. They did not usually bury thralls in the graveyard outside the town walls.

Thora frowned at her aunt, who nodded. She remembered

Sven coming into the room a few days before, covered in blood and dirt, but she had thought it had been a dream. 'Sven is back?'

'Aye, the old bastard is back. Came rushing in with Rollo like they were being chased by the ice giants three days ago.' Ingvild shook her head.

'How many days have I missed?'

'Four days. We were worried for the first few of them, weren't sure if you would make it, but the Norns decided it was not your time.'

Thora bit her cheek as she worried about what had happened while she had been sleeping. 'What did I miss?'

'They hung all the warriors who didn't help when Ivor's men attacked us. Well, the ones that didn't run away,' Jorlaug said, and Thora raised her scarred eyebrow at the glee she detected in the girl's voice.

'Sven did that?' Thora asked Ingvild.

Ingvild shook her head. 'Not Sven. Rollo. He strung every one of them up himself.'

'Rollo?' Thora's brows creased together and then she remembered one of Ivor's men had killed Rollo's mother when she had tried to protect Charles.

'Aye. By Odin, I've never seen the young man so furious. No one could stop him. It didn't matter how much those spineless worms had pleaded with him.'

Thora wasn't surprised. Rollo was a large man with shoulders broader than most. 'And Sven?'

'Sven is sad,' Jorlaug said, staring at her own feet as if she felt the old man's pain. Thora glanced at Ingvild.

'It's best you see for yourself.'

'He is here?' Thora asked. 'I thought he'd be tearing Denmark apart to find Charles.'

Ingvild shook her head. 'He is here. Not left the hall since he returned from the battle.'

Thora frowned as she wondered what impact losing Charles had had on Sven, and then turned to Jorlaug. 'Get me some more water.'

Jorlaug took Thora's cup and rushed to the bucket by the door while Thora forced herself to get up. She winced as she struggled out of bed and once she was up, she had to close her eyes to stop the room from spinning. 'By Frigg, it feels like I've been asleep for too many winters.'

Ingvild smiled. 'You are lucky Ivor keeps his knife clean, so we didn't have to worry too much about an infection, but your wound was deep and may take some time to heal properly.'

'I'll remember to thank him for that next time I see him. Where are my trousers?' Thora realised she was only wearing a sweat-stained tunic. She saw the scar on her leg, a recent wound from trying to protect Charles from warriors from Hedeby, and shook her head, wondering how many more scars she would get because of the small red-headed boy. Not that she lacked scars anyway. Thora had been a warrior once, many winters ago until her husband died. She had met him in the shield wall and that was where he had died as well. After his death, Thora had sworn never to fight again, but she had been forced to pick a sword up on a few occasions since she met Charles outside the Christian church in Hedeby. Jorlaug handed her clean trousers, and Thora struggled to get them on. Bending caused her pain, but then so did any movement, including breathing. 'What happened with the battle?' Thora asked to distract herself from the pain as she got dressed. 'Do we have a new king?'

Ingvild chewed her bottom lip as if she was debating what to tell Thora. But then she said, 'We have no king.'

'No king?' Thora's brows furrowed as she tried to make sense of what her aunt had said. 'What do you mean no king? Who won the battle, Guttrom or Horik?'

Ingvild sighed. 'Both bastards are dead, so neither won the battle, I'd say.'

Thora's head swam as she tried to digest this and she was forced to sit down again. 'Both Guttrom and Horik are dead?'

'Aye, and so are most of Denmark's jarls. Only a matter of time now before East Francia marches her army into our lands and forces us all to kneel to her nailed god.'

'How many men?'

Ingvild sighed. 'They say a countless number of warriors were lost. Many of Ribe's warriors did not return and of those who did, some can never fight again.'

Thora wished she had something stronger than water to drink as she listened to her aunt. 'How?' was all she could think of saying as she tried to make sense of everything. Thora knew Horik had no heirs, but more worryingly were the deaths of the jarls and their warriors. They kept order in their lands and protected those who paid landgilde, a land tax paid by farmers, to them.

'The battle lasted for three days, they say. Thousands of warriors died and all for nothing.' Ingvild spat to the ground in disgust. 'Neither Horik nor Guttrom cared about the men who died for their greed, and now both bastards are dead and we have no one to protect us.'

'What happened, Aunt Ingvild?' Thora asked again.

Ingvild shrugged. 'I wasn't there, was I?' The old lady sighed. 'From what I heard, Horik died on the third day. The old bastard decided to stand in the shield wall and a spear opened his throat.'

'And Guttrom?' Thora asked, but was sure she already knew the answer.

'Killed by Sven, some say. But others say different. Only the gods know what really happened. And Sven, but he has said little since he returned.'

'They say Sven killed more than a thousand men when he found out Guttrom had Charles,' Jorlaug boasted, but then looked at her feet when Ingvild glared at her.

'Guttrom had Charles?' Thora rubbed her temples and was tempted to ask Jorlaug to fetch her some ale. The last she saw of Charles, he was being carried away by Ivor, but she had passed out from her wound before she could contemplate where Ivor was taking him.

'Aye, Alvar said that during the battle, Halstein told Sven that he had seen Ivor ride into the camp with Charles on his horse. Sven left the battle to find out if that was true, but Alvar was too busy fighting to follow. After the battle, they found Halstein dead outside Guttrom's tent and Guttrom's corpse nearby. Guttrom's men left as if Thor was chasing them, so no one really knows what happened. Some warriors had told Alvar that Sven and Guttrom were fighting and that Sven had accused Guttrom of taking money from the West Franks, but no one is really sure what was going on.' Ingvild stared at Thora, her eyes searching Thora for the answer to that mystery.

'The West Franks?' Thora struggled to make sense of everything her aunt was telling her. She had known that the East Franks were after Charles, but now the West Franks as well?

'Why did Ivor take Charles?' Jorlaug asked, her face scrunched up, before Ingvild could say anything.

Thora wondered how much she could tell them as she felt their eyes on her. Did it really matter if they knew the truth? 'I think it was because of Charles's mother. She lives, and it seems she is someone very important.'

'We know that much,' Ingvild said, surprising Thora.

'How?'

Ingvild glanced at the door which led to the main hall. 'Because she is here, and she's not alone.'

'She's here?' Thora's head spun so much, she thought she might vomit and, without thinking, she jumped to her feet. But the pain tore through her and she dropped to her knees, clutching her stomach.

'Aunt Thora!' Jorlaug rushed to her side, while Ingvild only tutted.

'Told you to be careful.' Ingvild scowled at her.

'Why is she here? What does she want?' Thora asked, ignoring her aunt's scowl. Her eyes darted towards the chest with Charles's belongings.

Ingvild shrugged. 'I'm not even sure the gods know. But I think she is waiting for you.'

'For me?'

'Aye. Every day for three days, she comes in and sits in the hall and all she does is stare at that door.' Ingvild pointed to the door which led to the room.

'She's been here for three days?' Thora frowned, wondering why Charles's mother was sitting here and waiting to talk to her. Did she hope Thora could lead her to Charles? Thora clenched her teeth and struggled to her feet. After a few deep breaths to ease the pain, she smiled at the worried face of Jorlaug. There was only one way to find out what the woman claiming to be Charles's mother wanted. 'Come, let's go meet this mother of Charles.'

'She's very serious. Just like Charles.' Jorlaug looked at Thora, her eyebrows drawn together. 'Are all Christians so serious?'

'Aye, sour bastards, all of them,' Ingvild said and got off the chair she'd been sitting on to follow Thora.

Thora pushed the door open and stood there as she took in the sorry sight in the main hall. The hearth fire was nothing but a weak flame, while a few of the benches were filled with hunched-over figures. Old men and women, their faces pale and with blue rings under their eyes. Thora looked at the raised seat at the rear of the hall and was surprised that it was empty. She had expected to see Sven sitting there, but then turned her attention to the young man sitting by a table near the entrance of the hall. She ground her teeth as the dark-haired man stared back at her, his dark eyes wide and mouth open. Gerold. The young bastard had been with Charles when Thora had found him wandering around and asking about Sven. Gerold had told them he was a slave, and he had claimed to want to help Charles. But in the end, he had been a spy for the East Franks and was leaving a trail for those hunting Charles to follow. The woman sitting beside Gerold put a hand on his arm and Gerold glanced at her before he returned Thora's stare. If she could, Thora would have leapt across the hall and killed the bastard where he sat. *By Odin, what is the bastard doing here*, she wondered, and then looked at the woman sitting next to the slave or spy. She wasn't really sure what he was. Thora raised an eyebrow as she scrutinised the woman, sitting straight-backed with an air of discontent about her. Thora couldn't tell the colour of the woman's hair because of the head covering she was wearing, which matched the black dress she had on. On her chest was a golden cross and Thora had to resist the urge to glance over her shoulder at Charles's chest in the room. She had not thought of the cross that had started all of this. The Cross of Charlemagne that had been given to Torkel, Charles's father, and that had led to his death. Thora wondered if the cross would be safe in the chest with Gerold around.

She pushed the cross out of her mind and focused on the woman again. Thora did not need to be told that she was Charles's mother. She could see some of him in her face, especially her eyes and her nose. Next to the woman was an old man, a priest judging by his black dress and the cross, similar to Charles's mother's, around his neck, but Thora paid little attention to him as she eyed up the two Frankish warriors sitting near the group, both of them scowling at her. Jorlaug was right. The Christians were too serious. Not that the rest of the people in the hall were cheerful.

'You're awake,' a rough voice said, and Thora was stunned to see Sven sitting on a bench near the back of the hall. But it wasn't that he was sitting there that surprised her, it was the way he looked. Sven reminded her of the drunk he had been before Charles had come along. His face was dirty, and the large sweat stains and dried blood on his tunic told Thora that he had not bathed or changed since he had returned. His grey beard, tinged with the red it had been once, was bushy and all over the place and he had a few days' worth of stubble on his head. Enough to reveal the large bald patch where an old, faded tattoo of a raven was while bloodshot eyes stared at her over a nose made large from too much drink. Sven was shorter than most, with a round waist and a large stomach. His limbs were thick, both from muscle and fat and Thora knew he had earned his nickname, the Boar, both from the fact that he resembled one and that he was as stubborn and as dangerous as the woodland creatures. Sven was a man who enjoyed his drink as much as he had once enjoyed standing in the shield wall, and neither had been good to him. His arms and hands were covered in old scars and Thora raised an eyebrow at the fresh scabs on his knuckles.

'By Thor, Sven.' Thora walked towards him and winced as she sat down, both at the pain from her wound and from the stench coming off Sven. 'Charles is missing and here you sit, drinking your life away again.' Thora had hoped that Sven had broken the spell that ale had over him. After the death of his wife, Sven had spent almost a lifetime wandering around Denmark, drinking his way to what he hoped would be an early death, but the gods had kept him alive. When Charles had found them, Thora had believed that that had been the reason and as they had travelled north towards Ribe, the old Sven, the warrior he had been before, had returned. But that warrior was gone again and the pathetic drunk had returned. Thora couldn't help but pity Sven, though. Most men would have drowned themselves if they had suffered like Sven had, but the gods had kept him alive.

Sven looked at his cup, and Thora noticed the blood on the front of his tunic. She looked him over and saw another blood patch on his back. 'I failed him, Thora. I failed him, just like I failed my son.' Sven hung his head low as he took a shuddering breath and fresh tears ran down his cheeks and soaked into his beard. 'I should have listened to the boy. I should never have gone to fight Horik. By Odin it was dumb and the boy knew it. I knew it, but all I thought about was getting my revenge on Horik. And now Charles is gone and I don't know where he is. I failed him. I failed my son. His dying wish, and I failed him.' Thora knew Sven believed that Horik had played a part in Torkel being taken hostage by the Franks. The old king most likely had, but there had been nothing Sven could do about it until Guttrom had arrived.

Thora glanced at the woman, and Gerold, as she tried to find the words that might comfort Sven. But they could not come, because she knew she had failed Charles as well. 'We both failed him. We both should have seen what Guttrom was up to. He never needed you for that battle. He just wanted to get you away from Ribe so that Ivor could take over the town.'

Sven emptied his ale, and a thrall rushed to get him another one.

'Been drinking non-stop since he returned. Even Thor must be impressed that the bastard hasn't passed out yet,' Ingvild said with a curled lip. 'Should be out there searching for his grandson or at least do more about the raids.'

'Raids?' Thora asked.

'Aye, told you, didn't I? Most of the jarls died in that battle. There is no one to keep the peace and now many warriors are taking advantage of it and are raiding all over the place. They say it's mostly Guttrom's men, leaderless and with nowhere to go now that their paymaster is dead.'

Thora scowled at this and couldn't help but look at Charles's mother again. This was exactly what the Frankish kings would want. 'What is being done about it?'

'I had him. I had Charles. He was there in front of me in Guttrom's tent,' Sven said, ignoring what they had said. He looked at Thora again with fresh tears streaming down his face. 'Charles was there and I couldn't save him. I tried Thora, fought as hard as I could, but I couldn't save him.'

Thora felt the kick in her chest. She could have said those exact words, but she knew now was not the time to be sitting around and feeling sorry for themselves. They had to act now. They had to find out where Charles was. 'Where is Rollo, Alvar? The other senior men?'

'Rollo has gone to Hedeby, left two days ago on his own before all the warriors could return. We tried to stop him, but he refused to listen. Sven, in his rare moments of not drinking, arranged for the rest of the warriors to patrol the region and to protect the farmsteads from the raiders after they returned from the battle yesterday. The men barely had enough time to rest,' Ingvild explained.

Thora nodded, glad that something had been done to protect those who couldn't protect themselves. 'Why did Rollo go to Hedeby? To find Charles?'

'To find the bastard responsible for the death of his mother,' Ingvild said. 'But I'm sure if he finds Charles, he will bring him back.'

'So Ivor still has Charles?' Thora asked.

'He ran away before I could kill him,' Sven said, and then he surprised everyone by jumping to his feet and throwing his cup at the hearth fire. The weak flames sizzled, but stayed alive and Thora was glad to see that Sven still had some of his anger in him. But it didn't last long as Sven just slumped down again, with his head low. 'He got away.'

'He's been like that for the last few days. One moment raging like a sea storm, the next crying like a child.' Ingvild shook her head. 'What has happened to him?'

Thora sighed. 'He's a broken man, Ingvild. Charles was meant to fix him, or at least that was what I had hoped.' She put her hand on Sven's shoulder and glared at Charles's mother as if it was her fault that all of this was happening. 'We'll find him, Sven. By Thor, I swear we will find Charles.'

## 2

## HEDEBY, THE DAY BEFORE

Charles sat on the bench in the small wooden church in Hedeby and stared at the crude carving of Jesus. He remembered the first time he had seen it. When he and Gerold had come to Hedeby to find his grandfather. Charles had run into the church after some old men had told him his father had lied about his grandfather. The old men were right, though. His father had lied to him, but not intentionally, or at least Charles didn't think it was intentional. Before he died, killed by the men he had thought of as friends, Charles's father had told him to find his grandfather, a powerful jarl in the north. But the man Charles had found was a fat, old, smelly drunk and afraid of his own shadow. Charles looked at Jesus's face, but he didn't expect to find any comfort from the carving. The two holes which Charles guessed were the eyes were as empty as Charles felt.

Behind him, Ivor hawked and spat and Charles felt his irritation grow, but then glared at the wooden Jesus again. This was His house and yet He allowed these men to do that. Charles thought of the large golden cross his father had given him before he died. It had a large ruby in the centre, just above the sign of Charlemagne and the edge of the cross was rimmed with different-coloured gems. It was the most beautiful thing Charles had ever seen and had been given to his father by his mother when he was just a baby. Although Charles was beginning to wish she hadn't. All the cross had brought him was the deaths of those he loved. His father, Thora, Oda and Alfhild, all dead because of the cross, which was back in Ribe. He didn't even know if his grandfather had survived his fight with Guttrom. The last Charles had seen of him, Guttrom had the upper hand, but Ivor had dragged Charles out of Guttrom's tent before he could see how the fight had turned out. Charles wondered why God was allowing all these bad things to happen. He knew the Danes believed their gods were cruel, but he had always been taught that God was loving and protective of His people. But perhaps the priests were wrong. Perhaps God was as cruel as the heathen gods and enjoyed watching people suffer. Charles gripped the small wooden cross around his neck and his eyes darted to the wooden Jesus, but nothing happened. Although he wasn't sure what he thought would happen.

'What are you doing here?' Charles jumped as a voice hissed behind him. The man spoke Danish as he glared at Ivor, but his Frankish accent sounded different from where he had grown up in East Francia. 'You were supposed to wait for me in Ribe. That was the deal I made with your father.' The man looked like every other Frankish man Charles had ever seen. He was the same height as most, and his face was unremarkable. The cloak that covered his narrow shoulders was covered in dust, but otherwise seemed clean, and his light-coloured hair and beard were neatly groomed. But it was his eyes that stood out, because they reminded Charles of Gerold's eyes. Always scanning the surroundings, always searching for a threat. At first, Charles had thought that was because Gerold was a slave and he needed to be careful, otherwise he would be beaten by his master, but then

Charles had learnt it was because Gerold and his dead master were spies sent to capture him and take him to those responsible for his father's death. Charles decided he did not like the man who was now studying him, with his nose crinkled in disgust. Charles could not blame the man, though. His clothes reeked because of the horse's sweat and because he had peed his pants a few times as Ivor and his men raced to Hedeby and had refused to stop. They had only stopped when the sun had set and the horses were too exhausted to continue. Charles's red hair, which had grown long in the weeks since he had come to Denmark, was matted with sweat and dust and, even though he had not seen his face, he was sure it was dirty as well. And swollen from when Guttrom had struck him the day before. The man looked almost disappointed as he studied Charles. Charles was small for his age, just like his grandfather and his father had been. And unlike them, he was thin and narrow-shouldered, but he had the same blue eyes they had.

'We had no choice. Ribe became unsafe. We had to leave,' Ivor, the son of a man who had pretended to be his grandfather's friend, said. But just like Gerold had betrayed him, Ivor's father had betrayed Charles's grandfather. That was why Charles was now sitting in the church in Hedeby, and was surrounded by a handful of Danish warriors. Ivor was tall and thin, but had long, muscular arms. His light-coloured hair and beard were dirty from dust, sweat and blood, which made his eyes seem harder than they already were. Ivor also had a cut on his leg, given to him by Sven, which had been bound but was still bleeding. At first, Charles had been frightened of men like Ivor, but not any more. Especially because he knew his grandfather was more dangerous than any of them.

'This is not what I had agreed with your father!' the Frank said again, his eyes darting around the church, which was quiet because Ivor's men had chased everyone out.

'Well, Loki decided your plan didn't work for him and messed things up. We couldn't stay in Ribe and then that little bastard's,' Ivor jabbed a finger at Charles, 'grandfather made sure we couldn't stay in my father's camp at the battle.' An image of his grandfather, exhausted and covered in blood, fighting Guttrom after discovering that he had really been sent by the king of West Francia, came to Charles.

When they had arrived in Hedeby that morning, Ivor had tried to find out about the battle, but news had not spread this far south yet. Not knowing what else to do, Ivor had come to the church as he believed no one would look for them there and had sent one of his men to find the Frank. But Charles believed his grandfather still lived. Thora had told him that their gods were not ready for him to die yet.

'Sven still lives?' the Frank asked as he glanced at Charles with a raised eyebrow.

'I doubt it.' Ivor grinned. 'My father would have killed him by now. The fat bastard spent too many years drinking instead of fighting.'

'Then why are you here?' the man asked again. 'Tainting the house of God with your filthy presence.'

Ivor clenched his fists. 'I'm staying here until I hear from my father. Thought it would be safer hiding in a church, nobody would look for us here. What does it matter anyway? We have the boy, just like you wanted.'

The Frank's mouth twitched as he looked at Charles again. 'It's not just the boy I want.'

Ivor shrugged. 'You never told my father that.'

'No, I didn't,' the Frank said, and walked towards Charles.

Charles kept his eyes fixed on the wooden Jesus as the Frank sat down next to him. The bench creaked and Charles sensed the man's eyes on him, but he refused to look at him. Charles was determined not to tell him anything. He would not make the same mistake as he had done with Gerold.

'What's your name?' the Frank asked in Frankish, which sent Charles's heart racing. The man waited for a few heartbeats. 'They think your grandfather is dead. If they are right, then there is no one to keep you safe from them but me.'

Charles glanced at the Danes standing behind him and saw Ivor watching them while the other six looked bored. Charles hated how much he looked like Guttrom. 'My grandfather is not dead and when he finds you, he will kill you and Ivor and his men.'

The Frank smiled, but it was not a friendly smile. It was more like the ones Charles usually got from adults when they thought he had said something dumb. 'That's not very Christian of you, to wish others dead. And I've been told that you are a very good Christian.'

Charles glanced at the wooden Jesus, but this time he did not expect it to do anything. Not like before. It was just a simple wooden carving. And not even a good one. 'You're not a Christian,' he said.

'Oh, but I am.' The man pulled a small golden cross out of his tunic and showed it to Charles. 'I go to church every day when I can, and even when I don't, I say all my prayers. Do you do that?'

'I...' Charles started and then stopped. He had not prayed in days. Charles wasn't sure if praying really did anything any more. He remembered what Gerold had told him soon after they had first met. *Neither God nor any of his angels will come down here and save us.* Charles hadn't believed Gerold then, but now those words felt like the only true thing Gerold had ever said to him. 'Praying does nothing. It doesn't help.'

The Frank stayed silent for a while and Charles had to look to make sure that he was still there. The man smiled when he saw Charles glancing at him. 'Then you are praying for the wrong reasons.' Charles frowned at this, but stayed silent. 'My name is Roul, and unlike those men behind us, I don't want to hurt you.'

'Then what do you want?' Charles knew the man was after the cross, but he didn't say that.

'For now, I would like to know your name.'

Charles thought about it and decided that nothing bad could happen from the man knowing his name. 'Charles.'

'Charles,' Roul repeated as he twisted in his seat so that he could face him. 'Like Charles the Great, or Charlemagne, as we know him?' Charles nodded. His father had named him after the great Frankish emperor. 'Do you know much about Charlemagne?'

'No,' Charles said. He only knew that Charlemagne had built a large empire which had comprised what was now West, Middle and East Francia. But that empire was gone now, broken apart by the grandsons of Charlemagne, who could not agree with how the empire should be ruled and, more importantly, who should rule the empire. Charles's father had fought for the king of East Francia, Louis II, in the civil war which led to that break-up.

'Perhaps I can tell you more about him. Would you like that?'

Charles shrugged. He wanted to know more about Charlemagne, but he didn't trust Roul.

'But for me to take you away from this place and tell you those stories, I need one thing from you.'

'I don't have anything,' Charles said, which wasn't a lie. All he had were the dirty clothes he wore and the small wooden cross around his neck.

'We both know that's not true, Charles. Now tell me where I can find the cross and we can leave this godless place.'

Charles pulled the wooden cross from his neck and showed it to Roul. 'This cross?'

Roul's mouth twitched, but then he composed himself again and smiled. 'No, not that one. You know the one I am talking about. Charlemagne's cross. The one your mother gave you.'

Charles's heart skipped his chest, and he had to hide his hands so that Roul couldn't see them shaking. 'I don't know what you are talking about.'

'Now is not the time to be smart, Charles. Tell me where the cross is and I can take you to your mother.'

This time, Charles's heart felt like it was going to break out of his chest. His wide eyes snapped towards Roul before he could stop himself and he saw the smile of satisfaction on the man's face. Charles had been told his mother had died when he was born and he had been raised by his father, who knew more about fighting battles than children. Although, recently, Charles was beginning to wonder if that was really true. He wanted to believe Roul, only because he wanted his mother to be alive. But Charles had been lied to too many times over the last few weeks to believe the man he had just met. Charles took deep breaths to calm himself, just like Thora had taught him to do when she was teaching him to defend himself, and held up the small wooden cross he wore around his neck again. 'This is the cross my mother gave to me.'

The smile fell from Roul's lips and was replaced by a snarl. 'I'll only ask you one more time. Where is the cross?'

Charles shrugged. 'I don't know what you are talking about.'

Roul lifted his hand as if he was going to backhand Charles across the face, and Charles surprised both of them when he didn't flinch. Instead, he glared at Roul, daring him to smack him. Not that it would have made much of a difference to Charles, anyway. Half his face was already bruised and swollen from when

Guttrom had smacked him. Roul's hand hovered in the air for a while before he sighed and lowered his hand.

'If you don't have the stomach to beat information out of the little piglet, then let me do it,' Ivor said in Danish as he pressed his fist into his hand. His men grunted in approval, but Charles doubted they even knew what Roul and Charles were talking about.

'What makes you think I need to beat information out of the boy?' Roul asked in Danish.

'I'm not dumb.' Ivor limped closer. 'I might not understand what you are talking about, but I can see that you are getting nowhere. Leave the boy with us and he'll soon tell you everything you need to know.' Again, his men grunted in approval.

Charles glanced at the wooden Jesus and then at the warriors, all of them covered in dirt and stinking of sweat. But he did not feel afraid, not like he had done before. He wasn't sure if it was because he had seen more death and violence than a boy of nine should see, or just because he didn't care any more. So many people had died because of him. Perhaps this was his punishment from God. Although Charles didn't know what he was being punished for.

'No, the boy doesn't need to be beaten,' Roul said as he looked at Charles. Charles saw something different in Roul's eyes, something he had not seen before, and he frowned as he tried to understand what it was. 'The boy is brave, and he is doing what any good Christian should do.'

'And what is that?' Ivor glared at Charles.

'He is putting his faith in God and trusting that the Almighty will protect him.' Roul smiled, but Charles knew that wasn't true.

'No, not in God,' Charles said. 'In my grandfather. He will find me and kill all of you.'

The Danish warriors laughed as Ivor said, 'The old bastard is dead. There is no way he could have defe—'

Before Ivor could finish his sentence, they heard a cry outside the church. The men tensed and their hands went to their weapons as they looked at Ivor, who shrugged. The cries were not war cries or warriors calling for blood. They were men and women wailing as if some great tragedy had happened. Ivor looked at one of his men.

'Go find out what's going on.' He then turned to Charles and Roul. 'You two stay where you are.'

They waited in silence as one of Ivor's men ran outside and, when he returned a while later, he wore a frown which suggested he was struggling with some internal thoughts.

'What is it? What in Odin's name is going on?' Ivor asked, holding his leg as he limped towards the man.

The man stopped and frowned at Ivor. 'Jarl Torgeir has returned. They say Horik is dead.'

The church was filled with a sudden silence as everyone took in the news. Charles glanced at the wooden statue of Jesus and it seemed like even Jesus was holding His breath to see what would happen now. And then the silence was broken by Ivor's laugh.

'My father did it. He defeated the old bastard. My father is the king of Denmark.' He clasped the man's shoulders, but then stopped when the man did not celebrate with him. 'What, in Odin's name, is it?'

'Your father is also dead.'

'My father... dead?' Charles could not see Ivor's face, but he imagined the man's eyebrows were drawn together as he tried to make sense of what he had just been told. Charles, though, could not help but smile. He knew his grandfather would kill the man who had betrayed him. Roul glanced at Charles and scowled at his smile. 'How?' Ivor turned and glared at Charles.

Ivor's red face would have frightened Charles before, but it didn't this time.

'I told you my grandfather would kill him. Just like he will kill you.' Charles's heart raced in his chest as he spoke the words.

Before anyone could react, Ivor launched himself at Charles. He jumped over the bench and grabbed Charles by his tunic before lifting him up and screaming in his face.

'Impossible! There's no way that fat bastard could have killed my father.'

Charles closed his eyes as Ivor's spit splattered his face, but then heard Roul say, 'Let go of the boy, heathen.'

Ivor ignored the Frank and turned back to the warrior who had given him the news. 'How did it happen?'

The man shrugged. 'No one knows what had happened, but there are rumours that one of his jarls killed him. They say the man wanted to be king himself.'

'My father is dead.' Ivor let go of Charles, who collapsed onto the bench he had been sitting on before, and hunched over and his shoulders shook. Charles moved back to make sure he was out of Ivor's reach as Ivor said, 'My father... dead.' Ivor's remaining men stared at each other and could only shrug, as they didn't seem to know what to do. Ivor looked up and glared at Charles. His tear-streaked eyes creased and his face reddened. 'You little bastard! This is all your fault! My father died because of you! My... my future gone. I would have been the next king if it weren't for you!' Ivor pulled his sword from its scabbard. 'You will die for this, little piglet.'

Roul then surprised all of them when he yawned and stood up from the bench. 'No, he won't. And none of this is the boy's fault.'

Ivor lowered his sword and glared at the smaller Frank. The blade trembled in his hand and, for a heartbeat, Charles thought Ivor might attack Roul. 'I was supposed to be king. My father was going to share the crown with me. You cannot speak to me like that!'

Roul shrugged, and Charles couldn't help but admire the man's bravery. He looked weak compared to the seven large Danish warriors, yet he still faced them. 'I doubt your father was ever going to do that. And the truth, Ivor, is that you and your father failed. I gave your father a lifetime's worth of gold to find the boy and the dumb heathen decided to raise an army against his uncle instead. And to make things worse, he failed in that and failed to do the one thing that I required of him.' Roul sighed. 'I guess that is the price I pay for trusting heathens to do God's work.'

Charles scowled at that. He didn't understand why he was so important. Why Roul would pay Ivor's father so much just to get to him? He wondered if it was because he had the Cross of Charlemagne, but something told him there was more to it than that. Roul had said that he wanted Charles as well. Charles kept his thoughts to himself as an ugly sneer spread across Ivor's red face.

'By Thor, I've had enough of you Christians. You've been nothing but a thorn in my side. I do not need you any more! After I deal with you, I'll kill the fat pig in Ribe as well. Arvid, kill this bastard and grab the boy.'

Arvid, a large warrior with broad shoulders and a shaved head, grinned as he walked towards Roul. 'Time to d—'

Before he could finish his sentence, Roul's hand shot out, moving so fast that Charles never saw the knife he must have had. He only knew of it when the hairs of Arvid's beard fell to the ground and blood started leaking from the large cut across his throat. Arvid's eyes bulged as he struggled to breathe before he collapsed to the ground. A gasp made them all turn to the rear of the church where three priests had walked in. Charles recognised

Father Leofdag, the young priest who had gone to Ribe to build a church. He had left shortly before the battle, saying that he needed to see a friend and ask for help to build it. Father Leofdag and the other priests gaped at the scene in front of them, and then they all turned and rushed out. Father Leofdag glanced at Charles as he fled, his face almost apologetic, but Charles wasn't surprised. The young priest couldn't defend himself when he had been attacked by Haldor, a drunk who wasn't even a warrior.

Ivor tried to use the distraction to his advantage and roared as he charged at Roul. Charles turned in time to see the smaller man duck under Ivor's sword and rush past the Dane. Roul turned and grabbed Ivor by his long hair, before kicking the cut on Ivor's leg. Ivor cried out and dropped to his knees, his eyes wide as Roul pressed a bloodied blade against his neck.

'God will forgive me for killing you heathens in His church, even if this is just a modest one. If your men take one step closer, then I'll slit your throat and your dreams of being king will go with you to hell.'

The warriors behind Roul hesitated as Charles gaped at Roul's skill. He had never seen anyone move like that, not even Thora or his grandfather. Roul leaned closer to Ivor. 'You and your father were supposed to wait for me in Ribe with the boy. It wasn't just him I needed, but something he has, something he left behind in Ribe. And now I need to go to that cursed town and find the item he is hiding from me.'

'B... but you never told us about it. If you had, we could have got it for you,' Ivor protested, his wild eyes fixed on Charles as if he was blaming him for this.

Roul laughed. 'I would never trust you with something that sacred.' Roul glanced at Charles as he gasped. Charles wished he knew why the cross was so important to the kings of Francia. He remembered the old godi his grandfather had taken him to, saying that there was something inside the cross. An old magic that had made even the godi nervous. But Charles had refused to believe the godi. It was just a cross. One that his mother had stolen from King Louis and given to his father.

'We can go back. We can get this *thing* you want,' Ivor said.

Roul shook his head and pressed the knife harder against Ivor's neck. 'You heathens are really dumb, aren't you? What do you think would happen if you return to Ribe now, especially if Sven the Boar still lives?'

'I'll kill the bastard. I'll take Ribe for myself and then you can search for this... thing.'

'And how will you take Ribe?' Roul glanced dismissively at Ivor's remaining men. 'You barely have a handful of men left.'

'Support me, like you supported my father. I can get more men. I can buy the support of other jarls. That way I can take Ribe. Even become king of Denmark.'

Even to Charles, Ivor just sounded desperate. But he still looked at Roul to see how the Frank would respond.

Roul sighed and let go of Ivor, who rubbed his neck. 'No, Ivor. Your father failed me and my king. I'll stand in a pit of snakes before I trust you heathens again. And besides, you are not the man he was. No, I must go myself and find it myself.' He looked at Charles. 'Which I will.' Roul turned his attention back to the Danes. 'You will stay in Hedeby and guard the boy until I return.'

Ivor glared at Roul as he gripped his injured leg and struggled to his feet, but he kept his distance. 'And why would we do that if you refused to support me?'

Roul smiled. 'Because you have nothing left, Ivor. That is why. But if you succeed in this one small task, then I can make sure my king still has some use for you. And before you think of betraying me, just remember I have men in this town. Men who can kill you before you even know they are there.'

Ivor hesitated for a heartbeat, his eyes darting around the church, and then nodded. 'Fine, but you better return. Otherwise we kill the piglet.'

Roul smiled and walked towards Charles. In Frankish he said, 'Now, tell me where I can find the cross.'

Charles clenched his fist as he fought to stay strong. 'My grandfather will kill you when he finds you.'

This time Roul smiled. 'There is something I like about you, Charles. You are a very brave boy, but you are naïve. You better hope your grandfather doesn't find me, not if you still want him to live.' With that, Roul turned and walked out of the church. Charles looked at the wooden Jesus again. He hadn't prayed for days, but he prayed now. He prayed his grandfather was on his way to Hedeby and that he would slaughter all these men.

## 3

Rollo clenched his fists as he walked through Hedeby, his scowling eyes scanning the busy streets for Ivor or for any of his men. Traders in Ribe had told him many things about the large trading town which bordered the East Frankish kingdom. They had told him of the large market in the town centre, larger than the one in Ribe, filled with people and goods from all over Midgard. Men who looked so strange that you would think they were from one of the other eight realms which were connected to the great tree. They had told Rollo of the magnificent hall of Jarl Torgeir, and of the many places where a tired man could get a drink and a woman to warm his bed. For as long as he could remember, Rollo had wanted to come to Hedeby, but now that he was here, all he wanted to do was burn the town to the ground. It would have been easier to do that to find the men he was hunting, than walking through the endless streets hoping that the gods smiled on him.

Rollo was wearing his brynja, the one he had taken from his father's old war chest, and his helmet. His Dane axe was strapped to his back and his small one-handed axe he used in the shield wall was tucked into his belt. The brynja Rollo wore was too big for him, though, something that had surprised Rollo the first time he had put it on. He had always imagined that his father was a giant, especially as he couldn't remember much of the man who had died when he was just a small boy. But the brynja that was too large for him showed Rollo that his father had been even bigger than what he was. Rollo had often wondered if his son, Sigmund, would grow up to be just as large as him, or perhaps larger. The boy was only eight winters old and was already bigger than others his age, bigger even than some boys two winters older. He pictured Sigmund standing in front of their house, his face bruised and with a large lump on his head, but it was the tears in his boy's eyes that tugged at his heart. Sigmund felt guilty that he had not been able to defend his grandmother, and it didn't matter how often Rollo or his wife had to tell him he had done all he could. Rollo couldn't even blame Sven or Charles for his mother's death. She had been a stubborn woman who had done what she believed was right, and Rollo had to honour her for that. But first he wanted to find the bastard responsible for her death and gut the man slowly and painfully. Unfortunately, that man was dead, killed by Ribe's Christian blacksmith. But Ivor still lived and Rollo was determined to hack him into pieces so he could never reach Valhalla.

Rollo still wasn't sure what any of this was about or why Guttrom, Ivor's father, had wanted Charles. The boy was smart and could be a talented warrior one day, but he was still a child. Rollo had tried to get answers from Sven as they raced back to Ribe after the battle, but Sven had refused to tell him anything. So, Rollo had decided to wait until Sven had calmed down, hoping that his jarl would tell him then. But when they had reached Ribe and Rollo found out about the death of his mother, everything changed. She had died to protect Charles, and

Sigmund had been hurt. Rollo wanted the truth. He wanted to know what Sven was hiding from him. But that had to wait until Rollo found Ivor because it was Ivor's man who had struck his mother. Rollo had spent the first night back in Ribe mourning with his family, but when the sun rose the next day, he could no longer just sit back and do nothing. Not with the rage and anguish coursing through him. Even after hanging every one of those bastards who had stood by while Ivor's men attacked the people of Ribe, Rollo still wanted revenge. He had never felt anger like that before, but now that he had savoured it, he did not want to let that feeling go. It made him feel stronger than he had ever done before, and Rollo knew he would need that strength for what was to come. Even if he didn't know what that was yet. So, he had dressed for war, his brynja still covered in blood and dirt from the battle at Jelling, and mounted his horse. People had pleaded with him to stay in Ribe, to wait until the warriors returned from the battle, but his wife and Sven had remained silent. They both had known he needed to do this and had done nothing to stop him from leaving Ribe on his own and racing towards Hedeby.

Rollo still remembered Sven's last words to him before he had left.

'Find my grandson while you search for your vengeance. Find my grandson and bring him back to me.'

Rollo had raced through the night and only rested for a short while when his horse reached its limit, and then had arrived in Hedeby long before midday. The sun had reached its zenith and had moved on, although it was hard to see through the clouds, and Rollo had seen no sign of Ivor. He stopped in front of the small Christian church and stared at it. With his nostrils flared, Rollo hawked and spat towards it.

'To think they want to build one of these in Ribe. By Odin!' Rollo had never cared much about the Christians and never understood why so many hated them. He knew some of the Christians in Ribe and had always liked them. But his mother was killed by men paid by a Christian king, and Rollo knew he couldn't just ignore them now.

The church was larger than the surrounding houses but smaller than Jarl Torgeir's hall, although its pointed roof stood taller. Unlike the houses they had in Denmark, the church had holes in the wall to provide more light, although they were now shuttered, as were the doors. Rollo glanced at the large wooden cross outside the church, which matched the cross on the roof, and rubbed the Mjöllnir around his neck. He thought of the woman who had arrived in Ribe the same day he and Sven returned, claiming to be Charles's mother, and wondered what she would think of it. Then he remembered Gerold, the bastard who had given him many of the small scars on his arms that night when Sven had first returned to Ribe, and a growl escaped from his throat. If Rollo hadn't been so caught up with his grief, he would have strangled Gerold for that. He still might when he got back to Ribe. Rollo turned and walked away, ignoring the glances many of the people gave him.

As the day went on, Rollo grew more frustrated. There were no signs of Ivor or his men, and all Rollo could see were frightened people and empty taverns. And Rollo understood why. Denmark had lost her king and most of her jarls in the battle near Jelling. As he had raced to Hedeby, he saw the devastation caused by warriors who had suddenly found themselves leaderless and homeless. Farmsteads burnt down, dead livestock and people littering the ground. Women raped and abused and children shipped away on warships to be sold as thralls elsewhere. Most of the warriors had returned to their homes to defend their families, but there were many, mainly Guttrom's mercenaries, who were trying to take advantage of the situation to grab land and riches for themselves. He gripped the Mjöllnir around his neck and prayed to Thor, the protector, that Ribe and the surrounding farmsteads were safe. *Denmark needs to find a new king soon, otherwise she will burn to the ground,* Rollo thought as he walked past a small boy sitting on the ground, his knees pressed against his chest as he cried.

Rollo carried on walking, his eyes still scanning the side streets and scrutinising any warrior he saw, but he was losing hope. Hedeby was too large and there were plenty of places for Ivor to hide. That was assuming that Ivor was even in Hedeby. Rollo had only guessed that he would be here, because he could think of no other place where Ivor could go. As he walked past one house, the woman inside screaming at someone, he glimpsed something that sent his heart racing. Standing near the market was a warrior, his leather jerkin covered in dirt and dried blood, his face just as dirty. The warrior had an axe tucked into his belt, which his right hand was resting on as he scanned the market. 'By Odin,' Rollo said as he recognised the man who had been in Ribe with Guttrom's men before the battle.

As if warned of his presence, the warrior turned and looked straight at Rollo. His eyes widened as he mouthed something, before he shoved people out of his way and took off.

'Bastard!' Rollo chased after the man. People screamed in shock and outrage as Guttrom's man barged them out of the way, even throwing a few of them onto the ground in hopes of slowing Rollo down. Children cheered as a large hound snapped at Rollo's heels, but Rollo ignored the beast and used his long legs to jump over those on the ground when Guttrom's man disappeared around a corner.

As Rollo rounded the corner, he caught the glint of sunlight on metal and ducked in time for the axe to swing over his head. Rollo turned and threw a punch at Guttrom's warrior. The man dodged Rollo's punch and tried to slice his neck open with a back-handed chop of his axe. Rollo jumped back and before the warrior could recover from his own momentum, he skipped forward and landed a jab on the man's cheek. The warrior's head snapped back and he hit his head on the timber wall of the house behind him. Stumbling forward, he walked into another punch and dropped to his knees, his axe falling from his hand.

Thinking the fight was over, Rollo looked around to make sure he had alerted none of Hedeby's warriors, when the warrior jumped to his feet and drove his shoulder into Rollo's stomach. Rollo grunted as the air was knocked out of him and as Guttrom's man pushed him back a few steps, he clasped his hands together and struck the bastard on the back. But instead of letting go, Guttrom's warrior punched Rollo between the legs. Rollo's eyes bulged and his legs buckled under him, but he had enough sense to grab the bastard around the chest as he collapsed on top of him. The man struggled to get Rollo off of him and was rewarded with a knee to the head, which Rollo repeated for good measure. Rollo waited a few heartbeats before he rolled off the man and cupped his crotch.

'Bastard,' Rollo complained as Guttrom's warrior struggled to his knees.

The man shook his head and got to his feet, but was too dazed to know what to do or where to go.

'Where is he?' Rollo croaked as he struggled to his feet. The warrior shook his head again and then focused on Rollo, before he roared and attacked again. Rollo blocked the warrior's punch with his left hand and, with his right, he grabbed the man by his jerkin before headbutting him. Even though he was wearing a helmet, sparks still flew in his vision as the warrior's legs buckled underneath him and he collapsed. Rollo dropped to his knees and cupped his crotch when he heard shouts from the people of

Hedeby, who were outraged by the outsiders wreaking havoc in their market. Taking a deep breath, Rollo struggled to his feet because he knew it was only a matter of time before Jarl Torgeir's men came to investigate.

'Call that a fight!' an old voice barked and Rollo glanced over his shoulder to see three grey beards sitting outside a quiet tavern. All of them shaking their heads in disapproval.

'I could do better than that and I've only got one leg!' One of the grey beards patted his stump.

'Oleg, if you could do better then you would still have two legs,' another of the grey beards retorted, and the one-legged man scowled at him as he laughed.

Rollo shook his head. At least his pain amused the old bastards, but now he had to find out where Ivor was. After hopping from one foot to the other to relieve the pain in his groin, Rollo walked to Guttrom's man and grabbed him by his hair. He leaned in closer and glared at the dazed warrior. 'Do you know who I am?'

The warrior stared at him for a few heartbeats as his eyes struggled to focus and then he spat in Rollo's face.

'I guess that's a yes.' Rollo wiped the bloody spit from his cheek. It was a good thing he was already dirty, otherwise that would have annoyed him, Rollo thought as he backhanded the bastard, which only made the old men laugh.

'That's it, you show him who's boss!' one of them shouted.

Rollo sighed and tried to ignore the grey beards. 'Where is Ivor?'

'Fucking your mother,' the warrior said and Rollo kneed him in the face. He screamed at the unconscious man before stamping on his chest. The sounds of bones breaking as the man's chest caved in snapped Rollo out of his rage and he cursed himself for killing the bastard. Especially as the dead man had been his only lead on where Ivor was.

'He'll not tell you anything now,' the one-legged grey beard shouted and Rollo had to fight the urge to go take his other leg. But then Rollo took a deep breath as he tried to calm his racing heart. He looked around the small street, trying to figure out which was the best way to go, when one of the grey beards shouted, 'You better run, boy. The jarl's men are coming and they don't like others fighting in their town.'

'Aye, only they're allowed to do that. Not that they're any good at it.' The one-legged man scowled. 'Got beaten by a fat drunk not so long ago.'

Rollo nodded his thanks to the grey beards before he rushed away from the dead warrior. Hedeby's warriors would be looking for him now, and Rollo didn't want to fall into Torgeir's hands. He was sure the bastard would love to make an example of him, especially after Sven stabbed him in the foot during the battle.

He walked away from the market, towards the quieter part of Hedeby while keeping his head down and trying not to draw attention to himself. Something which was not easy for Rollo as he stood head and shoulders above most. But as he rushed to get as far from the bastard he had killed as possible, he bumped into a small man who somehow stayed on his feet.

'Forgive me...' Rollo started and then frowned as he took in the tonsured head and the brown robe, along with the crooked nose. 'Father Leofdag?' He grabbed the young priest before he could run away and sneered at him. 'Sven and I were wondering why you were so quick to leave Ribe before the battle.'

Father Leofdag lifted his pale face and swallowed down his fear as he stared at Rollo. 'R... Rollo. Please don't hurt me. I kn... know where Ch... Charles is.'

## 4

Charles was still staring at the wooden carving of Jesus when the church doors burst open. The candles by the altar fluttered and Charles felt his heart skip a beat at the fright of the sudden noise.

'What in Odin's name?' Ivor shouted as everyone turned towards the church doors and gripped their weapons.

Charles jumped to his feet, his heart racing in his chest. 'Grandfather!'

'Sven?' Ivor scowled and pulled his sword from its scabbard. His men all scrutinised the giant warrior who walked into the church, a large Dane axe in his one hand.

'That's not Sven!' one of Ivor's men said and Charles's shoulders dropped when he realised the man standing in the doorway, his face hidden by the eye guards of his helmet, was far too large to be his grandfather. Even from where Charles was, he could see the man was bigger than Ivor and his men.

'Ivor!' the large warrior roared and Charles recognised Rollo's voice.

'Rollo?' Ivor said, realising the same. 'What in the gods' names are you doing here?'

Rollo strode into the church, his angry eyes fixed on Ivor, as the dim light in the church reflected off his axe. Charles glanced around the church, sensing what was about to happen, and looked for a place to hide. 'I've come to kill you, Ivor!'

'Kill me? Like you can!' Ivor said and his men laughed. 'It's just you against me and my five men.'

'I see only four men,' Rollo growled. Charles wondered where the other man was – the one Ivor had sent to the market to get them some food after Roul had left – and hoped he wasn't behind Rollo, preparing to stab him in the back.

'I have one more man outside, Rollo. He'll be back soon, don't you worry.'

Rollo hawked and spat. 'I doubt it.' The way he said that made the rest of Ivor's men glance at each other.

Ivor shrugged as if that meant nothing to him. 'Why do you want to kill me, Rollo? Did Sven send you? Is he too afraid of facing me himself?'

Charles's heart raced in his chest as he wondered if his grandfather had sent Rollo, but then he wondered why Sven wasn't there himself.

'Your man killed my mother, Ivor!'

'That man is dead.' Ivor shrugged again. 'You have no quarrel with me.'

'Wrong.' Rollo stopped a few paces from Ivor, who had his sword in his hand still but kept it low. 'He was your man, there on your orders. He also struck my boy. I have plenty of quarrel with you.' Charles peered out from the bench he was hiding behind and couldn't stop his hands from trembling at the sight of Rollo's bared teeth. It reminded him of the night when he had first met the giant warrior. When Rollo had fought the Frankish spies who wanted to kidnap him. But since that night, Charles had only ever seen Rollo with a smile on his face and he had forgotten how terrifying the man could be. Not that Ivor seemed fazed by Rollo. Even though he was half a head shorter and his shoulders were narrower and his limbs much thinner than Rollo's.

'I'd be careful if I were you, Rollo. I could be the next king of Denmark. Drop your weapons and stand with me. You will be richly rewarded, that I swear by Odin.'

'You're not worthy to be king of my horse's shit, you worm!' Rollo shot forward and swung his Dane axe at Ivor, who ducked underneath it and stabbed at Rollo's exposed stomach. The stab was so fast that Charles barely saw Ivor's sword move and knew that neither had Rollo as he staggered back, his hand clutching his stomach. Charles's mouth dropped open when he thought Ivor had landed a killing blow on his rescuer, but then Rollo lifted his hand and Charles saw no blood on Rollo's stomach or his hand. Rollo's brynja had done its job and saved him, but from the grimace on Rollo's face, Charles could tell the blow still hurt him.

'You're no match for me and my men!' Ivor said, and Charles could hear the smile in his voice. But Charles also saw how Ivor gripped his injured leg and backed off so his men were facing Rollo and not him.

Rollo responded by charging at Ivor's men, his roar vibrating off the timber walls of the church. He swung his axe in a wide arc, forcing Ivor's men to either jump back or duck underneath it. Halfway through the swing, Rollo shifted the axe into his left hand, and with his right hand, he grabbed the nearest of Ivor's men by his hair and yanked him backwards. The man screamed and dropped his axe as he tried to free himself from Rollo's grip, who threw him into one of the other warriors who was about to charge at Rollo. As the two men collided, Rollo brought his Dane axe around and buried it deep in the chest of the first man. The second could do nothing as the top of the axe's head cut into his shoulder. Rollo stepped forward and pulled his sax-knife free from its scabbard before stabbing the second man in the throat. Blood sprayed over Rollo and the benches and before he could free his axe, another of Ivor's men rushed at him and stabbed at his exposed side.

Rollo let go of his Dane axe and twisted out of the way of the sword coming at him, but could do nothing as Ivor appeared behind him and swung his sword at Rollo's back. Somehow, Rollo sensed the attack and instead of jumping forward, he fell back into Ivor before his sword could complete its arc. The warrior who had tried to stab Rollo hesitated as Rollo pushed Ivor back and tried to elbow him in the head. But then Ivor's injured leg gave way and he collapsed. Rollo tripped over Ivor and the fourth warrior, who had been waiting for an opening, pounced on Rollo and chopped down with his axe. Rollo grabbed the man's axe before it got near his face and Charles marvelled at his strength as Ivor's man tried and failed to force the axe down and kill Rollo. Just then, Charles spotted the other remaining warrior, the one who had stabbed at Rollo, rush around so he could finish Rollo off. Charles knew he had to do something, but knew he could never hope of surviving in a fight against the Danish warriors. His eyes wide, he took a step back and felt something hitting the back of his foot. Looking down, Charles saw a large wooden cross which must have been dropped by someone. Without thinking, Charles grabbed it and threw it at the warrior who was about to stab Rollo. As if God was guiding the cross, it flew true and struck the warrior on the side of his head. The man cried out as his head snapped to the side, which distracted the warrior who was trying to kill Rollo with his axe. As that warrior looked up to see where the cross had come from, Rollo pulled the axe to one side, causing the warrior to lose his balance and fall over. Rollo jumped to his feet and kicked the axe warrior in the stomach when Ivor appeared from somewhere and stabbed at his face. Rollo ducked under the sword and tackled Ivor to the ground. But before Rollo could take advantage of the situation, the man Charles had struck with the cross, his head bleeding from the blow, jumped on his back and wrapped his arm around Rollo's neck.

Transfixed by the chaos in front of him, Charles didn't notice the figure creeping towards him and screamed when a hand gripped his shoulder. With bulging eyes, he turned to face his attacker, only to see the frightened face of Father Leofdag, who held a finger to his lips.

'Come, we must get you out of here,' Father Leofdag whispered. With a glance towards the fighting men, he tried to pull Charles in the direction he had come from, but Charles refused to go. With lowered brows, Charles stared at the young priest, wondering why he was helping him now and where he wanted to take him. He glanced at the fight and saw that Rollo had freed himself from the man choking him and had his one-handed axe in his hand. Father Leofdag sensed Charles's apprehension, and said, 'There's a back door. We can sneak out while these heathens kill each other. But we must hurry, before Jarl Torgeir's men show up.'

But Charles still refused to go. Father Leofdag had done nothing to help him earlier, and besides, he'd rather go with Rollo, whom he was sure would take him back to his grandfather.

'Come, Charles. We must go now!' Leofdag grabbed Charles again and pulled him harder.

'Rollo! Help!' Charles screamed.

Rollo looked his way while still fighting Ivor's man, a move that almost cost him his life as he narrowly avoided the sword aimed at his face. 'Go with him!' Rollo roared before he turned and chopped down with his axe. Ivor's man jumped back, but Rollo had expected that and rushed forward before shoulder barging him to the ground. The warrior rolled out of the way before Rollo could stomp down on his chest and, while still on his knees, swung his sword at Rollo's legs. Rollo barely reacted as the tip of the man's sword sliced his thigh and he punched the warrior on top of his head. But before Charles could see what happened next, Father Leofdag dragged him away.

'By God! Come on, Charles. You heard Rollo.'

This time, Charles nodded and followed the priest to a door in the back corner of the church. Father Leofdag shoved Charles through the door, which led to a small room at the back of the church. There was another door which led to the street and as Father Leofdag and Charles ran for it, they heard Ivor scream.

'Don't let that bastard boy escape!'

'Come on, Charles! Run!' Leofdag urged him as Charles shoved the door open and sprinted through it, not caring if the priest was behind him or not.

* * *

Rollo saw one of Ivor's men run after Charles and the priest and hesitated. He glanced at Ivor, who was leaning against one of the wooden posts that supported the church roof, his leg bleeding heavily and his face grimacing with pain. Rollo knew he had to make a decision and wavered as he fought against himself. Part of him knew he had to go after Charles and protect him from Ivor's man. But Ivor still lived and Rollo couldn't leave the church until Ivor was dead.

Ivor seemed to sense what Rollo was feeling and smiled. 'What's it going to be, Rollo? Kill me or protect the boy? You can't do both.' Ivor's remaining man got to his feet and shook his head. He took a deep breath and positioned himself between Rollo and the door Charles and the priest had used to escape. Rollo gritted his teeth and knew then he had failed Sven. He looked at his own thigh, which was bleeding heavily, and knew he would weaken soon. His mother had always taught him to be calm in any situation, to not give in to his emotions, like he had seen Sven do so many times. But Rollo did just that when he found out his mother had been killed and now he wondered if he would leave this church alive. He almost smiled at the fact that he might die in a Christian church and just imagined the other warriors in Valhalla making fun of him for it. Then Rollo glanced at his one-handed axe and took a deep breath. He had to trust that the priest would get Charles to safety and back to his grandfather. But if Rollo was going to die here in this church, then he was going to take Ivor with him.

Summoning what was left of his strength, Rollo made to go towards the back door and, as the warrior blocking his way tensed, Rollo turned and rushed at Ivor. Ivor's eyes widened and he rolled out of the way as Rollo's axe buried itself in the post Ivor had been leaning on. Knowing he could not free the axe, Rollo let go of it and turned in time to see Ivor stabbing his sword at him. Rollo batted the blade away with his arm before he punched Ivor in the face. Ivor staggered back, the punch not hard enough to knock him out, when his man roared and came at Rollo from the side. He swung his axe at Rollo's head, who winced as he ducked under the swing and then pushed the man away. The warrior took a few steps back and was about to charge at Rollo again when someone shouted, 'By Thor! What is going on here?'

Rollo and the warrior facing him turned towards the church door and saw nine warriors standing by the entrance of the church, all of them with their weapons in their hands. A few of them had recent injuries which suggested they had fought in the battle at Jelling and before Rollo could even wonder if they would recognise him, one of the Hedeby warriors said, 'Wait. Isn't that one of Sven's men? One of the giants that fought beside him.'

'Aye, I think that's him. He killed Ove. Almost chopped him in half.'

Rollo cursed and before he could say anything, Ivor took advantage of the situation.

'Thank the lord, you came. This mad man just attacked us. He killed my men as we prayed to our god!'

Rollo saw Ivor's man quickly tuck his Mjöllnir into his tunic and would have laughed if he wasn't in so much trouble, but luckily for him, Loki was in a mischievous mood and wasn't about to let Ivor get away with that.

'Do you really think I was born yesterday, Ivor Guttromson? My left testicle has more faith in the Christian god than you. Jarl Torgeir is in a terrible mood, but I have a feeling that seeing you will make him feel much better.' The warrior glanced over his shoulder. 'Get them and make sure you take them alive.'

The Hedeby warriors spread out as they approached Rollo and Ivor's man. Behind him, Rollo heard Ivor moving away, but didn't want to take his eyes off the Hedeby warriors to see what Ivor was doing. Then he caught movement out of the corner of his eye and turned in time to see Ivor's man striking at him with the head of his axe. The blow caught Rollo above his right eye before he could react and then it was all noise as the Hedeby warriors attacked. Rollo still wore his helmet with its eye guard, but that didn't stop the church from spinning and disorientating him. He felt hands grab him and swung his fist out, feeling it strike some-one, before one warrior struck him on the cut on his leg.

Rollo cried out and dropped to his knees and before he could do anything, punches and kicks rained down on him.

'Don't let Ivor get away!' someone shouted before Rollo's world went dark and he collapsed on the church floor.

## 5

Charles bolted out of the church and into the street, with Father Leofdag right behind him. The people of Hedeby scowled and dogs barked at them in excitement, but Charles soon forgot about them when Ivor's warrior shouted behind them, 'Get back here, you little bastard!'

Charles glanced over his shoulder and saw one of Ivor's men chasing them and gaining fast. This was just like in Ribe a few days ago. The only difference now was that Father Leofdag was behind Charles, his habit lifted to his knees as he tried to keep up.

'Run, Charles! Run!' the priest shouted and Charles lowered his head and ran as fast as he could. He rounded a house and almost ran into an old woman who swore at him, but her words were lost in the wind that rushed past his ears. Charles hoped that Father Leofdag was keeping up, but didn't want to look back again to make sure. He had learnt it was never good to look back when you were being chased and being chased was something that happened a lot to Charles. In the past, it was boys who wanted to beat him up because he was different to them, but now it was men who wanted him for reasons he didn't understand.

Charles was about to make another turn when Father Leofdag cried out behind him. He stopped and looked back to see the priest on the ground, his mud-covered face pale as he urged Charles to keep going.

'Run, Charles! Get away while you can!'

Father Leofdag's cries reminded Charles of the last time someone had urged him to flee a town. His father. That was the last time Charles had seen his father, covered in his own blood and barely able to stand. But he still fought off the warriors chasing them so Charles could escape Hügelburg, the last town he had lived in in East Francia. The last home Charles had. The memory made Charles hesitate. He had always regretted leaving his father to die, even if he knew he couldn't have done anything to help him, but perhaps he could help Father Leofdag. His mind made up, Charles was about to run towards the fallen priest when Ivor's man appeared. The tall warrior, his face swollen from Rollo punching him, stood over Father Leofdag, his boot on the priest's back, and glared at Charles as he panted.

'For God's sake. Run, Charles!' Father Leofdag screamed and Charles was about to turn and flee when the warrior knelt down and pressed the point of his sword into the back of Father Leofdag's neck.

'You run, boy, and the priest dies,' the warrior said with a vicious grin. To Charles, it looked like the man wanted him to run so that he had reason to kill Father Leofdag. Not that he really needed a reason, Charles was sure of that. Just as he was sure he could not run away and let Father Leofdag die, no matter what the priest was saying. 'Now come to me!'

'Don't worry about me, Charles. God will protect me. You get away!' The words that came out of Father Leofdag's mouth did not match the terror in his eyes, though.

Charles stood there, his hands trembling and unsure of what

to do. He did not want to go with the warrior, only to be taken back to Francia. But he could not let Father Leofdag die because of him, not like his father had, or Thora and Oda. Even Alfhild. All dead to keep him safe, and he still didn't even know why. Charles still didn't know why the cross his mother had given his father was so important or why so many people had to die because of it. As he stood there, struggling with the thoughts in his mind, the warrior pressed the sword harder into Father Leofdag's neck, causing the priest to scream out again. The townspeople all walked away, none of them willing to help Charles or Father Leofdag. Charles glared at them and wanted to curse them. He wanted to believe it was because they were heathens, but there were many times when he had been beaten in Hügelburg and the people there had done nothing to help him. And they were all Christians. Charles realised his grandfather had been right when he had told him that all people were the same, no matter their faith.

'Come here, boy. I don't have all day and neither does your friend.' The warrior pressed the sword down a bit more. Tears streamed down Father Leofdag's cheeks as his eyes implored Charles to help him. And Charles knew he would. He knew he could not run away. Not now. He looked to the heavens, just like he had seen his grandfather do many times, and just like his grandfather, Charles did not see any sign from God to show him what he should do.

*God, why do you punish me? What did I do to make you angry,* Charles wondered as he lowered his head and walked towards the smiling warrior.

'Good boy,' the warrior said, and then took his sword away from Father Leofdag's neck. Charles saw the blood on the tip of the blade and the small wound on the back of the priest's neck before he helped Father Leofdag up.

'Forgive me, Charles,' Father Leofdag said, his eyes looking at his feet and not at Charles. 'I'm not as strong as you.'

Charles frowned at that, but before he could say anything, Ivor and the other warrior appeared. Charles's heart dropped as he wondered what this meant for Rollo. Would Rollo now haunt his dreams like the others did?

'What happened to that whoreson, Rollo? Did you kill the bastard at least?' the warrior who had chased Charles and Father Leofdag asked.

Ivor shook his head, and Charles couldn't help but smile in relief. Ivor saw this and sneered. 'I wouldn't be so happy if I were you, piglet. I didn't kill him, but Torgeir's men might have done. And even if they don't, the gods know that Jarl Torgeir will, only because he hates your grandfather.'

'Torgeir's men?' The warrior frowned at Ivor.

'Aye, the bastards came out of nowhere. But luckily for us, they were more interested in Rollo than us. Now let's go. We need to lie low until the excitement dies out,' Ivor said to his men.

'What do we do with the priest?' the warrior asked.

'Kill him,' the other one said, but Ivor shook his head.

'No, he wanted to interfere, so now he comes with us. He might prove very useful.'

Father Leofdag paled, and he almost collapsed as he looked at Charles. For a moment, Charles saw the regret flash in his eyes and wondered if it was because they couldn't get away or because he had tried to help Charles. 'Wh... what wi... will you do to us?' Father Leofdag asked.

Ivor's smile sent a shiver down Charles's spine, but he did his best to hide it. He did not want these men to know that he was afraid, not like what Father Leofdag was doing. 'Well, the boy we need alive, so he is safe for now. But you, priest, you we don't need alive, so I suggest you do what we say, or...' Ivor left it there, not that he needed to say the rest of the sentence. Charles was sure that Father Leofdag's imagination was doing that for him.

'We need to get out of Hedeby. Torgeir's men will be looking for us,' Ivor's man said as he glanced over his shoulder towards the church. They could not see the small building from where they were, but the others all followed the warrior's gaze.

Ivor shook his head, though. 'No, they'll be happy enough with capturing Rollo. What we need is to figure out what to do next.' Ivor's forehead creased as he pulled on his beard, while his two men frowned. Charles glanced towards the church again and hoped that Rollo did not come to any harm. He did not know the jarl of Hedeby, but knew that the man was cruel. Thora and his grandfather had told him that, so he prayed Torgeir would spare Rollo.

'We should wait for the Frank to return,' one of Ivor's men said after a while. 'Isn't that what he told us to do?'

Ivor grabbed him by his brynja and snarled in his face. 'And since when do we do what the Franks tell us to do?'

'Since they pay us to do so,' the man said, glaring at Ivor. He wasn't much taller than Ivor, but was broader at the shoulder. The two men glared at each other, and Charles hoped they would fight so that he could get away. But, as usual, God ignored him as Ivor let go of the man.

'Aye, that was a mistake my father made. And Odin knows I'll not make the same mistake as well. I will not be the dog they send to do their dirty work, not any more.' Ivor hawked and spat.

'But what about the men he has watching us?' the warrior with the swollen face said.

Ivor smirked. 'You believed the bastard?'

'You don't?'

Ivor frowned. 'The Frank could have been lying to get us to do what he wants, or to set us up.'

'But why would he do that?'

'To get us out of the way. He said himself that his king wants something that is more important than the piglet. Who's to say he doesn't go straight back to West Francia once he finds this thing, or that he even survives, leaving us stranded here?' Ivor looked at Charles with a raised eyebrow. 'And besides, why would Sven's grandson be so important to the king of West Francia, anyway?'

The other two glanced at each other and then nodded as they agreed.

'Perhaps he even told Rollo where to find us?' one of the warriors said.

'Aye, it does seem strange that Rollo barged in there shortly after the Frank had left.' The warrior with the swollen face scratched the back of his neck.

Charles glanced at Father Leofdag and wondered why he said nothing. He was sure that the priest had told Rollo where to find him, even if he didn't know how Father Leofdag had found Rollo. Hedeby was a large town, larger than any he had ever seen. The last time Charles had been in Hedeby, it had taken him many days to find someone who knew about his grandfather, and even then, Thora had found him. Charles looked up and realised Ivor was still staring at him.

'Ivor? What are you thinking?' one of the men asked when they realised the same.

'There's something we are missing. This feels like one of Loki's schemes and there is something that only he knows while we blunder around in the dark.'

'What do you mean?' his man asked.

Ivor crouched down so he was face to face with Charles, who had to fight the urge to take a step back. Up close, Ivor was even uglier, with the dirt trapped in his pores and the stench of dried blood and sweat coming off of him. 'Who are you really, piglet? Why are you so important?'

Charles did not answer the question. Not only because he didn't want to, but also because he didn't really know. He suspected it had something to do with his mother, that she was more than what his grandfather had let on, but Charles didn't really know.

Ivor grabbed Charles by his tunic and brought him closer. 'You better tell me, boy, or the priest dies.' One of Ivor's men grabbed Father Leofdag and held a knife near his throat.

Again, Father Leofdag paled and his eyes pleaded with Charles.

Charles glared at the young priest and then said, 'I don't know.' Father Leofdag screamed and the man holding him pressed the knife into his throat. 'I don't know!' Charles said again. 'I really don't know!' Tears formed in his eyes as the events of the last few days threatened to erupt in him again. 'I don't know anything! Nobody told me anything! They think I'm a dumb child, even my grandfather and Thora! I don't even know who my mother is!'

Ivor smiled and let go of Charles. 'So this has something to do with your mother?' Charles's eyes widened as he realised he had said something he shouldn't have, but when he thought about it, he wondered why it mattered. He didn't know who his mother was or why she had the cross that had belonged to Charlemagne.

'Who is his mother?' Ivor asked Father Leofdag.

Father Leofdag shook his head and then winced as the movement made the knife dig deeper into his throat. 'I swear on the Almighty, I do not know. I was only asked to go to Ribe to build a church, nothing more.'

Ivor curled his upper lip. 'Forgive me if I don't put much faith in your god.' Ivor looked at his man, who had the knife, had the priest's throat. 'Kill him.'

'No! No! I know what the other man is after!' Father Leofdag screamed before the warrior behind him could open his throat. Both Charles and Ivor frowned at Father Leofdag as the man holding him hesitated.

Ivor signalled for him to wait and asked Father Leofdag, 'What is that bastard after? What is more important than the boy?'

'A cross,' Father Leofdag said and Charles gasped. How could he know about the cross? What did he know about the cross?

Ivor smiled, and Charles realised he had given himself away again. 'What is so important about this cross?' Ivor asked the priest.

'I... I don't know. But I know it is. I heard Sven and Thora talk about it in the hall. They didn't know I was there. The Frankish kings are searching for it.'

Ivor rubbed his beard and glanced at Charles, but this time, Charles swore he would not answer any more questions. He glared at Father Leofdag, who looked away, and Charles wondered why priests always seemed to betray him. Men he believed he could trust, men who spoke for God, and yet they always lied to him.

Ivor smiled, though, pleased with what he had heard. 'So, there is a cross that is important to the kings of Francia. The piglet here is also important to the king of West Francia. And I'll give my right eye to Odin to say that the piglet and the cross are connected somehow.'

'But how?' one of his men asked.

Ivor, still smiling, shrugged. 'I don't know, and I doubt the boy knows either. Sven was secretive about him and told my father nothing, no matter how much my father asked about the piglet. The old bastard is clearly hiding something.'

'But how does this help us?'

Ivor's smile grew wider as he stood up and looked around him as if he was trying to get his bearings. 'I know how we can use this to our advantage.'

'How?'

'Simple. If the king of West Francia is so desperate to get his hands on the piglet and this cross, then who's to say the other Frankish kings aren't either?'

The warrior with the swollen face scratched his head as he frowned at Ivor. 'Aye, but we can't just walk up to them and say here's a boy that is important and we don't know why and there's this cross we don't know much about either.'

Ivor nodded, but the smile stayed on his face. 'We don't need to. We know of another man who would be eager to see the old boar dead. Someone who can get word to the king of East Francia. My father told me about the history between Sven and King Louis.'

'Who?'

Ivor smiled at Charles, who again had to suppress the shiver he felt down his spine. 'Jarl Torgeir of Hedeby.'

## 6

Hildegard winced at the foul-tasting wine and put her cup down. She had been in Ribe for three days, which was longer than she had planned to be here, and for once, she did not know what to do.

When she had first set off from Bremen, she believed Charles would be here and that he would want to leave with her. He was Christian after all, and no Christian would want to live amongst the heathen Danes. Hildegard still remembered how she had trembled with nerves as her ship travelled up the river and she had her first sighting of Ribe. She had to admit, the town was larger than she had expected, with tall wooden walls on earth mounds, and a large wharf which was strangely empty, apart from a few Danish warships. Hildegard had never seen these long, sleek vessels before, but had been told enough about them to know that their draught was shallower than the ship she was in, making it easier for them to travel far upriver, and that they were much faster than her ship. She was surprised, though, that there were no monster heads on the prows of the ships. All the stories she had been told always described the many beasts' heads the

Danes liked to put on their prows. Sometimes it would be drag-
ons, other times wolves and even eagles. The ships sitting in the
wharves, though, had none, and she didn't understand why until
Bishop Bernard had explained to her that the Danes only
mounted the beasts' heads when they were in enemy waters and
they always removed the prow beasts when they returned home
because they didn't want to frighten the spirits of their lands.
Hildegard remembered how absurd the heathens were in their
beliefs of spirits and other false gods, but she'd had no time to
mention that as they spotted a large group of people walking
towards the wharf. At the head of the group, Hildegard had seen a
short man who walked with a limp and had a sword in his hand.
Gerold had told her the man was Torkel's father, Sven the Boar,
and she had worried at the fear in his voice. Because of that,
Hildegard had asked God to protect her as she stepped off the
ship and faced the man even the most hardened warriors of her
father had feared. Yet the man she saw that day was no evil
warrior with a lust for blood and a hatred of Christians, but a
father and a grandfather broken by the loss of his grandson. And
as much as Hildegard had wanted to be angry with Sven for losing
her son, she could not. Sven the Boar had done more to protect
Charles than she had ever done. Unfortunately, though, her
companions did not see him the same way she did.

Gerold had spent the entire time in Ribe cursing the Danes,
especially the woman whom they had been told had been injured
trying to protect Charles, and even Bishop Bernard found it hard
to keep the sneer from his face. It was even worse for the bishop
when they found out there was no wine in the hall, only ale,
which he had refused to drink. But Gerold had once again proven
how resourceful he was when he found some wine and information about what had happened from the few remaining Frankish
traders in Ribe. The wine, though, was disgusting, and the news

had left Hildegard furious. If they had left Bremen when she wanted to, then they would have arrived in Ribe before Charles was taken. And Sven would not have been here either, which would have made it easier to convince Charles to go with her. But God was testing her. Hildegard knew that. Why else would He have delayed them by bad weather?

Sven had barely spoken to them since they had arrived, and if it weren't for the Christian Danes, they wouldn't have anywhere to stay. They had been given an empty house to sleep in and had been told a young priest had stayed there before. Hildegard had wondered what had happened to that priest when she saw dried blood on the table in the house. But apart from bringing them food in the mornings and in the evenings, the Christians in Ribe had spent little time with them. The sailors and most of the warriors Duke Liudolf had sent with her had stayed on their ship and constantly asked Hildegard when they would be leaving. But Hildegard did not have the answer to that question. She did not want to go back to East Francia without her son because that would feel like a defeat, but she also knew that they couldn't stay here for much longer. Her absence in East Francia would be noticed and when her father found out that she was in Denmark and why she was in Denmark, then he would be furious. From what Hildegard had learnt, she was sure that Charles would be sent to West Francia, somewhere Hildegard could not go herself, especially as the tension between East and West Francia was already high. Even worse, she knew that if her son reached her uncle's kingdom, then he would be lost to her forever. So she had stayed longer than she should have, hoping – no, praying – that she could rescue Charles while he was still in Denmark.

Hildegard glanced at the two warriors, who stayed with them in the house, as one of them burped. She was not happy about their presence because the small house only had one room and she had no privacy, but the bishop insisted on them being there. Not knowing what else to do, Hildegard had gone to the hall every day, hoping that she might learn something about her son, but all she had learnt was that Sven loved to drink.

'Pathetic,' Gerold growled beside her, not for the first time since they arrived in Ribe. 'Charles is gone, and he sits there, drinking cup after cup. I knew he could never look after Charles.'

'These heathens have no sense of duty or honour.' Bishop Bernard grimaced as he drank his wine. 'But how can they if they don't follow the path of the Almighty? All their gods teach them about is violence and an unnatural lust for gold.'

Hildegard almost shook her head at the men sitting on either side of her. 'Gerold, you seem to have forgotten that you were the one who told me that Sven would kill anyone who tried to take Charles from him, and bishop, you make it sound like all Christians have honour and a sense of duty, but you forget it was a Christian that betrayed Duke Liudolf and killed Torkel. That it is because of a Christian king, my uncle, that Charles had to flee into the arms of the heathens.' Both Gerold and Bishop Bernard had the sense not to argue, which made Hildegard smile. 'And besides, you are both wrong about Sven.'

'Wrong?' Bishop Bernard asked. 'What do you mean, wrong? The man is a heathen known for torturing Christians.'

'And my great-grandfather was a Christian known for torturing heathens,' Hildegard retorted before she could stop herself. She took a deep breath to calm herself before she explained what she meant. 'Sven is a father and a grandfather mourning the loss of his grandson. Just like I'm sure he mourned the loss of Torkel after my father took him hostage.'

'The heathens don't understand these emotions,' Bishop Bernard said with a sneer in his voice. 'He lost and now he is licking his wounds.'

'No, bishop. You misjudge Sven, and that is dangerous.' Hildegard sensed the bishop frown at her. 'My father and his people
always wondered what happened to Sven after that day on the
beach. He simply disappeared, and many believed he was dead.
And yet, Gerold and Charles found him. An old, broken drunk
trying to kill himself.'

'You forgot to mention smelly as well,' Gerold put in and then
turned away as Hildegard scowled at him.

'Losing his son broke him, and I believe Charles had given
him a new sense of purpose. He killed his brother to regain his
position of jarl after Charles met him, did he not?'

Gerold's cheeks reddened after that comment and Hildegard
understood why. Gerold had been here that night and had barely
escaped. And then, even after his return to East Francia, Duke
Liudolf had blamed him for the deaths of the men he had sent to
find Charles and had thrown him in prison. The only reason the
duke had not hung Gerold was because Hildegard thought he
could be useful to her and, so far, she had been correct. 'Sven is
still a dangerous man. Never forget that.'

'What do you mean?' Bishop Bernard asked as he attempted
to drink more of the foul wine.

Hildegard watched as the woman who Charles believed was
his guardian angel spoke to Sven. A woman she was eager to meet.
'Sven the Boar has nothing to lose and everything to gain. As long
as he is sitting there drowning in his sorrows, then we have a
better chance of finding my son and taking him to where he
belongs. But if Sven comes to his senses, which she is no doubt
trying to get him to do, then the rivers will be red with blood, and
both my uncle's and my father's kingdoms will burn.' Hildegard
wasn't sure if she really believed the words she had spoken, but
everything she had learnt about Sven had told her never to underestimate him. All those who had done so were now dead,

including the king of Denmark. 'Tomorrow, we leave. We'll go back to Saxony and pray that Duke Liudolf has learnt something about Charles's whereabouts. I think we won't learn much by staying here any longer.'

'Finally,' Gerold said, but Bishop Bernard wasn't so sure.

'What about the cross? We don't know where it is.' Bishop Bernard had been dismayed when Sven had told them that the Cross of Charlemagne had been taken with Charles. It almost felt like the bishop cared more about the cross than her son.

Hildegard tensed. 'I only care about finding my son.'

'But we must find the cross, Hildegard,' Bishop Bernard said. 'The fate of Francia depends on it.'

Hildegard glanced at the old bishop, seeing the seriousness in his still-sharp eyes. 'Why, bishop? Why does the fate of Francia depend on a cross no one has seen for almost ten years?' Hildegard had never understood why the cross was so important or why Torkel had to die because of it.

'That cross helped the great Charlemagne to build his empire. It helped him spread the light of Christ to the darkest corners of our world. It protected us from the heathen scum which plague our shores today. We must find it if we want to free ourselves from the godless men in this town who want to rape our women or plunder our churches.'

Hildegard scowled as the warriors who guarded them stared at the bishop with wide eyes. 'It's just a cross, bishop. No item can hold so much power. And besides, my father has many more.' Even Hildegard noticed the lack of conviction in her own voice. Her entire life, she had been told of the power of the Cross of Charlemagne. But while many believed that the cross would save Francia and unite the three kingdoms again, she knew that the real reason the empire had broken up in the first place was because of the Cross of Charlemagne. Hildegard remembered how her mother had told her that the reason the sons of Emperor Louis had started the civil war was because he had given the cross to his oldest son, Lothair. But somehow, during the civil war, her father had got his hands on it and had been forced to keep it hidden ever since. That was why, to this day, no one knew the cross was missing. And since Charlemagne's cross had gone missing, there had been no more wars between her father and her uncles. Hildegard kept all this to herself, though. 'Now come. I'd like to meet Charles's guardian angel.' Hildegard stood up and walked towards the bench where Sven and the woman were sitting, and did not see the scowl on the bishop's face.

* * *

Sven's knuckles turned white as he gripped his cup when he saw the woman claiming to be Charles's mother approach them, with that snake and the old priest behind her. He had done his best to avoid them since the day they had arrived. Not just because every time he spoke to her, he was reminded again of how he had failed his son, Torkel, but also because he had to speak to Gerold. Charles's mother claimed she did not speak the Danish tongue and so Gerold translated for her, even though he knew Sven spoke Frankish. But it took too much for Sven not to beat the bastard to death with his bare hands. Sven glanced at his knuckles, which had almost healed from his fight with Guttrom. The scabs were gone and now only the white lines of the fresh scars reminded him of that fight. As well as the cut to his stomach and the stab wound to his back. His brynja had done what it needed to that day, though, as both wounds would have killed him if he had not been wearing the chain-mail vest.

Thora frowned as Charles's mother stopped by their table. Sven had hoped that they would leave as soon as they had found out that Charles was gone, but the woman had stayed, despite the protestations of the old priest and Gerold. That was another reason Sven spent all his time in the hall drinking. To avoid them. But instead, they came to the hall every day and sat near the door. Watching him and waiting, although Sven didn't know what for. He did not know where Charles was. If he did, then he wouldn't be here. He'd be ramming his sword down the throat of that bastard Ivor. But he didn't know where Ivor was either, and Sven was too exhausted and too old to be rampaging around Denmark. Or Francia, because he was sure that was where the boy was headed. His body ached more than ever and even the ale and mead did nothing to numb that pain. Not like it had done in the past. Sven could barely put any weight on his left leg. The old wound that Sven could not even remember getting was plaguing him even more, as if the gods were punishing him. Perhaps it was Thor, the protector, angered that he had failed to protect Charles. Then there was his back, his shoulders, his knees and even his wrists. Everything hurt and now he had a constant headache from the ale, but Sven did not want to stop drinking.

'You must be the woman who was injured trying to protect my son,' Charles's mother said, and Gerold translated the words. Sven sensed his glare, which only annoyed him even more.

Thora scrutinised Charles's mother and nodded, but Sven sensed she didn't want to speak to Gerold either. Thora took a sip from her cup and said, 'Your son?'

Gerold translated Thora's response and Charles's mother tensed. 'Yes, Charles is my son.'

Thora's brows creased. 'Then why did you abandon him? What kind of mother would choose her god over her own son?' Gerold's face went red as he translated the words, which made the old priest gasp and the woman glare at Thora.

'Heathen bitch,' Gerold hissed in Frankish. 'Just say the word and I'll kill her for you.' Before Charles's mother could respond, Sven exploded.

The rage he had tried to drown out with ale and mead took hold of him, overcoming his aches and making them seem like distant memories. Sven jumped to his feet and grabbed Gerold by the throat, while the old priest screamed and dropped to his knees. Everyone else in the hall stopped what they were doing and watched Sven lift the taller man off his feet and drag him out of the hall. The two Frankish warriors that were sitting with Charles's mother jumped to their feet but then remembered they didn't have their weapons on them as Sven forbade them from bringing their weapons into the hall. Not that it would have helped as Alvar and four of Sven's men rushed towards them and grabbed the Frankish warriors before they could do anything to stop Sven.

Gerold tried to free himself from Sven's grip. He struck Sven's arm with his fist, even kicked Sven in the stomach, but Sven felt none of it as he roared at Gerold. 'You'll kill her, will you?' He noticed Gerold's hand go to his stomach and saw the hilt of the knife that Gerold had hidden in his tunic, but before Gerold could pull the knife out of its scabbard, Sven gripped his hand, already around the hilt, and squeezed as hard as he could. Gerold cried out as he tried to pull his hand and the knife free, but he could not.

Outside the hall, the dull light of the clouded sky briefly blinded Sven as he threw Gerold to the ground. Gerold grunted as he hit the ground and somewhere a woman screamed. Just like inside the hall, everyone stopped what they were doing as Sven rushed at Gerold and kicked him in the stomach. The kick lifted Gerold off the ground and, as soon as he landed, Sven kicked him again. He leaned down and took Gerold's knife and with his other hand he grabbed Gerold's hair and lifted his face so he could see

Sven's anger. Gerold's face paled as Sven pressed the point of the knife against his throat. 'You threaten my people in my hall!' Alvar and the others dragged the Frankish warriors out of the hall and forced them to their knees while Alvar ordered other warriors to grab the remaining Frankish warriors.

'Stop! In the name of God, stop this now!' Charles's mother ordered in Danish as she rushed out of the hall, which only angered Sven even more. He glared at her, before turning his attention back to Gerold, who looked like a terrified child as the knife broke the skin of his neck and a trickle of blood escaped. As much as Sven hated Gerold for his part in this thing that Sven still did not understand, Gerold's wide eyes and trembling chin reminded him too much of Charles. It was the same look his grandson had that day in the forest when Jarl Torgeir's men had tried to kill them. The memory was like a wave that washed his rage away, and Sven's hand trembled as he thought of Charles. His grandson, lost and frightened, and here he was, drinking his sorrows away while others had to search for the boy. 'Please, stop. Gerold misspoke,' Charles's mother said once more, and again in Danish.

'Sven,' Thora said, and he saw her standing in the hall's doorway, her face strained from the pain while her hand clutched her stomach.

A growl escaped from Sven's throat as he pulled the knife away from Gerold's neck. He leaned closer to Gerold. 'My grandson saved your life today. Don't you ever forget that.' Gerold frowned, but Sven wasn't paying attention to him any more. He stood and glared at the people of Ribe, even though he knew they suffered much from what had been happening. Many returned his glare, blaming him for their fates, and Sven knew they were right. He turned his attention to the woman who claimed to be Charles's mother and remembered how her father had taken his son away from him and changed his fate. Or perhaps the Norns had decided long before that that would be Sven's destiny. 'So you speak our tongue.'

The woman found her composure faster than Sven would have thought possible and lifted her chin. 'Just like you speak mine,' she responded in Frankish. Sven growled and walked past her as he went back to the hall. 'Alfhild! Ale! Now!' He walked to the back of the hall and stopped in front of the raised seat when he remembered the young woman had died and that he had buried her the day before. None of the townspeople had protested that he had given a thrall the honour of a burial in the town's graveyard and Sven himself had been surprised by how many people had shown up for her funeral. Audhild, Thora's cousin, had even provided one of her dresses, so Alfhild wasn't dressed like a thrall when she reached Hel. Sven looked up at the stuffed boar's head that was mounted on the wall above the jarl's seat. It had a spear in it now, although Sven didn't know who had thrown it. He guessed it was Ivor and swore that he would stick his own spear in Ivor's head. Sven returned to the bench he had been sitting on for the last few days. He did not deserve to sit in the jarl's seat. Not any more. The people of Ribe needed someone who could protect them now with all the chaos caused by the death of Horik and his jarls. And Sven was not that man. He wondered if Loki was enjoying what was happening in Denmark. The trickster was the god of chaos, after all.

## 7

Sven collapsed onto the bench and noticed that the many empty cups that had been there before were gone and the table had been wiped clean as a thrall handed him the ale he had asked for. The few people still in the hall quickly left, not wanting to be on the wrong end of Sven's temper. They all still remembered what had happened to Haldor, the husband of Thora's cousin, when he had angered Sven.

He glanced at the thrall, who was older than Alfhild, as she returned to her task and remembered the first night he had met Alfhild earlier in the summer. Already that felt like it had happened so long ago and it was hard to believe they were still in the same season. For so many winters, nothing had happened in Sven's life. Just endless wandering around, avoiding trouble as he searched for enough ale to drown his memories in. Yet, since Charles had come into his life, it had been nothing but chaos. There had barely been a moment where Sven could just sit and stare at the stars. Sven missed those days, something which had surprised him when he became the jarl of Ribe again. But now, as he sat there on the bench, ignoring those in the hall who were still staring at him, he missed his grandson even more. The boy's inquisitive blue eyes which seemed to catch everything. His constant questions as he tried to understand the Norse gods, only then to dismiss them as false idols. But he would give anything to have Charles ask him about Thor, Loki or Frey, just so he could hear his voice again.

Thora sat down next to him, her face pale and grim, but she said nothing as the Franks entered the hall, followed by Alvar and another warrior dragging the Frankish warriors with them. A few more of Ribe's warriors came in and formed a half-circle around the Franks. Charles's mother had regained her composure and looked as stern as before, whereas the old priest could not keep his fear from his face, as his chin trembled and his eyes darted around the hall like he was expecting the warriors to attack him. Sven could almost smell the fear coming off the old priest, and prayed he wouldn't shit in his hall. Gerold glared at Sven as he used his tunic to wipe the blood from the small cut to his neck.

'I apologise for Gerold,' Charles's mother said to Thora in Danish. 'That was not very Christian of him.'

Thora barked out a laugh. 'No, that was very Christian of him. That's all he ever did when we first met. Look down on us, but then he turned out to be a bigger snake than any of us.'

Gerold opened his mouth to respond, but Charles's mother stopped him by raising her hand. 'That was wrong of him. Gerold has told me much about you, Thora. How you put yourself at risk to protect my son. Even going as far as dressing and fighting like a man.'

'I did not dress or fight like a man. I dressed and fought like a warrior. We Danish women are not servants to our men, not like you Christians.' Thora sneered as she said the words, which surprised Sven. He had never seen her angry before.

Charles's mother nodded as she accepted what Thora had

said, but again, Gerold could not help himself. 'It's not womanlike to dress like that.'

Sven looked up from his ale, his face creased as he glared at Gerold, who took a step back. He tried to understand if Gerold was trying to be brave in front of Charles's mother or was he just too dumb to realise the situation they were in? But he did not need to say anything as Thora responded, 'And it wasn't very manlike for you to squeal like a baby when we were attacked and I had to protect you.'

Gerold's face turned red and Sven prayed to Týr that the Frank was dumb enough to attack. Or even just to take a step forward because Sven would gladly send him to their heaven. His hands trembled as he wished he had done it outside the hall.

'Enough,' Charles's mother said, her eyes hard. 'We do not have time to squabble like children. We have much to talk about.'

'We have nothing to talk about,' Sven said. He looked at the woman, her hair covered by her hood and with the large golden cross hanging around her neck, and wondered what his son had seen in her.

Charles's mother glared at him in return. 'I have to find my son.'

'Why do you suddenly care about your son?' Thora said, sneering. 'Where were you when his father was killed? Where were you when he walked around Hedeby, frightened, and crying? You call him your son, but by Frigg, you are no mother of his!'

The words seemed to knock the wind out of Charles's mother, but she took a deep breath and looked at Thora. 'You know nothing of the sacrifices I had to make to keep Charles safe!'

Thora glared at Charles's mother. Sven knew Thora and her husband never had any children of their own, and wondered if that had anything to do with her anger. 'Sacrifices?' Thora hawked and spat. 'You gave your son away so you could follow your god.'

Charles's mother turned away and stared at the weak flames of the hearth fire. Sven saw how she clenched her fists and the tear that ran down her cheek. She then took a deep breath and turned to face Thora, her mask back. Sven understood then how dangerous this woman could be, and understood why the West Franks wanted Charles. 'I do not have to explain myself to a heathen who understands nothing of our faith or of my life.'

Thora jumped to her feet, her face grimacing in pain, but she kept her eyes on Charles's mother. 'This heathen bled for your son! What have you done for him?'

Charles's mother looked like she was about to launch herself at Thora, but again, she held her nerve. 'I bled to bring him into this world and since then, I have done everything to keep him safe. Even letting him believe I was dead so that others would not find out who he is.'

'But someone still did and his father died because of it,' Thora said.

'Enough!' Sven slammed his fist onto the table, which made everyone jump. Even those on the other side of the hall. Sven did not want to hear about the death of Torkel, not again. 'Enough of this!' He glared at Thora, who looked away when she realised her mistake, and then at Charles's mother, who only stared back. 'We all failed that boy. You,' he glared at Charles's mother, 'and me. And all you do is argue over who is to blame.'

'All you've been doing is drinking all week,' Gerold said and then took a step to the side so that he was almost hiding behind Charles's mother when Sven glared at him.

'Boy, if you say one more thing in front of me, then I'll rip your tongue out and feed it to the dogs.' Sven faced Charles's mother. 'Odin knows, I don't care if you really are his mother, or just someone pretending so you could stab me in the back, just like everyone else. All I care about is finding out where my grandson is.'

Charles's mother took a deep breath as her hands gripped the sides of her dress and said, 'So do I, but at least I know where he is going.'

'Aye, so do we.' Sven drank some of his ale as he tried to calm down before he killed the woman standing there. One, because of what had happened to his wife, Eydis; and two, because she might just actually be Charles's mother and Sven knew the boy had enough reasons to be angry at him. 'To West Francia.'

Charles's mother raised an eyebrow at him. 'How do you know this?'

'Because that snake Guttrom boasted about how you lot paid him to come here and to find my grandson.'

'Not us. My uncle, the king of West Francia. He is the one behind all of this. My father knows nothing of what is happening.'

Sven waved a hand at her. 'Pah! West, East, all you Franks are the same.'

The woman went red in the face and Sven found some grim satisfaction that he was getting to her. 'We are not the same as the West Franks.'

Sven leaned forward. 'You are all Christians and you think you are better than us Danes. And you all are the reason my son was killed.'

Charles's mother lowered her head and stood like that for a short while. He glanced at Thora, who only shrugged, but then Charles's mother sat down and stared at her hands. When she looked up again, her eyes were as hard as the stone in the mountains. 'I am not the reason Torkel was killed.'

Sven drank from his cup as he stared at the woman. Her stern face reminded him of her father, which only angered him even more. 'You gave him the cross, and that was why he died.'

Charles's mother only stared at Sven, but he saw battle raging in her mind, as she must have thought the same. He wanted to feel sorry for her because he knew what it was like to live with that kind of guilt. He still did himself.

'Why did you give the cross to Torkel?' Thora asked. 'You must have known what would happen.'

Charles's mother took a deep breath and glanced at the old priest, who looked like he was about to faint from his fear. She fingered the golden cross she wore around her own neck and just when Sven thought she would not answer, she said, 'So that when Charles was old enough, he could bring the cross to me and I would know who he is.'

Sven narrowed his eyes. 'But why that cross?'

Charles's mother stared at him. 'That has nothing to do with you.'

Sven jumped to his feet and again slammed his fist on the table. 'It has everything to do with me! My son died because of that! First, your father took my son from me and then you killed him!' Sven turned his attention to Alvar, who still had one of the Frankish warriors in his grip. For many winters, he had dreamt of getting his vengeance against the Frankish bastard who had taken his son from him. Sven never had the means to do that though. But now he did. He nodded to Alvar, who understood what Sven wanted. Alvar pulled the sax-knife from his belt and stabbed the Frankish warrior in front of him. One of the other Danish warriors did the same, as the old priest cried for mercy from his god and even Charles's mother paled when she must have realised what was about to happen. Gerold's eyes darted around the hall as if he was looking for a way to escape, but then he stepped closer to Charles's mother and put himself between her and the rest of

Ribe's warriors. That surprised Sven, but he said nothing as Charles's mother turned to him.

'What are you doing?'

Sven smiled at her. 'I'm making sure that you don't get in my way.'

Charles's mother stood up and took a step towards Sven. 'You cannot do that! I am the daughter of the king of East Francia!'

Sven clenched his fists. 'Aye, you are. Your father took my son from me and now I'm taking his daughter from him. You will stay in Ribe until I know exactly why that cursed cross got my son killed and my grandson kidnapped.' Sven looked at Alvar, who was cleaning his sax-knife on the trousers of the dead Frank. 'Alvar, take them and lock them up. Make sure no one goes near them, especially the Christians in this town.'

Alvar nodded. 'What about the rest of her men and their ship?'

Sven turned his attention back to Charles's mother, who was doing her best to look strong, but he still saw the fear in her eyes. 'Kill them. Kill them all.'

Alvar turned and left the hall with enough warriors while a few stayed and made sure that Charles's mother couldn't go anywhere.

Thora stepped closer and in a soft voice asked, 'Are you sure this is a good idea?'

As she spoke, there was a spark from one log in the hearth fire, and Sven wondered if that was an omen. 'No, Thora. I'm not. But I have no other ideas.'

## 8

Duke Liudolf sat in his library, as he often did since the death of Torkel, poring over messages sent to him from all over his duchy. As he finished reading the latest report from the south of Saxony, he leaned back in his chair and ran his hand through his greying hair and thought again about the moment that changed everything. The death of a man he had considered a friend. A man who had saved his life. Liudolf looked around his table for his cup, but scowled when he saw it was empty. A quick glance at the beaker lying on its side told him he had no wine left. He wondered where his servant had gone and then he remembered he had ordered that no one disturb him, not even his wife and children. Sighing, Liudolf picked up another message, this one from a town in the east, which, just like Hügelburg, was supposed to protect the eastern border of East Francia.

Since the death of Torkel, Duke Liudolf had worked his agents hard, sending them all over Saxony to root out any other traitors who had sold themselves to King Charles of West Francia. It wasn't just his duty that drove this, but also his guilt. The day Charles had been born, Liudolf had promised Hildegard that he would protect Torkel and their son. And that promise had been broken.

It had been easy at first to watch over them, when Torkel had joined his forces in Ehresburg. The man had been a talented warrior and, despite his origins, a devout Christian who was easy to like. But then King Louis had arrived on a surprise visit and had been furious with Liudolf for allowing Torkel to stay in his capital. In the end, both Torkel and Liudolf had agreed that it would be best if Torkel took Charles somewhere else. Somewhere where he was not known and where the king would never go. That way, the king would forget about Charles and the boy had a better chance of becoming a man. Liudolf had then remembered that one of his border towns had just lost a senior warrior in a skirmish against the Abodrites, the Slavic people to the east who were once allies of the great Charlemagne, but switched their alliance to the Danes so often it was hard to know where they really stood. So he had sent Torkel to Hügelburg. Lothar, the man he had appointed as the new chatelaine, was not pleased to have an outsider as his second in command, especially when that man was a Dane. Liudolf had ignored his complaints, though, and things between Torkel and Lothar had seemed to settle down. For many years there were no problems from Hügelburg other than the constant raids by the Danes and the Abodrites, though Duke Liudolf could never understand how his men always arrived too late to deal with the raiders. Lothar had suggested that some had been betraying them and had even suggested that it was Torkel. Liudolf had laughed at that notion, but never would he have imagined that it was Lothar all along. The man had always been loyal and a solid warrior.

The death of Torkel and the betrayal of Lothar had shown Duke Liudolf how little he knew of what went on in his duchy. So he had sent his agents out to scour Saxony for any other official or warrior who wasn't completely loyal to him and the king. So far, over twenty traitors had been found, most of them in the border towns and at least fifteen of those had been hanged. The rest still waited for his judgement. But the new message he was reading made him forget about all that and curse himself for his weakness when it came to Hildegard. It was a message from Bremen saying that his ship had not returned yet. It had been more than a week since it had left Bremen with Hildegard and Bishop Bernard on board, along with Gerold, and after the reports of the outcome of the battle between the Danish king and his nephew, Duke Liudolf had expected Hildegard to return immediately.

Frustrated, Duke Liudolf got up so he could get another jug of wine when the door to his library opened and his servant poked his head in. Liudolf scowled at the man and was about to berate him when the man said, 'Duke Liudolf. King Louis is here. He has just entered through the south gate.'

The duke scowled again while his servant waited by the door. He glanced at the message from Bremen and thought he knew why King Louis of East Francia had arrived unannounced. Again, Duke Liudolf cursed himself for being so weak when it came to Hildegard. But he could not help it. He had always been in love with her, from the moment he had first met her in her father's court so many years ago. But she had already chosen another man, and it wasn't until after the birth of Charles that Liudolf had discovered it was the small Danish warrior, Torkel. Liudolf had offered to marry Hildegard and pretend the boy was his own, but Hildegard had refused and had gone to a nunnery instead. 'Make sure the king is comfortable and has everything he needs,' Duke Liudolf said and ran a hand through his messy hair. He needed to freshen himself up before he met the king. The servant nodded and left while Liudolf glanced at the note again. *Where are you, Hildegard?*

Liudolf made his way to his room on the second floor of his house, where he found his wife, Aeda, playing with their four-year-old son, Otto. Aeda was the daughter of one of the Frankish princes and it had been a political marriage, made by Liudolf's father to bring him closer to the Carolinians. Liudolf never felt the same way for Aeda as he did for Hildegard, but he was still glad for the marriage. She had given him five children so far and had been a good companion to him over the years.

'Something the matter, husband?'

Duke Liudolf sighed before he rinsed his face in the bowl of water on the table. 'King Louis is here.'

'Now?' Aeda looked towards the door as if she expected him to walk into their room. 'But we were not told that he was coming.' She jumped to her feet, the movement so fast it made little Otto cry, and rushed for the door. The nursemaid appeared and collected Otto before calming him down and leaving the room.

'Because he wanted to surprise me.'

Aeda stopped and stared at him, her brows drawn together. 'Because of Hildegard?'

Duke Liudolf nodded.

'I warned you not to give in to her.'

Duke Liudolf said nothing as he combed his hair. They had had this fight already, and he had no time to do it again, especially not with the king of East Francia waiting in his hall. But he knew Aeda was right, and she knew he knew, which was why she didn't push any further. Instead, she headed to the kitchens to make sure the servants prepared a good meal for the king. Liudolf looked at himself in the small mirror and knew he had to be very careful with how he played this. His father had worked very hard to get him into this position and Liudolf had done everything he could over the years to foster a good relationship with the king and his children. He had provided Hildegard with information and spies so that she knew everything that went on in her father's kingdom. Liudolf wasn't the only duke to do so, but he was the only one who knew about her son and had kept her updated on the boy. He wished, though, she had told him about the cross. If he had known that Torkel had it, he would never have sent the man to Hügelburg. Now the Danes had the cross which could alter the destiny of Francia and he had to lie to the king about it. Although, it wouldn't be the first time he lied to the king to protect Hildegard.

Taking a deep breath and checking himself in the mirror to make sure he was presentable, Duke Liudolf left his room and made his way to the hall. There, he raised his eyebrow at the king's warriors guarding the door and wondered where his own men were. Most likely in the nearest tavern, enjoying their sudden freedom from their duties. The warriors greeted him respectfully, but Liudolf knew they would kill him in a blink if the king ordered them to. The duke's hall, which had belonged to his father, was decorated like most in Francia. Banners and flags showing the emblem of Saxony, a white steed on a red background, hung from the beams which supported the roof, while the walls were painted in bright colours to bring as much light into the large room as possible. Large windows with plain glass aided the banners and the colourful paint, while a large hearth fire heated the hall during the cold winter nights. As Liudolf entered his hall, he saw men he recognised from the king's court and a few he had never seen before. Newcomers trying to work their way into King Louis's good graces. There had been many of them over the years, but they never lasted long. King Louis was a hard man to please and most failed to understand that for the king to trust them, they first had to earn the trust of Hildegard. But many disregarded her because she was a woman and paid a heavy price for that. Duke Liudolf straightened his back and squared his shoulders as he walked to the rear of his hall, where King Louis was sitting in his chair and holding a cup of wine in his hand. Liudolf was glad he could rely on his servants and wife to know what to do in situations like this.

King Louis was a year younger than Liudolf and about half a head shorter, but his dominance always made him seem taller in Liudolf's mind. Like all the Carolinians, King Louis had dark hair and dark eyes, although his eyes were much harder than those of his brothers. His hair was cropped below his ears, just like Liudolf's and all the other men in the court, and his short beard was well groomed.

The king had the broad shoulders of a man who had fought many battles against his enemies and his brothers, but he had to give up the sword to watch over his domain, just like Liudolf had done. Although Liudolf had done it willingly. The last battle he had fought in was the final battle between the sons of Emperor Louis, before the Treaty of Verdun was signed. Liudolf had almost died in that battle and was only alive because of Torkel, and he still had nightmares of that day. That was the last time he had the strength to face another in combat, but no one could know that. Liudolf regularly sparred with one of his most trusted men to keep up appearances, but he always sent others to fight the actual battles.

'Duke Liudolf,' the king said in his deep voice, which lacked warmth.

'My lord king.' Liudolf stopped a few paces away from the king and bowed deeply. Two giant warriors stood on either side of the king, both men with long two-handed axes that would take your head from your shoulders before you could even get near the king. And they both scowled at Liudolf as if they had forgotten that they were in his hall.

King Louis took a sip from his cup and smacked his lips before he turned his attention back to Duke Liudolf. 'I was in Frankfurt, spending some time with my grandchildren, when I heard the news of what had happened in Denmark. I thought with King Horik dead and Denmark having no king, it would be a good time to do what my father and grandfather could never achieve. Conquer Denmark and make those heathen scum finally bend the knee to our beloved God.' The people in the hall cheered and a few even crossed themselves, but Liudolf steeled himself for what he knew was coming. 'But first, I wanted the advice of Hildegard. Perhaps she knew of a way I could do that without having to spill the blood of good Christian men on heathen grounds. So, I assembled my entourage and set to pay her a visit in Fraumünster.' King Louis took another sip of his wine and his face turned red. Duke Liudolf knew it was not because of the wine. 'Do you know what I discovered in Fraumünster, Duke Liudolf?' The king glared at him and Liudolf took a deep breath. He was tempted to lie, but he knew the king was aware of his close friendship with Hildegard. And besides, Liudolf had to protect his position so that his sons and their sons could rule Saxony. So he knew that lying would be the worst option for him.

With another deep breath, Duke Liudolf nodded. 'Yes, my king. I do.'

King Louis jumped to his feet and threw his cup at Duke Liudolf, who barely flinched as it struck his chest and wine sprayed his face. 'Where is my daughter?'

## 9

Hildegard paced around the house they were kept prisoner in, her arms crossed and with a scowl on her face, but her heart was still racing with the events from earlier in the day on her mind. Things had not turned out the way she had expected them to. She had wanted to leave Ribe and find her son, but God had decided against that plan. For a reason she could not understand, He had decided that she had to stay in Ribe. Or perhaps it had nothing to do with the Almighty, she thought as she glanced at Gerold.

The young man was sitting on a stool, his head leaned back against the wall and his eyes closed as if this imprisonment was nothing to him. But then perhaps it wasn't. He had spent many weeks locked up in one of Duke Liudolf's prisons before Hildegard had ordered him released. Now she was wondering if that had been such a smart move. She had believed that Gerold would be valuable to her in her quest to find Charles. He had been here before and knew the language, so she wouldn't have to give away the fact that she did as well. Torkel had taught her the Danish tongue, and it had been useful to her many times in the past. But Hildegard had not considered that the Danes would despise Gerold as much as they did, even though Gerold had tried to warn her. Hildegard had believed that she could overcome that. She might have done if Gerold had learnt to keep his opinions to himself. His insolence and disrespect towards the heathens might have pleased some, but Hildegard was not amused by it. Especially not after it got all of Duke Liudolf's sailors and warriors killed. Innocent and god-fearing men slaughtered just because of Gerold's hatred of the heathens. But not really because of that. It was her decision to come here, and she knew it had been her indecision on what to do next that had got them killed. If she had left sooner, then those men would still be alive. Wives would still have their husbands and children would still have their fathers. Hildegard knew she should pray for their souls and more than that, she should ask the Almighty for forgiveness, but she could not. Not with her anger at the situation still clouding her mind.

She glanced at Bishop Bernard, who wasn't as calm as Gerold. The old priest sat on a bench, his hands clasped before him and his eyes squeezed shut and lips moving fervently as he prayed. Hildegard hoped it was for the men who had died needlessly, but the way the bishop's hands trembled told her the old man was praying for himself. The bishop was frightened, though, and Hildegard could understand why. Sven the Boar was angry, and he was known to torture priests. Stories of his cruelty had been spread across Francia for as long as she could remember. Although she also remembered how Torkel would laugh when he heard them. Once she had asked him why and he told her the stories were never true. Hildegard prayed Torkel was right, because right now they were at Sven's mercy. She studied the house they were in, the one they had been told had been given to a priest from Hedeby. If Sven was really as cruel as the stories made him out to be, would he have allowed a priest to stay here? Hildegard had tried to find any proof of this priest, but the house was empty. *As barren as Sven's soul*, she thought.

'Fucking heathens! Who do they think they are? Holding us hostage like this!' Gerold's sudden outburst made Hildegard realise that the young man was not as calm as she had believed. She looked at him and saw his brows creased and his mouth set in a thin line. The blood had dried on the cut on his throat and it didn't seem to bother him.

Hildegard decided not to respond, but Bishop Bernard did. 'They do not understand what is right or what is wrong. How can they if they don't have God's book to guide their lives? I don't think the savages can even read.'

'I should have slit the old bastard's throat the last time I was here, while he was still a drunken old fool.'

'Yes,' the bishop agreed. 'You would have done us all a favour then. And the whole of Christendom. Sven the Boar is a minion of the devil and my heart breaks when I think of the horrors Charles must have experienced living here amongst the heathens.'

Hildegard took a deep breath as she tried to calm her racing heart. She turned and sat down on the bench on the opposite side of Bishop Bernard so she could see both the old man and Gerold. 'Do you remember that old warrior that used to fight for my father, Baldwin?'

Bishop Bernard frowned and nodded, the question seeming to catch him off guard. 'Yes, I remember him. A good Christian, never missed a service and donated much to the church.'

'Yes. Also known for stamping on the heads of small children and being one of the most ruthless of my father's warriors. That was why my father liked to send him when the Abodrites raided his kingdom. Because he knew Baldwin would do what was needed to make the Abodrites regret raiding East Francia. The man was a brute, vicious and cruel to his core. He reminds me of Sven.'

'But he was a Christian! He was a good man who did God's work!' the bishop said, showing some of the old fire in his veins which had helped him reach his position.

'Yes, but he was known for killing women and children. Many warriors have spoken of the things they have witnessed Baldwin do, but the stories we have of Sven are just stories. The towns and farmsteads he raided in Francia had suffered no worse fate than when other Danish jarls raided. Yet Sven, we fear the most.'

'What are you saying?' Bishop Bernard asked, his eyebrow raised.

'Do not judge Sven based on his faith and stories told to frighten children. I told you before. He is a grandfather mourning the loss of his grandson.'

'He is a pig who should be gutted,' Gerold retorted.

Hildegard felt a hot flash of anger engulf her and before she could stop herself, said, 'And you are a child who needs to learn when to speak and when to stay silent!'

Both Bishop Bernard and Gerold's eyes widened at her outburst.

'But—' Gerold started, but was silenced by Hildegard.

'No! You complain about being held prisoner by these heathens, yet if you had kept your opinions to yourself, then we might have been on our ship and trying to find my son, and not locked in this small house with heathen warriors guarding the door! Duke Liudolf's men would still be alive and their blood would not be flowing down the river!'

'You can't blame Gerold for this.' Bishop Bernard tried to defend Gerold.

'I do blame Gerold for this.' Hildegard glared at Gerold. 'Sven was just sitting there, drowning his sorrows in his drink. Then you

angered him with your empty threats and now we are locked in
here and have no way of finding Charles before he does! Not to
mention the men he had killed, innocent sailors and warriors
tasked with keeping us safe, because you can't control your
tongue!' Gerold looked away, his cheeks turning red as Hildegard
turned on the bishop before he could say anything. 'And you,
bishop. All you care about is the cross! My son is missing. Only
God knows where and you just keep asking about the cross. Is that
the real reason you insisted on coming with us?' Hildegard had
never planned on the bishop joining them on their journey to
Ribe. But she had visited the bishop to tell him of her plans and to
ask him about the cross that seemed to curse her family. Bishop
Bernard had insisted that he knew nothing about why they
believed the cross was so important and that he should come
along. Hildegard had been suspicious about that, but thought it
would do no harm for the old man to join them. She even thought
it might help Charles to see someone he knew and trusted. But
now, as the bishop struggled to find the words to defend himself,
Hildegard realised he had been lying to her. 'You know about the
cross. You know its story.'

Bishop Bernard's mouth fell open, but he quickly closed it and
shook his head. 'No, I already told you I know nothing about the
cross. I didn't even know Torkel had it until you told us after he
was killed.'

That was the only part Hildegard believed, but she had made
it her mission to learn when men were lying to her, as they often
did. Hildegard might have been an abbess and the daughter of
King Louis of East Francia, but she was still a woman and many
men believed they were better than her for that reason alone.
Only two men had never lied to her or treated her as less than an
equal. Torkel and Duke Liudolf. She had believed that Bishop
Bernard also treated her as an equal, but now realised otherwise.

Like with Gerold, Hildegard wondered why she had brought the bishop with, as he sat there, his mouth open and trying to find the right words. But before she could press him more, the door opened and the woman warrior walked in carrying a jug and some cups. She stopped and raised an eyebrow at them and Hildegard felt Gerold tense and prayed that the young man would do nothing foolish.

Thora seemed to sense the same as she said, 'You can try whatever you are thinking, Gerold, but I swear by Thor you'd be dead before you reach the door.'

Gerold bared his teeth and, again, Hildegard lost her patience with him. 'Gerold, don't.'

He glanced at her, his eyes widening as if he was about to protest, but Hildegard shook her head.

Once the door was closed, Thora walked towards the table and put the jug on the table. 'I thought you'd like something to drink. You'll be brought food twice a day, but don't try anything dumb. Sven doesn't need much to be angered.'

'The old bast—'

'Gerold!' Hildegard silenced him and wondered how his former master had tolerated him. She had known the old man, had used him often to deliver important messages to Duke Liudolf. She was upset when she heard about his death. Hildegard wondered if it was because of her respect for the old spy that she had given Gerold a chance. A choice she was starting to regret. Thora stared at them for a few uncomfortable moments as if she was trying to work something out when Hildegard asked, 'Are you wondering why I gave Torkel that cross and not something else?'

Thora nodded, and Hildegard took a deep breath.

'It's a question I have asked myself since I found out about Torkel's death.'

'You cared for him?' Thora asked.

Hildegard nodded. 'I did once, maybe even loved him. He was a good man.' She scrutinised Thora, taking in her wide hips and muscular frame. She looked at the old scar on Thora's eyebrow and wondered if she had got that in battle. 'You care for Charles?'

This time Thora took a deep breath. 'I do. The boy has suffered much, always being picked on by others and lied to by those pretending to be friends. And then to witness the death of his father. Charles deserves better.'

'All children do,' Hildegard said and glanced at Bishop Bernard. Throughout the years, he had kept her informed of Charles and Torkel. He had told her of how Charles was doing, how he had learnt to read the Bible and how proud she should be of him. But never was there a mention of the boy suffering or being picked on by others. She wondered what else the bishop had hidden from her about Charles.

There was another moment of silence, and then Thora asked, 'So why that cross? You must have known it was important.'

'I knew it was important. That was why I chose it over all the other things I could have given Torkel. It was my father's most precious item,' she said, almost in a daze as she remembered the day she had her maid take it from her father's room. Hildegard had known exactly where her father had kept the cross. 'I wanted to hurt him as much as he had hurt me by forcing me to give up my son.' She spoke in Danish so the bishop would not hear her words, but knew there was nothing she could do about Gerold. Gerold, though, looked away and pretended not to listen to their conversation. 'But I never would have imagined that it would cause the death of Torkel and my son fleeing Francia. I was young and foolish then. I wasn't able to think of the consequences of what I was doing.'

'What is so special about that cross? That is the one thing

Sven and I can't understand.' Thora had sat down and poured herself a drink.

Hildegard shrugged. 'I have spent many days since the death of Torkel trying to find the answer to that question. But I don't know. All we've ever been told was that the cross was blessed, and that it helped my great-grandfather build his empire. My father believed it would help him rebuild the empire. That was why he took it from his father during the civil war.'

'He didn't know that Torkel had the cross?' Thora asked.

Hildegard had often wondered the same, but she was convinced he didn't. Otherwise, Torkel would have been killed a long time ago. 'He didn't know. He believed it was stolen by someone sent by one of his brothers. For many years, he had sent men to scour the other Frankish kingdom for the cross.'

Thora drained her cup and stood up, but before she could leave, Hildegard asked:

'Do you think Sven will help me find Charles?'

Thora shook her head. 'Sven believes the gods sent Charles to him so he can make amends for failing his son. And besides, what life can you give him in Francia?' Thora left before Hildegard could even answer the question and as she sat there, staring at the closed door, it rung in her head.

'Bitch,' Gerold muttered.

## 10

The sun was setting by the time Ivor felt it was safe for them to approach Jarl Torgeir. They had gone back to the stables where their horses were while Ivor and his two men cleaned themselves up and dealt with their wounds. Father Leofdag had checked the wound to Ivor's leg, which, unfortunately for Charles, was healing well, although Ivor still walked with a limp. Much like Charles's grandfather. Charles couldn't understand why Father Leofdag was helping them, even though earlier they had threatened to kill him and the young priest had simply said that it was his Christian duty to help those in need, regardless of their faith. But Charles wondered if it wasn't more because the priest wanted to be useful to them so they wouldn't kill him. Charles was also worried about Rollo. He hoped that the giant warrior still lived, but he couldn't ignore the empty feeling in his stomach when he remembered what Ivor had said about Hedeby's warriors capturing him.

Charles's stomach growled, and he put his hand on it as if that would silence it, but his stomach only seemed to make more noise.

'Either stop that or lose your stomach.' One of Ivor's men

glared at Charles, who frowned as the comment made no sense to him.

'I'm hungry.' Charles had eaten nothing since the morning, and even that was only a small piece of stale bread given to him by one of Ivor's men. The only one that had been nice to Charles, but he was dead, killed by Rollo during the fight in the church, and Charles doubted Ivor cared about feeding him.

'We're all hungry.' Ivor glowered at him. 'But there's nothing to eat. We finished the last of our food this morning.'

'I could go to the market. Get some food for everyone,' Father Leofdag said, his eyebrows high as he saw an opportunity, although Charles wasn't sure what that was. To escape or to be even more useful to Ivor.

Ivor scowled as he scrutinised the priest and then shook his head. 'Do you really think I am that dumb, priest?' Ivor walked to the door of the stable and looked outside. 'Besides, it's time we go visit Jarl Torgeir. And if Odin is with us, then by this time tomorrow we'll be living in comfort again and plotting how to kill that fat boar.' Charles gritted his teeth at that, but kept his thoughts to himself.

'Or we'll be hanging from the biggest tree,' the man with the swollen face said, and then shrugged when Ivor glared at him. 'What? It's not like Odin has been on our side lately, is it?' The swelling had reduced, but had been replaced by a large red bruise that Charles knew from experience would be purple in a day or two. His own face was most likely more yellow than purple by now, and soon Charles would be without a bruised face for the first time in many weeks. If someone didn't strike him again.

Ivor took a deep breath. 'Aye, the All-Father has been against us, but I have a feeling that's all about to change.' Charles saw the way the thin warrior rubbed the Mjöllnir around his neck and wondered if Ivor really felt that way or was just trying to reassure his remaining men. Not that he cared, anyway. Charles already realised that God had abandoned him. Perhaps He had no power in the lands of the Norse gods. The thought sent a shiver down Charles's spine, and he gripped the small wooden cross around his neck. Ivor saw him do that and said, 'There's no point praying, piglet. Neither your god nor your grandfather can save you now.'

Charles glared at Ivor as he laughed at his own words and walked out of the stable. Father Leofdag put his hand on Charles's shoulder. 'Have faith, Charles. God will never abandon us.'

Charles shook his hand off and turned his glare on the priest. 'Why are you helping them?'

Father Leofdag's hand froze for a few heartbeats before he lowered it. 'Because I'm afraid, young Charles. You, they need alive. Me not. Ivor said so himself. I need to do what I can to be useful.'

'What happened to being martyred in the name of God?' Charles remembered what Father Leofdag had said to him in Ribe after he was attacked by Haldor and Charles had asked him why he didn't protect himself.

Father Leofdag gave him a sad smile. 'Words are often easier than actions, Charles. The idea of being martyred for my faith seemed so glorious when I read about those who had died in the name of Christ. People like Perpetua. But when I faced death, I found I did not want to die yet. Is that wrong?' Charles looked away, not wanting to hear Father Leofdag's response. He had heard of Perpetua. The priest in Hügelburg had told her story many times before, and Charles admired her bravery. She was a Christian who had lived a long time ago, in the days of the Romans, although Charles didn't really know who the Romans were, only that they were the ones who had crucified Jesus. Perpetua had been imprisoned because of her faith and had been told to give up God and swear to the Roman gods, but she had refused. The Romans executed Perpetua, but she had stood tall and strong until the end. Just like Thora. Charles felt the lump in his throat and swallowed it down. 'I'm not brave, Charles. Not like Perpetua or you.'

Charles looked at Father Leofdag with raised eyebrows and remembered his grandfather telling him that all men felt fear, even him. And Charles was afraid as well as he sat there, unsure of what his fate was. But he felt certain that his grandfather would find and save him. Thora had promised that before she had died, and he believed her because she was his guardian angel. 'I'm also afraid,' Charles said, but before Father Leofdag could respond, Ivor walked back into the stable.

'It's time to go.'

Ivor's men grabbed Charles and Father Leofdag and led them out of the stables and towards the hall of Jarl Torgeir. The people of Hedeby watched them as they walked towards the hall, with Ivor leading them. People frowned and whispered to each other, a scene that reminded Charles of Ribe because that was what he saw every time he walked anywhere, especially with his grandfather. But unlike in Ribe, Charles saw curiosity in the faces of the townspeople instead of hate.

'Father Leofdag?' one man asked, but quickly ran away when one of Ivor's men growled at him. Father Leofdag did not respond or even look at the man. Instead, he walked with his head down, his hands clasping the cross around his neck.

'What is Jarl Torgeir like?' Charles asked. He remembered what his grandfather and Thora had said about the jarl of Hedeby, but wondered if the man was really that bad.

'I don't really know,' Father Leofdag said. 'I've only seen him a few times, when my brothers and I went to his hall to ask for provisions or support. He always listened to us and sometimes gave us bread, but he never looked like he really wanted to.'

'My grandfather said he is a cruel man.'

Father Leofdag nodded. 'Yes, for once I will agree with your grandfather. The jarl can be very cruel if you break his laws.'

'Quiet, you two!' Ivor glanced over his shoulder at them. 'There's no point plotting an escape.'

Charles frowned and then realised that he and Father Leofdag had spoken in Frankish and that Ivor would not have known what they were saying. He thought that was strange, because he had been told that Ivor and his father had often taken money from the Frankish kings to attack their enemies. But before Charles could say anything, they reached the hall. Charles's eyes widened as he looked at the enormous building in the centre of Hedeby. It was the same shape as his grandfather's hall in Ribe; the sides being longer than the front and with the bowed roof, but this hall was much larger. Charles remembered Gerold telling him about churches in Francia being large enough to fit entire villages in and, as Charles looked at the hall in front of him, he wondered how many villages would fit in there.

Four warriors stood on either side of the hall's large door, which was open, two men on each side, and all four of them were dressed in their war gear, with shining brynjas and helmets. They had swords on their hips and each held a long spear in their right hands and a shield in their left. Charles looked at the images painted on the shields and realised they all had the same image: a white raven on a blue background. Two of the warriors stepped forward to block Ivor and his men, while the other two stayed by the door. Charles looked at the inside of the door and saw it was carved with what looked like a scene from a forest. He saw trees and deer and even something that looked like small angels, but Charles knew those were the forest spirits the Danes believed in. Thora had told him about them after they arrived in Ribe.

'Who are you and what do you want?' one warrior said. The

man stood taller than Ivor, but Charles thought Rollo was bigger than him and his companions.

'I know you,' one of the other warriors by the door said as he came closer. 'You were here before the battle. Ivor Guttromson.'

The first warrior smiled. 'Well now. Loki must be in the mood to be a right bastard today if you are here. What do you want, Ivor Guttromson?'

Ivor smiled at the men and raised his arms away from his sword and sax-knife. 'I'm here to see your jarl. I have a proposition for him.'

'The last time you came here with a proposition, Jarl Torgeir chased you out of Hedeby. Or did you forget about that?' the second warrior asked.

'Aye, he did, and look where that got him. Has he regrown his toes yet?' They had discovered more news of the battle during the day, although what had happened to Ivor's father was still unclear. What was clear, though, was the army of Guttrom had scattered and Ivor was on his own. There were rumours that most of Guttrom's surviving men were now rampaging across Denmark, killing and robbing helpless farmers wherever they went. Although the news that Jarl Torgeir had lost some of his toes in the battle did amuse Ivor and his men.

The warriors all growled at Ivor, and his two men looked nervous, as they must have realised they would not survive this fight. But before anyone could do anything, a loud voice shouted from inside the hall. 'Let the snake in!'

Charles frowned and saw that one of the four warriors was missing and guessed the man must have gone inside to tell Jarl Torgeir of his visitors. Ivor smiled at the other three warriors as they stepped aside, but Charles felt more nervous than he had ever done before. He wanted to pray as Ivor took him to the man who hated his grandfather, but knew there was no point. God would not listen to him.

The inside of the hall looked almost the same as the hall back in Ribe. There was a large hearth in the centre, its tall flames roaring as they fought the darkness away, and with a large hole above it to let the smoke escape. Although the hole was not big enough and Charles coughed as he breathed in the smoky air in the hall. The walls of the hall were lined with benches and tables, all of them filled with warriors and old men, and above their heads hung old swords, spears, axes and shields. The only difference between this hall and his grandfather's was that this hall was larger and did not have the stuffed boar's head at the back of the hall. Banners hung from the walls, all of them with the same white raven on blue as the shields of the warriors who guarded the door. Two of those warriors followed them in, although Charles wasn't sure why. There were plenty of men in the hall to protect their jarl if Ivor attacked. As Charles's eyes adjusted to the dim light inside, he scanned the hall, hoping to see Rollo tied up and alive. But there was no sign of his grandfather's man and Charles worried about what that meant.

Jarl Torgeir sat on his seat at the end of the hall, his left foot heavily bandaged and resting on a stool in front of him. Charles wondered if that was where the sickly-sweet smell was coming from. Jarl Torgeir looked tall as he sat in his chair, glaring at them, and his shoulders were almost as wide as the back of his chair. His long dark hair was tied neatly behind his head and his long beard was braided. When Charles had first come to Denmark he had been surprised at how much effort the warriors put into their appearances, almost more than the women back in Francia, but now he understood the Danes were not the filthy and stinking barbarians he had always been told about. They washed daily, constantly changed into clean clothes and regularly combed their hair and beards during the day. And Charles had to admit, they smelt better than most of the people he had known in Hügelburg.

'You must be keen to join your father in Valhalla, Ivor Guttromson.' Jarl Torgeir's voice echoed around the large hall and the warriors inside laughed.

'Maybe he misses his father,' one warrior from the benches said, and the others laughed even more. Even Jarl Torgeir smiled at that.

'I doubt he'll recognise him, though,' Jarl Torgeir said, his dark eyes fixed on Ivor. 'Not after Sven beat his face to a pulp.' The laughter in the hall reached a new height, and Charles noticed how Ivor clenched his fist and could almost hear him grinding his teeth. It must have been hard for him to hear his father mocked like that and Charles surprised himself when he realised he felt sorry for the warrior who had kidnapped him. Charles had lost his own father in the beginning of the summer, a pain he was still not over, but had only been distracted from by everything else. But in the quiet moments, Charles still cried for the loss of his father.

'Sven will pay dearly for that, as Odin is my witness.' Ivor's voice was strained, as he must have been struggling to contain his anger at Jarl Torgeir's taunts. 'One day, I'll slaughter the bastard and feed him to the pigs.'

Jarl Torgeir raised an eyebrow and then his hand to silence the men in the hall. Everyone fell silent, with only the flames daring to defy the jarl in his own hall. 'And how do you plan to make that happen when all you have left are two injured men, a boy,' Jarl Torgeir frowned at Charles, 'and a priest who seems familiar to me?'

'Is he not the priest that travelled to Ribe?' one of the older men asked who was sitting on a bench near the jarl.

Father Leofdag nodded. 'Yes, I went there to oversee the building of the new church.'

'I'm surprised you still live, priest. I was sure that Sven was going to kill you,' Jarl Torgeir said, and Father Leofdag paled as the warriors in the hall laughed again. Charles glanced at the jarl's foot, which seemed shorter than it should be, and wondered if he had really lost his toes during the battle. Jarl Torgeir noticed and his face darkened. 'I'd be careful where you stare, boy. Or it will be the last thing you ever see.'

Charles's heart raced in his chest and he did his best not to show the fear coursing through him, but he must have failed as the jarl smirked at him.

'I wouldn't threaten to kill the boy if I were you, Jarl Torgeir,' Ivor said. 'He's much more useful to both of us alive.'

Jarl Torgeir's brow creased at this. 'And why is this runt so important?' Charles felt the eyes of everyone in the hall on him, as many others must have wondered the same.

Ivor smiled. 'Because this runt is the grandson of Sven the Boar.'

A sudden silence filled the hall, as if the air had been sucked out of it. Even the flames of the hearth fire seemed to flutter and Charles had to resist the urge to grip the cross around his neck.

'Is this true, priest?' Jarl Torgeir asked Father Leofdag, who nodded. Jarl Torgeir leaned forward so he could get a closer look at Charles. 'By Odin, yes. I can see the bastard's ugly face in the boy.' He then looked at Ivor, the frown still on his face.

'Is that why Sven's man was killing people in my town?' Jarl Torgeir glared at Ivor. 'It was your men he was fighting in the Christian church?'

Charles's heart raced at the mention of Rollo and before he could stop himself, he asked, 'Rollo is still alive?'

Jarl Torgeir glanced at him before turning his attention back to Ivor. 'For now. So tell me, Ivor Guttromson, why do you have Sven's grandson and why are you coming to me with him?'

Ivor grabbed Charles by his red hair and dragged him forward. Charles winced, but did his best not to cry out. 'Because this little bastard will help us break Sven. To beat him down so hard that he will beg us to kill him.' The anger in Ivor's voice made Jarl Torgeir sit back again and glance at the old man who had spoken out before.

'What stops me from just killing you and taking the boy?' Jarl Torgeir had a small smile in his beard. 'Your father fought against me, after all.'

Ivor did not hesitate, and Charles guessed he had expected this. 'My father didn't fight against you, Jarl Torgeir. He fought against old Horik, and if you remember, he offered you his hand in friendship. You sided with the old king instead.' Some warriors cried out at his response, one even threatening to kill Ivor and his family, but Ivor ignored them as he stared at the jarl. 'And besides, like the boy, I am more useful to you alive than dead.'

'How so?' Jarl Torgeir frowned and silenced his men.

'Because I know you want to kill Sven for what he has done to you and what he has taken from you.'

Jarl Torgeir leaned forward again and took his foot off the stool with a grimace. 'What are you talking about, Ivor Guttromson?'

'Don't listen to him, jarl,' one warrior said, and those around him agreed, but Jarl Torgeir ignored his men.

'What are you talking about?' he asked again.

'I know you lost your son during the battle, Jarl Torgeir. I heard it was Sven who cut him down,' Ivor said, and Torgeir's face went dark.

'Aye, I lost my boy to Sven's sword. And you're right, I want my revenge. Everyone knows that. But I don't want to kill the bastard.

He would only then go to Valhalla and spend the rest of his days fighting and drinking with his forefathers and mine until Ragnarök. No, I don't want to kill Sven the Boar.' Torgeir leaned back in his seat again. 'I want to break him. I want to take everything away from him. I want him to wander my streets again as a broken old drunk so I can piss on him and laugh at his misery.' The flames seemed to flutter at Jarl Torgeir's words, and Charles had to suppress the shiver down his spine. Especially when Torgeir glared at him.

Ivor smiled, and to Charles it looked like the smile of a victor. 'Then I believe we can help each other, Jarl Torgeir.'

Charles's hand went to the cross around his neck, and he prayed. But not to God, not like he used to. This time he prayed to his grandfather, begging him to hurry and rescue him.

## 11

Torgeir sat in his hall, alone in the darkness, but he was not really alone. The snores of the sleeping warriors echoed around the building while the few torches still lit fluttered in the breeze from the open door. He knew his wife was waiting for him in their bed, but Torgeir was in no mood to sleep. He had not been since he had returned from the battle at Jelling that saw the death of not only his closest friend but also his oldest son. And both at the hands of that short bastard. Torgeir was glad he had kept his other sons in Hedeby to watch over his town, otherwise he would have no sons left. That was what many of the few remaining jarls faced. Their sons and grandsons killed, all so that Denmark could have an empty throne. But at least Torgeir still had two sons left, of that he thanked Odin and Thor. Torgeir glanced at his foot and grimaced. Sven had cost him more than he knew. Three toes were cut off, and another had to be removed. Now Torgeir had to walk around with a stick and already the people of Hedeby had a new name they called him behind his back. Torgeir Clubfoot. Torgeir wouldn't have minded if that had actually been true, but he still had one toe left, the big one, so it wasn't exactly a club foot.

'It doesn't matter how long you stare at your foot, your toes will not grow back.' A woman's voice broke Torgeir from his thoughts, and he was surprised to see Helga, his second wife, approach him. Torgeir frowned, concerned that he had not heard her approach. He had three wives, but the first was his true love. Helga was a cousin of the dead king Horik and was a political marriage, but she had given him one of his sons and two daughters. She was also the most intelligent of his wives, and he often sought her counsel. She had been the reason he could not have joined Guttrom in his rebellion, even if he wanted to. But as much as he disapproved of Horik's tolerance of the Christians, he disapproved more of Guttrom's links to the Frankish kings.

'You are still awake?' he asked as Helga sat down and filled a cup with ale. Torgeir looked around and wondered where the thralls were, but then realised they must have all gone to bed already.

'I knew you would be, so I thought I'd come keep my husband company.'

Torgeir glanced at Helga and sighed. 'Sleep does not come easy any more.'

'Sleep rarely does to troubled minds.' Helga scrutinised him as she drank from her cup. 'So what troubles you, my husband?' Torgeir wondered how much he should tell his wife, but then knew it didn't really matter. She would find out anyway. 'Is it about Ivor and the boy?'

Torgeir grunted and wondered how much she knew. Helga wasn't in the hall during the day when Ivor had shown up. Torgeir never allowed his wives in the hall when he was dealing out justice. But he imagined Helga was like Frigg, the mother goddess, all-knowing and all-wise, a match only to the All-Father. Perhaps that was why Odin and Frigg shared the throne of Asgard and perhaps why, of all his wives, Helga was the only one to talk about politics. Torgeir glanced at his injured foot again. 'I'm wondering if I should trust Ivor or cut his head off as you would to a snake.'

'You really believe what he says about the boy being Sven's grandson?' Helga tilted her head as she waited for the answer.

Torgeir shrugged. 'The boy is the grandson of Sven. You can see the ugly bastard in the boy's face and his lack of height. But what I don't understand is why would the grandson of that short bastard be so important?'

Helga drank from her cup as she considered his words. 'Wasn't Sven's son taken hostage by Louis of East Francia?'

Torgeir frowned and wondered why that was so important. 'Aye. Sven raided Saxony, and Louis had set a trap for him. After Sven lost a battle against Louis, the king of East Francia, who was only a young prince then, he demanded that Sven hand over his son. That broke the bastard.' Torgeir couldn't help but smile at that. He had not been jarl when that had happened. His father was still the jarl of Hedeby, but he had hated Sven. Sven was more powerful than he had been, and Torgeir's father had not liked that because he wanted to be the most powerful jarl in Denmark. It hadn't helped that Horik had executed one of Torgeir's uncles for raiding Francia, and yet to all, it had seemed that Sven was getting away with doing what he had wanted. But no one had realised that the king and the gods had other plans for the boar. Plans much worse than chopping his head off.

'And Louis raised Sven's son?' Helga asked.

Torgeir nodded. 'They say the prince took a liking to the young boy and raised him as if he was one of his own sons. Even convinced the boy to become a Christian. Why are you asking this?' Torgeir looked at his wife, who made a show of thinking about the answer, but he knew she had a reason. And it annoyed him he did not see it.

'Louis has two daughters, does he not?' Helga asked instead.

'What are you getting at, woman?' Torgeir was losing his patience.

Helga smiled her best smile. 'Think about it, husband. Sven's grandson appears out of the blue, as if the gods had plucked him out of the seas, says something to Sven who returns to his old self and kills his brother. And now we find out that the kings of Francia are after this boy.'

'And?'

Helga sighed and shook her head. 'Sven's son grew up in the hall of Louis, surrounded by his family and his two daughters, both of whom were sent to nunneries just as they became women. One of them you've met often when you dealt with the East Franks. The Abbess Hildegard.'

'So?'

'The question you should ask is not whether or not you should trust Ivor. It's who is the mother of this boy if the kings of Francia want him so desperately.'

Torgeir raised his eyebrows at this and cursed himself for not thinking of that. 'You mean the boy is the son of Louis's daughter?'

Helga shrugged. 'Only the gods will know the answer to that, but you have to admit, he resembles her a little.'

Torgeir scratched his head as he tried to recall what the oldest daughter of Louis looked like, but he could not. He never really paid any attention to her every time he had met her. She was always so sour-looking and serious, but he knew she was a dangerous woman and that she had the ear of her father. But then he thought of something else. 'But what does it matter? Louis and his sons will have plenty of bastards running around. Why is this one so important?'

Helga nodded. 'Aye, men may breed as many bastards as they want. Even you have more than you know of in Hedeby. Don't look so surprised,' Helga said when Torgeir's eyes widened. 'We all know about your other women and the thralls you bed, but you treat us well, so we don't complain. Not yet, anyway. But remember how the Christians think. It's fine for their men to sleep around, but the women should be faithful only to their husbands and they should definitely not lose their flowers before they are wed. Especially not if you are the daughter of the king.'

'So King Louis of East Francia hid his daughter so that no one would know she gave birth to a boy?'

Helga nodded again. 'We can't know for sure, but it makes sense if you think about it. Even more curious is the arrival of a Christian woman and an old priest in Ribe shortly after the battle.'

Torgeir frowned. 'How do you know this?'

Helga smiled. 'Husband, while you were sitting here brooding over your lost toes, I was walking around the market and talking to the few traders still brave enough to travel our hostile land. And a few of them told me of a stern-looking Christian woman in Ribe. One who Sven has been avoiding.'

'Hildegard?' Torgeir asked.

'None of the traders I spoke to could tell me who she was, but it is interesting considering everything we now know.'

Torgeir had to admit it was, but then he thought of something else. 'But why did Louis not just kill the bastard child after he was born?'

Helga shrugged. 'The Christians are strange in their ways, husband. But if we are right and the boy is the son of one of Louis's daughters, what do you think he will do to keep that from coming out and ruining his reputation?'

Torgeir grunted at how Helga said we, even though she was the one who had seen something they had all missed. 'Reputation is everything,' Torgeir mused while stroking his beard. He wondered how he could use this information to his advantage and what he could gain from it. Torgeir didn't need money. Being the jarl of the largest trading town had made him one of the richest men in Denmark. In fact, only Horik had been wealthier.

'You could use the boy to make yourself the new king of Denmark.'

Torgeir glanced at his wife as she smiled at him, her mind probably filled with the vision of her being a queen. 'I don't want to be king. A king's position is too fragile.'

Helga took a sip of her ale. 'Horik was king for a long time.'

'Aye, but he was hated by most of his jarls. No, I don't want to deal with the weight of the throne on my brows.' Torgeir stared at the embers of the hearth fire. 'I want to be the man who decides who the new king will be. I want to be the most powerful man in Denmark.' For many winters, Torgeir had been one of the most powerful men, but not the most. That honour had gone to Bjarni, Sven's brother, and Torgeir had never understood the close bond that Bjarni and Horik had shared. But if the stories he had heard before the battle were true and Bjarni had helped Horik by betraying his own brother, then that explained everything. But Bjarni was dead and so was Horik, and chaos reigned in Denmark. 'Nothing will hurt Sven more than giving his grandson to the man who took his son away from him.' Jarl Torgeir smiled at that. 'But perhaps the king of East Francia will reward us for saving his honour and reputation.' Torgeir stroked his beard as he thought about what he could gain from this. 'New trade deals with East Francia, more trade with Hedeby. The wealthier Hedeby becomes, the more powerful I'll be. Perhaps even a marriage between his sons and my daughters.'

'Your daughters aren't Christians. Would King Louis marry his sons to them?'

'My daughters can convert.'

'But what if King Louis kills the boy?' Helga asked.

Torgeir shrugged. 'Even better. Sven will be so blinded by rage that he won't realise what's happening until it's too late.'

Helga drank from her cup as she considered his words. 'And what does Ivor get out of this?'

Torgeir thought back to the conversation they had earlier in the hall. 'He claims he just wants to avenge his father, but I feel like there is more to it. There is something else he is after. He wants to be king. I'm sure of it.'

'Then why make a deal with him?'

'Because he is useful. He knows other jarls who hate Sven as much as I do. Jarls who can attack Sven while I keep my distance. And if he succeeds and makes himself the king of Denmark, then he will be in my debt and I will control him.'

Helga nodded, as if she thought that was a good idea. 'But there is another who claims the crown. A young man from Jelling. He might be a problem.'

'Aye,' Torgeir said. He had heard of the young man very few knew about who claimed to be a nephew of the old Horik. 'They say he is travelling around Denmark, trying to get the jarls to support him and proclaim him king at the next Landsting. Your brother, Hovi, is with him, is he not?' Torgeir liked Hovi and Hovi liked him. They shared a hatred for the Christians and had spent many nights by the hearth fire talking about how they wanted the Christians gone from Denmark.

'I believe so. The young man is very fond of him.' Helga's brows came together, and Torgeir wondered what she was thinking. 'There might be an opportunity for you there, husband. But you need to be careful, especially of Sven.'

'Sven?' Torgeir raised an eyebrow at Helga.

'Even the gods fear what he will do if he finds out you have his grandson or what you are planning.'

Torgeir waved a hand at his wife. 'Sven can't do anything. He has no power. They say even the people of Ribe despise him.'

Helga glanced at the embers of the hearth fire that had died a long time ago. 'You could say the same about those burnt-out logs. Now they are no threat, but with the right encouragement, they could burn this hall down.' Torgeir scowled at his wife, wishing she would get to the point. 'Horik and Guttrom underestimated Sven, and both are dead. They say he killed most of Bjarni's men the night he returned to Ribe.'

Torgeir stroked his beard again and realised she was right. He had underestimated Sven during their battle. He had believed he could kill the short bastard quickly, but Sven had surprised him. 'So what do you suggest?'

'You still have his man locked up?'

Torgeir nodded. 'I am going to hang him tomorrow for fighting in my town.'

Helga drank from her cup. 'I suggest you free him and send him back to Sven. Do not give him a reason to come here and learn what you are planning.'

'But Rollo knows Ivor is here with the boy. He will tell Sven that.'

Helga nodded. 'But he does not know about the deal you are about to make with Ivor, so your hands will be clean. He will tell Sven that he saw Ivor, assuming that was who he was fighting in the church, and that Ivor fled. Sven will believe they have gone to Francia and will search for them there.'

'And why will he think that?'

'Because you will tell him that. When you escort the future king of Denmark to Ribe.'

Torgeir's brow creased as he thought about this and realised Helga had a point, as usual. He wondered if this was how Odin felt about Frigg, especially when she saw something he had missed. 'I'll need to make sure then that Rollo doesn't see me talking with Ivor.' He stroked his beard as he thought of the solution. 'Ivor will want to talk to Louis himself. The bastard is arrogant enough to think it's his right.' Helga nodded, but said nothing. 'I will send him south, with one priest and Steinar.' Helga frowned as he mentioned their son. 'Steinar will make sure that Ivor believes he has my support and, more importantly, he will make sure Ivor doesn't double-cross us. And, with the help of your brother, I will befriend the other contender for the crown. Make him believe I support his bid and, in time, I will find a way to control him. That way, it doesn't matter which of the two becomes king.' Torgeir sent a silent prayer to Thor, asking him to make sure that Loki stayed away from this plan. Because the last thing he needed now was for the god of mischief to ruin his plans.

## 12

Sven lifted his shield and grunted as the sword struck it. The force of the blow almost caused his arm to drop, and it took all of his strength to keep it up. Sweat poured down from his freshly shaved head and stung his eyes, but he couldn't wipe it away as the sword was raised and brought again. This time, Sven's shield arm did drop and there was nothing he could do about the shield boss aimed at his chest. The blow knocked the air out of Sven and sent him stumbling backwards. Sven cursed at how weak he had become as he glared at his attacker, who stood over him with a cocky grin on his face. Alvar was almost twice his height and much broader at the shoulder, and he was fast and strong.

Sven shook his head to clear it and to get the sweat out of his eyes before he attacked. He stabbed with his sword, which Alvar dodged, but could do nothing as the young warrior brought his own sword around to take his head off. Sven tried to lift his shield, but his arm refused to obey, leaving Sven with no option but to drop to his knees. He grimaced at the pain when his knees hit the ground and almost missed the change in the sword's direction as Alvar turned it into a stab. Instinct, honed by many winters of fighting and not as dormant as Sven had thought, made him flick his own sword up and deflect Alvar's sword away, before he rolled forward and tripped the blond warrior. As Alvar's back hit the ground, Sven jumped on top of him, his sword at the man's neck.

'You're supposed to let me win, Alvar.' Sven tried to spit to the ground, but his mouth was too dry and Alvar had to turn his head out of the way, otherwise the spit would have landed on his face.

The large warrior smiled. 'Where is the fun in that?'

Sven growled and struggled to his feet. Again, he felt like he was too old for this life. His left shoulder had never really regained its strength after it was cut during a fight soon after meeting Charles, and every new wound just seemed to take more of his strength away. Sven wiped the sweat from his forehead. 'It's not about fun. It's about making me look good to the younger warriors so they don't stick a knife in my back.' Sven looked across the quiet market towards the main hall when he saw a man standing by one of the market stalls, watching him. Sven frowned, wondering who the man was, but did not recognise him. Not because of his weak eyes, but because the man looked like every other Frank he had ever met and Sven knew the man was a Frank because of his neatly trimmed beard and the clothing he wore. The man turned and walked away, most likely back to his stall, and Sven forgot about him. Over the last few days, some traders from Francia had arrived in Ribe, most of them with armed men to protect them from the leaderless men raiding Denmark. Ribe's territory had been spared the worst because Sven sent out regular patrols to protect the farmsteads. Not that the farmers thanked him for that. They blamed him for the raids because they didn't like him and because they believed it was his fault that King Horik was dead and the raids were happening.

'The warriors respect you, jarl. They all saw how you fought during the battle.' Alvar got to his feet and wiped the sand off his shoulder.

'Respect can disappear as fast as snow in the summer's sun.' Sven turned towards Hedeby and tried to see the large trading town to the south in his mind. 'Now where in Odin's name is Rollo? He should have been back days ago.' It had been a few days since Thora had woken up, and Sven had imprisoned Charles's mother. After that, Sven had finished his ale and ordered for the bathhouse to be prepared. Sven had decided that he'd wallowed enough in despair. Thora had been right, as always. She had promised Charles that he would find him, and Sven did not want to let either of them down. But first Sven had to find out where Charles was. He hated to admit it, but the gods knew he was too old to be rampaging around Denmark. That was why he was anxious for Rollo to return from Hedeby, hopefully with Charles or at least some information about where Charles was. Sven had also sent men he trusted to towns whose jarls were allies of Guttrom and Ivor, hoping that they might learn something. But the waiting drove him mad. Sven had never been a patient man, so he trained with Alvar every day to distract himself and to regain his strength.

'Perhaps he found a trail and is following it?' Alvar suggested as he studied the edge of his sword.

Sven nodded. He had wondered the same. 'But then why not send a message to let us know?'

'Who could he send? He went by himself.' Alvar shrugged as Sven glared at him. 'Do you want me to send some men to Hedeby to look for him?'

Sven scratched his head. Did he really want to risk sending more men away from Ribe? 'Let's wait another day before we think about doing that.' He turned and walked back to his hall, and Alvar followed. 'How are our guests doing?'

'They still live. The woman keeps insisting that she speak to you. She demands that you let them go before her father sends men to look for her.'

Sven almost smiled at that. He prayed that the king of the East Franks came here himself so that Sven could kill the bastard for taking his son away from him. 'I doubt her father even knows she's here.'

'So why keep them here, then?' Alvar asked as he and Sven walked back to the hall.

Sven rubbed his temples, trying to force the headache away. He had cut back on his drinking, wanting to keep his mind focused on what he needed to do, even if he didn't know what that was yet. But that left him with a constant dull pain behind his eyes. 'Because we both want the same thing and as long as I have her locked up here, then she can't get to Charles before me.' And that was Sven's greatest fear. Charles was all he had left of his son and his long-dead wife, and he doubted he would survive if the boy chose to be with his mother instead of him. But then, why would Charles decide to stay with Sven if he had the choice? Sven had been a terrible grandfather, just like he had been a terrible father and husband. He had put his own needs ahead of Charles's and, because of that, the boy was in the hands of Ivor and Sven did not know where to find him. So Sven decided it was best if Charles never learnt that his mother was still alive, and that she was in Ribe. When he found Charles, they would get on a ship and go as far north as they could. Sven had heard rumours of a land far to the north, a land of ice and fire where only the strongest could survive. He didn't know if the stories were true or just tales told by the skalds to entertain, but if this land existed, it would be as far from Francia as they could get, and Sven was certain that there the Frankish kings could never find him or Charles.

'A boy needs his mother, especially one like Charles,' Alvar said and then stopped in his tracks when Sven turned on him, his brows furrowed.

'What in Odin's name do you mean by that?' Sven tightened his grip on his sword, still in his hand, because the scabbard was back in the hall.

Alvar shrugged. 'Forgive me, Jarl Sven. I just mean that Charles is very quiet. He doesn't fit in here, even you must have seen that. A mother would provide him with the comfort he needs to deal with that.'

Sven wondered when these young people decided they could speak their minds to him. He blamed Thora for that. Everyone saw her do it and now they believed they could do the same. 'Charles has me and Thora!'

'Aye, he does. But you are not exactly...' Sven gritted his teeth as he waited for Alvar to find the right words, 'motherly and Thora is not Charles's mother.'

Sven glared at Alvar, who found something interesting elsewhere to look at, and then sighed. The giant warrior was right, and that only annoyed Sven even more. 'Alvar, your job is to kill bastards trying to kill me, not to be smart. Remember that. Now, let's go to the hall. I need a drink.' Sven turned and walked away, so he didn't see the smile on Alvar's face. But Alvar's words stuck in his mind as Sven glanced at the house Charles's mother was kept in. *The boy needs his mother.*

The hall was livelier than before. The hearth fire was burning strongly, and the thralls were preparing a large pot of pottage for their dinner. Thora had been keeping herself busy ensuring that things returned to normal, and Sven guessed it was to distract herself from her own guilt. He knew she wanted to ride out with the warriors Sven had sent to find Charles, just like he wanted to, but Sven needed her here, in Ribe. Only the gods knew if Charles was still in Denmark. It had been more than a week since Charles had been taken and, for all they knew, he could already be on his way to West Francia. Sven stopped and looked back towards the wharves at the three ships moored there. He was tempted to take those ships and sail to the land of the Franks, but he doubted he had enough men to fill even one warship. Sven was stuck, and he had too many unanswered questions, and that angered him. He wondered if he should speak to his uncle, Odinson, again. The old godi might have heard something from his many birds, as he called those who spied for him.

Thora sat by the table close to the jarl's seat, her fingers drumming on the table and her brows furrowed. She was frustrated, just like he was, but he knew it was worse for her. Thora wanted to train. She wanted to get her strength and skill back because she somehow believed that if she had been the warrior she once was, then she could have saved Charles. Sven had been told how she had killed more than a handful of men, including Oleg, and the only reason that Ivor could stab her was because one of Ribe's warriors was holding her. That traitor was dead now. Rollo had hung him, along with the other warriors who had stood by and watched as Ivor's men kidnapped Charles and killed people they were supposed to protect. Sven, though, wished Thora had not killed Oleg. Because he had wanted to do it himself. Oleg had once been Sven's hirdman, back when Sven had been a young jarl. But for many years, Oleg had been one of Bjarni's men, until he betrayed Bjarni and gave Sven his old Dane axe. Sven had used that axe to kill his brother and become jarl of Ribe once more. But Sven could never really trust Oleg after that. Especially not after Guttrom had arrived. The two of them were always locked in some conversation, which had made Sven feel uncomfortable. Sven thought he was smart by leaving Oleg behind when he and Guttrom marched their armies out to meet the king of Denmark in battle. But Sven had been a fool, because that decision had played right into Guttrom's hands. Sven never knew what arrangement Guttrom had with Oleg, but he guessed Oleg had hoped to become the jarl of Ribe after Guttrom became king.

Sven pushed the thoughts out of his mind. Both bastards were dead now, and none of that mattered. The only thing that did was finding Charles and Sven wondered if Rollo's absence had something to do with that.

'She's demanded to see you again,' Thora said as he sat down beside her.

'Aye, so I keep hearing. She can wait.'

Thora stared at Sven, and he knew what she was going to ask. 'Do you really think she is his mother?'

Sven took his ale from the thrall and drank before he responded. 'Aye, she is. She knows about the cross.'

Thora nodded. 'He has her eyes and nose.'

'That as well,' Sven said, drinking more of his ale.

'So what do we do with her and him?'

Sven raised an eyebrow at her. *Him* was Gerold and Sven wanted to cut his head off. 'For now, nothing.'

'By Frigg, Sven. You can't keep them prisoner. She's the daughter of the king of East Francia. The old bastard is some important priest. Soon the East Franks will come looking for them.'

Sven shrugged. 'Let them come. I'll kill them all.'

'With what army? Ribe lost a lot of good men and the few she has left are needed to protect the farmsteads until a new king can be crowned.'

Sven looked at his cup and then pushed it away. 'You want another king of Denmark? Another bastard who thinks we should do as he commands?' Just asking the question annoyed him.

'It doesn't matter what I want. Denmark needs a king before

she fractures into smaller kingdoms, like Norway. As one, Denmark can stand against the Christian aggression. As separate kingdoms, Denmark can't.'

Sven shrugged. 'Norway has managed well so far.' Unlike Denmark, Norway was not one kingdom, but a collection of smaller kingdoms, constantly fighting each other for land, unless they decided there were better rewards somewhere else. Then the different kings might join forces and go on raids together.

This time Thora took a drink from her cup. 'Norway doesn't sit next to Francia, but her time will come. The Christians are greedy. They want to control all of Midgard and chase our gods away.'

'That will never happen. Our gods are too strong for the weak Christian god.'

Thora stood up, wincing. 'I'm sure that's what the Saxons thought as well.' She walked away before Sven could say anything.

Sven sat alone, enjoying the silence. Alvar was sitting with some of the other warriors, laughing at something one of them said, and there was no one else to bother him. He looked at his half-empty cup and decided he might as well empty it before he cleaned himself up. Sven reached out for his cup when he heard a noise in the sleeping quarters. Frowning, Sven looked around the hall, but no one else seemed to have heard anything. Thora had already left the hall, and the nearest people were the thralls cleaning or preparing the evening meal. The young warriors on the other side of the hall were making too much noise to hear anything. Sven wanted to believe that he had heard nothing, but something made him feel he should investigate. He was not a smart man, but Sven knew to trust his instinct. It had served him well when he was a young warrior and even better when he was a drunk roaming around Denmark. Ignoring his ale, Sven stood up and, as quietly as his round frame could, he limped towards the door. He paused outside, holding his breath, and listened for a few heartbeats, but heard nothing. Sven shrugged. Perhaps this was one time his instinct was wrong. He was getting old, after all. He was about to return to his ale when there was a scraping noise on the other side of the door. Sven turned and rushed through the door, and stopped in his tracks when he saw a short man rummaging through Charles's chest. Sven realised it was the Frank that he had seen before, the one who had been watching him train with Alvar, although Sven couldn't be certain. What he was certain about was that the Frank was there for the cross. He knew this because, as the Frank scowled at him, he pulled it out of the chest.

'Bastard!' Sven roared, and charged at the thin man. The Frank reacted faster than Sven had thought he would as he side-stepped Sven and struck him on the back of the head with the cross. Sven, his vision blurred from the blow, tripped over the chest and fell onto the bed behind it. He shook his head to chase the stars away, before he jumped to his feet and launched himself at the Frank again, who was rushing towards the back door. Sven could not let that bastard escape, not with the cross. Charles would never forgive him for that. The Frank grunted as Sven crashed into him and they rolled around on the floor, before Sven ended up on top of him. He punched the Frank on the cheek and the man's head snapped to the side. He threw another punch, but this time the Frank got his head out of the way and Sven punched the floor instead. The Frank freed his legs and kneed Sven in the side. Sven grunted, but ignored the pain as he tried to get his hands on the cross. But the Frank kept on kneeing him and in the end Sven had to forget about the cross and roll off the bastard before he broke his ribs. The Frank moved faster than Sven and before Sven could get to his feet, he was already up and with a knife in his hand. Sven ignored the wicked-looking blade and charged at the Frank, who seemed to be surprised by that, but he quickly recovered and sliced at Sven with his knife. Sven twisted out of the way, but the knife still sliced his arm, before he punched the Frank in the stomach. The man staggered backwards, grimacing, but still rolled out of the way as Sven tried to kick him.

'Who sent you?' Sven roared as Alvar and the other warriors rushed into the room.

The Frank eyed them before he glanced at the door. Sven rushed at him again, as did the warriors who had barged into the room. In the blink of an eye, the Frank turned, threw his knife at the oncoming warriors and then struck Sven on the side of the head with the cross.

Sven dropped to his knees, his head swimming, and could do nothing as the Frank escaped. Alvar and the others gave chase, and Sven saw one warrior lying on the floor with the knife in his chest. Sven shook his head and struggled to his feet. He felt his rage taking over as he stormed out of the hall and was met with wide eyes and open mouths as the townspeople stared at him in shock. 'Where is he?' Sven looked around and then rushed after Alvar, who was chasing the Frank. He ran as fast as his old legs could take him, but was soon left behind. Sven rounded one house and saw a dead body, but the corpse was too large to be the Frank. Somewhere a dog barked and Sven set off again, hoping the hound had got hold of the Frank, but soon he tired and had to stop. As he struggled to catch his breath, he glimpsed a movement nearby, and Sven gave chase as the other warriors were calling out to each other. Sven's heart raced in his chest and his breath was so ragged he worried he might collapse, but he could not give up. He had to find that Frank. Sven ran around another house, not knowing where he was going and following the cries of his men, when he bumped into Alvar, whose face was red with exertion.

'The bastard got away. We lost him between the houses.'

Sven clenched his fists as his eyes darted around the houses surrounding them, angered that the gods had done this to him. Had they not tormented him enough? 'Find him! Find the bastard, even if you have to pull every house apart! He cannot get away with that cross!'

'What cross?' Alvar asked.

'Just find him!' Sven turned and marched to the one place he thought he might get answers from.

## 13

Roul rubbed his stinging cheek where the old heathen had punched him and knew he was going to have a large bruise there soon. That was not ideal because it would make it harder for him to hide, especially with all the shouting he could hear from his hiding place as warriors searched for him. But none of that mattered as he studied the large golden cross in his hands and felt the smile spread on his face.

It hadn't taken him long to find out where the cross was. Roul had arrived in Ribe a few days ago, having travelled with a large group of Frankish traders and their armed escort. The journey here from Hedeby had been uneventful, although Roul had enjoyed the chaos he saw as they travelled north. All across the horizon he had seen more than a dozen smoke plumes as buildings burnt and the sky filled with carrion birds. Bands of warriors were roaming all over the countryside, looking for easy plunder, and the large caravan Roul had joined had been too much of a risk for them. And once in Ribe, Roul had spent a few days wandering around and listening to people as they gossiped about current events. He quickly found out who Sven was and was surprised at how short and round the man was. From all the stories he had heard about the monstrous jarl, Roul had expected him to be a giant. But the man spent most of his time in the hall and drinking ale. That was until a few days ago when Sven threw a young Frankish man out of his hall. A woman had run out after them, an abbess judging by the way she was dressed and the daughter of King Louis of East Francia, Roul had guessed. As surprised as he was to see her in Ribe, Roul had kept his distance as they spoke. He was even more surprised when Danish warriors ran out of the hall and slaughtered the men on board a ship docked on the wharf. Their bodies were taken downstream and thrown into the river, but the ship still sat there. Empty and stained with blood. It was only after that that Roul had realised the ship belonged to Duke Liudolf of Saxony, confirming that the woman was Abbess Hildegard.

After that, Sven had been out training every day, and Roul wondered what had been said in the hall to force the change. That was when Roul had heard the man muttering about how he wanted to kill Sven. Roul had followed the man as he stumbled towards a house away from the river and near the town wall. The house wasn't as big as the other houses and Roul saw a small red-headed girl sitting outside and playing with two straw dolls. At first, the scene reminded him of one he had seen many times in Paris. A young girl dreaming of the man she would one day marry, but then he realised this girl was making the dolls fight. One doll even had a small stick stuck in its hand which looked like a sword. Roul could only shake his head at that point. How he despised the heathens. Even their children only cared about slaughtering others.

Roul had waited a while for the large man to leave the house again and had approached him with a skin of ale he had bought from a trader. The man had been suspicious at first, but Roul's drunk impression quickly fooled him as he pretended to be lost. After a few careful questions, Roul had learnt that the grandson of King Louis had stayed with the man and that the cousin of his wife was the boy's protector. The man had kicked them out because he hated Sven and refused to have a Christian living in his house, no matter how much the jarl had paid him. Roul sensed the story wasn't true, but he played along and complimented the man on his strong values. The man, Haldor, his name was, had told Roul that the boy and the woman had moved to the hall and were sleeping in the sleeping quarters in the back of the hall. Roul had thanked the man by giving him the rest of the ale and went back to the hall. It hadn't taken him long to find the small door at the back of the hall, one often used by the slaves. Roul waited two more days, just to make sure the room would be empty, and this morning while Sven was training again he searched the room. The cross had to be amongst the boy's possessions. He was sure of it. He had searched in the room carefully, checking under the rushes for signs of a recent hole being dug. Roul even searched the Christian shrine in the room's corner, something he had not expected to find before he searched the large chest he assumed belonged to Sven. He had raised an eyebrow, though, when he found the chest was filled with children's clothing, and then he saw it. Roul's heart had beaten harder than it had ever done in his life as he reached for the large golden cross, but just when his hand had gripped it, the door opened and there stood Sven, his fat face with his bulbous nose creased and his teeth bared. Roul had to admit that he'd felt a moment of fear, especially when Sven had charged at him. The old man was faster than Roul had thought he would be and when the other warriors rushed into the room, Roul had thought he had made a mistake by coming to Ribe. But God was on his side and he had escaped with the cross.

Roul ran his finger along the small gems that edged the cross as he stared at it, feeling his lust for wealth tugging at him. It was not the most beautiful cross he had ever seen, but that was only because he had seen King Charles's collection and he guessed that, to common people, this cross would stand out. But it was magnificent. Again, he wondered why his king believed this cross would help him rebuild the empire of Charlemagne. Roul pushed the question from his mind and put the cross in the large pouch he wore around his waist. It was not his job to decipher the mind of the king of West Francia. His job was to do as his king commanded, and Roul had now done that. He had the boy safely in Hedeby and now he had the cross. More importantly, Roul also had news that he was sure King Charles would be interested in. All Roul had to do was wait until nightfall, then he would sneak out of his hiding spot and leave this town. He frowned when he remembered the fat drunk. The man would need to be dealt with before Roul left, especially as things had not quite gone to plan for Roul. He fingered the scabbard where his knife would be, but it was gone now. Stuck in the chest of a heathen warrior. But Roul could always get another one. And soon he would be back in Paris, the capital of West Francia, and be named as the new head spy of King Charles.

God was smiling on Roul and, with His blessing, Roul would become the most powerful man in West Francia. Even more powerful than the king himself.

* * *

Sven barged into the house where Charles's mother was kept prisoner. She and the old priest were sitting by the table while Gerold was on a stool at the far end of the room and all of them jumped to their feet and gaped at him.

'Where is he?' Sven scanned the room, even though he knew the Frank could not have entered before him.

'Where is who?' Charles's mother asked, her eyes wide. The old priest paled and clasped his hands in front of him while Gerold scowled at Sven.

Sven, angry at what happened and needing to take it out on someone, stormed across the room, but Gerold was faster as he grabbed the stool he had been sitting on and attacked Sven.

'Gerold, stop!' Charles's mother shouted, but Gerold ignored her, just like Sven had hoped he would. He was convinced that the man who had stolen the cross was with them, even if he didn't know who the bastard was or how he had known where the cross was. Gerold moved fast, but Sven expected his move and let the young Frank swing the stool at him. He twisted out of the way and grabbed Gerold's arm before punching him hard in the side of his head. Gerold's head snapped to the side as his legs wobbled underneath him, but Sven did not let go. He was too angry and not just at the bastard Franks for ruining his life, but also at himself for not thinking to hide the cross somewhere else. Sven should have known that others were still looking for it. He should have expected something like this. He punched Gerold again before grabbing his hair and dragging him to the table where he smashed Gerold's face on its surface.

The old priest wailed and Charles's mother jumped back, her hand covering her mouth, as Gerold's limp body fell to the ground.

'Where is he?' Sven demanded again.

Before anyone could answer, Thora appeared by the door. 'Sven, what in Thor's name are you doing?'

Sven glared at her, his nostrils flared. 'They took it!' He jabbed a finger towards Charles's mother. 'They sent some bastard to take the cross!'

Thora took in the fresh cut on Sven's arm before she asked, 'Who took it?' Her eyes flickered towards Charles's mother, who sat stunned by the table, her eyes fixed on Gerold.

'Some Frankish bastard! They must have sent him! One of their men from their ship!' Sven turned his attention back to Charles's mother and the old priest. 'Where is he?'

'I... I... don't know what you're talking about,' Charles's mother finally managed, but Sven didn't believe her. He should never have let them stay in Ribe. He should have sent them away the moment they had arrived. But he had been too weak. Too caught up in his grief to see the danger they posed. Sven's eyes went to the old priest, who was on his knees, his hands clasped in front of him, and his lips quivering as he muttered a prayer.

'Take the priest,' Sven ordered Alvar, who had followed him into the house. 'It's time we make a proper sacrifice to the gods!'

The priest howled as Alvar grabbed him and lifted him up as if he weighed no more than a small child. Charles's mother tried to stop him, but Sven stepped in front of her. Before Alvar could take the priest out of the house, Thora blocked his way.

'Alvar, put the priest down!'

The old priest wailed while kicking his legs and swinging his arm. His robe rose to reveal thin white legs and if Sven hadn't been so angry, he might have found the sight amusing. Alvar hesitated and glanced at Sven, not sure what to do.

'Don't look at me! Take the bastard out!'

'Alvar, no! Put the old man down before I hurt you!' Thora stood her ground by the door as she squared her shoulders and scowled at the younger warrior. Even though she only came up to Alvar's chest and was still recovering from her stab wound, he took a step backwards and Sven knew she had won this. But Sven refused to give in so easily.

'Thora, get out of the way! It's time to make these bastards pay for what they have done!'

Thora glared at Sven. 'And what have they done? How do you know the man that took the cross works for them?'

'Because he was a Frank!' Sven looked around for something to throw, but there was nothing within reach, so he just clenched his fists.

'By Frigg, Sven! There are many Franks! Just like there are many Danes!'

'Please, she speaks the truth,' Charles's mother pleaded. It was the first time since she had arrived that Sven saw her show any fear. Gerold stirred on the ground and Sven was tempted to kick him in the head, but then the young man stopped moving. 'Your men have been guarding the door the entire time. There was no way we could get a message to anyone.'

'You could have ordered the bastard to steal the cross before I locked you up!'

Charles's mother shook her head. 'You told us that Charles had the cross.' Sven hesitated when he realised she was right. He didn't want them to know that he still had the cross, so the day they had arrived Sven had told her that Ivor had taken the cross when he took Charles.

'Sven, killing the priest will not bring Charles back.'

Sven ground his teeth. 'Perhaps not, but someone still has to pay for killing Torkel! Alvar, come and bring the priest!' Sven stormed to the door, but Thora refused to move.

'You'll have to go through me if you want to sacrifice the priest.' Thora prepared herself as if she expected Sven to charge at her. But Sven could not. Thora's injury was healing well, he had been told, but he knew she still didn't have all her strength back. He stood in front of Thora, his fists clenched by his side, while Alvar was behind him with the wailing priest over his shoulder.

Outside, Sven saw the townspeople hovering near the house, all of them eager to see what was happening. 'Sven, they are not to blame for Torkel's death and you know that.'

Sven glanced over his shoulder at Charles's mother. 'No, I don't. Charles heard the old bastard talk about killing Torkel. He told us so!'

Thora shook her head, her expression softening. She turned to Charles's mother. 'Ask the priest what he and the duke spoke of when Charles overheard them in the church the day after Torkel's death.' Sven heard Charles's mother ask the priest in Frankish, but the priest was too busy wailing to hear the question. 'Alvar, put the bastard down.'

'Sven?' Alvar frowned.

'Just do it.'

Alvar put the priest on the floor, making sure to drop him the last few feet, and Charles's mother repeated the question. The old priest frowned and then seemed to remember.

'We spoke about Torkel's death, yes. But not because we were plotting it. We were trying to understand what had happened. Duke Liudolf and I couldn't understand why Lothar had attacked him. If Charles hadn't run, then we would have explained it all to him. We would never have harmed Torkel. By God, we spent many years protecting him and Charles.'

Sven took a step towards the old priest, who cowered behind his hands. 'You're lying!'

'What did he say, Sven?' Thora asked because she didn't speak Frankish. Charles's mother translated when Sven stayed silent, and when she was done, he nodded to confirm that what she had said was true. Sven's anger left him, and he felt exhausted. He looked around the room, hoping to find some ale, but there was none.

Charles's mother went to the old man and wrapped her arms

around him, before she asked, 'Who took the cross?' Sven noticed she asked in Danish so that Thora could understand what she was saying.

'A Frank. That's all I know. A small man who looked like every other Frank I've ever seen. He looked just like that snake.' Sven pointed at Gerold. Charles's mother frowned. 'What?' Sven asked her.

'We are not the only ones who want the cross.'

'I know,' Sven said. 'The king of West Francia wants it as well. Enough to pay Guttrom to start a civil war so that he can get my grandson and the cross.' Sven made sure to refer to Charles as his grandson. 'But why? Why is everyone after that cross? Why was my son killed?' Charles's mother hesitated, and Sven looked at Alvar. 'Grab the priest. Looks like we'll be making a sacrifice after all.'

The old priest wailed as Alvar grabbed him again, and Charles's mother pleaded. 'Please, my uncle wants the cross because he believes it will make him emperor!'

'Why?' Sven asked as Alvar hesitated.

'I don't know. It's just a cross.'

Sven shook his head. 'No, it's not just a cross.' He remembered what his uncle, the old godi, had said about the large golden cross and then had an idea. 'Alvar, get the horses ready. We're going on a trip.'

Alvar frowned. 'And what about the priest?'

'Don't worry. He's coming with. All of them are.' He smiled and turned to leave the house.

'Sven, what are you doing?' Thora asked him with a raised eyebrow.

'We're going to visit Odinson.'

Thora's eyes widened. 'Odinson! Sven, no.'

'Who is this Odinson?' Charles's mother asked.

Sven smiled as he glanced at her over his shoulder. 'Someone who's going to make you wish you told me everything you know.' This time Thora let Sven leave the house and once outside Sven glared at all the townspeople who were standing around, many of them glaring back and one even spitting at the ground. Sven sneered at the man, who stepped back, and decided he had nothing to gain from confronting the people of Ribe. His fight was not with them, and they had suffered enough since he had returned. So, he just shook his head and went to the hall so he could prepare for the visit to his uncle.

'Sven, are you sure this is a good idea?' Thora asked as she followed Sven into the hall.

Sven did not look at her as he responded. 'I want to know the truth about that cross! I want to know why it got my son killed and I'm tired of the Christians lying to me about it.'

'But you don't know what that old godi might do. He might decide to kill one of them.'

Sven stopped and faced Thora, his eyebrows creased. 'I don't care what the godi does to them. As long as I get my answers.' He went to a bucket of water near the hearth fire and cleaned the cut on his arm, before he took the clean tunic from a thrall. Sven glanced at the woman, still expecting to see Alfhild, and wondered how long it would take for him to get used to the fact that she was dead. Or perhaps he never would because she had died trying to do what he couldn't. Protect Charles. He shook the thoughts from his mind as he put the clean tunic on and then brushed his beard with a fine-toothed bone comb handed to him by the thrall. Sven rubbed his head and felt the stubble, but knew he had no time to shave his scalp. The sun was past the midpoint, and he wanted to get to the godi before sunset.

'I'm coming with,' Thora said, and Sven wasn't surprised. As much as she dismissed the cross, he knew she also wanted the truth. He nodded and went outside to see Alvar bring enough horses for everyone, including Thora. Even the large warrior had expected Thora would join them. Alvar had also brought two other warriors with him which Sven thought was probably a good idea. There were still raiders rampaging around the countryside, despite regular patrols going out, but if there was one thing Danes were good at, it was raiding a settlement and then disappearing before the defenders could arrive.

'Where are you going?' Ingvild, Thora's aunt, appeared with the small red-headed girl behind her. Sven wondered how the two of them always seemed to show up when he least wanted to see them.

'Nowhere,' he said and walked to his horse. The animal seemed to glare at Sven, who just growled at it as he took the reins from Alvar and mounted the beast. 'Alvar, you stay here,' Sven said to the giant warrior, who seemed relieved that he did not have to go to the godi with them. 'Search every bloody house in this town, break doors down if you need to. But find that bloody Frank before he escapes!'

'Can I come with?' Jorlaug asked when she saw Thora get on her horse.

Thora shook her head. 'Not this time, Jorlaug.'

The small girl crossed her arms and puffed her cheeks out. 'Not fair. I never get to do anything.'

Sven shook his head and turned to Ingvild as Alvar brought Charles's mother and the old priest out. 'Tend to the injured snake inside the house. Make sure the bastard lives. I might still have a need for him.'

'What need?' The old lady scowled at him.

Sven waited until everyone was mounted and ready to go. 'I might still need to make a sacrifice to the gods and you know they like them young and strong.' Ingvild smiled as Sven rode off

without seeing if the others were following him. As he rode
towards the gate, he saw Rollo's wife and son standing by the road,
both of them staring at him. The boy's face had healed from his
fight with Charles, and Sven saw no sign of the lump he had from
trying to avenge his grandmother. Sven had been told how
Charles had beaten the boy and wished he had been there to see
it. But again, Sven wondered where on Midgard Rollo was. He
should never have let the bastard race off on his own like that, but
he had been in no state to stop the large warrior. Sven prayed
Rollo would return soon. He needed the man for the storm he
knew was coming, and young Sigmund needed his father.

## 14

The sun was starting its descent and soon Sol's brother, Mani, would be dragging the moon through the sky as they reached the place where the godi worshipped the gods. Sven felt unsettled as he remembered the large ash tree covered by more ravens than he could count. All of them enticed there with food by the godi, just so he could scare those who came to seek his aid. Thora had said nothing, but Sven sensed her eyes on him the entire ride through the forest and occasionally the old priest would whimper. But Charles's mother had not said a word either.

Sven dismounted near the path which led to the raven tree and was surprised to see fresh tracks on the path. Small footprints which suggested a child or a small woman. Sven knew the godi got his information from somewhere, most likely thralls, and often wondered who in Ribe was spying on him for the godi. He glanced over his shoulder and saw that everyone was ready, although he noticed how the two warriors hung back, neither of them eager to go into the clearing that was beyond the trees. Even from here, they could hear the ravens, but Sven knew it would be much worse in the clearing by the tree. He scrutinised the surrounding trees, wondering if his uncle's young servant was watching them, or if he had already run off to warn the godi of their arrival.

'Sven?' Thora asked after she had helped Charles's mother and the old priest off their horses. Their hands were tied in front of them, and Sven was determined to keep it that way. Not that he expected the old priest to do anything, but he had learnt never to underestimate women.

'Let's go.' Sven gripped the large ivory Mjöllnir around his neck before he led the way. The air along the path was heavy and Sven wasn't sure if it was just his imagination, but it felt like it was getting harder to breathe the closer they got to the clearing. He wanted to glance over his shoulder, to see if the others felt the same, but did not want to appear afraid. Not like the old priest, who was whimpering with each step.

It did not take them long to reach the clearing, and by the time they did, the cries of the countless ravens were deafening. Sven felt Thora grab hold of his shoulder, and when he glanced at her, he saw she had a hand to her mouth and her eyes were wide. Charles's mother gripped the large golden cross around her neck as her face paled and the old priest collapsed to his knees. His eyes screwed shut and his mouth moved as if he was praying, which Sven was sure the man was. But he doubted the Christian god would hear the old bastard's words over the ravens, and the more the priest tried to pray, the louder the ravens got. It was unsettling even for him, and Sven felt the hairs on his arms stand up.

Sven turned his attention back to the tree again. It was the same as the last time he had been here, which had only been a few weeks before. The tree was large and old, its branches filled with fresh and decayed bones, some with scraps of meat still attached. Ravens filled every branch and the ground below was littered with more bones and raven shit. The trunk of the tree was dark red, stained by the blood of many sacrifices made to the gods, while the edge of the clearing was ringed with stones, each of them marked with runes, one for each of the gods. The stench of death and rotting meat was suffocating, and Sven knew he wasn't the only one who was struggling to breathe. But the clearing wasn't exactly as Sven had seen it last time. Near the trunk of the tree, he saw the rotten carcass of the calf he had brought last time and remembered how the godi's servant had carved it up and started cooking the meat while the godi had studied the cross.

As Sven crossed the stone ring, he noticed something else, something that hadn't been there before. A new skeleton hung from the tree, its bones picked clean by the ravens, but it still had some strand of black hair attached to the skull. Sven felt his anger engulf him and gritted his teeth as he recognised the dress the skeleton was wearing.

'Sven?' Thora had to shout to be heard over the screaming ravens as Sven rushed to the tree. He stopped below the skeleton and saw where it had been tied to the branch. 'Is that...?'

'It's Alfhild,' Sven growled as he stared at the dress he had buried her in. The skeleton still had the golden Mjöllnir he had put around her neck. With clenched fists, Sven turned and glared at the trees. Charles's mother and the priest were still by the edge of the ring, both pale and looking like they were about to collapse, but Sven ignored them as he searched for the godi. 'Odinson! Odinson! Get out here now or I swear by Odin I will burn this whole forest down!' He paced the circle as Thora stared at the skeleton, but there was no response from the godi. 'Odinson! Get out here now!' He scanned the clearing, looking for something to start a fire with, but couldn't see anything useful. In his anger, Sven picked up a stone and threw it at the tree. It struck a raven, which cried out and took to the skies, a few of its companions following it. This gave Sven an idea, and he searched for more stones and threw them at the ravens, most of which were taking to the skies now. 'Odinson!'

'Stop!' a voice thundered from the trees. 'You've brought no sacrifice, Sven the Boar.'

Sven glanced at the old priest and, out of the corner of his eye, saw Thora shaking her head. 'Come out or I will chase every single raven away from here!' He threw another stone to prove his point.

'Fine!' the old voice said and the godi walked out from the trees, his ancient face flush with his own anger, as he leaned on a tall staff. The godi was much older than Sven, his back crooked and stooped, and his head bare. He wore a tattered deer hide and his face was covered in tattoos. Sven rushed at the old godi, ignoring Thora's scream, and grabbed the bastard by his long grey beard, which came down to his knees, and shook the ancient godi as he roared in his face.

'What did you do to her? What did you do to Alfhild?'

Before the godi could respond, his servant, a young man who had a short beard and, like the godi, had his face covered in tattoos, stepped out from the trees and pointed an arrow at Sven. Sven pulled his sword from his scabbard and stuck the point under the godi's chin, which made the servant hesitate. The old godi held a hand up to stop his servant from doing anything, and in a voice soft enough for only him to hear, the godi said, 'I brought her home, nephew. She belonged to the gods, and that is where she went.'

Sven twisted the sword, but the godi did not flinch. Instead, he stared at Sven with wise eyes. 'You dug her up to feed her to your birds.'

'She was one of my birds. My eyes and ears in your hall. All my children come here when they die. What do you think all those bones are?'

Sven's hand trembled as his anger coursed through him. The ravens had landed on the tree again, but they were silent as if they were waiting to see what Sven was going to do. Even Thora had gone quiet.

'She is where she belongs, Sven. She is one of the ravens. You probably even struck her with one of your stones.'

Sven glanced over his shoulder at the remains of Alfhild. 'She was one of your spies?' The godi nodded and now Sven knew how the old bastard knew so much about what was happening in his hall. But she had still died trying to protect his grandson. 'She deserves better than to be strung up on your tree so the ravens can feast on her,' he said, his voice strained with emotion.

'No, nephew. There is no higher honour than to be feasted on by Odin's ravens and becoming one of them. She is where she belongs and she is happy.'

Sven roared and let go of the godi, who somehow stayed on his feet, and threw his sword at the tree. It flung through the air, its whirling noise drawing the attention of everyone until it buried itself in the trunk. The ravens erupted with a noise so loud it drove the Christians to their knees and even Thora had to cover her ears. Sven turned and faced the godi again, his face red. 'Godi, I want answers and I want them now.'

'What answers, Sven the Boar?'

A growl escaped from Sven's throat, and he had to stop himself from killing the godi. Not because he was afraid of the gods' retribution, but because the ancient bastard might have information that could be useful. 'I want to know why the bastard kings of Francia think that cross is so special.'

The old godi scowled. 'I told you to get rid of that cross. It will only bring death and misery.'

'Too late for that,' Sven muttered. 'The cross is gone. It was taken.'

'Was it now?' The godi glanced at Thora, who looked away. Sven thought nothing of it, as he believed his uncle was playing his games again. 'I told you everything I know about the cross, Sven.'

Sven shook his head. 'There's more to it. I know there is and I want to know what.'

'Why?' The godi raised an eyebrow at him as he leaned on his staff.

'Because they took my grandson,' Sven said through clenched teeth.

The godi did not respond. Instead, he stared at Sven as if he was searching Sven's soul, before his eyes drifted towards Charles's mother and the old priest. Sven had almost forgotten about them, and thanked Odin that they were too frightened to even think of running away. Not that they would have got far. The godi smiled, revealing black gums and missing teeth, as he stalked towards them. It was like a dance performed just to scare them even more as the godi took a few steps forward, almost skipping instead of walking, and then he would sniff the air. Sven doubted the man could smell anything over the stench of death and raven shit, but it had the desired effect, as the old priest cowered behind Charles's mother. She, on the other hand, stood straight and glared at the godi, who repeated his dance until he reached the edge of the stone circle where he stopped and sniffed the air once more. Sven glanced at the godi's servant, who had his eyes fixed on Sven, but then he turned his attention back to what his uncle was doing. Which was nothing. He just stood in front of Charles's mother and scrutinised her as she held her cross towards him and prayed to her god. Sven remembered what Alvar had told Charles the last time they were here, and wondered if he should tell her the same thing, but he decided against it. She would find out herself that her god was not here, not in this stone circle. This was a place for the gods of Asgard. The ravens screamed as if they read his mind, which sent a shiver down Sven's spine, and even Thora looked nervous as she gripped her sword and the small Mjöllnir she wore. Then the godi held up his hand and the ravens fell silent, as if they waited for him to speak. Sven wondered how his uncle had taught the birds to do that and had to admit it was very effective when he saw the fear on the face of Charles's mother.

'You are his mother,' the godi said in Frankish. It did not surprise Sven that his uncle knew the language, and was sure that if he asked how, then the godi would most likely say the ravens had taught him.

Charles's mother frowned before she recomposed herself and glared at the godi. 'How do you know?'

Odinson sniffed the air again, before he said, 'You smell like him.'

Charles's mother's eyes widened and Sven shook his head. 'Your *birds* told you, didn't they?' Sven said, and the godi glanced at him with a grin on his face.

'Sven the Boar, always eager to take the fun out of everything.'

Sven ignored that comment and limped towards the godi and Charles's mother. 'I saw the flesh tracks on the path. One of them was here recently.'

The godi did not respond to Sven. Instead, he looked at the old priest and an enormous grin appeared on his face. 'Bernard. I wondered if I'd ever get to see you again.'

Everyone, including the ravens, it seemed, stared at the old priest, who could only frown while his mouth opened and closed. 'I... I... do... don't know you.'

'What's going on?' Thora asked because she didn't speak Frankish.

Sven rubbed his head. 'I don't really know.' He walked towards the godi and said, 'How do you know the old bastard? And don't tell me about your eyes and ears everywhere!'

Odinson smiled, but his eyes never left the old priest. 'Look closely at my face Bernard and you'll remember.'

'No!' The old priest gripped his cross and held it in front of him. 'Get away from me, you spawn of Satan! God will protect me!'

'Step back!' Charles's mother said, holding her own cross towards the godi, who started laughing. The ravens in the tree went wild as the godi grabbed the cross out of the old priest's hands and ripped it from his neck. Thora made to rush towards them, but Sven held his hand up to stop her. He wanted to see what would happen next. The godi, still laughing, threw the priest's cross towards the tree and one raven swooped down and grabbed it out of the air before it flew back to its branch. Sven watched as the ravens fought over the cross and had to resist the urge to cover his ears from all the noise they were making. He turned back to the godi to see him grab the old priest from behind Charles's mother and drag him into the circle and towards the tree. Charles's mother was about to rush after them when an arrow struck the ground in front of her. Sven turned and saw the godi's servant aiming his bow at her.

'Sven, we should stop this!' Thora shouted, and Sven noticed how she didn't rush to do that. Like most in Ribe, Thora feared the godi and dared not to interfere. Sven, though, knew who the man really was, but he wanted the truth and he believed his uncle would get it for him, so he did nothing. He also wanted to know why the godi acted as if he knew the priest.

'You don't remember me, do you, Bernard?' the godi shouted over the din of the ravens and all the old priest could do was shake his head. The godi pulled a wicked-looking knife, its blade thin and sharp, from somewhere under his deer-hide dress, and raised it as if he was about to plunge it into the priest's chest.

'Sven, for Odin's sake, do something!' Thora shouted, the ravens making it hard for him to hear her words. Sven glanced at Charles's mother, who was frozen with fear outside the stone circle, and then at the godi's servant, who was glaring at him.

Sven shook his head and then glanced at the remains of Alfhild hanging from the tree. 'Odinson! Stop!' he roared, but the godi couldn't hear him, or didn't want to. Before Sven could rush towards them, not that he would have made it in time anyway, the godi brought the knife down.

The old priest's cries silenced the ravens and all Sven could hear was the godi laughing, a mad, maniacal laugh that made Sven regret not killing the godi a long time ago. But then the godi stepped aside and Sven frowned when he saw the priest was still alive. Although, his robe had a wet stain where he had pissed himself, and if it wasn't for the stench of death and the ravens already filling the air, then Sven was sure he would have smelt the old priest's piss. The godi held on to his hand, which had a deep cut in it, the blood pouring down the old priest's arm and soaking his robe. Thora raised an eyebrow at Sven, who only shrugged as he waited to see what the godi would do next.

Odinson glanced over his shoulder at Sven and winked, before he dragged the old priest closer to the tree and pressed his bleeding hand against its trunk. 'The gods accept your sacrifice, Sven the Boar,' the godi said, and Sven suddenly felt exhausted. It took all his strength not to collapse, something Charles's mother had no problem with as she dropped to her knees and prayed.

The old priest frowned at the godi. 'You didn't kill me,' he said in Frankish, and the old godi laughed.

'My dear Bernard. I would never kill an old friend like you.'

Sven and Thora glanced at each other before Sven asked, 'What are you talking about, you old fool?'

Odinson didn't respond, instead, he knelt down and grabbed the old priest's head and forced him to look at his face. 'Look at me, Bernard. No, open your eyes and look.'

The old priest did that and then his head jerked back as if he had been slapped. 'Od... Odimir?'

'Odimir?' Sven repeated and raised an eyebrow at Thora.

'Yes, Bernard, it's me.' The godi sat down and crossed his legs as he laughed. 'I had you, didn't I? You really believed I was going to kill you.' Odinson scratched his bearded chin. 'It was tempting, though. It's been a long time since the ravens fed on a Christian.' The godi looked at the countless black birds in the tree above him.

Sven limped towards his uncle, after indicating for Thora to fetch Charles's mother, who was still outside the stone circle. 'What in the name of Thor's balls is going on, Odinson?' He glanced at the priest, his face pale as he looked at his bleeding hand.

'It's a long story, Sven the Boar. One you don't need to know.' Odinson looked up at the tree as one raven cried out. 'Fine, Alfhild. If you say so.' He then looked at Sven, who was staring at the ravens, trying to work out if that was really the spirit of Alfhild or just another of his uncle's games. Thora brought Charles's mother to the tree, who dropped to her knees beside the old priest and grabbed his hand to check his wound. She looked around for something, but then used her dress to stop the bleeding, her face a grimace at the stench that surrounded them. 'You know my life story, Sven. That my mother was a thrall and that your grandfather rejected me.'

Sven nodded and felt Thora frown at him. No one in Ribe

knew Odinson was his uncle. The only ones who did had died many winters ago.

'When I came of age, I decided I had no reason to stay in Ribe and I was curious about the rest of Midgard. I was also curious about the Christians to the south. Even as a young child, I knew the nailed god would be a threat to our gods and way of life, so I wanted to learn more about them. I travelled south, learnt to speak their language as if I was one of them, and became one of their priests. That was where I met Bernard.' The old priest stared blankly at them, because the godi was speaking Danish, but Charles's mother quickly translated what he had said.

'You were always a heathen?' the old priest asked, his aged face even more wrinkled with confusion. 'But you said you came from the north of Francia. You knew so much about the Bible and our way of life.'

Odinson shrugged. 'I was never meant to be a warrior, but Odin has blessed me with some of his wisdom, so I learnt your customs, your language, even all of your prayers. I even learnt to write and read your words.'

Sven scowled as he thought about something, something that had been bothering him since the day he had come here with Charles and the cross. 'That's how you knew about the cross, about its secret?'

Charles's mother stared at Sven with wide eyes before she translated his words to the old priest, who closed his eyes and turned his face away.

The old godi smiled. 'Aye, that's how I knew about the cross. Bernard was one of its guardians, but in his youth, he was a slave to their wine and after a few cups, with the help of some of my own ingredients, told me everything I wanted to know. And he told me all about the Cross of Charlemagne and of its dark secrets.'

The old priest cried when the words were translated to him. 'I didn't know he was one of them. I thought he was a friend.'

Sven wanted to feel sorry for the old priest, because he knew how deceitful godis could be. Much like Loki. The thought made him look at his uncle and he wondered if the old bastard wasn't really the god of mischief in disguise.

'What did you mean by its dark secrets?' Charles's mother asked in Danish, which surprised Sven and Thora. 'My son was taken and the man I once loved was killed because of the cross. I want to know about it as much as you do. More even because it involves my family. So don't look at me like that.'

Sven was taken aback by her response, but Thora only smiled. 'You mean you don't know about the cross?' Sven asked.

'I only know the story that everyone else knows. That it helped my great-grandfather build his empire, but no one really knows why it is so special. I doubt even my father knows.'

Sven frowned as he looked at Thora, who only shrugged. Then he remembered what the godi had told him and Charles about the cross. 'You told us something was added to the cross, an old and dark magic. Older than our gods.'

The godi smiled and looked at the old priest. In Frankish he said, 'Are you going to tell them, or should I?' But the old priest only turned his face away and carried on crying. The godi shrugged and looked at the ravens above him, as if he was waiting for an answer from them.

'Talk, Odinson, or I swear by Odin, neither your ravens nor your servant will stop me from spilling your blood on this tree,' Sven said, which only made the old godi smile.

'Sven the Boar, making threats because he doesn't understand what is going on.' The godi stood up and walked towards the tree, where he pressed his palm against the trunk and closed his eyes. 'Have you ever heard of Irminsul?'

'It was a great tree in what is now Ehresburg,' Charles's mother said. 'The heathen Saxons worshipped it before my grandfather destroyed it and built a church in its place.'

'Aye, Hildegard is correct.' The godi smiled.

Everyone frowned at the godi.

'You know my name? How?'

The godi laughed, which sent the ravens wild again. 'They told me.' He pointed to the large birds, which had the desired effect as Charles's mother gripped the cross around her neck again. But Sven knew that one of his uncle's many spies most likely told him. And if what he had said about spending many years in Francia was true, then he most likely had many eyes and ears there as well. Sven wondered if his uncle knew about Torkel and Charles, but then his uncle carried on talking after the ravens had calmed down again. 'Irminsul, like this tree, was connected to the gods, but it was a great wooden pillar that reached far into the sky.'

'But what does this have to do with the cross?' Sven asked.

The godi smiled. 'Patience was something you were never good at, was it, Sven? Even as a young boy, you always had to rush into things. It drove your father crazy with all the problems you caused for him.'

Sven growled and clenched his fist. 'My father hated me because I was never tall enough for him.'

'Is that what you really believe, Sven?'

'Can we discuss that later?' Thora said, shaking her head 'Odinson, tell us what this Irminsul has to do with the cross.' Even Hildegard was staring at the godi as she waited for him to explain.

The godi seemed to enjoy the attention and paused for a few heartbeats too many, before he finally continued. 'The great Charlemagne understood the power of the old gods and he valued the Saxons for their fighting abilities. They did beat his vast army many times, before he could finally subdue them and that was only because of something he did before he had Irminsul destroyed.'

'What did he do?' Sven said, losing his patience even more.

The godi smiled at him. 'Before Charlemagne had the pillar destroyed, he cut a sliver of wood from its trunk and had his blacksmith add it to the back of that cross.'

'You're lying!' Hildegard shouted, but was ignored.

'Why that cross?' Thora asked.

Odinson shrugged. 'I don't know. Perhaps that was the only cross they had available. Old Bernard here told me the cross was made especially for that campaign, but I guess it was the only one big enough.'

'But how did you know it was that cross?' Sven asked. 'We could have brought you any cross.'

'Because old Bernard gushed over the beauty of the cross and especially the size of the ruby. But the back of the cross confirmed it when I saw where the gold had been melted away and added again.'

'You lie!' Hildegard shouted again. 'My great-grandfather would never do that! He was a devout Christian and would never taint a symbol of Christ with heathen objects.'

Odinson laughed again. 'Your great-grandfather's only religion was power. That was all he ever sought. He never cared about the word of your god or his weak son.' The ravens took to the skies, the sight of it enough to frighten Sven as Hildegard hid under her cross as if it would protect her. 'He knew he could never defeat the Saxons as long as they fought for their gods. So he sought a way to use their power against the Saxons.'

'But he built a church to show that our faith conquered yours.' Hildegard bared her teeth like an angry wolf and Sven wondered if she might attack the godi. He glanced over his shoulder and saw the servant had disappeared, but was sure the bastard was hiding in the trees, watching them. He could feel it. Or maybe it was the gods' eyes he felt in them. Sven glanced up at the tree and shivered.

'He did, but where do you think he got the wood to build that church? Our gods helped him defeat the Saxons, and he built them a new shrine. One of stone and wood that would stand forever. But Charlemagne was a smart man and knew he had to make it look like a Christian church, otherwise everyone would know about the deal he had made.'

'No!' Hildegard said and then told the old priest what the godi had said. 'Bishop, tell me he is lying,' she said in Frankish.

But the old bishop just shook his head. His shoulders shuddered as he sobbed, and then finally he looked up, his eyes red and puffy. 'God forgive me, but what Odimir said was true. My master, the former bishop to the king, was there. He pleaded with Charlemagne not to do it, but the emperor saw no other way to defeat the Saxons. But afterwards he repented. He prayed for forgiveness. That was the real reason he built the church where the heathen tree once stood.'

The godi laughed. 'No, I was there. I visited your church and felt the power of my gods in the wood. And they are angry! Angry that Charlemagne made promises to them and then abandoned them. Angry that his son and grandsons rejected their power. That was why the mighty Frankish empire broke apart. Why sons fought against father and brothers against each other. The cross that was once the power to build an empire became the curse that destroyed it. And as long as you have that cross, Sven,' the godi stared at him, his eyes hard and uncaring, 'it will curse you and your grandson. I told you to get rid of it, but you didn't listen and now your grandson is in the hands of your enemy.'

Sven gritted his teeth. 'The king of West Francia is only my enemy because he took Charles from me!'

Again, the godi laughed. 'Oh, Sven the Boar. You know so little. It's a miracle you're still alive. Your grandson is not with the king of West Francia. Your grandson is with the man who took your son from you.' The godi looked at Hildegard. 'And he is in more danger than he has ever been.'

Hildegard paled. 'My father has my son?'

Sven shot forwards and grabbed the godi by his beard. 'How do you know this?'

The godi smiled. 'Because I know everything that goes on in Midgard, Sven. The gods tell me everything. That's why you came to me, isn't it?'

Sven growled and let go of the godi. 'Then tell me how I get my grandson back.'

Odinson sat down and crossed his legs while he stared at the tree, his head tilted as if it spoke to him. 'You can't, Sven. Your grandson is lost to you because of your lies. But you have more important things to concern yourself with.'

Sven wanted to grip the hilt of his sword, but then remembered it was still stuck in the tree trunk. 'What's more important than my grandson?' he growled.

The godi didn't answer straight away. He stared at the raven tree, his eyes briefly stopping on the skeleton of Alfhild. 'Your own survival, Sven. Remember what I said about the cuckoo in your nest?'

Sven frowned and remembered the last time he was here with Charles. His uncle had warned him in his own way that there was someone he couldn't trust around him. 'Aye, that was Guttrom and the bastard is dead.'

'The nephew of Horik isn't the only cuckoo chick in your nest, Sven. There are many who want you dead.'

'Who are they?' Sven's knuckles whitened as he clenched his fists.

But the godi only shrugged. 'The gods have not told me yet.'

'And what of your birds, the unfreed ones that whisper in your ears?' Sven thought of the footprint he had seen on the path.

'They know nothing about this, but they did tell me something else that you might be interested in.'

'What?'

'A new king. One that bears the same name as the previous owner of Denmark's crown.'

Sven hawked and spat. 'Why should I care about a new king?'

His uncle stared at him, but Sven struggled to see what was behind his eyes. 'Because your enemies whisper in his ears and because he is on his way to you now.'

Sven glanced at Thora, who only shrugged. 'He is coming to Ribe? When?'

The godi stood up and stretched his back. 'The day has been long, Sven, and I need my rest.' Before Sven could say anything, the godi turned and walked away.

'Odinson! Tell me about this new king!' Sven's face turned red, but before he could charge at the godi, the ravens in the tree screamed their own anger at him and Sven couldn't help but grab the Mjöllnir around his neck.

Thora did the same and said, 'Sven. I think it's time to leave.'

Sven growled and knew that Thora was right. They had been there longer than he had realised as he saw the moon in the sky. As Thora collected Charles's mother and the crying priest, Sven glared at the back of his uncle as he disappeared amongst the shadows of the trees.

*One day, Uncle, I'll burn this tree down with you tied to it.*

## 15

Charles rubbed the palms of his hands as he waited to meet the last person he wanted to see. Duke Liudolf of Saxony. The man who had been a friend to his father for so many years until he and Bishop Bernard betrayed his father and had him killed. Or at least that was what Charles believed after he caught part of their conversation in the church in Hügelburg the day after his father had been killed. But Charles had never understood why Duke Liudolf and the bishop wanted his father dead, especially Duke Liudolf. Charles's father had saved his life in the civil war between the sons of Emperor Louis, and Charles had always believed they were good friends. It was one of the many mysteries that surrounded Charles and another one he was sure his grandfather had the answer to, but refused to tell him.

'How much longer do we have to wait for that bastard?' Ivor asked Father Egbert, the old priest who Jarl Torgeir had sent with them to Hamburg. Like Father Leofdag, Father Egbert was from the church in Hedeby, and Father Leofdag had told Charles that Jarl Torgeir would often use the old priest to send messages to King Louis of East Francia. Charles had asked what messages the jarl needed to send to King Louis, but Father Leofdag did not know.

They had been in Hamburg for four days now, locked away in a small room in one of the taverns, which smelt of sweaty men and farts. But that didn't surprise Charles. There were twelve of them in the room and most of them had to sleep on the floor. Ivor had demanded the only bed in the room, even though Steinar was the son of Jarl Torgeir, and his five large warriors outnumbered Ivor's two injured men. But Ivor had made himself the leader of the group, saying that he would be king of Denmark if his plan worked out. Although Charles didn't know what that plan was or what part he had to play in it.

And then there was Father Leofdag, who had refused to stay in Hedeby, even after he was released by Ivor at the request of Father Egbert. The old priest had been unhappy at Father Leofdag's disobedience, but the young priest had insisted on staying with Charles. Though Charles didn't understand why and was still unsure how he felt about Father Leofdag's presence.

'The duke should arrive soon,' Father Egbert said without opening his eyes. He and Father Leofdag were sitting together in one corner of the room in prayer, because Ivor refused to let them go to the church. No one could leave the room apart from Ivor and Steinar and his men. But Steinar always made sure that at least four of his father's men stayed behind to keep an eye on Ivor, something Charles found curious. He had believed that Ivor and Jarl Torgeir had made a deal, but perhaps the jarl of Hedeby did not trust Ivor. Charles couldn't blame him, though. His grandfather had trusted Ivor's father, and now Charles was in Hamburg. And Thora was dead. Her death still haunted his dreams, which made it even harder for Charles to sleep. Most nights, he would just lay awake until he could no longer and when he slept, all he saw was the raven tree and the many people that had died since his father had been killed.

'That's what you said yesterday!' Ivor took a step towards the priest, but one of Steinar's men moved so that he was between Ivor and the old priest. Ivor glared at the man, who was taller and broader than him, as Steinar said:

'The Christians always make us wait. They hope we might convert to their weak god if we stay here longer.' His men smiled at this and Charles wondered how often they came here to speak to the duke and what about.

Ivor glanced at Steinar and clenched his fists, but he turned and limped back to his two men. 'Aye, well, the bastard better show up today.'

'You're not praying, Charles.' Father Leofdag opened his eyes and glanced at him. Charles was sitting with the two priests because they had told him to, but he was not in the mood to pray. He doubted it would do anything. God had been deaf to his prayers since his grandfather had marched off to fight the king of Denmark, and Charles still struggled to understand what he had done to anger the Almighty. He had done his best to pray every day in Ribe before the battle, but he missed a few prayers because it wasn't always convenient. Not with the Danes staring at him. Or perhaps it had nothing to do with that. Maybe it was because he gave into his demons and got into a fight with Rollo's son. Or maybe because he wished for the death of Ivor for killing Thora.

'The boy's spent too much time amongst the heathens.' Father Egbert scowled at him. 'His weak mind has already forgotten the light of God. I think a few lashes should remind him of his duties as a good Christian.'

Charles glowered at the old priest, but Father Leofdag put a calming hand on his shoulder. 'Charles has been through much,

Father Egbert. He needs understanding, not a beating. Besides, he's had enough of those.'

The old priest grunted and went back to his prayers as Charles rubbed the right side of his face. He knew the bruises were fading, but they were still there. At least no one had struck him over the last few days, something he was grateful for. And for the fact that since they had left Hedeby, Father Leofdag made sure that Charles had enough food and water, something old Ingvild in Ribe would be pleased about. Charles smiled as he remembered how Thora's aunt always complained that he was too thin. And then the smile was replaced by a tear as he thought of Thora and realised he would never see her again. He wondered if she would go to their Valhalla, but thought more likely that she would go to heaven. He still believed she was a guardian angel, sent by God to protect him, and that was another reason Charles believed God was angry at him. Because he had got one of His angels killed.

Father Leofdag's face had healed as well. His bruises were gone, but his nose was still bent, which caused a whistling noise sometimes when the young priest breathed. Something the Danes complained about every night when they tried to sleep, but to Charles, their snoring was much worse.

Everyone in the room fell silent again. This was what it had been like for the last few days, but Charles noticed how Ivor was getting more irritated every day and hoped that Duke Liudolf would arrive soon. Even if he didn't want to see the man. The two priests carried on praying for a while, but Charles gave up and moved away from them. He went to the corner where he had been sleeping and scrutinised the men in the room. Steinar was lying on the floor near the bed, his eyes closed, while his men played some game Charles had seen the warriors in Ribe play, but he did not know what it was. Ivor sat on the bed, sharpening his sword with a stone he had taken out of his pouch, his eyes fixed on

Charles and when he saw Charles looking at him, he said, 'We're
not so different, you and I.'

Charles looked away, not wanting to talk to the man who had
killed Thora and caused the deaths of the others. But this did not
put Ivor off.

'I had to leave my home at a young age and live in a strange
place I did not understand.' Charles noticed how the others in the
room glanced at him, as if they were waiting for him to respond,
but before he could, the man Steinar had left outside came into
the room.

'He's here.'

'By Thor, at last!' Ivor jumped to his feet and winced as his
hand went to his leg.

'Where do you think you are going?' Steinar got up from the
floor. 'It's best that I speak to the duke. He knows me.'

Ivor smiled at the young warrior. 'The piglet is my prisoner. I
will speak to this duke.'

'I don't think that is a good idea,' Steinar said, which caused
Ivor to raise an eyebrow.

'I don't care what you think.'

'Enough!' Father Egbert said, his voice firm from many
sermons. 'I suggest that Steinar and Ivor come along and the rest
of you,' he cast a frustrated eye over the rest of the Danish
warriors, 'can stay here.'

'What makes you think that you're coming along, priest?' Ivor
asked.

The old priest sighed. 'Do you speak the Frankish tongue?'
Ivor shook his head. 'Well, neither does Steinar, and Duke Liudolf
is too busy to learn your vulgar language, so I have to translate.
That is the way it always goes.'

Ivor growled and glanced at Charles, who wondered what the
man was thinking, but then turned back to the priest. 'Fine, but by

Thor's ginger beard, if I feel you are double-crossing me, I will kill you slowly and painfully.'

Father Egbert paled before he nodded and walked out of the hall. Steinar signalled for one of his men to come with and left the others to watch over Ivor's men and Charles.

'Watch the piglet,' Ivor said to his men, who grunted in response.

'That man scares me more than your grandfather.' Father Leofdag offered Charles some cheese. Charles took the cheese and thought about it before he shook his head.

'You've not seen my grandfather fight.'

Father Leofdag nodded. 'True, and I thank God for that.' He then stared at Charles for a while. 'You know Duke Liudolf?' Charles shook his head, almost too quick, as he didn't want Father Leofdag to learn the truth, but the priest only smiled. 'I saw how you flinched when Steinar's man announced his arrival.' He waited, but Charles still said nothing. His grandfather had told him not to tell anyone about where he came from or why he had to go to Denmark. 'Does this have anything to do with the cross your grandfather and the woman spoke of?'

'Her name was Thora!' Charles snapped at Father Leofdag.

Father Leofdag held up a hand. 'I apologise, Charles. Thora.' The warriors glanced at them, but then all of them got back to doing what they were doing. Which was nothing. Charles never understood how warriors could just sit and do nothing as they waited for something. His father had been the same. He could just sit on the same spot for most of the day, his eyes closed, but not really sleeping, when he needed to wait for something or someone. 'Forgive my questions, Charles. But I'm trying to understand what this is all about, and why everyone is so interested in you. I thought it was because of your grandfather, but now I think there is more going on.'

Charles lowered his head and sighed. He wished he knew the answer to that question and the many others that had been plaguing him. 'I don't know. I don't know why they want me, or why the kings of Francia want me or my mother's cross.'

'The cross belonged to your mother?' Father Leofdag asked and Charles gasped when he realised he had said too much. 'Who is your mother?'

Charles looked away, not wanting to answer, but then wondered why it mattered. 'I don't know who my mother was. My father never told me about her.'

Father Leofdag frowned. 'Your mother is dead?'

Charles was about to nod, but then he thought about the question. 'My father told me she was, but I don't know.' He looked away from Father Leofdag, remembering what Roul had told him in the church. Not for the first time, Charles wondered who his mother was or if she was really alive. But he didn't know if he could trust the words of a man he knew worked for the king of West Francia. And then a thought came to him that made the breath catch in his throat. If she really was alive, would he want to meet her? Everything that had happened this summer was because of something she had done before he was born.

His whole life, all he had ever wanted was for his mother to be there. To comfort him when the other boys had picked on him and all his father would say was that he needed to learn to fight back. They fell into silence as Charles struggled with this question. Father Leofdag gripped the cross he wore around his neck and went back to praying, while the warriors just waited for the others to return, leaving Charles alone. He looked around the room and wondered if he could find a way out. Perhaps he could escape through the window. He was good at climbing, after all. Thora had said he reminded her of the squirrel that ran up and down the great tree to deliver messages, but Charles couldn't remember the name of the squirrel. To reach the small window, though, he had to walk past Steinar's men, and he doubted they would let him just climb out. With a sigh, Charles gave up and leaned back against the wall. He tried closing his eyes, like the warriors had done, but then the raven tree flashed in his mind and sent his heart racing. Charles wondered if he would ever forget the large tree filled with more ravens than leaves. He still saw the godi in his dream, laughing as a small creature feasted on the carcass of a calf under the branches of the tree while the ravens deafened him with their screams.

Charles must have fallen asleep at some point, because he woke with a fright when Ivor stormed into the room.

'Bloody bastard! Who does he think he is?' He stopped and glared at Charles, which made Charles wonder what he had done wrong.

'What did you expect, Ivor? That the man would just take your word that we have the boy? The Christians don't trust us, even less than we trust them,' Steinar said as he, too, stopped and looked at Charles. 'We have no choice. If you want the duke to agree to take us to his king, then we need to show him the boy.'

'No!' Charles said before he could stop himself. Everyone in the room stared at him as Ivor raised an eyebrow.

'You know the man?'

Charles shook his head and chided himself for his mistake. He glanced at Father Leofdag and saw the priest frown at him. But before Father Leofdag could say or do anything, Ivor rushed at Charles and grabbed him by his tunic. He plucked Charles to his feet and raised his hand to strike Charles. But Charles only glared at him, again, determined not to show fear to his abductors, even as his heart raced in his chest.

'Do not lie to me, piglet. Do you know this duke?'

Charles bit his lip, not wanting to answer when Steinar said,

'By Odin, Ivor. What does it matter? Just bring the boy so we can get this over with.'

Ivor glared at Charles and Charles was surprised to see the small smile in the corner of Ivor's mouth as he lowered his hand. Ivor then turned and dragged Charles towards the door, and no matter how hard Charles tried, he could not loosen Ivor's grip. The man was too strong for him.

Father Leofdag jumped to his feet and was about to rush after them, when Ivor turned and pulled his sax-knife from his belt faster than Charles could see. 'One more step, priest, and you die. Remember, I don't need you.'

Father Leofdag's eyes widened as he stared at the knife pointing at his face and took a step back. He gave Charles an apologetic look, but Charles ignored it. He had learnt not to expect the priest to help in situations like this. Father Leofdag was a man of words, not a man of action. He was the type of man that Charles had always wanted to be, just like Bishop Bernard. For most of his short life, all Charles wanted to be was a priest, but it seemed that he was destined to be surrounded by death and violence. And he should have known it would be like that. His father was a warrior and his grandfather was one of the most feared men in East Francia. Even though people had not seen or heard from him for many years, they still crossed themselves when they heard his name.

'Make sure the priest stays in his corner,' Ivor said to his men, who again only grunted as he dragged Charles out of the room. Charles tried to resist as they went down the stairs to the tavern below the room they were staying in. But when they reached the bottom of the stairs, Charles heard Duke Liudolf's voice, which almost made his heart stop and all the fight left his body.

'Charles?' Duke Liudolf jumped to his feet and knocked his chair over. 'By God, it is you!'

Ivor looked at Charles and smiled. He must have realised he had been correct about Charles's importance, even if Charles himself did not understand it. 'So you don't know the man then?'

Charles did not look at Ivor, though. His eyes were fixed on the man he believed was responsible for his father's death. A man his father had always thought was a friend. Duke Liudolf looked just like he had when Charles last saw him. Large and broad-shouldered, his black hair tinged with grey and his beard neatly groomed. He wore a dark-coloured tunic, with a leather belt and a fine sword on his waist. A dusty cloak covered his shoulders while leather riding gloves lay on the table closest to Duke Liudolf.

The tavern was empty apart from Duke Liudolf and his men, although Charles could not see how many there were. But even with his young age, he knew that Duke Liudolf would have more men than the Danes. All of Duke Liudolf's men wore chain-mail vests and had helmets on as they glared at the Danes, their hands never far from their swords.

Father Egbert sat by the table where Duke Liudolf was, his old face even more wrinkled as he frowned. 'Duke Liudolf, you know the boy?'

Duke Liudolf ignored the old priest and took a few steps towards Charles, who backed away. The duke noticed this and stopped. 'Charles?'

'Looks like the boy doesn't want to talk to you,' Ivor said in Danish, which the old priest had to translate for him.

'Charles?' Duke Liudolf held a hand out towards Charles.

Again, Charles took a step back and shook his head. 'Y... you had my father killed.'

Duke Liudolf's eyes widened. 'No... Charles, I had nothing to do with your father's death. You have to believe me. He was my friend.'

'But Lothar attacked us.' Charles glanced around the tavern, his heart racing as he looked for a way to escape. He had to get out of here. He had to get away from everyone who was using him and lying to him.

'I know, Charles,' Duke Liudolf said. 'But I never told him to. I swear on my eternal soul. I did not know what Lothar was doing until it was too late.'

'What is the bastard saying?' Ivor asked because Father Egbert had decided not to translate Charles and Duke Liudolf's conversation. He grabbed Charles by his tunic and pulled him away from Duke Liudolf, whose eyes flashed with violence. 'You've seen the boy, and I think you know why the boy is important. Now you run and tell your king that if he wants the piglet, then he must agree to our terms.' Ivor turned and walked away as Father Egbert translated his words.

But then Duke Liudolf spoke Danish, which made them all stop and turn.

'There will be no deal with you heathen scum.'

## 16

There was an explosion of noise as everyone reacted to Duke Liudolf's words. His men all drew their weapons and rushed at Ivor, while Father Egbert screamed in fright and dived under the table. Before Charles even knew what was happening, Ivor grabbed him and pressed a knife against his throat.

'One more step and I kill the piglet!'

Charles felt the sharp edge of Ivor's knife against his skin and tried to pull himself away from it, but he had nowhere to go as Ivor gripped him tightly. His heart raced as he glanced at the door to the tavern, almost expecting his grandfather to burst in and save him as he had done before. But there was no blood-chilling roar, no door breaking open and no Sven the Boar.

Duke Liudolf raised his hand, and his men stopped before he said in Danish, 'Kill the boy and you die, heathen.'

Charles felt Ivor shrug behind him, the movement causing the knife to press a little harder against his skin. 'If the Norns decide that today is my day, then so be it. But at least you won't be able to get the runt.'

Duke Liudolf hesitated before he took a deep breath. 'You really think my king will make a deal with heathens because of the grandson of a man too old to really be a threat? Sven the Boar is not what he once was.'

Charles felt his anger build as Duke Liudolf dismissed his grandfather so easily, and even Ivor seemed amused by the duke's words. 'My father underestimated the Boar, and now he is dead, and so is King Horik. And besides, I know there is more to the piglet. King Charles of West Francia paid my father a fortune to deliver the boy.'

Duke Liudolf signalled for his men to step back before he shrugged. 'I can't imagine why. I know the boy and his father. There is nothing special about either of them.'

With the knife still at his throat, Charles clenched his fists as he struggled to understand why the duke was saying these things. He wished his grandfather was there, or Thora, so they could kill the man responsible for his father's death, but they weren't. There was no one to help Charles, not even God.

'I know about the cross, Duke Liudolf. And I know where to find it.'

Duke Liudolf hesitated before he scowled at Ivor. 'What cross?'

Charles sensed Ivor's smile behind him. 'You know exactly what cross I'm talking about, Duke Liudolf. And if your king supports my bid to become the new king of Denmark, then I will give him the cross. If not, then I'm sure King Charles of West Francia would be very happy to receive it.' Charles wondered how Ivor could make a deal like that. Roul had told them he was going to Ribe to get the cross. 'So, tell your men to step back and take me to your king.'

Again, Duke Liudolf hesitated. He clenched his fist and glared at Ivor. 'There is no cross.'

Charles's mouth fell open as he struggled to understand why Duke Liudolf would say that. He wanted to scream out, but then a thought came to him. Maybe the duke didn't know about the cross.

Ivor didn't feel the same way as Charles, though, as he said, 'You're lying. Just like you lied about not speaking my language.'

Steinar took a step towards Ivor. 'Maybe he is right, Ivor. Maybe there is no cross.'

'I know there is a cross. My father and I were paid to find this cross.'

Charles frowned at Ivor's lie and wondered why he said nothing about Roul, the West Frankish spy.

'But you didn't find this cross,' Duke Liudolf responded.

Ivor shrugged. 'Only because the Norns had other plans for us. But if King Louis helps me become the new king of Denmark, then I'll personally hand him the cross after I take it from Sven's corpse.'

Duke Liudolf glanced at his men, who still glared at the Danes, their hands still on their weapons. His eyes then fell on Father Egbert who, though he was hiding under the table, seemed to follow the conversation with keen interest. Charles watched as Duke Liudolf's jaw muscles worked under his beard, before the duke took a deep breath. 'I'll deliver your message to my king on the condition that the boy stays with me.'

'No, I want to talk to your king or there is no deal and I take the boy to the West Franks.' Ivor tightened his grip on Charles's neck.

'King Louis never talks directly to you Danes. Not even to Jarl Torgeir. This is the way it is done,' Duke Liudolf said.

'He's right,' Steinar added. 'My father only ever gets to talk to the duke here or the king's daughter.'

Ivor paused for a few heartbeats and then shoved Charles

towards Duke Liudolf. The move caught Charles by surprise and he yelped as he tripped over his own feet. 'The piglet is our gift to your king, anyway. We know of his history with Sven the Boar and thought your king would like to raise another of his runts.' Charles glared at Ivor, but the thin warrior ignored him. 'Come then, Duke Liudolf. We have much to discuss.'

The tension seemed to go out of the tavern as Duke Liudolf's warriors relaxed. Duke Liudolf glanced at Charles and then said to Father Egbert, 'Father, if you could take the boy to the church. Perhaps they can clean him up and provide him with some food.'

'Gladly, Duke Liudolf.' Father Egbert crawled out from under the table, but before he reached Charles, Charles asked:

'What about Father Leofdag?'

'Who?' Duke Liudolf frowned.

'The foolish young priest who is determined to save the boy's soul.' Father Egbert grimaced as he said the words.

'The boy's soul does not need saving.'

The old priest scowled at Charles, who glared back. 'I'm not so sure. He has spent many weeks with the heathens.'

Duke Liudolf looked at the priest, his eyes hard. 'Careful, Father.'

The old priest paled and got to his feet. 'Forgive me, Duke Liudolf. If you think the boy's soul is secure, then you must be right.'

Duke Liudolf grunted before he knelt down in front of Charles. 'Where is this Father Leofdag?'

'In the room, up the stairs.'

Duke Liudolf nodded and then turned to Ivor and Steinar. 'There is another priest with you. Bring him down.'

Steinar nodded and sent his man up to the room, who returned a few moments later with Father Leofdag behind him, his hands trembling as his nervous eyes glanced around the tavern.

'Charles, I don't know what you have been told, but I swear I had nothing to do with your father's death. And neither did Bishop Bernard. We loved your father and would never hurt him or you.' Duke Liudolf spoke softly so that only Charles could hear him.

Charles stared at the duke, trying to find signs he was being lied to, because he was sure the man was lying to him. Everybody was lying to him at the moment.

'Charles, are you all right?' Father Leofdag asked as he rushed to Charles's side. Charles nodded, but his eyes were still fixed on Duke Liudolf, who patiently waited for him to respond.

In the end, Charles took a deep breath. 'Then why was my father killed?'

Duke Liudolf sighed. 'There is much you need to learn, Charles. But it is not my place to tell you.'

Charles felt his anger flare up again. 'Then who will tell me?'

'Only your mother can tell you what is really going on.'

'My mother is dead.' Charles clenched his fists.

Duke Liudolf's head jerked back before he said, 'No, Charles. She isn't.'

Charles felt the thud in his chest as Duke Liudolf's words sank in. 'My mother? She... she's alive?' Charles's head spun, and he felt like he was about to collapse. Since his father had died, he had suspected that his mother might be alive. He even thought that his grandfather knew and was keeping it from him. But Charles still struggled to believe what Duke Liudolf had just said.

Duke Liudolf gave Charles an incredulous stare. 'You didn't know?'

Charles shook his head, which only made the spinning worse.

He squinted as he tried to concentrate. 'Wh... where is she? Who is she?'

'Charles,' Duke Liudolf said and frowned even more. 'She went to Ribe. To find you.'

'Ribe?' Charles trembled and felt an arm wrap around him. He looked up to see Father Leofdag's concerned face.

'Charles needs to rest, Duke Liudolf.'

'Yes, you are right,' Duke Liudolf said. 'Charles, we will talk later, if you want to.'

Charles nodded as Duke Liudolf got to his feet and walked towards Ivor and Steinar, who were sitting at a nearby table and drinking ale.

'My mother is alive.'

'So it seems,' Father Leofdag said.

Charles rubbed his head and wished the spinning would stop. 'Did you know?'

Father Leofdag shook his head. 'If I knew, Charles, I would have told you. Now come, you need to rest.' His hands still trembling, Father Leofdag led him out of the tavern.

Outside, Charles squinted even though the sun was hidden by the thick clouds, which reminded Charles of his journey to Ribe. He pushed the thought away as he took a deep breath and felt his head clear. Father Leofdag offered him some water, which Charles greedily drank.

'Who do you think my mother is?' Charles asked as he wiped his mouth clean.

Father Leofdag thought about it for a short while, and then said, 'I'm not sure, Charles. But I guess she is very important.'

'Important?'

'Yes, Charles. Why else would Ivor go through all of this and if what he said about the king of West Francia is true, then that can only mean that your mother is an important person.'

Charles gripped the small wooden cross around his neck as he thought about what Father Leofdag had just said and wondered if it could be true. His grandfather and Thora had said that his mother had been a handmaid in King Louis's court who had stolen the golden cross before she had been sent away, but to Charles's young mind, that had never made any sense. He could not understand how a Christian king could chase someone away just for getting with child. And what about his father? If everything Charles had been told about him was true, then it made even less sense that King Louis would send one of his best warriors away. Then there was the cross itself. If it was so important to King Louis, then how did a handmaid get hold of it?

Charles scowled as he wondered if his grandfather knew the truth about his mother. Before he had left for the battle against the Danish king, Charles had felt that his grandfather was hiding something from him. Something important about his mother and the cross. Could this have been it? That his mother was not a handmaid, but someone more important? But then who was she and why had Charles been told that she was dead?

'Charles?' Father Leofdag's voice broke Charles's thoughts, and he frowned when he saw the look of concern on the priest's face. 'You looked...' Father Leofdag hesitated as he tried to find the right words. 'What were you thinking?'

Charles shook his head. 'Nothing,' he said, and followed Father Egbert and Father Leofdag to the church.

Charles spent the rest of the day in the small stone church outside Hamburg to pray. Just like in Hügelburg, the church was the only stone building in Hamburg, and Charles was surprised that it sat outside the town walls. When he had asked about it, the old priest had said that God protected the church from the heathen raiders, which Charles had thought was a strange thing to believe. Especially as the old priest had spent some time in Hedeby and lived amongst the Danes.

The church inside looked like the one in Hügelburg, with its tall ceiling and large decorated windows. Stone pillars with plenty of torches to bring the light of God into the building, but Charles could not feel the light. He only felt cold as they sat on a bench near the altar. Even the carving of Jesus seemed to scowl at Charles as if judging him. Charles shivered as he sat there, pretending to pray with the two priests. The priests of Hamburg gave them some food to eat, some bread, cheese and slices of cold meat, with some wine for Father Leofdag and Father Egbert and water for Charles. Charles also bathed, his first wash in many days, and afterwards his hair was cut by the priests who complained he looked like a heathen child. Something Charles was not happy about.

Father Egbert exchanged news and gossip with the other priests, but when the priests of Hamburg had to return to their chores, both Father Leofdag and Father Egbert looked concerned. Charles asked them about it and Father Leofdag was about to explain to Charles what the other priest had said, but the old priest told him to be quiet.

Charles thought about what Duke Liudolf had told him, that his mother had gone to Ribe to find him. He imagined being there when she arrived and tried to picture her on the wharf, but he couldn't, because he had no idea what his mother looked like. And then a question he had before came to him. Would he have been happy to see her? Charles still didn't know the answer to that. He glanced at the statue of Christ and saw nothing but judgement in His stony face, which made him feel guilty for feeling the way he did.

Charles had mixed feelings when Duke Liudolf walked into the church, his face drawn and eyes red. Charles wanted to get answers from him, but he was afraid of what those answers were, because he knew they would change his life yet again.

Duke Liudolf stopped in front of the altar and crossed himself before he sat down next to Charles. For a moment, he scrutinised Charles's short hair, and Charles worried the priest had done a poor job. 'Charles, how are you feeling?'

Charles shrugged. He was exhausted, but at least he had been fed and was clean. He almost smiled when the thought that Thora's aunt would be pleased about that came to him, but kept his face straight. 'I'm fine.'

Duke Liudolf nodded, and they sat in silence for a while until Duke Liudolf asked the priests to give them some privacy. Father Leofdag hesitated, but then followed the old priest out of the church. Satisfied that they were alone, Duke Liudolf turned his attention back to Charles.

'Charles—'

'Where is Ivor?' Charles asked before he could stop himself. He wasn't sure if he really wanted to know where the man who had kidnapped him was, or if he just wanted to delay the conversation.

Duke Liudolf frowned at the question, but responded anyway. 'They left for Hedeby a while ago. Don't worry, Charles. I'll make sure you never have to see that Dane again.'

Charles nodded and took a deep breath as he braced himself for whatever Duke Liudolf had to say next.

'Charles, what happened to your father... I can never forgive myself for not seeing Lothar's deceit until it was far too late. Your father was a good friend. A man I trusted with my life. I would never have done anything to harm him or you.'

Charles was staring at his hands while Duke Liudolf spoke and was not really listening to what he said, because there was one thing he wanted to know more than anything. He looked up and asked, 'Who is my mother?'

Duke Liudolf sighed as if he had been expecting this question. He looked at the statue of Christ, before turning his attention back to Charles again.

'Charles, your mother is Abbess Hildegard, the daughter of King Louis.'

## 17

Charles felt the air being sucked out of the church, or perhaps it was just sucked out of him, and he struggled to hear the words of Duke Liudolf as he asked him something. Charles had heard of the Abbess Hildegard. He knew who she was.

'Charles?' Duke Liudolf said.

'You're lying!' Charles jumped to his feet, his clenched fists trembling. 'You're lying!' The few people in the church scowled at him for his outburst, even the priests, but they soon turned away when he glared at them. 'She can't be my mother! My mother was a handmaid! My grandfather said so!'

Duke Liudolf gently shook his head, but he did not force Charles to sit down again. 'God knows I wish that was true, Charles. Your father might have still been alive if your mother was a handmaid. As God is my witness, Charles, Abbess Hildegard is your mother.'

'No!' Charles lost control of himself and struck out at the duke. Duke Liudolf barely reacted as Charles hit him in the chest, again and again. After a few heartbeats, Charles's fury was spent, and he just dropped back onto the bench and stared at the statue of Christ. Duke Liudolf just sat there, not saying anything, until Charles took a deep breath. 'Father Leofdag believed my mother was an important woman.'

'Father Leofdag seems like a smart man. A pity I can't say the same for Father Egbert.' Duke Liudolf smiled, but Charles could not return his smile.

'If the abbess is really my mother, then why was I told that she was dead? Why could I not be with her?'

'Those are questions only she can answer, Charles.'

Charles looked at the duke and saw his downturned face. He remembered something Duke Liudolf had said before. 'But she went to Ribe? Why?'

Duke Liudolf smiled, but to Charles, it looked like a sad smile. 'Because she is a stubborn woman, and she believed we weren't doing enough to find you. She took my ship and set off for Ribe so she could find you herself.'

Charles looked at his feet and wondered if his grandfather had met her and what he would do. He also wondered if Sven would give her the cross. Charles frowned when he remembered the large golden cross. 'What about the cross? Why did she give it to my father? Does she know it got him killed?' The questions came out faster than Charles could breathe, but he needed to know.

'I'm afraid I know little about the cross. I didn't even know your father had it until after he was killed, when Abbess Hildegard told me about it. But, by God, I don't know why she gave that cross to your father, that—'

'That is something I should ask her,' Charles interrupted the duke, who nodded. 'How long has she been in Ribe?'

Duke Liudolf looked worried for a heartbeat before he glanced at the statue of Christ. 'For too long, Charles. I expected her back days ago. I fear Sven the Boar might have harmed her.'

Charles shook his head. 'No. My grandfather would not hurt Abbess... my mother,' Charles corrected himself, but it felt strange to say those words.

'Charles, Sven the Boar is a cruel man known for his hatred of Christians. And don't forget, King Louis took his son from him.' Duke Liudolf punched the palm of his own hand. 'By God, I should never have let her go to Ribe. Gerold had warned us it was not a good idea.'

Charles's head jerked as if he had been slapped. 'Gerold?'

Duke Liudolf frowned. 'Charles? What's the matter?'

'Gerold lied to me. He wanted to take me...' Charles hesitated and then realised he never knew where Gerold was meant to take him. Gerold had only told him he was supposed to take him to a man in a different town, or at least his master was supposed to. But his master had been killed when bandits had attacked them and Charles had convinced Gerold to take him to Denmark.

'Gerold and his master were supposed to take you to one of my men, who was going to take you to my house in Ehresburg.'

'To your house?'

Duke Liudolf nodded. 'As soon as I learnt what had happened to your father, I knew I had to do something quick. By God's grace, I was in Hügelburg to meet an old informant, Gerold's master, who had brought me important information. I told him to find you, because I knew there were few men better at doing what he did. Even at his old age.' Duke Liudolf leaned back and sighed. 'But then something went wrong, and you ended up in Denmark.'

Charles looked at his hands. 'My father told me to find my grandfather. That he would keep me safe.'

'I know,' the duke said. 'Gerold explained what had happened.'

'So Gerold was one of your men?'

'Gerold was training to be one of my spies.'

'And what about the men that attacked us near Ribe and then in Ribe?' Charles still struggled to make sense of everything. He wondered how much of this his grandfather knew.

'They were my men as well. My best men. I sent them to Denmark after I found out that the old spy was dead and that you and Gerold were gone. I believed Gerold had betrayed his master. If I had known what was really going on, I never would have sent them. They were dangerous men, but I believed their skills were needed.' Charles nodded and remembered stabbing the leader of the group. If he closed his eyes, he could still see it as clearly as if it was happening there in front of him. He shuddered at the memory. 'It must have been terrifying for you, Charles. To have to live amongst the heathens.'

Charles thought about it. It was no worse than when he lived with Christians. They all treated him the same. But he did not say any of that. 'No, Thora looked after me, and my grandfather kept me safe. He is a good man, I think.'

'I pray you are right, Charles, because I fear for your mother's safety.'

Charles nodded and then looked at the statue of Christ. 'So now what?'

Duke Liudolf followed his gaze and then said, 'Now we rest. We will stay in the house of a noble who is a good friend of mine. My men will make sure you come to no harm. And then in the morning we go to Bremen.'

Charles had heard of Bremen. He knew there was a large church in the trading town and in the past would have been eager to see it. But now, even in this small church, he suddenly felt like he did not belong in the house of God any more. 'Why Bremen?'

Duke Liudolf rubbed his hands together and took a deep breath. 'Because I have to take you to your other grandfather, to King Louis.'

Charles's eyes widened. 'King Louis is m... my grandfather?' Charles felt like he was about to faint as Duke Liudolf nodded. The news that Abbess Hildegard was his mother had not really sunk in yet, so he never thought that he was the grandson of the king of East Francia. 'W... what is he like?' was the only question Charles could think of asking as he struggled to make sense of what was happening.

Duke Liudolf sighed. 'Right now, Charles, the king is angry. Very angry.'

'Why?' Charles rubbed his head. 'Because of me?'

Duke Liudolf bit his lip as he thought about something. 'No... and yes. He is angry at your mother for disobeying him and he is worried about her safety, just like I am.'

'But why? My grandfather would not hurt her.'

Duke Liudolf sighed. 'Charles, I pray you are right.'

'Did King Louis travel to Bremen because of me?'

'No, we were already in Bremen. The king is also angry at me, because he had discovered that I had helped your mother travel to Ribe. We went to Bremen to wait for her return.'

'So he won't be happy to see me?' Charles's hands trembled, and he tucked them under his legs so the duke wouldn't see it.

'I don't know how he would react to seeing you, Charles.' The church bells rung, signalling that it was time for the evening meal. 'It's been a long day, Charles. And I still have much to do. I have men outside. They will escort you and Father Leofdag to Lord Handolf's house when you are ready. Tomorrow we will travel to Bremen and, Charles,' Duke Liudolf said as he got up, 'pray for your mother.'

Duke Liudolf turned and left the church before Charles could respond. For a while, Charles just sat there, staring at nothing as he tried to understand everything he had been told. He still couldn't believe that Abbess Hildegard was his mother. Although, that helped to explain a lot of what had happened this summer. But then he didn't understand why he and his father had to live in Hügelburg, in a small, run-down house with a leaking roof, if he was the grandson of the king. He also wondered why everyone was so certain that his grandfather would hurt his mother. Charles knew Sven could be a cruel man and that he was vicious in battle. But Charles also knew what had happened in Sven's past and was sure that he would never hurt a woman, regardless of her faith. Gerold, though, Charles was sure, was dead by now. Charles thought about the young man and saw him slightly differently now that he knew Gerold was working for Duke Liudolf. But then Charles wondered if Gerold had known that at the time and, besides, Charles was still mad at him for pretending to be his friend. And then there was the man he had killed. Charles felt even more guilty about that now that he had learnt the truth. But he had feared for his life at the time. That was why he had done what he did. Again, he wondered why adults couldn't just tell him things instead of hiding everything from him. If the man had just told him, had just told his grandfather, then all the bloodshed could have been avoided.

Sitting there, lost in his thoughts, Charles did not notice Father Leofdag approach until the priest put a hand on his shoulder. Startled, he looked at the priest.

'Forgive me, Charles. I didn't mean to frighten you.'

'You didn't,' Charles lied and wished his heart would calm down.

Father Leofdag smiled. 'Come, let's go eat with the other priests. You must be hungry.'

Charles nodded and followed Father Leofdag to the mess, but he didn't feel like eating. His mind was still numb from what he had learnt and he was still trying to make sense of it all.

Charles remembered little of the meal and couldn't even

remember what they had eaten by the time Duke Liudolf's men took them to the house of Lord Handolf, which was near the centre of the town. He vaguely remembered Father Leofdag was asked to pray before the meal, but that was all. The house of Lord Handolf was larger than the rest and one of the largest Charles had ever seen, but he paid little attention to it, or the woman who greeted him and showed him his room. Father Leofdag apologised and told the lady of the house that Charles was exhausted and they were left alone after that.

The room he was in was larger than the one they had in the tavern, with a large bed, which he had to himself. Father Leofdag stayed with Charles instead of going back to the church and slept on the floor, but Charles still struggled to sleep that night. Every time he closed his eyes, his nightmares would return and Father Leofdag's presence did not reassure him. Neither did the two warriors outside his room. Not like Thora had. Charles realised that since his father had been killed, he had only ever really felt safe when Thora was around. He knew his grandfather would protect him, but there was a part of his grandfather that frightened Charles, which meant he never really felt comfortable around Sven. He felt the tears run down his cheeks and wetting his pillow when he thought of Thora and the others who had died because of him, but he was too exhausted to stop them. Charles missed Thora, just like he missed his father, and the news that his mother still lived did nothing to take that pain away. He also missed his grandfather. Even Jorlaug, who liked to scare him and asked dumb questions.

The following morning, Charles felt as tired as the day before and struggled to eat the morning meal. It was not because the porridge was bad. It was quite tasty and the berries and honey sweetened it nicely, but Charles just did not feel like eating. They were sitting at the main table in the hall as a slave rushed around to make sure everyone had everything they needed, even if it was just Charles and Father Leofdag. Unlike his grandfather's hall in Ribe, this hall had no weapons or shields on the walls. Instead, there were tapestries depicting stories from the Bible, with bright colours and rich details. Father Leofdag had marvelled at them and even named all the figures he recognised in the tapestries. Charles knew about most of them as well, but he wasn't as excited about them as Father Leofdag. But the tapestries and the large windows provided plenty of light, which meant there was no need for the hearth fire to be as large as the one in his grandfather's hall. Lord Handolf was away by the time they finished their breakfast, but his wife made sure that Charles had everything he needed for the trip to Bremen. She even gave him an extra apple and winked at him as if it was a big secret, but Charles did not really care. He wondered if his mother would have done stuff like that, but then forgot about the thought when he saw two older boys glaring at him.

Duke Liudolf was talking to Father Egbert while he waited for them outside the house, and Charles was surprised at how many men he had with him. The warriors were all on horseback and all of them dressed for war. Charles frowned at how similar they were to the Danish warriors. They all wore chain-mail vests, with swords or axes on their waists and spears in their hands. Even the helmets they wore were similar to those he saw in Denmark. Duke Liudolf was also wearing his war gear and Charles gasped at how intimidating the duke looked. His chain-mail vest glittered in the sun while stern eyes studied him from under the gold-rimmed helmet. Charles had never seen him dressed like that and even though he knew the duke was a warrior, he never really saw him as one.

'Come, Charles. We must go.' Duke Liudolf mounted his horse after he nodded at something Father Egbert had said. Charles nodded and was glad to see the cart waiting for him. He did not like riding horses and had not looked forward to the journey on horseback.

'I wonder what that is about?' Father Leofdag asked, but Charles didn't respond. He didn't really care. The young priest climbed on to the cart and then crossed himself as if that would protect them on the road. Father Egbert joined them on the cart as well and Charles wondered why the old priest had not returned to Hedeby with Ivor and Steinar. Father Leofdag must have thought the same as he raised an eyebrow at the older priest, but Father Egbert just ignored them as he made himself comfortable. Charles looked again at the number of men the duke had with him and wondered why the duke needed so many men. Did he fear that someone would attack them? Sven maybe? Charles wondered how he felt about that. A few days ago, he wanted nothing other than for his grandfather to rescue him, but now that he knew his mother was still alive, he realised he did not feel the same any more. Especially because he was certain now that his grandfather had lied to him about his mother.

Satisfied that everyone was ready, Duke Liudolf gave the order for them to leave and Charles had to grip the side of the cart as its sudden movement almost caused him to fall over. He clutched the cross around his neck as he watched Lord Handolf's wife waving them off and wondered how his life would change now that he knew he was the grandson of the king of East Francia.

They travelled slowly to Bremen, which meant the journey took them two days. Charles got the idea that Duke Liudolf did not want to rush and he wondered why. They spoke little during the journey, but occasionally the duke would leave the head of the column to check up on Charles. Neither of them wanted to speak of Charles's mother while the duke's warriors and Father Leofdag were nearby. Father Leofdag, as curious as ever, had asked Charles what he and the duke had spoken about, but Charles never responded. He was glad, though, that the priest had not pushed him and realised that he was starting to like Father Leofdag again. Father Leofdag was a calm and patient man, the opposite of Charles's grandfather, and he seemed to know when to give Charles his space, something which Charles appreciated. More than anything, he didn't treat Charles like a child, not like most of the other adults around. Charles also believed that Father Leofdag had sensed that he was drifting away from God, but unlike Father Egbert who believed Charles should be beaten because of it, and who had spent most of the time glaring at Charles, Father Leofdag tried instead to encourage him to pray with him whenever they had time to. So far, Charles had refused every time. He still felt that God was punishing him and the fact that his mother was now in Ribe and he in Francia only supported that idea. Because if God had been with him, then his mother would have arrived sooner and then perhaps they could have met, or she would have stayed in Francia.

For most of the journey, Charles tried to distract himself by watching the towns and farmsteads in the distance as they travelled along the road. He tried to work out which direction they were travelling in and, occasionally, he would ask one warrior to see if he had guessed correctly.

'We're here,' Duke Liudolf announced.

Charles sat up and scowled as they entered the town of Bremen. It was larger than Hamburg and busier, too. Just like Hamburg, though, the houses were all made of wood, but Charles could see the tall stone tower of the church sticking out over the thatched roofs and remembered how he had once been so eager to see the enormous building. People stopped and stared at Duke Liudolf and his entourage and Charles spotted many pointing at him on the cart. Dogs came rushing out of the side streets and barked as they chased after them, which encouraged some boys to do the same, until two of the duke's warriors chased them all away. Then Charles saw the large house they were travelling towards, with the king's banner flying above the roof of the hall, a signal that the king was inside, and his stomach suddenly felt empty at the prospect of meeting the king, his grandfather.

**18**

King Charles of West Francia rubbed his temples as the bishop droned on about the virtues of turning the other cheek. The bishop wanted Charles to forgive his nephew – well, his half-nephew, anyway. Pepin of Aquitaine. Charles and Pepin's father both shared the same father, but they had different mothers. Charles's mother was the second wife of Emperor Louis and he was much younger than his brothers, who all shared the same mother, the first wife of Louis. And because they didn't share the same mother, his brothers had never treated Charles as an equal. They had resented the fact that their father gave Charles land many years ago, especially Lothair, because that land had originally been promised to him. That was the first of many civil wars the sons of Emperor Louis had fought. Even the death of their father had not stopped the fighting between the brothers. It was only after Charles had convinced his brother, Louis, to join him against Lothair that they had finally brought an end to the fighting. That was when they had signed the Treaty of Verdun and had decided how to split their father's empire.

Charles had thought that most of his problems were over, but

God had other ideas for him. If it wasn't for the constant raids from the Norse and the Danes, who he usually had to pay to leave only for them to return the next summer, then it was his blasted nephew fighting him for Aquitaine. Emperor Louis had made Charles the king of that land when he had a falling out with Charles's brother and Pepin's father, who had been king of Aquitaine. But when Pepin's father died over ten years ago, the nobles of Aquitaine had decided that Pepin should be their king. Charles cursed those arrogant bastards for all the problems they had caused with that move, and even now, when Charles had defeated Pepin and had him in custody, they still caused problems for him.

Charles looked up when he realised his hall in Paris, the capital of his kingdom, had gone quiet and realised they were waiting for him to say something. The grand hall, its walls filled with colourful tapestries and painted with scenes of Charles's favourite pastimes, was empty apart from his closest advisers. There was the old bishop, a relic from his father's court, and Ignomer, one of Charles's generals and one of the few he trusted. And then there was Bero, his spymaster. Although, Charles never really knew if Bero worked for him or for himself. 'How is my nephew?'

The old bishop stammered as the question took him by surprise. 'He is living a life of solitude, as you had ordered, my king.'

After Pepin had been captured by Charles's men two years before, Charles had him tonsured and sent to a monastery near Paris. He had hoped that his nephew would spend his time contemplating his mistakes and would be forgotten about in Aquitaine. But the opposite had happened instead. The nobles of Aquitaine had so far refused to accept Charles as their king and neither had they accepted the authority of the man Charles had made duke of Aquitaine. The same man who had captured Pepin. And to make matters even worse, now Charles's brother, King Louis of East Francia, had sent his son to claim Aquitaine for himself.

But none of this was what bothered the king of West Francia. 'Where is Roul?' This question was directed at Bero, who could only shrug. 'He should have been back days ago with the boy and my grandfather's cross.' They had heard of the large battle between the king of Denmark and his nephew, the man Charles had paid to retrieve his niece's son and the Cross of Charlemagne, but Charles was unsure if the battle was part of the plan.

'Nothing has been heard of him since the battle, my king,' Bero answered.

'Perhaps he is dead?' Ignomer suggested, and Charles wondered the same before he dismissed the idea. No, Roul was one of his best, which was why the fact he had not returned yet was so worrying. Charles needed that cross, and he needed the boy. The boy he hoped he could use as leverage against Abbess Hildegard to convince her father to call his son back and not to interfere with Aquitaine. He knew she would not want word to come out that she had an illegitimate child, especially one fathered by a Dane. And not just any Dane, but the son of Sven the Boar. Charles had even wondered if he could use the boy to ally the Danes to him. He had their blood in his veins as well, if the rumours were true.

But the Cross of Charlemagne was what Charles was really after. With the cross, the same one his grandfather had built his empire with, he could quell the dissent in Aquitaine and do so much more. No one really understood what had made the cross so special, but they all knew that it was blessed by the Almighty and that whoever possessed it was the true ruler of Charlemagne's great empire. And to think that his brother, Louis, had possessed the cross, only to let it be stolen from under his nose. If Charles could get his hands on the Cross of Charlemagne, then he could defeat his brothers and reunite the kingdoms of Francia. He could rebuild his grandfather's empire and be the most powerful man in all of Christendom. But he needed to find the cross first.

'Bero, send men to Denmark. Find out where Roul is.'

Bero nodded as Ignomer said, 'We should send an army instead. Denmark is weak. They have no king and from what we have heard, thousands of warriors were killed in that battle. There will never be a better time to make Denmark part of your kingdom, my king.'

Charles scowled at the old warrior, the man who had been at his side the longest and who had taught him how to wield a sword, and knew he was right, but also knew that he couldn't. 'No, Ignomer. Not with my brother's army marching towards us or with the unrest in Aquitaine. And then there's Lothair as well.' Lothair was Charles's oldest brother, and although he had been quiet of late, Charles still didn't trust him not to be plotting something. But only because Charles was plotting to take his kingdom from him one day. Charles hit his fist on the armrest of his throne. 'By God! Where is that man and where is that cross?'

'May I make a suggestion, my lord king?' Bero asked, and Charles was already suspicious.

'What?'

'Perhaps it would be prudent to make a new cross and say that is the cross that once belonged to your grandfather.'

Charles's eyes darted around his hall, but he knew it was empty. Even his guards had been sent away. 'Would that even work?'

'Nobody has seen the cross since the days of Charlemagne.' Ignomer scratched his grey beard. 'Your father kept it hidden while he was emperor.'

Charles glanced at the bishop who seemed to have paled at this talk. 'Bishop? You've seen the cross before. Do you recall what it looks like?'

The bishop's mouth dropped open, and he glanced at the men around him as if searching for support. And when he saw he would not get any, he turned back to King Charles. 'I... I... no, my lord king, I cannot. It's been many years since I've seen Charlemagne's cross.'

Bero smiled. 'You see, my king. Who will know that is not the real cross?'

Ignomer nodded as King Charles thought about it. 'And when Roul returns with the real cross, then we can just swap them.'

'If Roul returns,' Charles said, more to himself. He did not like the fact that the spy had not returned yet when it had been more than a week since the battle in Denmark that killed their king. And that the man Roul had paid with Charles's gold had died as well after deciding to take the crown for himself only made Charles feel more nervous. The men in the hall waited patiently as King Charles considered his options. 'Ignomer,' he said at last. 'Find the best goldsmith in Paris and bring him here. Bishop, I believe there are some references to the cross in some documents in the library in your church. Find them so the smith has an idea of how the cross should look. And Bero, send men to Denmark and find Roul!'

'And the boy?' Bero asked as the other two left the hall to do as the king commanded.

'Find him as well. The boy might not be as important as the cross, but we still need him to keep my brother at bay.'

Bero bowed and left the hall as King Charles leaned back on his throne and dreamt of being a mighty emperor, just like the great Charlemagne.

## 19

Charles swallowed back his nervousness, or perhaps it was nausea, as he entered the great hall in the centre of Bremen, behind Duke Liudolf and flanked by his warriors. Father Leofdag walked beside him with his hand on Charles's shoulder for support and his other hand holding the large wooden cross around his neck. Charles was glad the priest was there with him, because he wasn't sure if he could do this on his own. His legs trembled and with each step it felt like he might collapse, but he tried to remember the breathing exercises Thora had taught him to calm his nerves. His hand went to brush the stray hair out of his face when he remembered his hair was not long any more. To his surprise, he missed his longer hair. He had got so used to constantly clearing the hair out of his face that he still did it now, even though he didn't need to any more.

When they had arrived, Duke Liudolf had Charles and Father Leofdag wait outside, guarded by his men, while he went inside the hall to speak to King Louis. Father Egbert had gone to the church and wanted Father Leofdag to accompany him. But the young priest had stayed with Charles. After a while, Charles could hear the king's voice booming inside the hall and then the doors slammed open and people streamed out as if they were chased by Danish warriors.

'That's our signal to enter,' one warrior said. Charles's legs suddenly felt weak, and he prayed he would not collapse. After taking a deep breath to steel himself, Charles followed the warriors into the hall.

The hall was larger than any building he had been in before and Charles could not help but look around him, his eyes wide as he took in the large wooden posts and beams which supported the roof. The wooden walls were all decorated with white plaster and adorned with paintings of both King Louis and religious figures, while banners of different colours and designs hung from the beams. Fresh rushes had been laid on the floor, their scent mixing in with the small fire from the hearth and the musty smell of a room filled with men for most of the day. The hall had plenty of windows which, along with the white plaster and colourful banners, brought plenty of light into the building. It was so bright that Charles almost had to squint as he looked around. Occasionally, something sharp would dig into Charles's bare feet and he winced as he wished the priests had given him shoes, along with the itchy new clothes they had given him. Charles fought the urge to scratch as he sensed that Father Leofdag was just as nervous, because he could feel the priest's hand tremble on his shoulder.

Charles was so focused on the hall that he did not notice that the duke's men had stopped and would have walked into the warrior in front of him if it had not been for Father Leofdag. He tried to get a look at King Louis, but unfortunately, his view was blocked by Duke Liudolf, who was walking towards him. The duke knelt down in front of Charles and, after a quick glance at Father Leofdag, the duke whispered, 'Charles. Whatever you do, do not mention the cross to the king. Understand?'

Charles frowned. 'Why? Would he not want to know about it?'

Duke Liudolf quickly glanced over his shoulder. 'The king does not know that your mother gave your father the cross. As far as he is concerned, someone else had stolen it a long time ago. For now, let him think that, because—'

'Duke Liudolf.' The deep voice of the king stopped Duke Liudolf mid-sentence.

Duke Liudolf stood and turned before he bowed to the king. The warriors around Charles did the same, as did Father Leofdag, but Charles only stood there and studied his other grandfather. A stern face stared back at him, while dark, creased eyes seemed to reach into his soul and judge him. Charles gripped the small wooden cross around his neck and felt its corners dig into his hand. King Louis was taller than Sven, much taller. That was something Charles could see, even though the king was sitting down. His dark hair was cropped below his ears, much like most men in Francia, and he had a neatly groomed beard which, like his hair, was speckled with grey. Charles had seen paintings of King Louis in the past, but the man seemed much larger and fiercer in real life. His shoulders were broad and his arms thick, and even the relaxed posture of the king told Charles that this was a man who, like his father and grandfather, relished being in the middle of a battle. 'My lord king,' Duke Liudolf said as he straightened.

'So what is so urgent that I had to empty the hall?' King Louis asked, his eyes still on Charles. 'And who is the boy you bring with you? Not another of your bastard children, I hope.'

'Not my bastard son, my king,' Duke Liudolf said, which made King Louis frown. Charles began to wonder if he had made a mistake by coming here as the king glared at him, the sudden hardness in his eyes sending a shiver down Charles's spine. Perhaps he should have tried harder to escape in Hedeby and then looked for Rollo. He wondered again what had happened to the giant warrior and hoped that Jarl Torgeir had not killed him. 'The boy is the reason that the Danes wanted to talk. They were hoping to broker a deal with you in exchange for him.'

King Louis raised an eyebrow. 'What deal?'

'Jarl Torgeir wants a partnership that he believes would benefit both you and himself.'

'A partnership?' King Louis leaned back in his chair and crossed his fingers under his bearded chin. 'Do we not already have an agreement with him?'

Duke Liudolf nodded. 'We do, my king. But Jarl Torgeir wants new terms.'

'New terms?' There was a hint of annoyance in King Louis's voice as he said the words. 'What new terms?'

'New trade agreement between your kingdom and Hedeby and... a proposal for one of his daughters to marry one of your grace's sons.'

King Louis said nothing for a while and then asked, 'Are his daughters Christian?'

Duke Liudolf shook his head. 'No, my king. But I've been told they would be happy to convert.'

King Louis glanced at Charles as he considered what he had been told, and Charles wondered what the king was thinking. 'Is that all?'

'No, my king. There is also Ivor Guttromson who wants you to support his bid to take the throne of Denmark.'

'Did Ivor's father not recently attempt the same thing?' King Louis asked.

'He did, my lord king. And though we are not sure what happened, both King Horik and Guttrom are dead.'

'And now Ivor wants to attempt the same.' King Louis looked

at Charles again, who felt even smaller under the king's gaze. 'And where are they now? These Danes?'

'Steinar, the son of Jarl Torgeir, and Ivor Guttromson have returned to Hedeby, but they left a priest behind who will deliver your grace's response.'

King Louis glanced at Father Leofdag standing beside Charles, who was the wrong priest, but at least now Charles understood why Father Egbert had travelled with them to Bremen. His gaze fixed on Charles again. 'And why is this runt so important?'

Charles felt a flash of annoyance at being called a runt and wondered why everyone always believed he was weak just because he was short for his age. His grandfather was short and was a great warrior, as had his father been.

This time Duke Liudolf took a deep breath. 'The boy is the grandson of Sven the Boar, my lord king, and the son of Torkel the Dane.'

King Louis raised his brows as he leaned forward in his chair. His eyes flashed at Duke Liudolf and he clenched his jaw. Charles wondered what was going through the king's mind as he gripped the armrests of his chair and glared at Charles. Charles could not stop the shiver which ran down his spine and felt Father Leofdag stare at him. But Charles did not want to look at the priest. He did not want to be there either. He wanted to turn and run for the door as fast as he could and, in his mind, he heard his father's last words. *Now run, my son. Run like the devil's minions are chasing you.*

'Priest, I think you should leave the hall,' King Louis growled at Father Leofdag, who paled but stood his ground.

'Forgive me, my lord.' Father Leofdag bowed. 'But I stay with the boy.'

King Louis stood and took a menacing step forward as Charles realised he had been right. The king was a large man, even though he was shorter than the duke. 'Priest, this conversation is not for you. But if you insist on staying, then you'll meet the Almighty much sooner than you'd want. Now, get out!'

Father Leofdag gave Charles an apologetic glance before he scurried out of the hall. Charles wasn't surprised though, and neither did he blame the priest this time. He wanted to do the same thing, but couldn't because the duke had his hand on his shoulder. Duke Liudolf gave a signal to his men who followed Father Leofdag out, leaving only the three of them. To Charles, it felt like the hall doubled in size and all he wanted to do was hide from the hard eyes of King Louis.

For many uncomfortable heartbeats, King Louis stood where he was, his dark eyes scrutinising Charles. Charles tried to find the same courage he had found when he had faced Ivor and Roul. But he struggled under the weight of the king's glare.

'Yes, I see it now. I see her in his face and him.' King Louis turned and walked back to his seat before he collapsed into it. Just like Charles had seen his grandfather do many times. He rubbed his temples with his left hand before he looked at Charles again. 'Why did you bring him here, Duke Liudolf? You told me the boy was with Sven in Denmark.'

Duke Liudolf dipped his head. 'That is what I believed as well, my king.'

'So why did Jarl Torgeir and Ivor Guttromson have him?'

'From what we can tell, King Charles of West Francia paid Guttrom to find the boy. I believe that was how Guttrom funded his rebellion against King Horik.'

A vein bulged on King Louis's head and Charles was worried it might burst and kill the king as he glared at Duke Liudolf. 'My brother knows about the boy! How in God's name does he know?'

'We don't know, my king.'

'Then you are a fool!'

Duke Liudolf dropped to his knees. 'Forgive me, my lord king.

But that is why I believed it best to bring Charles to you.'

'Charles?' The way King Louis said his name sent a shiver down Charles's spine and he knew then that he would have no relationship with King Louis. 'And how is bringing the bastard child to me going to solve our current problem? Sven, that bastard boar, has my daughter and Bishop Bernard. The old fool. And now I find out that my brother, the king of West Francia, is aware of his existence.'

'Yes, my lord king. And we have Sven's grandson.' Charles glanced at Duke Liudolf and did not like the way this conversation was going. Once again, he wished he had run when he had the chance.

'Do you really think that heathen cares about this boy?' King Louis glanced at Charles again.

Duke Liudolf nodded. 'From what we have learnt, Sven the Boar has gone to great lengths to protect Charles. I believe that is something we can use to our advantage, my lord king.'

King Louis raised an eyebrow as he considered what Duke Liudolf had said. 'You think we can trade the boy for my daughter? You really expect Sven to go for that? For all we know, he has already sacrificed her to their false gods.'

'My grandfather would never do that!' Charles said before he could stop himself. He was tired of everyone thinking his grandfather was a monster, even when he himself had felt that recently. Charles clenched his fists as King Louis glared at him again.

'How are you so certain of that, boy?' The king leaned forward in his chair as he waited for Charles to respond.

Charles took a deep breath to calm his heart before it broke out of his chest. 'My grandfather is not a monster.'

'He is a heathen!' the king thundered as he slammed his fist on the chair's armrest.

Charles jumped and just wanted to turn and run, but he tried to remember what Thora had taught him. Taking another deep breath, Charles said, 'Not all heathens are monsters. Some are good people.' Charles thought of those who had died trying to protect him from Ivor's men. Alfhild, Oda and, most importantly, Thora. 'Thora was a good person,' he said as a tear ran down his cheek.

'Charles?' Duke Liudolf said, but Charles ignored him as he returned King Louis's glare.

'My grandfather would not kill my mother!'

King Louis almost flinched at those words and looked like he was about to launch himself at Charles.

'Charles is right,' Duke Liudolf interjected before the king did just that. 'There is no reason for Sven to kill your daughter.'

King Louis glared at Charles for a short while, his nostrils flared, before he responded, 'I took his son from him.'

'Yes, my lord king. But you treated Torkel well.'

'Something I've regretted ever since he betrayed my trust with my daughter.' King Louis turned his attention back to Duke Liudolf. 'Do you really believe that you can get that heathen bastard to trade Hildegard for him?'

Duke Liudolf nodded. 'I've spoken to the priest that accompanied Charles. He told me that Sven threatened to kill anyone who harmed Charles. I believe he will trade the abbess and the bishop for Charles.'

King Louis stroked his short beard as he thought about it, and then he nodded. 'Fine. You leave today, Duke Liudolf. Tell that bastard to meet me on the beach where we first met and to bring my daughter and the bishop if he ever wants to see the runt again. And in the meantime, I will consider Jarl Torgeir's proposal.'

Duke Liudolf dipped his head. 'Yes, my king. We will leave today.'

'The boy stays, Liudolf. I'm not letting him out of my sight.'

Charles's heart skipped a beat in his chest and he looked at Duke Liudolf with wide eyes.

'My king?' Duke Liudolf frowned.

'The little bastard has caused enough problems for me. This time, I make sure that I know exactly where he is.' King Louis turned his attention to Charles. 'And, boy, if you tell anyone who you think your mother is, then I'll personally make sure that no one ever hears or sees you again. Understand?'

Charles glared at King Louis and wished his grandfather was there. Sven would never let anyone speak to him like that. But Charles was on his own and he knew there was nothing he could do. For him, it was more proof that God had abandoned him. Even a Christian king was threatening to kill him. So in the end, Charles nodded, because there was nothing else he could do.

'My king, if I may. Permit Father Leofdag to stay with Charles. The boy needs guidance.'

King Louis scowled but nodded. 'Fine.'

'Thank you, my lord king.' Duke Liudolf knelt down and whispered, 'Forgive me, Charles. I thought this would go differently. Remember what I said. Do not mention the cross to the king.' Charles nodded, but he wasn't really listening as he stared at King Louis, who was glaring at them. 'Good. May God be with you, Charles. And soon, maybe even your mother.'

Charles frowned at Duke Liudolf. 'But you are going to trade me for her. How can we be together?' *Would we want to be together*, he thought as well, but did not say.

'Do not underestimate your mother, Charles. She will make sure the king does not hand you over to that heathen. I promise you that you will never have to spend time with any of the heathens again. Your mother and I will make sure of it.'

Charles looked at Duke Liudolf and then at King Louis. *But what if I'd rather be with the heathens?*

## 20

It was the day after they had returned from their visit to the godi and Sven and Thora were sitting on a bench near the jarl's seat, which had been collecting dust over the last few weeks as Sven had forbade the thralls to clean it. Hildegard and the old priest were back in their house again, the one Sven was using as a prison, but he allowed them to walk around the town, guarded by four warriors who kept them away from the market. Gerold still lived, unfortunately, but his face was heavily bruised and he had a cut on his forehead. Ingvild had treated him, but had told Sven it would have been better to just kill the ungrateful bastard.

Thora had said little since they had returned, which Sven was happy about because he didn't feel like talking either. The only one at the table who was talking non-stop was Jorlaug, the daughter of Thora's cousin, who insisted on following Thora around. Sven wondered why she didn't play with other children her age, or why at least she didn't stay at home with her parents, but then Ingvild had said that since Sven had beaten the girl's father for his attack on Charles, the atmosphere at home was not healthy for the small girl. And now her father had disappeared, and no one knew where to. Audhild had asked Sven to send men out to look for him, which he had done, or at least, Thora had. But Sven would rather the drunk bastard not be found.

'I hope they're feeding the poor boy,' Ingvild said of Charles and not for the first time, as she sat on a stool nearby mending one of Sven's tunics. She was another of that family who had been spending more time in the hall instead of the house they all shared. Thora smiled at her aunt's comment. The old lady was obsessed with feeding Sven's grandson, as if she believed he would grow taller if they gave him more food. Sven had tried that and knew it didn't work. The only part that grew had been his stomach.

'Where is Charles? I miss him. Even though he is a Christian.' Jorlaug looked at Sven as if he knew the answer. He thought about what his uncle had said about Charles being in East Francia and wondered if the godi had spoken the truth. And then he wondered how Charles would have ended up with there when they had all believed the boy would be on his way to West Francia. King Charles of West Francia had paid Guttrom to find the boy, so it made sense for Ivor to take Charles to the king of the West Franks. Even Charles's mother had been shocked by that. After they had left the godi and her courage had returned, she had demanded that Sven free her. But now that her father possibly had Charles, she was even more important to him.

'If I knew, then I'd be on my way there now to get him,' Sven grumbled, which earned him a glare from Thora.

'We all miss him,' she said and stroked Jorlaug's head.

Sven drank his ale and saw Rollo's wife hovering near the door of the hall, her eyes fixed on him. She looked like she wanted to talk to him, but when she spotted Sven looking at her, she turned and walked away.

'She worries about her husband, the oaf. What was he

thinking rushing off on his own like that?' Ingvild said and, for once, Sven agreed with her. Although he knew he was also to blame for Rollo leaving. If he hadn't been so caught up in his grief of losing Charles, then he would have stopped the young warrior. But he had hoped that, by letting Rollo go to Hedeby, Rollo might have found Charles and brought him back.

'You should go talk to her, Sven,' Thora said.

'What can I say to her? I don't know where Rollo is.' Sven looked at his cup so he couldn't see the scowl on Thora's face.

'Sigmund is also sad,' Jorlaug said. 'I saw him yesterday, sitting outside his house. He doesn't want to play with the other boys any more.'

'You're the jarl, Sven,' Thora said. 'You should comfort her.'

*I'm no jarl*, Sven was about to say when a horn blew from the town gates. 'What, in Odin's name, is happening now?'

Thora frowned and, like everyone in the hall, she looked at the hall doors. Sven wondered if Ribe was being attacked, but then he dismissed the idea. No one would be that dumb. Even the bands of leaderless warriors.

'Jarl Sven! Jarl Sven!' A warrior ran into the hall and stopped in front of Sven.

'What is it?'

'At the gate, jarl. A large force is by the gate.'

'A large force?' Thora asked, her brows furrowed. 'Who is leading this force?'

The warrior took a deep breath. 'A man claiming to be the future king of Denmark. Jarl Torgeir is with him and so are other jarls.'

Sven scowled as he glanced at Thora and thought about what the godi had said. He wondered which of the jarls were whispering things into this would-be king's ears. Sven was sure Torgeir was one of them, especially after Sven had killed his close friend and cut most of his toes off during the battle at Jelling.

'They have Rollo,' the warrior added.

'Rollo?' Sven asked, his heart racing in his chest. 'He's still alive?' Sven asked before he could stop himself. He had not realised that he believed Rollo was dead, but the man had been gone for too long. 'Get Alvar and tell him to get the men ready quick. And then return to the gate and don't open it. No matter what.'

'And what if they threaten to kill Rollo?' the warrior asked.

Sven clenched his fists. 'Do not open that gate.' The warrior nodded and ran out of the hall.

'So we finally get to meet this new king we have been hearing about.' Ingvild stared at Sven as she put his tunic down and stood up from her stool.

'Aye, we finally do.' Sven felt his battle lust taking over him, even though he wasn't sure why. It might have been because of what his uncle had told him or because he knew many of the jarls with this young king wanted to see him dead, especially if they had sided with Horik before the battle. Or perhaps it was just because he had arrived with an army, and that made Sven nervous. 'Alfhild, my armour!' he shouted and stopped when he realised he had called out for the young thrall. Sven shook his head and ignored the look of sympathy that Thora was giving him. He wondered how long it would take him to get used to not having the young woman seeing to all his needs.

'I'll help you get ready, Sven,' Thora said and helped Sven put his brynja on and handed him his sword and helmet. Thora then put her own leather jerkin on and fastened her sword belt around her waist. Sven raised an eyebrow at her, and she shrugged. 'The gods are determined to make me fight, so I might as well be ready this time.'

'Your wound?' Sven asked.

Thora put a hand on her stomach. 'I'll be fine.' She then turned to her aunt and Jorlaug. 'You two stay here, especially you, Jorlaug.'

'But Aunt Thora,' the young girl complained.

'No, Jorlaug. Your mother will not forgive me if something happens to you as well.'

Sven put the felt cap over his scalp and then put his helmet on before he left the hall. Outside, Alvar was waiting with as many warriors as he could muster. Which wasn't much because many of the warriors were patrolling the farmsteads. Alvar raised an eyebrow at Thora walking out of the hall dressed for war, but then shrugged and asked Sven, 'Do you really think he is here to fight?'

Sven shook his head. 'No, but I want to make sure the other bastards with him don't give him that idea.' Sven ran his eyes over the men Alvar had gathered and nodded his approval. These men had all fought in the battle at Jelling and Sven knew they would do what was needed if they had to defend their town. 'Let's go meet this new *king*.' Sven turned and walked towards the gate, ignoring all the stares and whispers from the townspeople.

'Off to kill more of our sons, are you?' a grey beard said as he walked past Sven. 'You were a curse to us then and you are a curse to us now, Sven. Your father should have drowned you when you came out of your mother.' The man spat at Sven's feet.

Sven clenched his jaw as he fought the urge to kill the old bastard, but then he took a deep breath and walked towards the gate. The people of Ribe hated him even more than they had before. And Sven knew they had good reason too. About a third of Ribe's warriors had died during the battle, and many had come back badly injured. It would take many winters before Ribe's forces recovered, but then the other jarls had not fared better either. The few that had survived were weakened as much as Sven was and he was glad the Frankish kings were too busy fighting each other because the gods knew it would not take much for them to take over Denmark and force them all to kneel to their nailed God.

'The people should show you more respect, jarl,' Alvar said as he walked beside Sven, but Sven only shook his head.

'Many of them lost children and husbands in the battle. Let them be angry.' Sven glanced over his shoulder, searching for the old man, but could not see him. 'Our anger is what makes us strong. The gods thrive on that. That is why they make our lives difficult. And that is the reason we are not as weak as the Christians.'

Alvar nodded, but Sven doubted the young warrior really heard what he had said as they approached the gate. Sven grimaced as he tried not to walk with his customary limp, but it was difficult. His left leg ached more than ever and he prayed to the gods that there would not be another battle, because Sven doubted he could stand in a shield wall again. He still had nightmares of the last battle, something Sven never really had before. Although his dreams weren't really about the battle itself, but of Charles being carried away and his wife, Eydis, standing in the tent as he fought Guttrom, shaking her head in disappointment.

Sven pushed the thoughts from his mind as he walked up the wooden steps which led to the top of the earth mound wall that surrounded the landward side of Ribe. On top of the earth mound wall was a wooden wall which stood as tall as Alvar and Rollo and Sven was glad for the platform behind it which he could stand on so he could see over the wall. Once up the stairs, Sven climbed onto the platform, with Thora and Alvar standing on either side of him, and looked over the wall. Sven did not look at the small army which stood there, with the group of richly dressed men in front of it. Instead, his gaze was fixed on the graveyard to his right. Countless of Ribe's generations were buried there. All the way back to the first people that settled on the banks of the Ribe River and started the first market. Sven's ancestors had been amongst the first of Ribe's people, and all of them were buried in that graveyard. All of them apart from those lost in distant lands during raids, and his son Torkel. Sven's father was there, along with all his brothers, all of them dead by his hands, even Bjarni. But Torkel was not, and Sven doubted he himself would ever be buried there alongside his kin. *Would they even accept me after all I have done*, he wondered as his eyes turned to the forest not far from the graveyard where the last of his family lived. The old godi who was too old to still be alive and yet the bastard still lived. Perhaps he did belong to the gods, after all. Sven was aware of the men on the wall shuffling uncomfortably. Even Alvar fidgeted as they waited for him to greet their visitors, but Sven was in no rush as he took in the lands of his ancestors. When he wandered Denmark, drunk and lost, he had refused to come to this region, afraid of what he might find. But now, as he saw the many smoke plumes in the distance from farmsteads which had been attacked, he knew he could not just leave Ribe undefended. He needed to make sure she was protected before he left to find his grandson.

Only then did Sven turn his attention to the group of men standing ahead of the army. His eyes found the would-be king quickly enough. He was in the centre of the group and the youngest of them all. Sven raised an eyebrow, wondering how the man with his thin beard and unlined face could be a nephew of the dead king. His brown hair lifted in the breeze as his angry eyes glared at Sven. But Sven was in no rush to bow to another of Horik's kin, if this man was indeed of that bloodline. Jarl Torgeir of Hedeby was next to the king, his shoulders broader and his face more lined and Sven felt the smile in the corner of his mouth when he saw the bastard's foot still wrapped in a bandage from when Sven stabbed him during the battle. There were other jarls as well, some of them Sven recognised, others he didn't. The one that did surprise Sven, though, was the bastard called Hallr Red-Face. He had been one of Guttrom's strongest supporters before the battle, but here he was with the would-be king. Sven wondered what that meant when he spotted Rollo and frowned. He had expected to see his hirdman tied up with warriors on either side of him, but apart from his bruised face and cut lip, Rollo seemed fine. He was on a horse which looked too small for him, but then all horses did, and his hands were untied. Rollo even had his weapons with him.

'Is this how you greet the man who will be your new king?' the young leader of the army shouted at Sven. 'Making him wait while you admire the countryside?'

Sven hawked and spat. 'This is how I greet any man who arrives unannounced at my gate with a small army. And besides, you're not king yet. Not until the next Landsting and only if the jarls vote for you.' Alvar sucked in his breath beside Sven and even some warriors on the wall gasped at Sven's response. Jarl Torgeir snarled, but the young man only smiled.

'You are correct. I'm not the king, not yet anyway. And these are dangerous times, Jarl Sven. I need to make sure I have enough men to protect me and my guests from the bands of wolves ravaging the country.'

Sven raised an eyebrow at being called a jarl by the would-be king. 'Those men are not wolves. They are weasels who steal eggs from the hens while the wolves are away.' Sven turned his attention to Rollo. 'Rollo, you are well?'

Rollo raised his hand. 'Aye, Jarl Sven. I have been treated well. Jarl Torgeir even showed me his famous hospitality.'

'You see, Jarl Sven. I bring you your man back. Mostly unharmed, even though Jarl Torgeir has good reasons to hang him.'

Sven ran his eyes over the army again. They outnumbered the fighting men and women he had in Ribe, but the look on Rollo's face told Sven that he had important news for him. Sven took a deep breath as he resisted the urge to rub the large ivory Mjöllnir around his neck. It had belonged to his father and his father before him. Sven's grandfather was said to have killed a walrus with his bare hands, and then made the pendant from one of its tusks. The wind picked up and Sven glanced at the sky, wondering if that was a sign from the gods. And then wondered why he still looked for signs when he never understood what they meant, anyway. Sven turned and stepped off the palisade and as he made his way to the steps, he said to Alvar, 'Open the gates.'

Alvar gave the order for the gates to be opened and then glanced at Sven. 'So what do you think he wants?'

'To buy Sven's support,' Thora said as Sven watched the would-be king march his army into Ribe. 'That's why he brought all the other jarls with him. To show Sven that he will be outnumbered if he stands against him.'

Alvar scratched his head. 'So what do we do?'

'We throw a feast for the bastard and his followers and we listen to what he has to offer.' Sven turned and looked at the forest, wondering if his uncle was watching them, as the gates were opened and the new king entered with the jarls, while the warriors stayed outside the gates. Sven knew they would find somewhere to pitch their tents and make themselves comfortable, as warriors did.

'But do we trust him?' Alvar asked.

Thora looked at Sven as if she, too, wanted to know the answer to that. Sven thought about the godi's words.

'Alvar. Never trust any man who wants to wear a crown on his head.' Sven watched as Rollo stopped his horse and jumped off before embracing his wife and son. He rubbed the Mjöllnir around his neck as he glanced at the clouds and wondered what price he would have to pay for Rollo's safe return.

## 21

Roul cursed himself for trusting the men he had left behind to
watch those heathen bastards in Hedeby. He glared at the body of
one of them, the man's eyes still open in shock as his blood leaked
out of the stab wound in his chest where Roul had stabbed him.
The man was supposed to watch Ivor and the boy while Roul
went to Ribe for the cross. He had strict orders to kill the heathen
scum as soon as they stepped out of line. But instead the bastard
had got drunk and while he was whoring with heathen women,
Ivor had slipped away. Roul's other men had fled before he
returned, no doubt certain of their fates for failing, but Roul knew
he only had himself to blame. He had underestimated the thin
heathen bastard and now his life was on the line, because Roul
knew that if he returned to King Charles now, he would be
executed. But he had to get the cross. He could not return to Paris
without it. Now Charles was gone, though, and Roul had to decide
what to do next.

Roul cleaned the blood from his knife while he thought about
what the dead man had told him. Ivor had gone to Jarl Torgeir, a
move that Roul had not expected, but should have done. But the

one thing he never could have expected was the fight in the church soon after he had slipped out. Roul wondered who the large warrior he had been told about was and whether this was what drove Ivor to Jarl Torgeir. Did Ivor believe he had sent the man? Again, Roul cursed himself for being so foolish.

It had taken Roul two days to get back to Hedeby. He had stolen a horse and had left Ribe as soon as the sun had set. He had almost run into Sven again as he and a group of people returned from somewhere. Luckily, one of their horses whined, which had warned Roul of their approach. Roul had to resist the urge to follow them back to Ribe, just to confirm his suspicion that the woman he saw was the daughter of King Louis of East Francia. But instinct had told him it was more important to get back to Hedeby, grab the boy and go back to West Francia. Once he had reached Hedeby, Roul had gone straight to the church and was surprised to find it empty. What surprised him even more was the dried blood on some benches and the story of the fight that one priest had told him. Roul had sought his men out then and had found one of them drunk in a tavern. The man, who had been working with him for many years, told Roul how Ivor had gone to Jarl Torgeir the following night, but he did not know what they spoke of. What concerned Roul more was the news that the following day Ivor, along with the jarl's youngest son, travelled south. Roul had plunged his knife in the man's chest before he could even tell him that the boy had gone with him, but Roul did not need to hear that.

Roul thought about the cross in his pouch and wondered if that would be enough to save him from King Charles's wrath. But it wasn't just the king he had to worry about. The king's spymaster, Bero, hated Roul because he was a threat to his position and Roul knew the man would make sure the king was displeased with him. Roul shook his head. No, he needed to get the boy back. He could only return to King Charles with the grandson of King Louis of East Francia and the Cross of Charlemagne if he wanted to live and, more importantly, avenge his master, who had been murdered by Bero. Roul took the cross from his pouch and ran his fingers over the different-coloured gems that rimmed the edge of the cross. The more he looked at it, the more beautiful it became. He couldn't tell any more if it was the allure of the power it possessed that drew him in more or just because it truly was the most beautiful cross he had ever seen. Roul had studied every inch of the cross, determined to discover its truth, but saw nothing to explain why his king thought this cross could make him an emperor. As Roul stared at the cross, an idea came to him that made him smile for the first time in many days. But for this idea to work, Roul knew he had to be very careful.

Putting the cross away, Roul left the room he was in and slipped out of the tavern. The tavern owner was too busy dealing with others to even notice him leave, and once outside, Roul wrapped his cloak around his shoulders as a thin rain fell. He made his way to the market, ignoring all the traders who were shouting at him, many of them with strange accents from lands far away and with goods on their stalls he had never seen before. Roul was tempted to steal one brooch, which looked like a unicorn yet had two horns instead of one, but decided against it. He needed to focus and forced himself to turn away from the stall and head towards a trader he knew very well.

Roul soon reached the stall he was aiming for and browsed the contents on the stall as the trader spoke to a potential buyer. He didn't have to wait long as lumps of silver were soon swapped for a new pair of leather shoes and the pleased buyer walked away. The trader turned to Roul and was about to greet him warmly when he recognised him and scowled.

'Surprised to see you here. Thought the north was too cold for you,' the Danish trader said as he put the silver in the bulging pouch he wore on his waist.

Roul shrugged as his eyes scanned the market. The Danish trader had been his main source of information from Hedeby for many years, as he often travelled between Hedeby and Paris. That he was a red-headed Dane made it easier for him to get information from drunken warriors and other traders who would be more wary around Frankish traders, but Roul knew he wasn't the only trader here that traded in more than just goods. But of all the spies, this was the man he trusted the most. Because no one else knew the man worked for Roul, not even Bero.

'I'm looking for something in particular,' Roul said, his eyes glancing around to make sure no one was within earshot. 'Something from Paris.'

The trader scratched his short beard with his rough hands as he studied the contents on his stall. 'You see nothing on here that you like?'

'No, I'm afraid not.'

'That's a pity. But luckily for you, I depart for Paris tomorrow and if you tell me what it is you are after, I'm sure I can find it for you, for a price, of course.'

Roul smiled. That was just what he was hoping for. Now he just needed one more thing and the grace of God, and then his plan might just work. 'Of course.'

'Have you heard of this nephew of old Horik who aims to be the next king of Denmark?' the trader asked, and Roul raised an eyebrow.

'A nephew of Horik, you say?' Roul kept his voice casual so that anyone walking past would think they were just gossiping about recent events.

'Aye, although few have heard of him before and some even think he is too young to be his nephew.' The trader moved some of the items on his stall around and nodded a greeting to a passer-by.

'His grandson then, perhaps?' Roul mused and wondered if this information could be useful to him.

The trader shrugged. 'Might be. If you were here a few days earlier, you might have seen him.'

Roul raised an eyebrow again. 'He was here?'

'Aye. Arrived with a small army. Jarl Torgeir entertained him for a few days and then joined this Horik on his journey north. They say the new king was heading to Ribe to speak to Sven the Boar.'

'And Torgeir went with him?'

The trader nodded and Roul wondered how he had missed them on the road. But then, he had avoided the main roads and even if he had seen a large force, he would have done his best to avoid them as well. 'But if you ask me, Torgeir is up to something.'

'Up to something?'

The trader paused as a woman stopped and glanced at the products on his stall. She smiled at him and then moved on. 'Shortly after they had left for Ribe, Torgeir's youngest son returned to Hedeby with a man who looked a lot like Ivor Guttromson. They stayed barely long enough to drink a cup of ale before they raced north.'

'To join Torgeir with this new Horik?'

The trader shrugged, as Roul had to calm his racing heart at the fact that he had just missed the bastard Dane. 'It's strange though, because I heard a rumour they were in Hamburg.'

Again Roul frowned. 'Hamburg? Who?'

'Ivor.' The trader glanced around before he leaned in closer and held a hand out for Roul. The man knew he had important information and, like the trader he was, he wasn't going to give his product away for free. Roul was tempted to pull his knife out and stick it under the man's throat, but he quickly dismissed the idea. The trader had always been an excellent source of information. Roul reached into his pouch and pulled out a few gold coins with the face of King Louis on them. He never used West Frankish money when he was in this part of the world. The trader put the coins in his pouch without looking at them and said, 'I heard that Ivor and Steinar had a meeting with the duke of Saxony. And at the end of that meeting, the duke of Saxony had a boy in his possession.'

'A boy?' Roul did his best to keep his face passive, but knew this boy could only be Charles. So, Ivor and Torgeir had hoped to trade Charles to the East Franks. *What for, though*, he wondered. 'And what is so special about this boy?'

The trader shrugged. 'They say the boy was heavily guarded by the duke's men and that the next day, they left for Bremen where King Louis was.'

'King Louis was in Bremen?' Roul asked and knew there was only one reason for the king of East Francia to be in Bremen. Because he knew his daughter was in Ribe. Which also meant that, by now, Charles would be in the possession of King Louis and it wouldn't take long before King Charles found this out. This changed everything for Roul. He frowned as he considered what the trader had just told him. But Roul knew there was only one thing he could do right now. He had to go back to Paris and face his king. And more importantly, Roul had to pray that the cross was enough to save him. 'There's a change of plan.' The trader raised an eyebrow. 'I need passage to Paris and we need to leave as soon as you can.'

## 22

The flames of the hearth fire leapt high as they feasted on the wood the thralls had fed them. They moved in no particular pattern as they danced this way and that, their heat relentless as they fought the darkness away. But the roar of the flames was drowned out by the noise of a hall filled with the people of Ribe as they all came to see the man who wanted to be the new king of Denmark. There was not an empty bench to be seen as thralls rushed from table to table, filling cups with ale or mead, while four thralls sweated near the hearth fire as they turned the large pig over the flames. People talked and laughed, and if Sven ignored much of what had happened since he had returned, he would have believed that Ribe was a happy place. But he couldn't as he sat there and stared at the flames leaping towards the roof of the hall, desperate to get to the old wooden beams so they could burn the hall down. Something even Sven had been tempted to do in the past.

Ribe had been a hive of activity since Sven had opened the gates to the young Horik. That was the name of the would-be king, which meant that Sven already didn't like him. Apart from a few of Horik's hirdmen, his army was camped outside the town and Sven had made sure he had enough men on the town walls to watch them, just like he made sure that he had men he trusted near him. Sven wanted to relax. He wanted to talk to the young man who had the seat of honour in his hall, to learn more about him and so he could decide if young Horik would be a good king or not. But he could not. The scene in the hall reminded him too much of the night he had returned, seeking his brother's aid so that he could protect his newly discovered grandson, which only fed his anger like the wood fed the flames in the hearth fire. Sven was forced to push the memories of that night from his mind when he noticed the young Horik talking to him.

'This is a fine feast, Jarl Sven. I'm surprised you got so much food together on such short notice.'

Sven grunted. It had not been easy. Men had been sent out to the nearest farmsteads to buy as much meat and vegetables as they could. Many of the farmers weren't happy about it as the end of the summer was near and they were preparing their winter stores. But the farms near Ribe had been spared from the raiders because of the patrols that Sven had sent out every day and so there was plenty of food available. The rest of the day had been spent preparing the feast. Pigs had been slaughtered and fish gutted. Vegetables boiled or roasted and barrels of ale and mead had been opened. The thralls had worked hard to prepare the hall under the watchful eye of Ingvild and Thora. The tables, benches and the walls had been cleaned, the old weapons dusted, and they had even hung Sven's banner on the back wall, a black boar's head, its mouth open and tusks sharp on a red background, below the boar's head. Thora had wanted to remove the spear that someone had thrown at it, but Sven had refused. He wanted the spear to stay to remind him of what had happened the last time he had trusted those who came pretending to be friends.

Sven had spent the day getting himself ready for the feast. He had bathed and shaved his scalp, brushed and braided his beard. Somehow Ingvild had found a new tunic that fit him, a finer one than any he had worn in a long time, and Sven felt uncomfortable as he sat next to the young king wearing it. On both his arms, he wore gold and silver arm rings, but had refused to wear the rings Ingvild had found for him. He was not the only one who had dressed for the occasion. Thora, who was sitting on Sven's right, wore a green dress with golden brooches and a glass bead necklace Sven knew belonged to her mother. Her hair was braided and tied back, apart from the stray strand that hung over her scarred eyebrow. It was the first time he had seen her in a dress since he had returned from the battle and Sven had to stop himself from staring at her, but he knew she most likely had a knife hidden away somewhere.

Alvar was also dressed in his best as he sat with the other warriors not far from Sven. His blond hair was tied back and his beard had been cropped and decorated with lint. Sven knew he was trying to impress a young woman whom he had his eye on for a while, but the girl's father did not approve because of Alvar's loyalty to Sven. Sven searched the hall for Rollo, not for the first time since the feast had started, and knew the giant warrior would not be there. He was with his wife and son in their house, where he should be, even if Sven would have preferred to have Rollo near him.

'I noticed a house near the market guarded by your warriors,' young Horik said, and Sven raised an eyebrow at him. 'I am curious about who or what you are guarding.'

Sven scowled and saw that Torgeir, who was sitting near Horik, was leaning towards them. 'Unwanted guests.'

'Well, if they are unwanted, then why not let them leave?'

Torgeir asked after he wiped his mouth clean with the sleeve of his tunic. But Sven did not like the glint in his eyes.

Sven scrutinised Torgeir while he thought of the answer, but then young Horik asked, 'Does that have anything to do with your grandson?' Sven scowled at him again and Horik explained, 'I heard he was taken by Ivor Guttromson. Rollo told me he went to Hedeby to find Ivor so he could avenge his mother and find your grandson.'

'Aye, they have something to do with Charles.' Sven wished he had talked to Rollo before the feast to find out what had happened in Hedeby, but there had been too much to do, and Rollo needed to be with his family.

'Ivor went to East Francia, did you hear?' Torgeir said.

Sven raised an eyebrow and sensed Thora turning her attention to them. 'East Francia?'

'Aye.' Torgeir drank from his cup before he continued. 'My men chased him out of Hedeby. If I had known he had your grandson, I would have told my men to grab the boy so I could bring him to you.'

Sven drank his mead as he wondered why Torgeir was telling him that and whether he was telling the truth. He glanced at Thora, who frowned at him, and then turned his attention back to the jarl of Hedeby. When he arrived with young Horik, Sven had watched as his men had to help him off his horse and hand him a crutch so that he could walk. Sven had heard that he had lost three of his toes, although he wasn't sure which ones, but that was nothing compared to the loss of his oldest son during the battle at Jelling. And then there was the death of Ketil as well. The man had been an old friend of Torgeir and had been a fine man. Sven still regretted having to kill him during the battle.

'Why did he go to East Francia?' Sven's uncle had told him that Charles was now with Louis of East Francia, and again he wondered how the ancient bastard knew so much. But Sven still couldn't understand why Ivor had done that.

Torgeir shrugged. 'Only the gods will know. Perhaps he realised he could not stay in Denmark any more and, seeing as his father's rebellion had failed, he probably couldn't go back to West Francia either.'

'He must have believed he could sell his sword to the king of East Francia,' the jarl sitting between Horik and Torgeir said. The man's name was Hovi and Sven wasn't sure what he was jarl of, but he had been told that Hovi hated the Christians more than he did. Sven wanted to like the man for that reason, but he couldn't. Especially not after he had found out that Hovi was the brother of Torgeir's second wife.

Sven glanced at Thora again and saw her eyebrows drawn together.

'You think it has something to do with your grandson?' the young Horik asked.

'Ivor fled the battle with my grandson.' Sven's eyes were fixed on Torgeir as he felt his body getting warmer, although he wasn't sure if it was because of the hearth fire or his anger. Somewhere, a young woman squealed and men roared with laughter. Everyone looked towards the interruption, apart from Sven and Torgeir who glared at each other.

'You think Ivor took your grandson to the East Franks?' Horik asked after a thrall put more meat onto his plate.

Sven took a bite of the fish in front of him and thought of the answer as he chewed. 'I can think of no other reason he would go there.'

'The gods are cruel, if that is the case,' Torgeir said, although he didn't hide the smile from his face. 'Didn't the king of the East Franks take your son away from you?'

Sven gritted his teeth as his knuckles whitened around his

eating knife. If it wasn't for Thora putting a hand on his arm and shaking her head at him, he would have launched himself at the jarl of Hedeby and buried his knife in the bastard's arrogant face.

'As you say, Jarl Torgeir. The gods are cruel,' Thora said, her eyes darting to the crutch behind Torgeir's seat. Torgeir's face turned red as he drank from his cup. His youngest son, Steinar, who was sitting next to him, glared at Thora as Torgeir smiled.

'Thora Haraldsdóttir, I was upset when I learnt you tied your fate with Sven's. My shield wall still misses your sword.'

Thora had been one of Torgeir's warriors when she was younger. Her father would have preferred that she fought for Ribe, but Thora had spent most of her life in Hedeby after they had left Ribe and so she had fought first for Torgeir's father and for Torgeir. 'My sword doesn't miss your shield wall.'

Horik cleared his throat to stop the conversation from turning ugly and turned to Sven. 'Well, if there is anything I can do to help you get your grandson back, Jarl Sven, don't hesitate to ask. Isn't that so, Jarl Hovi?'

'That is so,' Hovi responded, but Sven didn't like the glance he directed at Torgeir.

Sven nodded, and was about to thank the young Horik when he spotted Hallr Red-Face further down the table staring at him, his face creased in anger. He forgot about the young jarl and turned his attention back to the flames as they danced away and wished the feast would end and the bastards would leave. Then he could get on his ship and go find his grandson.

The following day, Sven stood in front of his hall and watched as the would-be king and his entourage left Ribe. The townspeople cheered for Horik as he waved at them. Many of them shouted the blessing of the gods on him while Sven prayed Thor strike Torgeir down with lightning.

'The people love him,' Thora said as she stood beside Sven,

dressed in trousers and wearing a leather jerkin again. Sven decided he preferred her dressed like a warrior.

'Aye, he made sure they would.' He thought of the raiders the young Horik had executed outside the town walls. Men who had raided farms and killed others for their own greed. Horik had captured the raiders as he travelled north and had them kept under guard with his main force. And in the morning, as the sun shone brightly, he had his best warriors chop their heads off, much to the delight of the people of Ribe. Sven had to admit it had been a good move, because it showed the townspeople that Horik would be a just king who punished those who broke his laws. He then clenched his fists when he remembered how people had commented that Sven had done nothing to protect them from the raiders. They had already forgotten the times when he had marched the warriors out to fight the jarls who had raided his lands before the battle at Jelling, and how after he had sent patrols out to protect the nearby farmsteads. But Sven knew the people of Ribe hated him and, no matter what he did, they would never see how he had tried to protect the town of his forefathers.

Sven studied the town as if he would never see it again. He took in the market, once filled with traders from all over Midgard, but which now stood empty apart from a few traders brave enough to travel to Ribe. The training ground near the river where he had spilled blood and sweat as he trained every day so he could stand up to his enemies. Even the hall behind him, built by his grandfather and a symbol of how he had failed his family.

'Sven.' Rollo startled Sven. He had not realised the giant warrior had approached him.

Sven scrutinised the blond-haired warrior, taking in his bruised and scarred face. 'We missed you at the feast.'

Rollo nodded. 'I felt it was more important to spend time with my wife and son.'

'Aye, family is important.' Sven glanced at the clouds as they sailed overhead.

'Sven, Torgeir is up to something. You can't trust him.'

'We know, Rollo,' Thora said.

'You know?' Rollo raised an eyebrow.

'Aye,' Sven said. 'The bastard was too nice. It's obvious he is hiding something.' Sven remembered his uncle's words, telling him he was in more danger than his grandson. He did not want to believe the bastard, but now he knew the godi was right. Sven needed to find Charles, but first he had to survive whatever Torgeir was planning. 'What happened in Hedeby?' he asked Rollo.

Rollo lowered his head. 'I failed, Sven. I failed my mother and... I failed you.'

'You still live, Rollo.' Thora smiled at him. 'You haven't failed anyone yet.'

But Rollo shook his head. 'No. I saw Charles, Sven. I saw him and Ivor. I could have saved Charles, but I let my revenge cloud my judgement and decided it was more important to kill Ivor. But the bastard still lives and Charles is gone.'

Sven took a deep breath to calm himself. But his anger was not at Rollo. 'You did not fail, Rollo. I did. I failed that boy the moment I let Guttrom and his bastard son stay in Ribe when I should have chased them away.' Sven looked up at the clouds again. There weren't many of them and the sun shone brightly above them, but Sven still felt there was a storm coming. 'Alvar! Make sure the men are ready at all times. I want their weapons sharp and their armour clean.' Alvar frowned as he nodded, but then ran off to do what Sven had asked. 'Rollo, I want you to tell me everything you learnt in Hedeby.'

'Aye, Sven. But there isn't much. They kept me away from the hall, so I don't know what Torgeir is planning.'

'But that already tells us he is planning something,' Thora said.

Sven nodded as he rubbed the Mjöllnir around his neck. 'And we'll have to be prepared for whatever that may be.'

They were about to enter the hall when Rollo pointed at the house with the two warriors outside the door. 'Are you going to tell me why they are guarding the house the priest had stayed in?'

'Sven decided to keep Charles's mother as a prisoner,' Thora said with a shake of her head.

Rollo raised an eyebrow. 'Is that a good idea? The last thing we need now is to anger King Louis of East Francia.'

'Aye, that's what I said. But Sven refuses to listen.'

Sven grunted as they talked around him. 'The king of East Francia can choke on his wine for all I care. The bastard took my son from me and now he has my grandson.'

'And you have his daughter. Sven, the gods know this will not end well.' Thora shook her head again.

'The king of East Francia has Charles? I thought Ivor and his father were working for the West Franks.' Rollo scratched his head.

'Aye, the bastards were. But something happened and now King Louis has my grandson. That's why I want you to tell me everything you saw while you were in Hedeby.' Sven turned and walked into the hall and towards his bench. A thrall spotted him and rushed to get him ale while another cleared the empty plates and bowls away from the morning meal Sven was forced to share with the young Horik and his entourage. Torgeir had not sat with them; instead, he had shared his meal with Hallr Red-Face. The two had been in constant conversation, and it bothered Sven that he didn't know what they were planning. As he sat down and took his ale from the thrall, he wondered if Torgeir was planning an attack on Ribe, but then dismissed the idea. Ribe might not be as big as Hedeby, and her walls might not have been as tall, but they were still formidable. Torgeir would need a large army to defeat the walls. Another option was to attack by the river, but Ribe had lookouts both up and down the river, which would warn her of an attack. All Sven then had to do was to form a shield wall along the riverbank and kill Torgeir's men as they jumped off their ships. The only way Sven could think of how Torgeir could defeat Ribe was by attacking from the land and the river at the same time as Sven did not have enough men to defend both positions, but then he was sure that Torgeir didn't have men to do that either. Even if he joined forces with Hallr Red-Face. Hallr might have had a reputation as a great warrior, but he was the jarl of a small town and, like most jarls in Denmark, he had lost many warriors in the battle at Jelling. *What are you up to, you club-footed bastard*, Sven wondered as Rollo and Thora sat down. Sven saw the serious look on Rollo's face and knew what he was going to say before he said it.

'I'll tell you all I can, but first I want you to tell me why everyone is after Charles. And don't tell me it's because of you. There's more to it and I want to know what that is.' Rollo emptied his ale and gave the cup to the thrall to refill as Sven stared at him. Rollo's son, Sigmund, was sitting next to him, and Sven wondered when he had shown up. He glanced around and was surprised not to see young Jorlaug there as well.

'Rollo is right,' Thora said. 'He deserves to know what this is all about.'

Sven sighed. 'Aye. Rollo does.' He took a deep breath and told Rollo everything he knew about Charles, his son and the cross. He also told him what had happened while Rollo was in Hedeby, how he had taken Charles's mother to the godi and what the godi had told them, and how the cross was stolen by a man Sven had believed worked for Charles's mother but now thought was a West Frankish spy.

'Charles is a Christian prince?' Sigmund asked, his eyes wide, when Sven had finished his tale.

Sven shook his head. 'No, Charles is no prince. Just a boy caught up in something that started long before he was born.'

Rollo stared at his cup as he processed what Sven had told him, and then he nodded. 'That all makes sense, I guess. So what do we do?'

Sven drank from his cup and looked at Thora, who only shrugged. He was about to answer when a warrior ran into the hall.

'Jarl Sven! Jarl Sven!' The man stopped and scanned the hall until he found Sven.

'What is it?' Sven asked, irritated by the interruption.

The warrior pointed towards the river. 'A Frankish ship is coming towards Ribe and she's filled with warriors!'

Someone dropped a cup and Sven thought he could hear the gods laughing in the sound it made as it bounced off the table. He gripped the ivory Mjöllnir around his neck and wondered why Odin loved to toy with him.

## 23

'To arms!' Sven roared as he jumped to his feet. He winced at the pain in his back and left leg, but pushed it out of his mind as he rushed to his war chest. Thora was right behind him as Rollo turned to his son.

'Run home. Tell your mother to block the door.'

'But, Father, I want to help,' Sigmund complained.

'You can help by keeping your mother safe, now go!'

Sigmund looked like he was about to protest, but his father's hard face made him change his mind. He nodded and ran out of the hall as if he was being chased by ice giants.

'Rollo, you need to get ready,' Thora said as she helped Sven with his brynja. Her face was strained at the pain Sven was sure she still felt from her wound.

'There's no time,' Rollo said as he glanced around the hall. The few warriors that were there already were all preparing themselves for battle as more rushed in from the training grounds. Alvar ran into the hall and when he saw Rollo had no brynja, he frowned.

Sven tied his belt around his waist and gave his large Dane axe to Rollo. 'Don't break it!'

Rollo smiled. 'I would have thought your words to me would be don't get yourself killed.'

Sven grunted as those within earshot laughed. 'Alvar, make sure we have enough men guarding the house with the Christians.' Alvar nodded and left as Sven turned to his warriors. 'Right, you bastards. To the wharves!' The warriors all rushed out of the hall, leaving only Sven, Thora and Rollo. Rollo gripped Sven's axe as if he was getting used to it when Sven said to him, 'Rollo, don't get yourself killed.'

Rollo smiled again. 'Aye, the same for you, old man.' He ran out of the hall as Sven shouted after him:

'Who are you calling old?' He and Thora left the hall and paused as Sven assessed the situation. Warriors were running towards the wharves while a few extra men joined those who were guarding the house where Hildegard was kept. The townspeople were all rushing away from the river, towards their houses, and more than a few glared at Sven as they ran past him.

'I hope they kill you!' a voice shouted, but Sven ignored it as he made his way to the river. Ribe had too many wharves to protect, so Rollo had the men stand back until they saw which wharf the Frankish ship used. Sven would have preferred to have all the wharves destroyed. They could always be rebuilt, and the debris from the broken wharves would make it more difficult for their attackers to control their ships. But Sven had been told about only one ship, so he didn't feel that was necessary.

'King Louis of East Francia?' Thora asked as they watched the ship come around the bend in the river.

Sven looked at the flag which hung from the mast and didn't recognise the white steed on the red background. 'Aye, the bastard must have found out I have his daughter.' Sven scowled as he scrutinised the ship. It was a similar shape to the warships the Danes used, but the sides were much higher and Sven knew the hull would be deeper as well. It had one mast, just like the Danish ships, but it had something the Danish ships didn't. A tower built on the rear of the ship. Sven glanced at the other Frankish ship that was still docked on the wharf, the one Hildegard had arrived in with the old priest and Gerold. It looked just like the one that was approaching them now. It even had the same flag. Sven was hoping to sell that ship because he was sure he would need more men to prepare for whatever Torgeir was planning, but now he had to deal with this new threat first.

The ship slowed down as it approached the wharf and Sven saw a tall man with broad shoulders standing in the tower at the stern of the ship, his hands on his hips as he was also scrutinising Sven. For a moment, Sven was reminded of the young prince on the beach in Francia so long ago, and he wondered if that was King Louis on the ship. But then he dismissed the thought. King Louis would not risk sailing to Ribe himself. No, he would send someone else.

'The duke of Saxony,' Thora said. 'I recognise his flag. I saw him many times when I was part of Torgeir's army.'

Sven nodded. He had guessed it was that man. 'What do you know about him?'

Thora shrugged as the ship stopped mid-river and oars moved up and down to keep the ship in place. 'He's smart, very serious. They say he was a good warrior once, but now prefers to talk to solve his problems.'

Sven frowned. 'That's the man Torkel saved.' Thora nodded and Sven said, 'Doesn't look like he came to fight.'

'My thoughts as well,' Rollo said, who was standing near them.

Sven walked towards the wharf nearest to the ship, his mouth tight as he tried to walk without his limp. Rollo and Alvar, who had arrived after carrying out Sven's orders, followed without him asking them to and he knew there was no point in sending them back, but he was glad that Thora stayed with the warriors on the riverbank. She would make sure no one did anything dumb.

The large man on the tower walked down and went to the side of the ship as Sven stopped at the edge of the wharf. He looked down at the water flowing past him and saw a fish's tail splash the surface. Sven didn't even try to work out if that was a sign from the gods.

'Are you Jarl Sven?' the large man on the ship asked in Frankish. The man's black hair was neatly combed back, but lifted on the breeze, and his tunic was pressed against him, showing a man who still trained often. That he was not wearing any armour was more proof that he had not come here to fight, despite the many warriors on his ship.

Sven glanced at the sky before he turned his attention to the man. 'Aye. Who are you and what do you want?' he responded in Frankish.

'I am Duke Liudolf of Saxony, and I come on behalf of King Louis of East Francia.'

Sven scratched the back of his neck and was tempted to take his helmet off, as the felt cap was making his head itch. 'And what does that bastard want?' He saw how the men on the ship bristled and almost smiled.

'My king has a proposition for you. One I suggest you listen to carefully.' Duke Liudolf leaned forward, his hand on the side of his ship.

Sven knew what Louis's proposition would be. If what he had been told about Charles being in East Francia was true, then there could be only one reason this Duke Liudolf would be here. To trade Charles for the woman. Sven's hands trembled at the thought and he prayed to Thor that he was right. He glanced over his shoulder and saw the townspeople were creeping closer so they could see what was happening. He guessed they realised this was no attack and were curious about the Frankish ship filled with warriors. 'Alvar, show the bastard where he can dock. Make sure you have enough men with you in case this is a trap.'

Alvar nodded and signalled for some warriors to join him on the wharf as Sven turned and walked back to his hall. 'Come, Rollo, let's see what this duke has to say.'

The townspeople parted so that Sven could walk past. No one said anything to him, but he could feel their glares on him. Before he reached the hall, Sven spotted Audhild near the hall. Thora had sent men out to search for Haldor, her husband, but there still was no sign of the drunk. Sven remembered almost killing the bastard for attacking Charles. The only real good that came out of that was that the people of Ribe were more wary of what they said to him, apart from those old enough not to care any more. Sven had not seen Haldor since that day and been told by Ingvild that the bastard drank more than before, but he kept his distance from the hall and the river.

Rollo and Thora followed Sven, neither of them saying anything, and when they reached the hall, Sven stopped and watched the Frankish duke disembark his ship with a handful of warriors behind him.

The duke walked towards the hall, keeping his head high, while his warriors kept their hands near their weapons. Sven tried to picture Torkel amongst the Christian warriors, but quickly pushed the image from his mind. It would only make him angry, and for this, he needed to stay calm. Killing some sailors and warriors was one thing, but if he killed one of King Louis's dukes, then Sven knew Charles would be in even more danger. Duke

Liudolf stopped near the hall and raised an eyebrow at the nearby house, which was guarded by a group of warriors.

Sven glanced at Rollo. 'Make sure they leave their weapons outside and double the men on the house. I don't want these bastards getting any ideas.' Rollo nodded and Sven went into the hall, with Thora behind him.

The benches were already filling with townspeople, those who felt they were important enough to sit in and listen to what the Frank had to say. Although Sven wondered how many could understand because he doubted the duke spoke Danish, and Sven would not have his words translated for them. Sven saw the scowl on Thora's face when he sat down by his bench. 'What?'

'Shouldn't you be sitting there?' She indicated to the raised seat at the back of the hall.

Sven glanced at the chair made of oak and covered in dust, and shook his head. 'No, only the jarl should sit there.'

'Sven, you are the jarl.'

Again Sven shook his head. The warriors might have been calling him jarl since the battle, but the people of Ribe had made it clear he was not their jarl. And Sven didn't want to be jarl either. Not any more. Before he could say anything though, Rollo walked towards them, his eyebrow also raised at Sven sitting by the bench, but he kept quiet about it.

'It's done,' Rollo said as he positioned himself behind Sven, with the Dane axe in one hand and his other hand on the one-handed axe he wore. Even without his brynja, Rollo still looked imposing and Sven knew that most men would hesitate to attack when they saw him.

The whispers in the hall stopped when Duke Liudolf entered, flanked by two warriors whose hands were twitching near where their weapons would be and their eyes darting all over the hall. The duke himself seemed composed as he walked towards Sven, his face stern and his hands relaxed. He glanced at the empty raised seat and then the stuffed boar's head on the wall with the spear in it, raising his eyebrow as he did so. Behind the Franks came Alvar with his own Dane axe and wearing his brynja. He nodded to Sven to tell him that the Franks had given up their weapons before he joined Rollo behind Sven, who smiled at the nervous glances the Frankish warriors gave the two giants.

Duke Liudolf glanced at them as well and then he frowned when he saw Thora, sitting beside Sven and wearing a leather jerkin. Sven never understood why the Christians believed women should only breed children and run the household. He couldn't imagine Thora being happy with that life. Like him, she had given up the sword, but since Charles came into their lives, she was drawn back to it like a moth to the flames of the hearth fire.

'Sit,' Sven said and indicated for the thralls to bring the duke some ale. The whispering picked up again as the townspeople discussed what they were seeing, while Sven and the duke scrutinised each other.

'Is Abbess Hildegard still alive?' the duke asked in Frankish after he took a sip of his ale. The thrall gave his men cups as well and at first they seemed uncertain, but then one of them took a sip and shrugged. After that, it didn't take long for both warriors to empty their cups, and the thrall was sent to fetch them more ale.

'She's not been harmed,' Sven said, also in Frankish. He heard someone translate the words to those in the hall and guessed it was one of the traders. 'I can't say the same for the snake that came with her.'

'The snake?' Duke Liudolf frowned.

'Gerold.'

Duke Liudolf nodded, but said nothing about that. Sven got

the idea he cared even less about the young Frank. 'And the bishop?'

Sven shrugged. 'Shat himself a few times, but he lives.' There was an outburst of laughter from two boys as Sven's words were translated, which stopped when a woman slapped one boy behind the head.

'And what of my men?' Duke Liudolf's eyes hardened when Sven did not respond. Not that he needed to. He was sure the Frankish duke already knew Sven had had his men killed. 'They were good Christian men.'

Sven shrugged again and wondered what their faith had to do with it. 'They were fighting men who were in the wrong place.'

Duke Liudolf bared his teeth at Sven. 'I want to see the abbess and bishop before I say anything else.'

Sven stared at the Frank as his two warriors glanced around the hall, their eyes taking in all the weapons that hung on the walls. He took a sip of his ale, pretending to think about it, and then glanced over his shoulder at Rollo. 'Go get the woman. And only the woman.'

'If that young bastard tries anything?' Rollo asked.

'Deal with him, but keep him alive.'

Rollo left while Sven and the duke just sat there, sizing each other up as they drank their ale. Duke Liudolf glanced at Thora, his eyes lingering on her longer than Sven liked. Longer than Thora liked as well.

'Tell him he'll lose his eyes if he keeps staring at me like that.'

Sven didn't need to say anything as Duke Liudolf got the idea from the tone of Thora's voice or perhaps he knew their tongue and pretended not to, just like Hildegard had done when she first arrived. But Sven couldn't help himself. 'She likes your eyes. She wants them for herself.'

The two warriors behind the duke glanced at each other and

one of them couldn't help but cross himself. But Duke Liudolf only smiled as he drank his ale. They waited in silence then, the only noise being the townspeople as they spoke to each other, the constant hum of their voices making it hard for Sven to concentrate. But perhaps that was a good thing. All he could think about as he stared at the duke was how this man had been a friend of his son and how he had let Torkel die.

'Ask him if they're feeding Charles enough,' Ingvild said, who was hovering nearby. Sven scowled at her as Thora shook her head. 'What? Somebody needs to make sure the boy gets fed. He's too small.'

There was snickering at that, but then the hall fell silent again as Rollo entered with Charles's mother behind him and three warriors behind her. The Frankish warriors growled at this as the duke studied Hildegard, no doubt trying to see if she had been harmed. But she hadn't been. Hildegard's dress had dried mud and other stains on it, and the cover she wore on her head didn't look much better. She had refused to wear any of the dresses that Thora had offered her, insisting that as an abbess of the church, she had to dress like one. But her face was clean and, apart from her tired eyes, she looked in good health.

Charles's mother stopped when she saw the duke, her eyebrows raised, and her hand went to the cross she wore around her neck. Duke Liudolf jumped to his feet.

'Hildegard!'

'Duke Liudolf,' she said and then glanced at the two Frankish warriors. 'My father sent you?'

Duke Liudolf nodded, and Sven wondered at the frown on Hildegard's face. The duke turned to Sven, his face now a scowl. 'Where is the bishop? I demanded to see both of them.'

Sven drank his ale, taking his time before he answered, but more to control his rage at being spoken to like that in his own hall. 'Duke Liudolf, you are in my town and in my hall. You do not get to demand anything. I allowed you to see the woman because she is the one you are really here for, isn't she?'

Duke Liudolf continued to scowl at Sven when Hildegard said, 'He knows who I am, and he knows who my father is, Duke Liudolf. Bishop Bernard is frightened, but otherwise he is in good health.'

Sven smiled as Duke Liudolf bared his teeth before he turned back to Charles's mother. 'Abbess, we have much to discuss.'

'You can discuss it all later, but first you tell me what your king wants,' Sven said. He glanced at Rollo, who stayed near Hildegard, sure that the young warrior wouldn't let the Franks try anything.

Duke Liudolf turned his attention back to Sven, but this time he stayed standing as if he wanted to intimidate Sven with his height. The duke was tall, but he was still shorter than both Rollo and Alvar, so no matter how hard he tried, he did not frighten Sven. 'King Louis demands that you return his daughter and the bishop.'

Sven stroked his beard as he pretended to think about it. There was a gasp from the townspeople when they heard that the woman Sven had been keeping prisoner was the daughter of the king of East Francia, and many glared at him as if they believed the East Franks would attack their town. But Sven ignored them. 'What makes your king think he can tell me what to do?' Sven remembered the day on the beach in East Francia so many winters ago when King Louis, a young prince then, demanded that Sven hand over his only son as a hostage. His heart thudded on his chest at the memory and Sven had to drink from his cup to calm his anger down.

Duke Liudolf crossed his arms. 'Because King Louis has something you want, and he demands a trade.'

'My son,' Hildegard said, and Duke Liudolf's head snapped towards her so fast, Sven thought the man would fall over.

His eyes wide, he asked Hildegard, 'You know he has Charles? How?'

Sven smiled at the duke's confusion and answered before Charles's mother could, worried that she would tell him about the godi. 'We have our source, Duke Liudolf. We've suspected for a while now that your king has my grandson and even thought that he might want to make this trade.'

'So you accept?' Duke Liudolf recomposed himself and ran a hand through his hair.

Again, Sven drank his ale before he answered. He looked at Hildegard, seeing traces of Charles in her face, but also traces of what he remembered King Louis looked like. 'To be honest with you, I don't care about this woman or the other two. If it had been up to me, I would have sacrificed them all to Odin so he would burn your kingdom to the ground. But I want my grandson back and I'll do everything I can to do that.' He took another sip of his ale and ran his eyes over the people of Ribe as they all waited for his response. 'So aye, I accept your king's offer. Just tell me where to go so we can get this done.'

Duke Liudolf nodded. 'The beach where you first met. My king assures me you will remember where that is.'

Sven heard the gods laugh in his head as he thought of that beach again and cursed King Louis for his arrogance.

## 24

Charles sat on the bed in the small room he had been given, which was really a thin straw mattress on the floor, and stared at the small wooden cross around his neck. His father had made it for him when he was only little, and Charles had often found comfort in it over the years. But now, as he played with it in his fingers, he saw nothing but a lump of wood.

The day before, Father Leofdag had taken Charles to the church in Bremen, accompanied by two warriors who never let Charles out of their sight. The stone church was larger than any Charles had ever seen before and was much bigger than the church in Hügelburg. He had wondered if it was as big as the churches Gerold had told him about, the ones he had seen in West Francia and in Frankfurt, King Louis's capital. Charles had gaped at the size of the church, especially when he had to crane his neck backwards just to stare at its high roof. The church had a large central nave with two side aisles, the same as the church Charles had seen in Hamburg. Large windows of decorated glass adorned the walls, and he had marvelled at the depictions of images from the Bible. Images of Jesus with fishermen on a boat in rough seas and of Jesus on the cross. But there was one image that caught his attention and Charles had spent a long time staring at it. It was an image of the Virgin Mary cradling the baby Jesus. Charles had seen the image many times before, but as he stared at it, all he could think of was the woman he had been told was his mother. He wondered if she had cradled him like that when he was a baby and then got angry when he remembered she had given him up and had chased his father away so she could join the church.

Father Leofdag had prayed with the other priests and had encouraged Charles to join him, but he could not. His whole life, all Charles wanted was to serve God, to become one of His priests, but as he stood in the large stone building, he felt nothing. He did not feel the presence of God or the security he had felt in the church in Hügelburg. Charles was sure it was not because of the two warriors, or because the church was unfamiliar to him. It was because God had abandoned him and now Charles sat alone in a room in a town he didn't know.

It had been two days since they had arrived in Bremen and since Duke Liudolf had set off for Ribe. The king was staying in the large house that belonged to one of the wealthier families in Bremen, and Charles had been sent to one of the rooms they used for their servants.

There wasn't much in the room, which reminded Charles of the bedroom he had shared with his father back in Hügelburg. Just a straw mattress on the floor for him to sleep on and a stool that had a used candle on it. In one corner of the room was a dirty bucket for him to piss and shit in, though it looked and smelt like it had not been cleaned for a while. Charles had gagged when he had first entered the room because of the stench from the bucket and had to take it to the river to empty and to clean. He wasn't sure how he had not puked, but the two warriors that had followed him had kept their distance. Charles had thought of running away, certain that he could lose the warriors in the busy streets where people gave him funny stares, but he had decided against it. Even if he escaped the warriors, he would have nowhere to go.

Father Leofdag had gone to stay in the church, but he visited him as often as he could. The first night Charles was here, he had tried to think of a way he could escape and slip on board the duke's ship and then he would be back in Ribe, but then he had wondered if he wanted to go back. Thora was dead and his grandfather had lied to him about his mother. And not just that. The only reason he was back in Francia was because his grandfather had decided that fighting a battle was more important than staying with him. And Ribe had never been a home to Charles. In the few weeks he was there, he had been bullied by Rollo's son and his friends and he had been attacked by a drunk. Even the people of Ribe had treated him with disdain and the only ones that were nice to him were dead. Oda, Rollo's mother, and Alfhild. And Thora. His guardian angel killed as she tried to protect him.

Charles sighed as he let go of the cross and felt it hit his chest. He had no home, just like he had no family, and he had no God.

There was a squeaking noise as the door opened and Charles barely looked up as he expected it to be Father Leofdag, most likely with a Bible again. The previous night, he had visited Charles and had tried to get him to read from the Bible, but Charles could not. The words were empty, the promises false. An enormous shadow loomed over Charles and when he looked up, he gaped at seeing King Louis standing in his room and scrutinising him. Hs nose wrinkled, and he glanced at the bucket before he ordered one of the warriors to get rid of it.

The king was wearing a fine tunic with gold-rimmed edges and leather boots that looked like they had only been made that morning. His hair was combed back, but he wore no crown as he stood there with his hands on his hips.

'Bow before your king!' one of the warriors that came into the room with the king said, his eyebrows crunched together.

Charles could only stare, his mouth still open, as he struggled to make sense of the fact that the king of East Francia, his grandfather, was standing in front of him. Apart from his height and the fact that he had hair, he reminded Charles of Sven. He had the same scowl on his face and the same hint of violence in his eyes.

'I said bow before your king!' The warrior shot forward and raised his hand to strike Charles. Charles jumped to his feet and clenched his fist as he waited for the strike, but he fought hard not to show any fear of the man that towered over him.

King Louis raised his own hand to stop the warrior and then, in a quiet voice, he said, 'Leave us and take the guards with you.'

'Yes, my king.' The warrior glared at Charles and then left the room. Outside, Charles heard him telling the two warriors to follow him.

For what felt like a long time, he and King Louis stood there, staring at each other as if neither of them wanted to speak first. Not that Charles knew what to say.

'You look like her,' the king finally said. His nose crinkled and Charles remained silent, not knowing how to respond to that. King Louis walked to the stool and, after wiping the candle and the wax off, he sat down. The stool creaked under his weight and Charles almost hoped it would break. 'You look like your father as well.'

'Why did you make us leave after I was born?' Charles asked as the question popped into his head.

King Louis raised an eyebrow at him as if the answer was obvious, but to Charles, it wasn't. 'Your father was about your age when I took him in.'

'Took him hostage,' Charles said and felt an anger he did not understand. 'Why did you do that?'

King Louis shrugged. 'Sven the Boar.' He scowled. 'That's a name I've not said for a very long time. Sven the Boar was a very dangerous man. Every summer his ships would raid our shores, killing men and taking women and children, only to sell them as slaves. He burnt farms, killed livestock and plundered every church in sight. Even the church here in Bremen had witnessed his violence. He needed to be stopped and my father tasked me with doing that, especially after it became clear that the king of Denmark could not control him.'

'So you took my father?' Charles remembered the story his grandfather had told him of that day. Of the battle he had fought and lost and how he had watched Charles's father disappear in the distance as he was forced to sail away without him. Charles had always believed what King Louis had done was a good thing. His father had found God and Charles had been certain his path lay in the church. But now, he wasn't so sure any more.

'We tried fighting him, but he always slipped away just before my men arrived. And then God smiled on us and we found an ally we did not expect. His own brother.'

Charles scowled as he remembered the first night in Ribe. How Sven's brother had laughed when Sven had discovered he had been the one who had betrayed him.

'He helped us set a trap for Sven and made sure that he brought his only son with. It was the only way I knew we could stop the attacks on good Christian people.' King Louis looked at him, his eyes searching Charles's. 'You are a Christian. Do you think what I did was wrong?'

Charles's eyes widened at the unexpected question. He stammered as he tried to find the right answer, but he took a deep breath and thought about it. The only reason he was here was because his father was raised by the king and because he had converted to Christianity. 'No, I guess not. But you had threatened to kill him. You told my grandfather that.'

King Louis nodded. 'Yes, I did.'

'But why?'

The king's face hardened. 'Because it is my God-given duty to protect my lands and people from the heathens that plague us every summer. If that means killing a child to do that, then that is what I must do. One day God will judge me for that action and only He can tell me if I was wrong in doing that.'

Charles frowned as he thought about that, but still he didn't agree. 'But killing children is not very Christian-like.'

King Louis gave him that look that Charles didn't like. The one adults liked to give children. 'Boy, there is much you need to learn about life.'

Charles clenched his fists again, something the king noticed and smiled at. 'Then why didn't you kill my father?'

King Louis shrugged. 'Because Sven the Boar vanished and over time, I came to like your father. He was smart and saw the light of God. And when he became a man, he turned into a fine warrior.'

'My father told me many stories about how he fought for you.' Charles frowned. 'If you liked my father so much, then why did he have to leave after I was born?'

Again, the king's face darkened and Charles wondered if it had been a good idea to ask that question. But it was one that had been burning inside of him since the day his father had told him he had once fought for the king of East Francia. 'Because of you, boy.'

Again, Charles's eyes widened. 'Me?'

'What your father did to my daughter was unforgivable. Even if she claimed she loved him. If it weren't for Duke Liudolf and

Bishop Bernard, both you and your father would have been killed.'

Charles was taken aback by the anger he saw in King Louis. He took a step backwards, instinctively making sure he was out of reach, and then he realised something. 'You're not going to give me back to my grandfather, are you?'

King Louis smiled. 'Boy, your grandfather will be lucky if he leaves that beach alive. I made the mistake of letting him live the last time we met. I thought that by taking his son, I had won. But the son of Sven hurt me more than Sven ever did.'

Charles gritted his teeth as his anger took hold of him. He tried to remember everything Thora had taught him, but then the king stood up and Charles realised he could never attack a grown man. Not physically, anyway. But there was one way he could hurt the king. Through clenched teeth, Charles said, 'My grandfather has your cross. The one that belonged to Charlemagne.'

King Louis shot forward and grabbed Charles by his tunic, and lifted him off his feet. It happened so fast that Charles didn't even have time to think of getting out of the way. Eyes, dark with fury, bored into him. 'You're lying to me, boy.'

Charles's heart raced, and he felt the blood drain from his face. Duke Liudolf had warned him not to tell the king about the cross. But Charles was angry at what the king had said and wanted to hurt him. 'My mother gave it to my father after I was born.'

King Louis glared at Charles, his face turning dark red before he let go of Charles. Charles hit the ground and grimaced at the pain as the king grabbed the stool in his room and smashed it against the wall. He turned to face Charles again, who jumped to his feet and wished he had kept quiet about the cross. 'Where is the cross?'

'My grandfather has it and he will kill you with it.' Charles tried to be strong and stood as tall as he could as he faced the furious king. But his heart was racing even faster now, and he felt like he might piss himself again, especially when the king took a step towards him, his hands balled into huge fists.

But then the door opened and the king's men rushed in. The king turned to them. 'I told you not to disturb me!'

'M... my king.' One of the warrior's eyes fell on the broken stool and he frowned.

King Louis glared at Charles before he took a deep breath. 'You just made sure that your grandfather doesn't leave that beach alive.'

The king turned and left the room; the warriors following him, after frowning at Charles. One of them threw the bucket back into the room, its newly added contents spilling all over the floor as Charles dropped to his knees and gripped the cross around his neck. This time, he did pray to God.

*I know you are angry at me, but I beg you. Protect my grandfather. Even if he is a heathen.*

## 25

Sven wiped the sweat from his brow and growled at Rollo's smirk.

'Are you sure you've been training while I was in Hedeby? You've got worse.' The young warrior checked his shield, pretending not to see any damage on it.

Sven resisted the urge to attack the bastard, and not just because he knew that was what Rollo wanted him to do. Sven's hand trembled from exhaustion as he glanced at Duke Liudolf's ship, still docked in the wharf. It was the day after he had arrived, and Sven was still furious. Although, he wasn't really sure who at. Louis of East Francia for using his grandson to control him, much like he had used Torkel to do the same? Duke Liudolf for delivering the message? Or because King Louis wanted them to meet on that beach. Sven should have known that Louis would make him go back to that beach on the north coast of East Francia. The beach that had started Sven's downfall. The beach the gods had used to punish Sven for his arrogance. Sven's hand went to the Mjöllnir around his neck as his eyes scanned the skies. In the distance, he saw an eagle hovering above the clouds while closer ravens circled where they had dumped the corpses of those the new would-be king of Denmark had executed a few days ago. But nothing to tell Sven what he needed to do.

'Do you think you can trust him?' Rollo asked.

'Trust who?' Sven shifted his attention to the house where Charles's mother was. The duke was in there now, talking to Hildegard. Sven wondered what plots they were hatching.

'King Louis.'

Sven saw the frown on Rollo's face. He shook his head. 'As much as Fenrir trusted the gods when they tried to bind him with Gleipnir.'

'Aye,' Rollo said and the two of them stood in silence. Around them, the warriors of Ribe were training hard under the watchful eye of Randolf, an old warrior who was too old to stand in the shield wall, so they used him to train the children and young warriors. The man was harsh and if you didn't do as he commanded, you were likely to leave the training ground with a few bruises. It didn't matter how old or experienced you were. Sven watched as Randolf barked an order and the warriors he was training all jogged in a shield wall, their faces strained as they all tried to keep pace with each other. Thora had believed it was unnecessary. The warriors of Ribe had proven themselves during the battle at Jelling and the fights against the raiders since, but Sven felt that something was coming and he wanted the men to be ready.

Thora was there as well, training by herself, which was something old Randolf was not keen on. He felt it distracted the men and when he had tried to force her to join the others in the shield wall, he ended up with a new bruise. So now he left her alone, but the other warriors were suffering for his humiliation.

'You know, I beat her in a fight,' Rollo said when he saw who Sven was looking at.

Sven glanced at Rollo. 'I'm sure that's what she wanted you to think.' He watched as Thora trained with a shield and sword, her movements crisp and swift. Sven might not have seen her fight in a shield wall, but he remembered how she had fought the men chasing them from Hedeby earlier in the summer.

Rollo raised an eyebrow, but before he could say anything, Alvar approached from the hall with a scowl on his face.

'Jarl Sven, the scouts have returned and saw nothing.'

Now it was Sven's turn to scowl. He was convinced that Torgeir was planning something and so he had sent scouts out to follow the king's entourage and to scout the nearby lands. He wasn't really sure what he had expected them to find, but that they found nothing only made him more nervous. 'Are you sure?'

Rollo scratched his head. 'Why do you think Ribe is in danger? I've spoken to this Horik. He seems like a good man. All he wants is to protect Denmark. And Jarl Hovi is keen on getting the Christians out of Denmark. Thought you'd approve of that.'

Sven scanned the skies again. 'It's not Horik or Hovi I'm concerned about.' What Sven didn't tell them was that his gut told him something was coming, but he was sure these young warriors would not understand that. They had not lived the life he had. They had not had to rely on their instincts like he had to to survive. And his uncle's words still echoed in his head, which only reinforced his gut feeling.

'You really think that Torgeir is planning something?' Rollo asked.

'You said yourself you saw Ivor in Hedeby. Why else would he be in Hedeby if not to make a deal with Torgeir?'

'Aye, but I never saw them talking to each other.'

'And neither did you spend any time in the hall. You said so yourself.'

Rollo nodded, and they all turned as Randolf berated a

warrior who had dropped to his knees. 'He's working them too hard.'

'Aye, well you go tell him that,' Sven said and then turned to Alvar, who was shuffling on his feet. 'What?'

'They found Haldor.'

Sven raised an eyebrow. Haldor had not been seen for many days and Audhild, Thora's cousin and Haldor's wife, had been worried sick. Barely a day went by where she didn't come to the hall and ask for Sven's aid to find him. But Sven had been glad that the bastard had gone, especially after he had struck Charles. 'Where?'

'In one of the abandoned houses near the wall. On the east side of the town. His throat cut open.'

Sven scowled and glanced at Rollo, who had the same response. Many of the houses in Ribe stood empty because many people had left after Sven had killed his brother Bjarni, who had been the jarl of Ribe. They had heard stories of what he had been like as jarl when he had been younger or they just didn't want him as their jarl. So they had left. But that had weakened Ribe because many of those who had left were warriors. Sven had believed they would find the bastard drunk in another town. But to find him dead in Ribe only made Sven more nervous. 'You still think I'm overreacting?' he asked Rollo.

Rollo frowned. 'How long has he been dead?'

Alvar shrugged. 'Looks like many days. He was definitely dead before Horik arrived.'

Sven and Rollo scratched their beards as they wondered about that.

'It could be the Frank that stole the cross,' Thora said, her face glistening with sweat and surprising all of them, as they hadn't heard her approach.

Sven grunted as he realised she could be correct.

'Someone must have told him where to find Charles's belongings,' Rollo agreed. 'And Haldor had reason to want to hurt you.'

Sven clenched his fist and wished that he had killed Haldor that day. But he didn't because he wanted to be different from the way he had been when he was younger. He wanted to be a better jarl, just like he wanted to be a better grandfather than he was a father. But Sven was failing at both.

'I should go to Audhild,' Thora said and walked towards her cousin's house. Sven watched her walk away and knew that he'd be seeing more of her aunt and Jorlaug in the hall now. Although he wasn't sure how he felt about that. As much as their constant presence in the hall was frustrating, they made the building seem alive again.

'You never found the Frank who stole the cross?' Rollo asked.

Alvar shook his head as Sven remembered fighting the bastard in the sleeping quarters. 'We searched all the houses and even the traders' carts.'

'And you didn't see Haldor when you searched the houses?' Rollo raised an eyebrow.

Alvar shrugged. 'I didn't search those houses, but I'm sure the men who did would have said anything if they had.'

'You're assuming they searched those houses, Alvar,' Sven said and walked back to the hall. He needed a drink and to make sense of what was going on. As he walked to the hall, Sven glanced at the warriors as they trained and wondered for the first time if he could really trust any of them. They had all fought hard during the battle at Jelling, but that had been for the gold he had promised them. But now, when there was nothing he could give them, could he really depend on them the same way he could depend on Thora, Rollo and Alvar? He shook his head to get the thoughts out of his mind and called for some ale before he sat down on his bench. His cup only just touched his lips when Duke Liudolf walked into the hall with two of his warriors on either side of him. Sven lowered the cup and sighed when the man stopped in front of him. 'You're still here then?'

Duke Liudolf nodded. 'I leave tomorrow.'

'Good.' Sven drank his ale and then raised an eyebrow when he saw the duke was still standing there. 'What, in Thor's name, do you want?'

'I plan to take the bishop back with me. You don't need him, it's the abbess you need and—'

'Fine, and take that snake as well, before he ends up dead.'

Duke Liudolf's eyes widened at Sven agreeing so fast, but he was right. Sven had no need for the old snivelling bastard and if he could get rid of Gerold as well, then Odin was, for once, smiling on him.

'So you're not going to argue about this?' Duke Liudolf's brow creased. Even the two warriors behind him looked confused, but Sven ignored them. Instead, he offered Duke Liudolf a seat.

'Charles told me you knew my son well.' Duke Liudolf nodded, but his face was uncertain. Sven called for a thrall to bring him and his men ale and then he said, 'Tell me about my boy.'

Duke Liudolf sat down. 'What do you want to know?'

'Everything since the day you first met him. I want to know what kind of man he was.'

'You want to know if he was like you?' Duke Liudolf almost sneered.

Sven glanced at the hearth fire a thrall was tending to, his eyes glazing over as he thought about his life. 'No, I want to know if he was better than me.'

Duke Liudolf hesitated and then nodded. He told Sven of how he had first met Torkel on the beach in Francia.

'You were there?' Sven asked as he searched his memory for Duke Liudolf's face, but he could not remember seeing him there.

'I was,' Duke Liudolf said and carried on with his story. He told Sven of how Torkel had been convinced that his father would come and save him and Sven felt his guilt eating away at him for letting his boy down. He had tried to get his son back, but the gods were against him and he had been stopped by a storm only Njörd could have sent. Duke Liudolf explained how, after a few years, Torkel had given up on his father saving him and had converted to Christianity when he realised he would spend the rest of his life living amongst the Franks. He told Sven how he had spent a lot of time with the young daughter of King Louis and how he earned a reputation as one of King Louis's best warriors. 'No one fought more fiercely than Torkel. It was like his short stature gave him the strength to fight like a bear.'

'Like a boar,' Sven said, but more to himself.

Duke Liudolf nodded and carried on telling the tale of Torkel. Sven felt the tears build up in his eyes as he listened to Duke Liudolf, and on more than one occasion, he had to cuff the tears away.

'One hell of a fighter the Dane was,' one of the warriors sitting with Duke Liudolf said. Sven looked at the man and saw he was older than the other warrior and appeared to be the same age as the duke. 'Got in a drunken brawl with him once. The bastard was muttering these words to himself, fight harder than him, fight harder than him, over and over.' The warrior laughed, and Sven smiled. That was the advice he had given to Torkel that day on the beach. Like him, Torkel had been short. Sven had learnt to use it as an advantage, and he was glad that his son had done so as well. 'Thought the Dane had lost his wits, but by God, did he batter me.' The man laughed even louder.

'Your son was a great man, Jarl Sven,' Duke Liudolf said. 'Great enough for the daughter of the king to fall in love with him. My heart broke the day he died.'

'He died protecting his son.' The words came out of Sven as he remembered what Charles had told him of that day.

'Charles meant everything to him.' Duke Liudolf nodded.

'As he does to me,' Sven said, and then sighed. He looked around the hall and saw that it had filled up with warriors and townspeople, all of them eating their evening meals. Rollo was there with his wife and son, sitting with Alvar and two other warriors Sven knew were close friends of Rollo's. He bent his neck and looked outside of the hall door and raised an eyebrow when he saw it had gone dark. He had not realised how long they had been sitting there and was about to comment on that when there was a scream from outside the hall.

Everyone jumped to their feet as Rollo started shouting out orders to the warriors. Sven and Duke Liudolf glared at each other, both of them suspecting the other of plotting something when Jorlaug came running into the hall.

'Sven! Sven! There's a crazy old man outside, and he's got another crazy old man with him.'

Sven's heart skipped a beat when he realised what the little girl was saying and knew he should have expected something like this to happen.

'What is the little girl saying?' Duke Liudolf asked, his hand on the knife in his belt. Even though his warriors weren't allowed any weapons in the hall, Sven had allowed the duke to keep the knife.

'That something bad is about to happen.' Sven rushed to the door, having to push others out of the way. Someone struck him on his weak leg and it took all of Sven's strength not to fall over, but when he glared at those around him, he saw only confused and frightened faces.

'By God!' Duke Liudolf exclaimed as they all got outside the hall and saw the old godi standing there, a sharp knife in his hand and the old Christian priest naked and on his knees in front of him.

'Odin's balls,' Sven muttered as he looked towards the house where his prisoners were kept and wondered how the godi had got hold of the priest. He prayed that the ancient fool hadn't harmed Charles's mother.

'Liudolf, save me! For heaven's sake, do something!' the old priest cried out, his thin, pale, wrinkled body trembling as the smell of piss filled the air. Wide eyes implored Duke Liudolf and his men to help him, as his hands were clasped in front of him.

Duke Liudolf glared at Sven as he jabbed his finger at the godi. 'What in God's name is the meaning of this? Who is that old fool?'

'He's one of our priests, a godi.' Sven kept his eyes fixed on his uncle.

'Tell him to stop this at once, or there will be consequences!'

Sven gritted his teeth at being spoken to like that in his own town by the Frank and was tempted to cut the bastard down, but he knew the man was right. Odinson could not do what he was about to do, whatever that was. Although Sven knew he could not stop the old bastard. 'The godi don't answer to any man on Midgard. They only answer to the gods.'

The duke's men came rushing towards the hall from their ship, all of them brandishing their weapons, which only angered the townspeople. Rollo summoned the warriors to block their path and the two groups of warriors stood facing each other, all the while Odinson was cackling over the chaos he had unleashed. Sven scanned the surrounding houses, wondering if the godi's servant was hiding in the shadows with his bow. He must have helped the godi slip into the house and strip the old priest.

Thora appeared by Sven's side, her cousin and aunt with her. 'Sven, you have to do something.'

Sven scrutinised the house and saw no sign of the warriors who were supposed to be guarding the Franks. But then, he knew they would not have stopped the godi. He spoke for the gods, and even the most experienced warriors feared him. Sven glanced at the night sky, but saw nothing to tell him what he should do. So he took a deep breath and walked towards the godi. 'Odinson, what are you doing?'

Odinson laughed and there was a gasp when his servant dragged Charles's mother out of the house, her hands tied behind her back and his knife at her throat. Sven shook his head and knew that was going to be too much for the Franks.

This was confirmed when Duke Liudolf shouted, 'Kill them all! Protect the abbess and the bishop!'

But before his warriors could charge at Ribe's warriors, the old godi screamed in flawless Frankish, 'Take one step closer and the ground will split open and you all will fall into the fires of your hell! That is my promise to you. A promise from your God and mine!'

The Frankish warriors all hesitated and looked at the duke, who had paled when he heard the words.

Sven scowled as he wondered why the gods enjoyed fucking with him so much. 'Odinson, in the name of the gods and the nine realms, what are you doing?'

The old godi stared at Sven, his eyes filled with fire. 'I am protecting you from what is to come, Sven the Boar. I am protecting what is yours and mine, so it can go on long after Ragnarök.'

The townspeople broke out in whispers, as they must have been wondering what the godi meant by that. Even Thora was frowning. Sven took a step back, his hand gripping the Mjöllnir around his neck. The Mjöllnir that had belonged to his father and his father before him.

'Liudolf, help me!' the old priest pleaded again, his eyes filled with terror as he sensed what was coming.

Duke Liudolf stared at Sven, his eyes wide and face pale. 'Jarl Sven, stop this at once!'

Sven stared at the godi, who brought his knife down and held it under the wrinkled chin of the priest. 'The gods demand this, Sven. Would you deny the gods again? Remember what happened the last time you turned your back on them.'

The people of Ribe fell silent as they watched, all of them knowing they were about to witness a powerful sacrifice. The Frankish warriors too were silent, many of them crossing themselves and a few even on their knees, their hands clasped in front of them as they prayed. Duke Liudolf looked like he was about to faint, but no one moved. Even Sven felt like something was gripping him, holding him in place.

'Sven,' Thora appealed, but even she must have known there was nothing they could do.

The godi looked up at the same time as the clouds parted to reveal a large moon. People gasped, and many gripped the Mjöllnir pendants they wore around their necks. 'Odin, All-Father, lover of the battle frenzy! Thor, protector of gods and men. Hear me now! See me now! Accept this offering in the name of Sven the Boar! Aid him as he slaughters his enemies and sends them to fill the benches of Valhalla! Open his eyes so he can see the danger he is in!' With one swift movement, the godi pulled his hand back and the old priest's eyes bulged as his blood leaked down his chest and soaked into the soil of Ribe.

'Bastard!' Duke Liudolf roared, and was about to attack the godi when a horn blew from the gates.

## 26

'We're under attack!' A warrior came racing down the main road, his leather jerkin covered in blood and with a large gash on his cheek. 'We're under attack!'

'What's happening? Who is attacking us?' Sven asked, his mind reeling at this sudden turn. He had been expecting an attack, but not this soon and not at night. Duke Liudolf stopped and turned to face Sven, his confusion all over his face.

Fear gripped the people of Ribe as women and children screamed and old men cried out in despair. Dogs barked from all over the town, a few even fighting with each other, as they must have sensed the sudden fear in the air, while people fell to their knees and prayed to the gods to protect them. But Sven felt like they were wasting their time. The gods allowed this attack to happen because it amused them.

Sven shook his head, trying to clear the fog caused by the shock of the attack. But that was what his attackers had wanted. That was why they attacked now. They wanted the confusion because that would be their biggest weapon. But Sven still struggled to get his thoughts together. Ribe had never been attacked, not in his lifetime, and in his shock, Sven couldn't picture the town in his mind, so he could get the defences ready. The warriors of Ribe, still facing the Frankish warriors, all looked towards Sven and Rollo as they waited for their orders, but Sven was too busy trying to make sense of what was happening. He turned to where the godi was, wondering if the ancient bastard had known about the attack, but then his eyes widened when he saw only the corpse of the Christian priest, his dark blood soaking into the soil. Sven glanced towards the house, where the godi's servant was with Charles's mother, but saw only the woman on her knees, eyes wide as she stared at the dead priest.

Thora pulled her sword free from its scabbard. 'All the women and children in the hall! Those too old to fight in the hall! Now!'

'Get to the ship! We'll meet you there!' Duke Liudolf shouted at his men who stood frozen as they still faced the Danes. His men were about to protest, but then the duke shouted, 'Now!' Duke Liudolf then grabbed the two warriors that were still with him. 'The abbess! Save the abbess!' He must have seen the same Sven had and saw his chance to get Charles's mother back for his king.

Sven felt his anger explode in him, as if Thor himself had taken hold of his body, and before Duke Liudolf could take two steps, Sven punched him in the side. Duke Liudolf grunted and, as he bent over, Sven punched him in the side of his head, knocking him to the ground. 'Don't let the Franks get the woman!' Sven roared but doubted anyone could hear him in the chaos of screams and people rushing to the hall. Duke Liudolf's two men realised what was happening and, as they hesitated, Sven pulled his sword from his scabbard and stabbed one of them in the back. Before the second warrior could retaliate, Thora stepped in front of him and opened his neck with her sword. The warrior gaped at her as he dropped to his knees, his blood soaking into his tunic that he wore under his brynja, and then he dropped to the ground as his life left him. *Another sacrifice to the gods*, Sven thought as he checked to make sure that Charles's mother was still where he had last seen her.

Rollo had snapped out of his shock and was repeating Thora's commands. Women grabbed their children and dragged them into the hall, while old folks rushed to join them as quickly as their old legs could take them. 'Alvar, take as many men as you need! Protect the gates! Asbjorn! Grab some men and get shields for everyone!'

Alvar nodded at Rollo and called for most of the men to follow him as they all ran towards the town gates. Only a few of the warriors wore armour and none of them had any shields with them. But they all had their weapons. Asbjorn, an experienced warrior, gathered some of the younger warriors and they rushed to the hall to get shields for everyone.

'Stop!' Sven ordered, his voice thundering over the chaos. Everyone stopped what they were doing, including the women and children rushing for the hall. 'The gates will be lost already. We need to protect the people in the hall.' Sven closed his eyes, trying to picture Ribe, but again, he couldn't. He turned to the naked body of the Christian priest, which was even paler in the moonlight. Sven wondered again if the godi had known about the attack and if that was the reason he had made the sacrifice to the gods. If that was the case, then Sven could only hope that Odin had accepted the godi's offering, because he knew he needed the gods' help to survive this. Shaking his head to clear his mind, Sven turned to the warriors. 'Get your armour on! Asbjorn, get those shields! We form a shield wall on the main road. We protect the hall and everyone in it!'

The warriors all hesitated at first, some of them even glancing at Rollo, but then Thora shouted, 'You heard the jarl! Move, now!' She handed Sven a shield which Jorlaug had brought her. Luckily for Sven, he was already wearing his brynja, as he had never taken it off after his training session with Rollo earlier in the day.

'Where's the godi?' Rollo stared at the corpse of the priest, only now realising the godi was gone. Everyone looked towards the square in front of the hall where the godi had been before. But before anyone could answer, the horns blew from the gate again. And then more joined them.

Sven ignored the question and turned to the warrior who had brought him news of the attack. 'How many men are there? Who is attacking us?'

'I... I don't know. They attacked us from behind, from inside the town. They opened the gates.' As the warrior answered, Duke Liudolf stirred and tried to crawl towards Charles's mother. Sven kicked him in the stomach.

'You're not going anywhere,' Sven said in Frankish, the words almost a growl. Duke Liudolf looked at Sven and bared his teeth. But before he could say anything, Sven knocked him out with the pommel of his sword. 'Rollo, tie the bastard up and put him in the hall. Thora, grab Charles's mother and do the same.'

Rollo nodded and got to it while Thora asked, 'What about Gerold?'

Sven gritted his teeth. He hoped the godi had killed the bastard, but knew he wouldn't be so lucky. Just like he knew Gerold could cause problems if Sven ignored him. 'Kill him if he still lives.' Sven turned to the warrior who came from the gate in front of him, the man's face pale with fear. 'Who attacked you from inside? Men of Ribe? How many were they?'

The warrior shook his head. 'I didn't really see them. They came out of nowhere.'

'The men are ready.' Alvar arrived at Sven's side with his brynja on and his sword in his hand. Sven scanned the open space in front of the hall and saw the warriors of Ribe wearing armour and ready for battle. He still had no idea who was attacking Ribe or how many men they had, but he knew these warriors would all die to protect their homes. Sven just hoped that would be enough.

'They're coming!'

Sven turned towards the gates and saw their attackers storming down the main road, brandishing their weapons in the air and crying out to the gods. He tried to see the leader of the group, but no one stood out.

'Shield wall!' Rollo ordered and the men of Ribe rushed towards the main road and formed a shield wall, with Rollo in the centre of the front rank. Sven scowled at the other streets that led to the hall and the market from between the other houses, and hoped that whoever led the attacking army was not smart enough to send men around the shield wall.

He then glanced at the moon and gripped the Mjöllnir around his neck, again praying that his uncle's sacrifice was accepted by the gods.

\* \* \*

Thora gripped her sword in front of her as she approached the house where Charles's mother had been staying with Gerold and the old priest. Hildegard was in the hall, her hands tied up and guarded by young men and girls who knew how to fight, but were still too young to stand in the shield wall. They would be the last defence, though, if their attackers got into the hall. Jorlaug was there as well, with an eating knife in her hand and threatening to kill the Franks if they moved. Thora struggled to understand why the young girl was so drawn to violence. But then she guessed the stories she had been told of Thora hadn't helped. Audhild, her cousin, had told her how Ingvild would tell Jorlaug all the stories she had heard in the market about Thora.

Thora still did not understand how the godi had got into the town and not only got the old priest out of the house, but got him to undress as well. She suppressed the shiver that ran down her spine as she wondered what magic he had used to do all of that. Her mother had told her enough stories about Odinson to know the man was connected to the gods. How else could you explain the fact that he still lived when he was already old, when her father had been young? But still, to do what he had done. This time, Thora couldn't stop the shiver as she pictured the old priest, frail and naked, and terrified. No man needed to die like that.

She hesitated as she got to the door of the house and held her shield in front of her. There was no light inside, which meant that Thora could not see if Gerold was still in there, or if he was still alive. She sniffed the air, but could not smell any blood. That didn't mean that Gerold was still alive though. The godi could have killed him in other ways. But Thora knew she needed to be wary. Gerold was as sly as Loki and just as dangerous.

Thora took a deep breath and stepped into the house. No sooner had she entered when her foot caught something on the floor. Suspecting an attack, Thora turned and ducked behind her shield. She waited a few heartbeats and when nothing happened, Thora kicked the object on the floor and realised it was clothing. She wondered if it was the old priest's and was about to kick it to one side when she sensed movement behind her.

She twisted out of the way as something missed her, but then Gerold crashed into her and she bounced off the wall of the house. Gerold reacted faster and stabbed at Thora with a broken chair leg, but Thora brought her shield up and as soon as Gerold's wooden stake struck her shield, she kicked him in the groin. Gerold made a noise as if the air had been sucked out of him and dropped to his knees.

'Still think you are better than me?' Thora sneered and, as he looked up, she struck him on the head with the rim of her shield, knocking him out and cutting his head open. But before she could do anything else, she heard the sounds of shields coming together and knew she had to get out there and defend Ribe.

Thora glanced at the prone Gerold. Sven had told her to kill him, but she felt he was no threat and decided not to. She would deal with Sven's anger if they survived the attack. After tying Gerold's hands and feet with the old priest's clothing, she left the house. Thora prayed it was not too late to save Ribe, especially her aunt, cousin and young Jorlaug. This world was cruel to women who could not defend themselves. That was the reason her father had taught Thora how to fight with every weapon known to man and it was the mockery of other men which had driven her on to become a better warrior.

But Audhild had never learnt how to use a sword or a spear, she had never learnt how to kill with an axe, and Ingvild was too old and even though her mind was strong, her body was weak. That was why Thora had to fight for them. Around her, she caught flashes as warriors ran between the houses. She heard metal striking metal and men cursing the gods and each other. Thora ran around one house and almost bumped into a warrior. The man screamed, more in fright, and swung his axe at Thora, who got her shield up to block the blow. She felt the strain in her stomach from her wound and prayed to Frigg that she didn't tear it open as she brought her sword around to kill the warrior in front of her. But then, in the dim light of the moon, she recognised him as one of Ribe's men and twisted her sword away from him.

'Thora, by the gods!'

'Aye,' Thora said, glad she hadn't just killed one of Ribe's defenders. 'Get to the hall!' she told the man. 'Sven and Rollo have formed the shield wall.'

'Sven and Rollo can fuck themselves!' The man's face

contorted with anger. He shoved her back with his shield and swung his axe at her head.

Thora ducked under the axe and sliced the warrior's leg open and as the man dropped to his knees, she grabbed his hair and pulled his head back, a scowl on her face. 'You fight with the enemy?'

The warrior grimaced. 'Sven is the enemy! The fat dwarf cursed this town and he must die for that!'

'Aye, you tell him that in Valhalla one day.' Thora stepped back and chopped her sword at the bastard's neck. Blood sprayed into the darkness as she pulled her sword free and frowned. How many more of Ribe's men were helping the attackers? And how many of them were standing beside Sven in the shield wall, ready to stab him in the back? Thora stood frozen as she tried to figure out what was happening. She had to warn Sven of the danger he was in. For a moment, she wondered if that was what the godi was trying to warn Sven of. As she struggled with her thoughts, another warrior shot out of the darkness and stabbed at her with his sword. Instinct made Thora lift her shield, but the blow sent her staggering backwards.

'Time to die, bitch!' the large warrior said, his face more of a leer than a smile. 'Then I will fuck you silly.'

Thora shook her head. She had heard this many times before. 'I bet that's the only way you get to fuck anyone.'

The warrior raised an eyebrow at her response and then roared as he attacked her. Thora deflected his stab with her shield and tried to cut his exposed side, but the man moved fast and twisted out of the way. He turned and brought his shield around to strike her with its rim, but Thora ducked under the shield and stabbed the larger man in the stomach. Unfortunately for her, the warrior wore a brynja, so even though he grunted and took a step back, her sword did no more damage other than to bruise him.

The warrior raised his sword and brought it down on Thora, who lifted her shield to block the blow, but the man's strength knocked her to her knees. Thora growled. She did not have time for this. She needed to warn Sven. Fighting this bastard was not part of her plan. As the man lifted his sword to chop down on her again, Thora said, 'Fuck this, you ugly bastard.' And she stabbed him between the legs. The warrior squealed as her sword severed his testicles, the blood reddening her blade before she pulled it free. He dropped to his knees, his hands cupping his crotch as he glared at her.

'You bitch!'

'Aye, tell me something I don't know.' Thora rammed her sword through the man's throat and then sprinted towards Sven to warn him of the real danger he was in.

## 27

Sven stabbed out with his sword and felt it strike a shield before he pulled it back.

'Die, dwarf!' His opponent chopped down with his axe, which Sven deflected with his shield before he headbutted the man in the chest because the warrior was too big for Sven to reach his face. As the man staggered back, Sven dragged his sword across the bastard's knee, causing him to drop to the ground, his eyes wide, before Sven crushed his skull with the rim of his shield.

Rollo, fighting on his right, buried his axe in another warrior's skull, the force of his blow splitting the man's helmet but leaving his axe stuck. As Rollo struggled to free it, another of the enemy rushed in to slay the giant warrior. But as he raised his sword to kill Rollo, Sven stabbed him through the armpit. The warrior's eyes bulged as he stared at Sven, and then he frowned before Sven pulled his sword free and he dropped dead to the ground. Rollo nodded his thanks and freed his axe before he charged at the enemy, calling for their deaths. Sven took a moment to get his bearings and see how the fight was going, but it was difficult to see anything as thick clouds now covered the moon. It was mayhem as they fought under the dim light of the night, barely able to tell friend from foe and on more than one occasion one of Ribe's men had attacked Sven, only to back off when they saw it was him, or when Rollo shouted at them. Men cursed those they were fighting, while some called out for the gods. Dogs barked and howled in the darkness and at one point Sven was sure he heard a cat screech. But the overwhelming sound was of metal striking metal and of shields coming together, which resembled the sound of Thor's fury. At least it was not raining, Sven thought, and then he wondered where Thora was. The last he had seen of her was when she went to kill Gerold, but he had been distracted by more warriors streaming out of the side streets and had not seen her leave the house. Sven could only pray to the gods that Gerold had not got to her as he blocked a spear aimed at his head. He cut the spear shaft in two and the young warrior wielding it paled. If it wasn't for the darkness, Sven might have seen him piss his pants before he sliced his neck open.

Sven still had no idea who he was fighting or how many of the bastards there were. But he was sure there were many more of the enemy than his own force. It didn't help that his army had to be split in two. Alvar led most of Ribe's warriors as they fought the enemy shield wall on the main road, while Sven and Rollo protected their rear from the enemy warriors who ran around the houses to get to the hall. But it was chaos, and it was a mess, and Sven knew the gods were enjoying this. Torches fluttered in the breeze, their dancing shadows playing tricks on his eyes and on more than a few occasions Sven thought he saw movement to the side as he fought, only to turn and face nothing.

Rollo kicked one man to the ground, the warrior beside him stabbing the enemy through the neck, as Rollo stepped forward and shoved another back by punching out with his shield. Sven ducked under an axe that swung at his head and knocked it away with the rim of his shield before he cut his attacker's leg. The man screamed, but before the scream could finish, Sven punched him in the face with the rim of his shield. The warrior dropped to the ground, most of his front teeth broken or missing.

'Protect the hall!' Sven roared as he blocked another attack and stabbed the warrior through the neck. Blood sprayed over Sven's face as he pulled his sword free, blinding him. His heart skipped when he heard another warrior scream for his death, but Rollo barged his attacker to the ground before killing him with his one-handed axe.

'There are too many of the bastards!' Rollo blocked another blow and kicked his attacker's legs out from under him, before stamping on his neck.

Sven wiped the blood from his face and wished he had his helmet. He glanced over his shoulder at the hall, his heart racing, as he feared he might not be able to protect the people inside. What made it worse was that Sven didn't know who he wanted to protect more. The people of Ribe who hated him and didn't want him here, or Hildegard, Charles's mother, and the key to getting his grandson back. 'Just keep fighting!'

'What do you think I'm doing?' Rollo roared back as he blocked a sword with his shield.

Sven shoulder barged Rollo's attacker out of the way before Rollo killed him. 'Fight, you bastards of Ribe! Fight for your homes and your family! Show these bastards who we are!'

Those around him who heard his call roared as Rollo called out to the gods and Sven rushed at warriors who came surging out of the side streets. But before he even reached them, he heard someone shout.

'The dwarf is mine!'

Sven stopped and growled when he saw the warrior stepping out of the shadows, his face painted red with fresh blood. 'Hallr. So you are Torgeir's pet?'

'I am no one's pet.'

Sven raised an eyebrow. 'So you attacked Ribe all by yourself?' Sven glanced around him as the fight for the town continued. 'I didn't know you had so many men.'

Hallr roared and attacked. He swung his sword at Sven's head, who blocked with his shield and stabbed at Hallr's leg. Hallr twisted out of the way, but Sven rushed him and shoulder barged Hallr before he could do anything about it. Hallr hit the ground, but quickly rolled to his feet and ducked behind his shield to block Sven's sword.

'Fall back! Fall back to the hall!' Alvar ordered and Hallr laughed.

'You're losing, Sven. The mighty Sven the Boar can't even defend his own town.'

Sven clenched his jaw and risked a glance to see the shield wall on the main road falling back and leaving many bodies behind, although Sven could not tell if the dead warriors belonged to Ribe or to Hallr. He gritted his teeth and looked at the naked body of the old priest, his skin as pale as the moon, but battered and bruised as warriors trampled over him. The godi had been convinced that by killing the priest, the gods would be on Sven's side, but so far it looked like they wanted him to lose. Sven growled, refusing to believe that the gods had turned against him. Not after a sacrifice like that. His family had held on to Ribe since his grandfather had first become jarl, and he would not dishonour them by letting it fall into the hands of the red-faced worm in front of him. Sven wiped the blood off his scalp, so the raven tattoo on his head was visible for Odin to see. The gods were with him. Sven was certain of it. He just needed to remind them of that. Turning his attention back to Hallr as the shield wall reformed by the hall with Rollo and Alvar at the centre, Sven said, 'The only way a worm like you could even think of winning is by attacking at night!'

'I am no worm, I am Hallr Red-Face!' Hallr roared. 'Kill them all!'

'Sven!' Rollo shouted. 'Get back! Get in the shield wall!'

But Sven ignored the giant warrior as he charged at Hallr. Hallr raised his eyebrows at the unexpected attack, but lifted his shield to block Sven's sword.

'This is my town!' Sven hacked at Hallr's shield, not giving the red-faced jarl a chance to attack himself, as he was forced to duck behind his shield. Sven beat his sword on the bastard's shield one more time before he shoulder barged Hallr's shield. The attack drove Hallr back, and he tripped over the body of the dead priest. Hallr's eyes widened as he fell, and he just got his shield up in time to block Sven's sword.

Sven felt the strike vibrate up his arm, and he had to grip his sword tightly as Hallr twisted his shield. Worried that he would lose his sword which was stuck in Hallr's shield, Sven stamped down on his enemy's leg, hearing the bone snap and Hallr's screams drowning out the sounds of the battle raging around them, and as Sven freed his sword somebody barged into him. Sven grimaced as the pain shot up his left leg, which had to take his weight to stop himself from falling over. He turned in time to see the axe coming for his unprotected head and thought he'd be seeing his son in Valhalla soon. And even with death so close, Sven found the time to wonder if Torkel was in Valhalla or if he had gone to the Christian heaven. As the thought ran through his mind, a shadow appeared over him and Sven's eyes widened when he thought a Valkyrie had come for him, but then she lifted her shield and blocked the axe before ramming her sword into the skull of Sven's attacker.

Sven shook his head and realised it wasn't a Valkyrie he was staring at, but Thora. She twisted out of the way of another attack before cutting her opponent's leg and cracking his skull with her helmet.

'Are you going to fight or just stand there gaping like a virgin?'

Sven tested his left leg, wincing at the pain, and decided he just had to deal with it. 'Was just wondering what took you so long.' Sven lifted his shield and looked for Hallr. He saw the red-faced bastard trying to crawl to safety and felt the growl escaping his throat. He was not done with the bastard yet.

'Sven, I need to—'

'Not now, Thora. I have a maggot to kill,' Sven interrupted Thora, and stalked Hallr, whose wide eyes were fixed on him. But when Sven was only a few paces away, Hallr's eyes shifted towards the hall, and the smile that appeared on his face made Sven stop. He turned his attention to the hall and his heart thudded in his chest when he saw the flames spreading across the thatch roof. 'No!'

'The hall is on fire!' someone shouted, and the warriors who had formed a shield wall in front of the hall all turned to see the burning roof behind them.

Rollo killed the man he had been facing before he shouted, 'We need to get everyone out of the hall now!'

'Ten men on me!' Alvar rushed inside the hall, a group of warriors following him, to rescue the people of Ribe.

'Sven, we need to help them!' Thora ran to the hall without waiting to see if Sven had heard her.

Sven turned and glared at Hallr, who was laughing despite the pain edged on his face. 'It's burning, Sven! It's burning and there's nothing you can do!' His laugh echoed in Sven's mind, and Sven imagined the gods sitting in Asgard and laughing as well. Especially when his eye caught a movement in the shadows behind the hall.

As the light of one torch flickered, Sven saw the Frankish duke, his head bleeding from where Sven had struck him and surrounded by his men, glaring at him. Sven knew then the Franks had set his hall on fire and, even worse, they were escaping with Charles's mother. 'The Franks! Stop the Franks!' Sven roared, forgetting about the battle being fought in the streets in Ribe as he set off after them.

'Sven!' Thora shouted at him.

'Go after him, we've got this,' Rollo shouted and sent men to join Thora as she rushed to catch up with Sven.

Hallr's men were backing off, all of them wanting to get away from the flames chewing their way through the roof and not wanting the bits of burning thatch to land on them as they floated down. Smoke started to come out of the hall as Alvar and the few men outside led the women, children and old folk out of the hall through the back door. He shouted for them to head to the river before he rushed back to the shield wall.

But Sven knew none of this as he chased the Franks towards the wharf. He gritted his teeth against the pain in his leg, but he refused to let them get away. One of the Frankish warriors turned and swung his sword at Sven. Sven took the blow on his shield and then barged into the man like a wild boar, knocking him to the ground. Another Frankish warrior turned and saw his companion was down and the Danes chasing them with Sven in the lead. He shouted a warning to the others and turned to face Sven.

The Frank jabbed at Sven with his spear, and Sven ducked under it before he stabbed the Frank in the stomach. Behind him, he heard Thora kill the warrior who he had knocked down before, and stopped when he saw the Franks form a shield wall along the wharf as Duke Liudolf helped Hildegard on board.

'You burnt my hall, you bastards!' Sven knew it could only have been them. Hallr or Torgeir, or whoever was behind the attack, would not want the hall destroyed. It was the centre of the town and the most important building. But for the Franks, it would have been the distraction they needed to escape. Which they would have done if Sven hadn't spotted them.

'Kill the Danes!' Duke Liudolf roared as he sent more of his men to the wharf to stop Sven.

Sven ducked behind his shield and ignored Thora's calls for him to stop as he barged into the Franks. The first man fell backwards and Sven killed another before he could react and then had to lift his shield to block an attack aimed at his head. Thora rushed in and sliced that warrior's arm and then kicked him to the side as the rest of Sven's men joined the attack.

The Franks didn't have enough men to deal with Sven's and soon they were backing off. Sven glanced up after he pulled his sword free from the chest of the Frank he had just killed and saw the pale face of Duke Liudolf when he realised he would not get away.

And then Hildegard pointed to something behind Sven and shouted, 'Behind you!'

Sven glanced behind him and saw a handful of warriors approach, although he was unconcerned when he recognised them as Ribe's warriors. But then he frowned as his instinct told him that something wasn't right. Thora must have sensed it as well as she turned. Sven wasn't sure what had warned him, whether it was the anger in their eyes and the way the men were sneaking up on them, as if they were trying to catch Sven by surprise. But at the last moment, the leading warrior roared, 'Die, Sven, you bastard!'

Just then, one warrior beside Sven turned and stabbed him in the side. Sven had sensed the movement and instinct had made him twist out of the way, but the warrior's sword still broke a few links of Sven's brynja and cut through his tunic. Sven screamed as he turned and punched the treacherous bastard with the rim of his shield, and as the warrior fell, he pulled the sword out of Sven's side. Thora blocked the next attack aimed for Sven, before kicking the man into the river. But not all the warriors around Sven had turned against him, as the few still loyal to Sven formed up around him and fought off the men who wanted to kill him.

'Why are you bastards protecting the dwarf?' one attacker shouted.

Sven glanced behind him and saw the Franks use the distraction to get back to their ship, but in their haste to get away, they forgot to untie the mooring line. Sven knew he had to act. Dropping his shield so he could put his hand on his wound, Sven limped towards the ship.

'Sven, what in Odin's name are you doing?' Thora asked as she opened her opponent's chest.

But Sven ignored her as he limped towards the ship. He reached the post where the ship was still tied to and then glared at Duke Liudolf. 'Tell your king I will be on the beach in five days' time. He better be there with my grandson or I burn every church in Francia and kill every priest I find.'

Duke Liudolf frowned, but nodded as he held his hand up to stop his men from jumping off and killing Sven. Sven glanced at Hildegard and nodded to thank her for her warning, which had saved his life, and then he cut the rope so the duke's ship could float downriver and away from the fight. Sven wasn't sure why he let them go. He would have preferred to have Charles's mother in his hands, but he knew he was going to lose Ribe. He had realised that when one of Ribe's warriors stabbed him. And if he lost Ribe, then the bastards who had attacked his town might have decided to have their fun with the daughter of the Frankish king before they killed her. It wouldn't have mattered then if Sven survived or not. Without Hildegard, he would never see his grandson again. At least this way, he hoped that King Louis would keep his word and still meet Sven on that blasted beach.

'Sven!' Thora shouted as she fought off one man. Dead bodies lay at her feet, but it looked like she and the few warriors still loyal to Sven had the upper hand. Sven gripped his sword and tried to push his wound out of his mind.

'Odin!' he roared and charged. He reached the small battle in a few steps and stabbed one attacker before he could react and then hacked another in the leg. This was too much for those attacking Sven as they turned and fled. But Sven didn't waste time celebrating the small victory. He knew Rollo and Alvar would be fighting a desperate battle in the centre of the town. Sven looked at the hall, seeing how the roof had been consumed by the flames and that the fire had spread to the wooden walls. He felt the knot in his throat as he thought of all the weapons that hung on the walls. Swords, axes and spears. Even the shields his ancestors had taken as trophies from those they had defeated. The history of his bloodline, all being eaten away by the flames just like Asgard would be destroyed by the flames of Surtr during Ragnarök. The roar of the fire drowned out the battle sounds as the few loyal men fought to protect the people of Ribe. Sven glanced to the side and saw the women and children cowering near the river. Amongst them were those too old to fight in the shield wall, but they still stood there with weapons and protected the townspeople. He felt some of their eyes on him, accusing him of this attack.

And they may have been right. But despite their hatred of him,
Ribe was still his town and even though he knew the town was
lost, Sven was determined to make Torgeir and Hallr pay a heavy
price for it. Sven picked up his shield and winced at the pain in his
side before he charged forward. 'To the hall!'

## 28

Sven charged towards the hall, with Thora and the handful of men behind him. With his battle rage coursing through him, the pain from his stab wound and the limp on his left leg were forgotten as he scanned the open space in front of the burning hall. In the light of the flames, he saw Rollo and Alvar standing side by side in the centre of their small shield wall that was outnumbered by the attacking army. Both Rollo and Alvar looked like the giants mothers warned their children about as they stood taller than everyone and killed any warrior that came into reach of their weapons. But they and the warriors of Ribe who were fighting with them were slowly being pushed back towards the burning hall.

Sven knew he had to help them, so he changed direction and aimed for the back of the enemy shield wall. Rollo and Alvar had saved his life more times than he could count in the many battles he had fought this summer, and besides, he would need his giants for what was to come. Thora sensed the same as she turned and followed him without him needing to give the order, and they reached the enemy shield wall in a few quick strides. The enemy was too focused on Rollo and Alvar's shield wall to even notice them as Sven put his shoulder behind his shield and he charged at the back of the enemy.

'What the—' the warrior Sven barged into shouted before Sven knocked him to the ground and stabbed him through the back. Thora hacked her sword into another's neck, his blood spraying everywhere as she freed her sword and punched another enemy with her shield.

'Behind! Behind!' another shouted as the rest of the warriors with Sven crashed into the enemy.

Sven stabbed one warrior in the back of his leg, and as he dropped to his knees, Sven cracked him on the head with the rim of his shield. He had enough time to see the dent in the bastard's helmet before he swung his sword into the side of another warrior. The warrior wore a brynja and Sven's blade was too blunt to break through the links, but the man still arched to the side in pain before one of Sven's warriors killed him.

The enemy, now aware of what was happening behind them, turned to face the new threat, which reduced the pressure on Rollo and Alvar's line.

'For Ribe! For Odin!' Rollo roared when he realised what was happening. He raised his axe and brought it down on the skull of the man he'd been fighting as the rest of Ribe's warriors took up his call. With renewed energy, they pushed the enemy back and got themselves away from the flames licking their backs.

'For Ribe!' Alvar stabbed with his sword and then jumped forwards into the breach he had caused before the enemy could close the gap. Not that any thought of doing that as they now fought a battle on two fronts, the same thing the warriors of Ribe had to deal with earlier.

Sven blocked an axe on his shield and stabbed his attacker in the stomach, his blow not hard enough to cut through the bastard's leather jerkin, but as the man bent over, Sven punched him in the head with the boss of his shield and stamped on his head as the warrior collapsed. All around him, the enemy was thinning as some died and others fled, having decided that the town with the burning hall wasn't worth their lives.

'They're running!' someone shouted and the warriors of Ribe cheered as they sensed that victory was in their grasp. But Sven refused to let any of the enemy get away as he continued to cut down any who came within reach. Beside him, Thora fought with the same ferocity, her face an ugly grimace as she bared her teeth. She lifted her shield to block a blow and Sven stabbed her attacker in the leg before she killed him, and the two of them pushed forward.

'Retreat! Retreat!' one of the enemy shouted and somewhere a horn blew.

Sven was about to give chase when Rollo shouted a warning he barely heard through the blood pumping in his ears, and someone knocked him over. Grimacing at the pain that shot through his shoulder as he landed on it, Sven struggled to his feet and glared at the bastard who had attacked him from the side. For a moment Sven believed it was another of Ribe's warriors who had betrayed him, but then he gasped when he took in the tall, narrow-shouldered warrior with a Dane axe in his hand. And not just any Dane axe, but Sven's.

'Ivor!' Sven almost choked on the name. He glanced at the battered body of the dead priest and almost heard Loki laughing at him.

'This is for my father, you fat dwarf!' Ivor attacked by chopping down with the Dane axe and Sven just twisted out of the way. But the shock of seeing Ivor there had killed his battle rage and his old body struggled to obey his commands. Ivor swung the axe, which Sven blocked with his shield, but the blow sent him staggering backward. He glanced around, trying to find someone who could help him, but everyone was busy fighting the new force Ivor had brought with him. He lifted his shield to block the next attack and felt the pain jolt through his shoulder as Ivor's axe bit into the wood. His fingers too numb to hold on to the shield, Sven let go of it and lunged forward, hoping to catch Ivor off guard, and stabbed at his stomach. But his old body moved too slowly, and Ivor laughed as he jumped out of the way.

'I find it hard to believe that you killed my father. He was a far better warrior than you.' Ivor freed the axe from Sven's shield and swung it at his head. Sven dropped to the ground and felt the axe just miss him, but before he could do anything else, Ivor rushed forward and kneed him in the face. His head snapped back and Sven fell backwards, doing everything he could to keep hold of his sword. As long as he had that, he could defend himself, but as Sven looked up and saw the sneer on Ivor's face, he knew he was going to die. The thought doused the last of his battle lust, and Sven suddenly felt far older than he believed he was. Or maybe he just was that old. Sven had seen more than fifty winters and had lived a life harder than most. He knew he was lucky to still be alive and had always believed it was because Odin was keeping him alive. But as he stared at Ivor, who lifted Sven's Dane axe to kill him, Sven believed Odin had decided that now was his time. That now he was going to die as the hall his grandfather had built burnt behind him.

\* \* \*

Thora twisted out of the attack and stabbed her opponent under the armpit. The man, young enough to almost be called a boy, shuddered as her sword ended his life and as she pulled it free, Thora turned in time to see Ivor knee Sven in the face. For a moment, she stood there, stunned at seeing Ivor in Ribe, when they had all believed he was in East Francia. But then she realised the danger Sven was in.

'Sven!' she shouted, but the old bastard just stared at Ivor, his face dazed as the tall warrior lifted the axe to kill him. Thora rushed at Ivor, at the coward who had stabbed her while another held on to her arms. Her anger erupted in a roar that made Ivor look her way and from under his helmet, she saw his eyebrows raise and his eyes widen before she barged into him with her shield.

Ivor staggered back a few steps, but quickly recovered and swung the Dane axe at her head. Thora ducked under the axe and rushed past the bastard who had taken Charles from her, her sword grazing along his brynja. She knew she wouldn't break any links, but she also knew the blow would hurt the bastard. And that was what she wanted before she killed him.

Thora swung her sword at Ivor in a backhanded attack. Ivor turned and brought the axe handle up to block her sword. He twisted the axe, hoping to pull her sword out of her grip as it got stuck in the wooden handle, but Thora tightened her grip and pulled her sword free before punching out with her shield. Her shield caught Ivor on the shoulder and he grimaced at the pain before he brought the axe around and swung it at her chest. Thora jumped back, knowing it would do her no good to use her shield to block the axe, not with Ivor's strength and the weight of the large axe head. She bumped into someone behind her and as she turned she glimpsed the one-handed axe coming for her head. This time, Thora used her shield to block the axe, and then she turned her sword around and stabbed the bastard wielding the axe in the stomach. The warrior's eyes widened in shock and then glanced at something behind her. Thora ducked as Ivor tried to use the distraction of the attack to kill her and heard his Dane axe bury itself in the warrior's chest who had attacked her.

Thora turned and dragged her sword along the back of Ivor's leg before he could pull his axe free. She grinned in satisfaction as he cried out and dropped to one knee. But instead of killing him there, she backed off and gave him a chance to get back to his feet.

'What? Too afraid to kill me?' Ivor said as he shifted his balance onto his good leg, his teeth bared in anger.

Thora smiled, remembering again how he had stabbed her in the stomach before carrying Charles off. 'I'm just not ready for you to die yet.'

Ivor hawked and spat as he limped closer, the Dane axe gripped in both his hands. 'You should have joined me, Thora. With you as my champion, and perhaps my wife, I could be a great king.'

'I'd rather be fucked by a goat than have you rutting me.'

Ivor grimaced at that. 'You know, at first I was glad when I heard you survived. But now, I'm going to make sure I kill you.' Ivor dropped the axe and pulled his sword out of his scabbard before picking up a shield from a dead warrior. But before he could prepare himself, Thora attacked.

She stabbed low, towards his injured leg, and when Ivor lowered his shield to block her blade, she punched him in the chest with the rim of hers. Ivor staggered back, barely staying on his feet and his eyes wide as he struggled to breathe. Again, Thora stepped back, smiling as she allowed Ivor to recover. The tall warrior glared at her as he clutched his chest. Both of them were oblivious to the battle raging around them as the warriors of Ribe, led by Rollo and Alvar, fought hard to protect their town. Ivor's men, on the other hand, were losing heart, especially when they noticed how Thora was toying with him.

'I heard your husband cried before he died. That you were the one with the cock and not he.'

Thora shrugged as the comment bounced off her like a raindrop bounced off the mountain. She had heard it all before. Many warriors had tried to use her dead husband to goad her, to anger her so that she would make a mistake, but her father had taught her to block it all out. 'My husband was more of a man than you'll ever be. And that's if you ever crawl out of your father's shadow.'

Ivor's eyebrows raised at that. 'Bitch.' The word barely was out before Thora launched at him again. This time she swung her sword at his head and Ivor ducked under it, before stabbing at her side. Thora blocked his attack with her shield and jumped back to give herself more space. She rushed at him a second time, aiming high again, and when Ivor lifted his shield, she turned her sword and slapped the wound on his leg with the flat of her blade. As Ivor cried out, she moved behind him and punched him in the back with her shield. Ivor arched backwards, but then pivoted on his good leg so he could swing his sword at her, but Thora blocked his attack before she struck him in his side. Again, her blow was not hard enough to break the links of his brynja, but she knew soon Ivor would beg her to kill him.

Ivor staggered back, his pain edged all over his face and something else in his eyes, which made Thora smile. Fear. Ivor had realised he could not defeat her, and she saw it all over his face. The way his eyes darted everywhere as if he was looking for a way to escape her and how his lips trembled.

'What's the matter, Ivor? You can only cut me when somebody is holding me?' She stalked him as he continued to stagger backwards, his shield in front of him as if he was hiding behind it.

'Bitch,' he muttered as his eyes darted around.

'You already called me that.' Thora was blind to the surrounding battle because at that moment, she only cared about one thing. She took a deep breath as she closed her eyes and saw Charles's terrified face as Ivor threw him on the back of his horse and rode out of the town gates while she lay on the ground, bleeding. *Thora!* Charles's voice came to her. With a roar, her eyes snapped open, and she charged at Ivor.

Ivor ducked behind his shield as Thora punched out with hers, sending the taller warrior backwards. As he struggled to stay on his feet, his arms out wide, Thora stepped in and drove her sword through his brynja and into his stomach.

Ivor grunted, his eyes wide as Thora twisted her sword and drove it in deeper. She felt his blood wetting her hand and let go of the sword and stepped back as Ivor dropped to his knees. He looked up at her, his eyes pleading for something he would never get from her. Thora wiped the stray hair from her face before she pulled her sax-knife out of its scabbard and walked towards Ivor. After knocking his helmet off, she grabbed him by his sweaty hair and pulled his face up so he was forced to look at her. Thora grimaced as she smelt his fear and wondered how Ivor believed he could be the king.

'When you see my husband in Valhalla, you better apologise for what you said about him. Otherwise, he will kick your arse every day until Ragnarök.' She stabbed up with the knife, driving it through his throat and into his skull. Ivor shuddered and when Thora stepped back, he collapsed. She stood there, glaring at his body as his blood soaked into the ground of Ribe, thinking of nothing else but of how that would not bring Charles back.

'Ivor is dead!' someone shouted, but Thora wasn't sure whom. Her hand went to her stomach, where Ivor had stabbed her. The muscle felt sore, but it held. The gods were with her, and she knew she wouldn't have to worry about the wound affecting her. All around her, more and more warriors cried out about the death of Ivor, but many seemed not to hear the call as the fight continued.

The shield wall had broken apart and Thora saw Rollo lift one warrior off his feet before throwing him to the ground and kicking him. She searched for Sven and found him lying on the ground where she had last seen him, with Alvar standing over him and killing anyone who tried to get near him. Her heart skipped when she thought the bastard was dead. Thora thought about freeing her sword, but then she realised she did not have enough strength left for that. So instead, she just picked up a one-handed axe and rushed to Sven.

'Ivor is dead! Retreat!' The call came again and was soon echoed by the enemy as they all turned and fled.

Thora reached Sven and dropped to her knees. 'Sven, you dumb boar.' She felt the tear running down her cheek as she lifted his head, but then Sven groaned.

Tired eyes stared back at her, which made her smile. 'Thank you.'

'I told you the gods aren't ready for you yet.'

Sven nodded and looked toward the river. 'It doesn't matter what they want.' He sat up, wincing as his hand held on to his bleeding side. 'She is gone, and so is the cross. We have no chance of getting Charles back.'

Thora knew he was talking about Charles's mother and also stared at the river. But Sven had no choice. He had to let her go. She knew that as well as he did. But she knew something that Sven didn't. Something that she'd been trying to tell him for many days, but he never wanted to listen. 'Sven, the cross is not gone.'

Sven frowned at her. 'It is. That bastard Frank stole it.'

Thora shook her head. 'No, he stole a different cross. The one I put in Charles's chest when I took the real one out. Sven, we still have Charlemagne's cross.'

## 29

Sven sat on a stool, his face, covered in sweat and dried blood, creased as he stared at the burnt remains of the hall. The battle for Ribe had ended a while ago and for the rest of the night, they had done nothing but wait. No one was really sure what for, though. For the enemy to regroup and attack again, or for Sol to pull the sun through the sky with her horse-drawn chariot. It had been a tense night and often someone would swear at the gods when they jumped at an owl hoot or a dog barking somewhere. The townspeople stayed near the river, guarded by Alvar and a handful of men, while Rollo and Thora stood by the gate with the rest of Ribe's warriors. In the end Sol had arrived and there was no sign of the army that had attacked them apart from the dead they had left behind.

Sven wore only his trousers and boots. His brynja and tunic had been removed so his wound could be treated by Audhild. They didn't speak to each other, neither of them wanting to talk about Haldor and what part he might have played in this. With tired eyes, Sven stared at what remained of the great hall of Ribe. A few blackened timber posts and the stones of the hearth fire.

Everything else had been chewed up by the hungry flames. All the benches, the tables and stool. Even the jarl's seat, which had warmed not only Sven's arse but also his father's and grandfather's. The shields and spears were gone and most of the other weapons that had hung on the walls were all damaged. The sleeping quarters were destroyed as well, along with the bed and Charles's chest, with his few belongings. Sven mourned the loss of that more than his own things. Even while all he had left were the sweat- and blood-stained clothes he had fought in and his brynja. He glanced at the Dane axe by his feet. His Dane axe with the boar engraved on the axe head and surrounded by a swirling pattern. Sven still didn't know how Ivor had got his hands on it, but guessed someone in Ribe had given it to him. He had wanted to shame Sven by killing him with his own weapon, and he would have done if it had not been for Thora.

Sven turned his attention back to the remains of the hall, glad they had kept the fire contained during the night. Those who weren't fighting or guarding the townspeople had spent the entire night running buckets to the river and back and pouring water over the houses nearest to the hall, so the flames couldn't leap to them as they looked for more nourishment. Perhaps the gods were with them, but Sven found little comfort in that. Ribe's hall was gone and her already depleted fighting force was reduced even more as they had fought to defend their town. What made things even worse was that some of Ribe's warriors had been part of the attack. Sven clenched his fist when he remembered the conversation they had with one of Ribe's men who had attacked him.

The warrior had been badly injured, a deep cut in the leg that was bleeding heavily, but Thora had got him to talk.

'Ivor approached me during the night of the feast. He knew I hated you.' The warrior had glared at Sven, even as his life was draining out of him. 'Told me if I helped him open the gates, then I'd be richly rewarded when he became king.'

'So you gathered others you knew felt the same?' Thora had asked.

The warrior had nodded. 'We attacked those who were guarding the gate and opened it for Ivor and Jarl Hallr.'

'And then you joined the defence and waited for the right moment to stick a knife in my back.' The words had come out as more of a growl, but the warrior had nodded again.

'It was Hallr's idea.'

Those were the last words the man had spoken because Sven had stamped on his face and had crushed his skull. Those they knew were part of the attack had their eyes stabbed out and their tongues removed. Sven had also ordered that their hands and feet were cut off. He did not want these men to reach Valhalla. Their punishment would be to forever be stuck on Midgard, unable to find their way to Odin's hall of the slain. No one had protested. They had betrayed their sword brothers and had tried to kill their jarl.

The dead were taken away, Ribe's warriors taken to one of the empty houses where they could be prepared for their funerals, while Hallr and Ivor's men were thrown on a cart and taken to the forest. There their bodies were dumped and left for the wolves, ravens and bears. Ivor's head had been chopped off and Sven had sent it to Hedeby as a gift and a warning for Torgeir, because Sven was certain he was behind the attack. Ivor had no men or gold to pay for an army and Hallr wasn't smart enough to plan this. And Sven knew Torgeir hated him, even if he had pretended to be friends when he was here with the new Horik. The Christian priest's body had vanished during the night. Sven wasn't sure if his uncle had come back for it or if the Christians in Ribe had taken it to be buried.

'Bet you're pleased with yourself,' an angry voice said behind Sven.

Sven glared at the source from over his shoulder and saw a group of townspeople had gathered behind him, their faces dark and many with snarls on their lips. He took a deep breath and struggled to his feet so he could face them. 'Pleased with myself?'

'Aye, this is all your fault! You should never have come back here!' One man in the group jabbed a finger towards the hall. Sven recognised the man as one of the prominent traders who often travelled north and returned with furs and ivory which he then sold to Frankish traders or traded for wine and Frankish jewellery. But Sven could not recall the man's name and doubted he ever knew it.

'My fault?' Sven took a step closer to the trader, his heart beating hard in his chest as he struggled to contain his anger.

The trader nodded as he stared down at Sven. The man must have felt some false sense of confidence just because he was taller than Sven. 'You brought nothing but death and misery to Ribe.'

Sven's hand shot out and grabbed the trader's beard and yanked the man's head down before he headbutted him. The trader's nose exploded in a spray of snot and blood, and the trader collapsed to the ground. Some women in the group cried out, which sent nearby warriors running towards the centre, while everyone just stared at Sven, their anger replaced by fear.

'My fault?' Sven glared at the people. 'This,' he pointed at the burnt-down hall, 'is not my fault. All I've been doing since I returned was shed my blood and the blood of Ribe's warriors to protect you and your lands. Battle after battle, I fought to keep you safe. Every day, I sent men out to protect the farmsteads and keep the raiders away. And all I ever got was anger and hostility.' Sven took a deep breath. 'But I accepted that. I know you never wanted me back, and I already told you I didn't want to be the jarl of Ribe. That had never been my intention. But this,' again he pointed at the hall, 'is not my fault.'

'Then whose fault is it?' a voice shouted, but Sven couldn't see who it came from.

He glared at the people as Rollo and Thora came rushing from the gate, a group of warriors behind him. 'This is your fault,' Sven said to the townspeople, who all gasped in shock. 'It was your sons who opened the gates to the enemy. It was your sons who knew there was an army camped near the town, waiting to attack, but took their gold and stayed quiet. It was your sons who tried to kill me while I fought to protect you and your homes. The gods know this isn't my fault. The gods know it all. They see your betrayal of Ribe and they will punish all of you for it. But I am done with you. You who did nothing while Ivor brought his men here and took my grandson.' And that was true. It was all Sven had been thinking about after the battle as he watched the hall burn down. The great hall of Ribe was the last thing that tied him to Ribe and now that it was gone, all he had left was Charles. He had no more reason to stay in Ribe.

'So you're just going to abandon us?' a woman asked, and Sven almost smiled at the fear in her voice. Many other people glanced at each other, frowning with concern.

He hawked and spat. 'You never wanted me, anyway.'

Sven was about to turn and walk away when someone asked, 'Who will be our new jarl, then?'

'Aye,' the others agreed with the question.

Sven shrugged and then looked at Rollo, who was frowning as he stared at the unconscious trader. Thora only shook her head as she must have realised what had happened. As he limped away, he said, 'If it was up to me, then I'd make Rollo your new jarl.'

'Me?' Rollo's eyes widened, but the townspeople nodded and

seemed to agree with what Sven said. Rollo chased after Sven. 'Why me?'

Sven sighed. 'The warriors respect you and the people like you. You are also a good leader and a great warrior, Rollo. I think you'd make a great jarl.'

Rollo then shook his head. 'I don't want to be jarl.'

'We never get what we want, Rollo. The gods make sure of that.'

'Aye, but I'm not staying here. I'm going with you. Wherever you go.' Rollo set his jaw to show that he would not be argued with, but Thora, who was with them, ignored that.

'Are you sure that's wise, Rollo? We might never come back and wherever Sven goes, death always goes.'

Sven raised an eyebrow at Thora for assuming that she would go with him.

Rollo stopped in front of them and crossed his arms. 'Sven, all I ever wanted was to fight by your side, just like my father had done.'

'Your father died fighting by my side. He never got to see the man you have become because of me.'

Rollo nodded. 'Aye, but that was his choice, and this is mine. And besides, these people did nothing when Bjarni left me behind when he took the warriors raiding. None of them stood up for me or my mother when she rejected Bjarni as jarl after you left. Like it or not, Sven, my fate is tied with yours, just like my father's was. I go where you go.'

'And me,' Alvar said, surprising them because they had not heard or seen him approach. Alvar had a cut on his face which would leave a nasty scar, but then none of them had come out of that battle without any injuries. Rollo had a cut to his arm and a new bruise forming on his cheek and even Thora had a few minor cuts.

'And what of your son and your wife, Rollo? You will leave them here? Never to see you again?'

Rollo smiled. 'No, they come with. I'm not leaving them in Ribe. And besides, my mother was the last of our kin to tie us to Ribe.'

'Your wife has no family in Ribe?' Thora asked, tilting her head.

'Her parents died many winters ago and her brother was killed on a raid before we wed.'

Sven stared at Rollo and realised he was not going to convince the giant warrior to stay. Even Alvar seemed determined to follow him to Francia. He glanced at Thora, who only shrugged, but the smile on her face told him he didn't really have a choice. 'Fine,' he said. 'But don't come crying to me when you die in Francia.'

They all smiled and then Alvar asked, 'So now what?'

Sven scowled. 'Let's go have a chat with Hallr. There are still a few things that need to be explained.'

'Aye,' Thora agreed, and they went to where Hallr was tied up near the hall and guarded by men Rollo knew to be loyal.

They had found Hallr alive and cowering behind one house after the battle. His men must have believed he was dead and had fled without him. His leg, swollen and with a large purple bruise, was broken from when Sven had stamped on it and he had a gash on his forehead.

As they approached him, he looked up from where he was lying on the ground, his face pale and jaw tense with the pain he must have been feeling. 'Ale,' he mumbled, as his eyes pleaded with Sven.

Sven nodded and one of the warriors guarding him went to find some ale as Sven glared at Hallr. 'Why did you attack my town? What did Torgeir promise you?'

'How do you know Horik wasn't involved?' Thora asked, and Sven frowned as he thought about it.

'Was Horik involved?' he asked Hallr, who refused to answer.

'Ale,' was all he said, and Sven felt his patience running out.

He pressed his foot down on Hallr's broken leg and Hallr cried out in pain. 'Answer my questions, Hallr.' Sven lifted his foot away from Hallr's leg.

Hallr shook his head. 'H... Horik knew nothing about this. It was Ivor. It was all Ivor's idea.'

Sven glanced at Thora, but he could tell that she didn't believe that either, so he stood on Hallr's broken leg again. The scream that came out of Hallr made everyone stop and stare at them. Mothers took their young children away as men rubbed the Mjöll-nirs around their necks. 'Torgeir is behind this. I know he is. I saw how you two spoke in my hall.'

'Torgeir told us Ivor was in East Francia,' Thora said as Hallr shook his head, tears streaming down his cheeks.

The warrior that had left to find ale returned and hesitated until Sven took the ale and drank half the cup before pouring the rest over Hallr's head. 'Why did Torgeir tell us Ivor was in East Francia?'

'Th... they had a deal. I... I don't know what it was. B... but Ivor came to me. S... said I'd be made jarl of Ribe if I helped him. They wanted you to think he was gone. Then you'd relax and drop your guard.'

Sven growled as Hallr spoke and glanced at Rollo, who was scowling.

Hallr kept on talking, the words flowing out of him like a river spilling into the sea. 'Ivor and Steinar caught up with us as we travelled north with Horik. That was when Ivor approached me. Told me he was going to be the next king of Denmark.'

'But why attack Ribe?' Thora asked.

Hallr licked his lips. 'They wanted you to suffer,' he said to Sven. 'They wanted you to suffer like you suffered when the Franks took your son. Then Ivor was going to slip into Ribe and kill you.'

'What deal did Torgeir make with the Franks?' Sven asked and lifted his foot when Hallr shook his head.

'I swear by Odin, I don't know! They never told me that.'

Thora looked at Sven. 'Do you believe him?'

Sven scratched the back of his neck as he thought about what Hallr had just said. 'I don't know. But it doesn't really matter though. Torgeir still won. They will still get Ribe and I will be gone.' Sven turned and walked away. He was tired of all this. He was tired of others feeling threatened by him and attacking his family because of it. All he wanted now was to protect his grandson. But others always had to interfere and ruin his life.

'What do we do with him?' Alvar pointed at the crying Hallr.

Sven stopped and, without looking back, said, 'Kill him and send his head to Horik. He wants to be king, so let him deal with this. I have other things to do.'

'What about Jarl Torgeir? Do we let him get away with this?' Rollo asked.

Sven sighed as he rubbed his face. He doubted he had the energy to take on Torgeir. And it wouldn't just be Torgeir, but his allies as well, because Sven knew there were many who would support Torgeir against him. 'Let Horik deal with him. All I want to do is get my grandson back.'

'So what do we do?' Thora asked.

Sven turned and looked at Ribe again. 'We do what we need to and be ready to leave as soon as we can. We get the ship ready to sail and see how many warriors we can get to join us.'

'Are you sure it's a good idea to take warriors away from Ribe?' Thora asked. 'Ribe needs to be able to defend itself.'

Sven hawked and spat. 'Ribe will be important to young Horik when he becomes king. I'm sure he'll make sure the town is protected. And besides, we're only taking those who will join us.'

'Still might not be enough,' Rollo said.

'Aye, but we'll deal with that later.' Sven turned and walked towards the gate.

'Where are you going?' Rollo asked.

'To make sure we can get more warriors.'

Rollo and Alvar looked at each other and shrugged before they went to do what Sven had asked of them, but Thora walked with Sven. As they walked up the main road, Sven saw the way the people of Ribe looked at him and guessed word of what he had said had already spread. But he did not care any more. All he wanted to do now was to find his grandson.

'You really think that King Louis will meet you, especially now that you don't have his daughter any more?' Thora asked.

Sven looked at the clouds that were forming and shrugged. 'Only the Norns will know, but what else can we do but go there and see? Perhaps the godi's sacrifice will give us some more luck.'

'Aye, if you want to call that luck.'

Sven smiled. 'We still live. That's luck enough.'

They walked in silence until they reached the gate. Sven stopped and stared at the warriors guarding it and wondered if they had really got all the ones who had betrayed them before he turned to Thora. 'What made you swap the cross?'

Thora smiled. 'When I woke and learnt that Charles's mother was here with Gerold, I decided it would be better if the cross wasn't in the hall, so I swapped it with one I found in your treasure chest. It looked similar enough, I thought.'

Sven grunted. 'You could have told me.'

Thora laughed. 'Sven, I tried. Many times, but you never wanted to listen to me.'

'Aye.' Sven rubbed his head. 'Where is the cross now?'

'I buried it in a place only I know of. It's safe.'

Sven nodded. 'You make sure it stays safe. That cross could be useful to us if King Louis decides not to meet us.'

This time Thora nodded. 'He has his daughter now, but if he finds out we have the cross, then he will definitely be at the beach.'

'Aye,' Sven said.

'Sven, what do we do with Gerold?' Thora asked before Sven could walk off.

Sven thought of the snake and felt his mood darken. They had found him unconscious and tied up in the house he had shared with Hildegard, and Thora had told Sven how he had attacked her. 'We take him with. Who knows, we might find a use for him.'

Thora nodded and walked towards her aunt's house and Sven limped out of the gate towards the graveyard. He took his time and felt the eyes of the warriors on the wall on him. Sven walked until he reached the grave of his father, and then winced as he got down on his knees. Using his sax-knife, Sven dug into the mound until he found the small chest he had buried there soon after he had returned to Ribe with Charles and pulled it out. That had been his insurance for if something like this happened. Sven opened the chest and scrutinised the contents. Cut-off chunks of gold and silver, arm rings and other jewels, and coins with markings he did not recognise but knew came from the Arab kingdoms far away. There were even coins from Francia in there and a dagger with a golden hilt. That was the last of his wealth, and he would need everything in there to get his grandson back.

Sven sensed movement behind and turned, wincing at the pain as he reopened the wound on his side, his sax-knife in his hand, and was surprised to see his uncle standing there.

'Sven the Boar,' the godi said. The man looked even older than he had the last time Sven had seen him, and Sven wondered again how the bastard was still alive.

Sven raised an eyebrow at him. 'How did you do it?'

The godi tilted his head and then smiled. 'The priest? I'm not going to tell you all my secrets, nephew. But it worked. The gods were with you and you still live.'

Sven shrugged. 'I live because Thora killed Ivor.'

The godi nodded and then glanced at the wall. Sven looked over his shoulder and saw that none of the warriors were there. 'So you go for your grandson?'

'Aye. I need to get him back. He is all I have left.'

'He is. I like the boy. He is very smart.'

Sven scowled at his uncle. 'How come you never told me you spent time in Francia?'

'You never asked me. And besides, it's not like you ever visit me without wanting something from me.'

'Is that why you are here? You want something from me?'

The godi smiled. 'No, Sven. I come to say farewell and to warn you.'

'Aye, I am still in more danger than I know.'

The godi laughed. 'That you are, Sven. Odin has his eye on you. You amuse him, but Loki is jealous of the attention you get from the All-Father.' The godi then turned serious as he glanced at the grave mound behind Sven. 'Your father would be proud of the man you have become.'

Sven grunted. 'My father hated me.'

'No, Sven. Your father feared for you. You were smaller than your brothers, and he was afraid that life would be cruel towards you. That's why he was. He hoped it would make you strong enough to deal with it.'

'Life was cruel to me.' Sven thought back to the day he had killed his father to become the jarl of Ribe. 'It still is.'

'Aye, but you are the last of your brothers still alive. Of all his sons, you are the only one that survived the cruelty of life. I think he would be proud of that.'

'I'll ask him when I see him in Valhalla.'

'Aye, Sven. You do that.' The godi laughed and then turned and walked away, leaning on his staff as he did so.

Sven glanced at his father's grave mound and shook his head before he returned to Ribe.

## 30

Charles glanced at Father Leofdag as the priest sat on his knees and prayed. He was supposed to be praying as well, but he didn't feel like it. It had been two days since his conversation with King Louis, and Charles still felt conflicted about what had happened. He had promised Duke Liudolf he would not mention the cross, but in his anger he had because he wanted to hurt the man that had hurt his grandfather. And as far as Charles was concerned, he only had one grandfather. Sven the Boar. King Louis of East Francia might have been the father of the woman Charles had been told was his mother, but he was not Charles's grandfather.

Charles remembered the first time he had seen his grandfather. He remembered how he had trembled as he followed Thora and then the shock he had felt when he first laid eyes on the short, fat drunk who was covered in dirt and dried blood. The stench had made him recoil, but most of all, he remembered Sven's eyes. So dull and devoid of life, the opposite of Charles's father that he had almost been glad when the fat drunk had claimed that Charles was not his grandson. But since that first day, as his grandfather changed and Charles learnt the truth of who the man was, he had realised that, like his father, Sven would do anything to protect him. Unlike King Louis, who had locked Charles away in this room and only allowed him out once a day to go to the church, but he was always escorted by at least two warriors. Charles rubbed the lump on his head where one of those warriors had struck him the day before when he had tried to run away. He had always been good at escaping those chasing him and at hiding, and he had thought he could get away from the warriors while they had been distracted by a woman calling out to them. But the guards reacted quicker than he had expected they would, and Charles had barely run five paces before they had caught him. One of them had struck Charles on his head with the hilt of his knife as punishment, and Charles had wanted to believe that his grandfather would kill the man for that. But as the days went past, Charles was starting to believe Sven would never find him. *Does he even know where I am?* The question came to Charles again.

When Ivor first took Charles, he had believed that his grandfather would never stop until he had found him. But that was weeks ago and still his grandfather had not rescued him. And now that he was in Francia, Charles wondered if Sven could ever save him. And then there was the other question that had been plaguing him. Did he really want his grandfather to rescue him?

Sven had treated Charles better than King Louis did, but he had still gone to fight a battle instead of staying in Ribe with Charles. And even before that, their relationship had been difficult. Charles, at first, didn't understand why Sven wanted him to train to be a warrior when he had wanted to be a priest. It wasn't until after Haldor had attacked Father Leofdag that Charles understood why he needed to learn how to defend himself. And now, Charles wasn't even sure that he wanted to be a priest any more. The other problem was that Sven was a heathen, and

Charles knew that no matter how hard he tried, Sven would never accept Christianity. Sven did make an attempt to accept Charles's faith, though, by making him a shrine in the room he had shared with Thora, but Charles wanted his grandfather to become a Christian, just like his father had done.

The thought of Thora brought a lump to Charles's throat again, and he coughed to clear it.

Father Leofdag opened his eyes. 'You're not praying again, Charles.'

Charles sighed and wondered again why Father Leofdag kept coming to him. The priest had been told to leave, but he had insisted on staying with Charles. 'Why do you care?'

Father Leofdag dropped his hands that had been clasped around the small cross he wore. 'I care because you are a good boy, Charles, and I want to make sure your eternal soul is not lost to God.'

'It already is,' Charles said before he could stop himself. 'God doesn't care about me any more.'

Father Leofdag stared at him, the look of pity in his eyes only annoying Charles even more. 'God does care about you. That is why he sent me to watch over you and to guide you back to Him.'

Charles jumped to his feet, his face turning red. 'How can you do that when you can't even protect yourself?'

With widened eyes, Father Leofdag stammered as he struggled to find the right answer. And then the priest lowered his head. 'You're right, Charles. I am no warrior like your grandfather or Thora. I can't protect you from fists and iron. All I can do is pray for your soul and do my best to bring you back into God's light.'

Charles glared at Father Leofdag, almost forcing himself to be angry with the priest. But he knew he could not blame Father Leofdag for what had happened. And maybe that was why

Charles had been angry and why he couldn't pray any more. He didn't know who to blame other than God. Just like he still struggled to understand why everything was happening to him. 'What if I don't want to go back to God's light? What if God has abandoned me and doesn't want me back in his light?'

Before Father Leofdag could answer, the door to Charles's room opened and Duke Liudolf walked in. Charles turned and forgot about his anger when he saw the look on the duke's face. His eyes went to the cut, surrounded by a bruise on Duke Liudolf's head, and Charles frowned.

'Out,' Duke Liudolf said, and Father Leofdag hesitated and then got to his feet. But before he left, he turned to Charles.

'That is why I keep praying for you.'

Duke Liudolf raised an eyebrow at that, but said nothing while he waited for the priest to disappear. Charles tilted his head and saw that the warriors outside the door were gone as well, and wondered what that meant. Duke Liudolf chewed on his lip as he seemed to struggle with some thought and Charles asked, 'You returned from Ribe?' He knew it was a dumb question, but he didn't know what else to say.

Duke Liudolf nodded. He glanced over his shoulder and Charles sensed there was somebody else out there. 'Charles,' Duke Liudolf said. 'There is someone here to meet you.' The duke stepped aside, and a woman walked into the small room.

Charles frowned as he scrutinised the woman, taking in her dark dress and the head cover. The large golden cross around her neck and the stern look on her face that reminded him of King Louis. Her hands gripped in front of her, with a slight tremble in them. It took Charles a few heartbeats to understand who he was looking at and, when it struck, he felt like he had been kicked in the chest. The flood of conflicting emotions made the room swim and for a moment Charles felt like he might faint. He took a step back as he sucked in the air, doing his best to remain calm, just like Thora had taught him.

The woman seemed to struggle with the same emotions as a small tear rolled down her cheek.

'I'll leave you two to it,' Duke Liudolf said and closed the door behind him as he left the room.

For a while, Charles and the woman stared at each other before she finally said, 'You look just like him.'

Charles tilted his head. 'Like who?' He tried to stay strong, but he struggled to understand how he felt seeing his mother, who he had always been told was dead, standing in front of him. He didn't know if he should be angry that he had been lied to. That she had been alive all these years and had never come to him. Or should he be happy that his mother lived and that he was not alone? But he had not been alone. Even after his father had died. He had Thora and his grandfather. Even Oda, Rollo's mother, and Thora's aunt, Ingvild, had been there for him. Jorlaug as well, as much as she annoyed him, had been as close to a friend as he had ever had.

'Your father, Torkel.' The abbess glanced at the small stool. Father Leofdag had brought him a new one after King Louis broke the old one. 'May I sit?'

Charles nodded, but stayed standing as she sat down and looked around the room. Her eyes fell on the Bible Father Leofdag had left behind. She smiled at that.

'I hear you want to be a priest.'

Charles shrugged, suddenly not trusting himself to speak, as his mouth had gone dry. He studied her face, seeing every line and her tired eyes. Her face was gaunt, and he spotted a smudge of dirt on her cheek that she must have missed.

Abbess Hildegard fell silent as she seemed to struggle to find the words and then the question came to Charles that he had wanted to ask since Duke Liudolf had told him about his mother.

'Are you really my mother?'

Abbess Hildegard took a deep breath, and then she nodded. 'I am.'

Charles's eyebrows furrowed as he scrutinised her, looking for signs that she was lying to him. Not that he knew what those signs looked like. He then thought back to his earliest memories, trying to see if he could remember what his mother looked like, but he could only remember life in Hügelburg. Everything before that was darkness and stories Bishop Bernard had told him. He thought of his life in Hügelburg, his father struggling to feed him, even though many other warriors seemed wealthy. Him being picked on by the other boys because of his height, his father and the fact that he had no mother. But yet, here she was. Sitting in front of him and watching him, her face unreadable. Charles saw none of the affection he had seen in the eyes of other mothers when they looked at their children. The way Audhild would look at Jorlaug. He tried to picture what his life would have been like if his mother had been there. Would he have been a prince, living in the capital with the king and his children? But that was pointless, and Charles knew that. His mother hadn't been there and his whole life he had been told she was dead. And not just by Bishop Bernard, but by his father as well. Charles's face hardened as he looked at the woman sitting on the stool.

'Why did you leave me and my father?'

Abbess Hildegard stared at him, her mouth open in shock, although she must have expected the question. She turned away from him and took a deep breath. 'I had no choice, Charles.'

That sentence again, the one he had heard over and over when adults couldn't explain their actions or choices. Next, she would tell him that God had chosen her path, and she had to follow it, just like his grandfather blamed his gods and the Norns for everything that had happened in his life. But she didn't because she didn't get the chance as the door opened and Duke Liudolf glared at Charles.

'The king is back from his hunting trip. They say he is furious. Charles, did you tell him about the cross?'

Charles thought about lying, but then decided there was no point. King Louis would tell them anyway, so he nodded. 'I did.'

'Why?' Duke Liudolf's face went red. 'I told you not to. By God, boy. Why did you do something so foolish?'

'It doesn't matter,' Abbess Hildegard said, fingering the cross around her neck. 'It's time my father learnt the truth of what I had done.' She stood up and looked at Charles. 'I promise that after I speak to my father that I will answer all your questions, but there is much that needs to be done first.'

She was about to walk out when Charles asked, 'How is my grandfather?'

Both Duke Liudolf and Abbess Hildegard hesitated and Charles felt his heart racing in his chest when he caught the glance between them.

Abbess Hildegard turned to him. 'I don't know. There was an attack on Ribe and we were lucky to escape ourselves. If it hadn't been for your grandfather, we might not have done. But things weren't looking good for them. The hall was burning and the last we saw, he and Thora were outnumbered and their own men turned on them.'

Charles's eyes widened. 'Thora lives?'

'The last we saw of them, she did. Now, I don't know.'

Charles felt his head spin and didn't hear the last words spoken by Abbess Hildegard before she and Duke Liudolf left the room. Neither did he hear what Duke Liudolf had said, but he caught the bishop's name. None of that mattered, though. Thora was still alive. His guardian angel still lived. And with a sudden certainty, Charles knew he still had hope that his grandfather, with Thora by his side, would find him and they would save him. Because he knew that his grandfather would have survived the attack on Ribe. And he knew that because of what Thora had told him before and the fact that she was alive meant her words were true.

*The gods aren't ready for him yet.*

# HISTORICAL NOTE

We can only imagine the chaos that might have ensued after an enormous battle that killed not only the king of Denmark but also most of his jarls and relatives (including his nephew and challenger to the throne). Power-hungry jarls would have used this as an opportunity to grab more land and wealth for themselves while droves of warriors, suddenly leaderless and homeless, might have raided across the Danish countryside, attacking small villages and farmsteads. The people of Denmark most likely lived in fear and believed that their gods were punishing them. Sacrifices would have been made to please the gods or to ask for protection until a new king came forward.

But the truth is that we don't really know what happened in Denmark after that battle (which we know almost nothing about) as there are no records that give us this information. The only real source of information that we have of this time is the *Vita Anskarii*, which is the hagiography of Saint Ansgar. Ansgar was the Archbishop of Bremen-Hamburg and was known as the Apostle of the North for his role in spreading Christianity to Denmark and the other Scandinavian nations. Ansgar had spent some time in the court of the old King Horik at the behest of the kings of Francia, and was said to have a close relationship with the king of Denmark. The *Vita Anskarii* tells us that a battle took place and that shortly after King Horik's death, his descendant, also named Horik, became the new king.

The *Vita Anskarii* doesn't tell us how old this new Horik was other than stating that he was young and that he was somehow related to the now deceased king, although again, it doesn't tell us what this relation was. In medieval Denmark, much like most of Europe at the time, the crown didn't pass down the hereditary line. New kings were elected during the Landsting, which was a governing assembly in the early Scandinavian society. The Landsting was held at regular intervals during the year and this was where the free people of Denmark would discuss the laws, settle disputes and vote for who they believed the new king of Denmark should be.

What the *Vita Anskarii* does tell us, though, was that the new King Horik did not support the spread of Christianity in Denmark and that as soon as he was crowned, he closed the church in Hedeby and chased the Christians out of Denmark. However, it was not Horik II to blame for this, but his close ally, Jarl Hovi, who had a hatred of Christians. After some time, Horik II banished Hovi and the king's attitude towards the Christians changed. This was possibly due to pressure he received from the East Franks to the south, although this is merely speculation on my part as we are told that Horik II had a good relationship with the East Franks. With Hovi's influence now gone, Ansgar persuaded Horik II to reopen the church in Hedeby and also give Ansgar land to build more churches in Denmark.

Meanwhile, Francia – modern-day France, Belgium, Germany and everything in between – had its own problems. In 838, after the death of his father, Pepin II claimed the throne of Aquitaine, which had been given to Charles the Bald by Louis the Pious in 832 after Louis had dispossessed Pepin's father. In 852, after years of battles between uncle and nephew, King Charles of West Francia came out victorious and had Pepin II imprisoned in the monastery of Saint Médard in Soissons. The nobles of Aquitaine, unhappy with Charles as their new king, went to King Louis of East Francia and asked for his aid.

King Louis sent his oldest son, also Louis, with an army to free Aquitaine from the clutches of King Charles, although I suspect he wanted the land for himself. However, the younger Louis didn't leave immediately and eventually reached Aquitaine in 855. The events of what happened then will be covered in novel four of the *Charlemagne's Cross* series.

# ACKNOWLEDGEMENTS

That is the end of *Thor's Revenge*, but Sven and Charles's story are far from complete. The stakes are getting even higher as more people learn about the Cross of Charlemagne and dream of the glory it might bring them, while all Sven wants is to find Charles and protect him like he never could his own son. And as for Charles, he has to deal with learning who his mother is and the consequences of a choice she made in anger so many years ago.

But before I start working on the next adventure for Sven and Charles, there are a few people I need to thank.

A massive thank you to my editor, Caroline, who gave me the time I needed to finish this novel and for her guidance and encouragement when I got stuck. To Ross and Susan for bringing the best out of my novel and always finding a way to cut through my ramblings as I write.

To my wife, Anna, as ever for her support and understanding. Writing a novel isn't always easy, especially when you don't always know where the story is going. I thank her for her patience and putting up with me being a bit difficult as I struggled with this novel. And to Joey, our French bulldog, for the long walks and being willing to listen to me work through the plot (in exchange for a treat, of course).

For the new friends I have accumulated over the last few years, MJ Porter, Peter Gibbons and JC Duncan, for making this journey feel less lonely.

And most importantly, to my readers. I've said this before and

I still mean it. I could not be doing this if it wasn't for your support and your kind words.

Happy reading and I hope you will all join me on the next adventure in the *Charlemagne's Cross* series.

Thank you.

# ABOUT THE AUTHOR

**Donovan Cook** is the author of the well-received *Ormstunga Saga* series which combines fast-paced narrative with meticulously researched history of the Viking world, and is inspired by his interest in Norse Mythology. He lives in Lancashire.

Sign up to Donovan Cook's mailing list here for news, competitions and updates on future books.

Visit Donovan's website: www.donovancook.net

Follow Donovan on social media:

 x.com/DonovanCook20
 facebook.com/DonovanCookAuthor
 bookbub.com/authors/donovan-cook

# ALSO BY DONOVAN COOK

**Charlemagne Series**

Odin's Betrayal

Loki's Deceit

Thor's Revenge

# WARRIOR CHRONICLES

WELCOME TO THE CLAN ✕

THE HOME OF
BESTSELLING HISTORICAL
ADVENTURE FICTION!

WARNING:
MAY CONTAIN VIKINGS!

SIGN UP TO OUR
NEWSLETTER

BIT.LY/WARRIORCHRONICLES

# Boldwood

Boldwood Books is an award-winning fiction
publishing company seeking out the best
stories from around the world.

**Find out more at www.boldwoodbooks.com**

Join our reader community for brilliant books,
competitions and offers!

Follow us
@BoldwoodBooks
@TheBoldBookClub

**Sign up to our weekly
deals newsletter**

https://bit.ly/BoldwoodBNewsletter